NEW YORK REVIEW BOOKS
CLASSICS

SAND

WOLFGANG HERRNDORF (1965–2013) studied painting
at the Academy of Fine Arts, Nuremberg. After graduating,
he moved to Berlin, where he worked as a magazine illustrator
and posted frequently on the Internet forum Wir höflichen
Paparazzi (We Polite Paparazzi). In 2001, Herrndorf joined
the art and writing collective Zentrale Intelligenz Agentur,
eventually contributing to their blog, *Riesenmaschine* (Giant
Machine). He published his first novel, *In Plüschgewittern*
(Storm of Plush), in 2002. This was followed by a collection of
short stories, *Diesseits des Van-Allen-Gürtels* (This Side of the
Van Allen Belt, 2007), which received the Ingeborg Bachmann
Prize Audience Award. In early 2010, he was diagnosed with a
brain tumor; his novel *Tschick* (*Why We Took the Car*) was
published just months later and would eventually be translated
into twenty-four languages. *Sand* was released in 2011; it was
short-listed for the German Book Prize and won the Leipzig
Book Fair Prize. Herrndorf committed suicide in the
summer of 2013. His posts on *Arbeit und Struktur* (Work
and Structure), the blog he started after receiving his cancer
diagnosis, have been published as a book of the same name.
An unfinished sequel to *Tschick*, *Bilder einer großen Liebe*
(Pictures of Your True Love), was released in 2014.

TIM MOHR has translated the work of such authors as Alina
Bronsky, Stefanie de Velasco, and Charlotte Roche, as well as

Wolfgang Herrndorf's novel *Tschick*. His own writing has appeared in *The New York Times Book Review*, *Playboy*, and *New York* magazine, among other publications, and he is the author of *Stirb nicht im Warteraum der Zukunft*, a history of East German punk rock. Prior to his writing career he was a club DJ in Berlin.

MICHAEL MAAR is a literary scholar and Germanist. A member of the German Academy, he is the author of a dozen books, of which *The Two Lolitas*; *Speak, Nabokov*; and *Bluebeard's Chamber: Guilt and Confession in Thomas Mann* have been translated into English.

SAND

WOLFGANG HERRNDORF

Translated from the German by
TIM MOHR
Afterword by
MICHAEL MAAR

NEW YORK REVIEW BOOKS

New York

THIS IS A NEW YORK REVIEW BOOK
PUBLISHED BY THE NEW YORK REVIEW OF BOOKS
435 Hudson Street, New York, NY 10014
www.nyrb.com

First published in the German language in Germany in 2011 as *Sand*.
This translation first published in the United Kingdom in 2017 by Pushkin Press,
supported in part by a grant from the Goethe-Institut London.

Afterword originally published in *Merkur*, number 755 (April 2012).

Library of Congress Cataloging-in-Publication Data
Names: Herrndorf, Wolfgang, 1965–2013, author. | Mohr, Tim, translator. | Maar,
   Michael, writer of afterword.
Title: Sand / by Wolfgang Herrndorf ; translated by Tim Mohr ; afterword by
   Michael Maar.
Other titles: Sand. English
Description: New York : New York Review Books, [2018] | Series: NYRB Classics
Identifiers: LCCN 2018004067 (print) | LCCN 2018010465 (ebook) | ISBN
   9781681372020 (epub) | ISBN 9781681372013 (paperback)
Subjects: LCSH: Hippies—Africa, North—Fiction. | Communal living—Africa,
   North—Fiction. | Murder—Investigation—Africa, North—Fiction. | Suspense
   fiction. | BISAC: FICTION / Historical.
Classification: LCC PT2668.E7572 (ebook) | LCC PT2668.E7572 S2513 2018
   (print) | DDC 833/.92—dc23
LC record available at https://lccn.loc.gov/2018004067

ISBN 978-1-68137-201-3
Available as an electronic book; ISBN 978-1-68137-202-0

Printed in the United States of America on acid-free paper.
10 9 8 7 6 5 4 3 2 1

CONTENTS

BOOK ONE

The Sea

1

Targat on the Sea

Each year we send a ship to Africa—sparing neither lives nor money— to seek answers to the questions: Who are you? What are your laws? What language do you speak? They, however, never send a ship to us.

HERODOTUS

ATOP THE MUD-BRICK WALL stood a man stripped to the waist, with his arms stretched out to the sides as if crucified. He had a rusted wrench in one hand and a blue plastic canister in the other. His gaze fell across tents and huts, piles of garbage and plastic tarps, and off out over the endless desert to a point on the horizon where soon the sun would rise.

When it was time, he banged the wrench and the canister against each other and shouted: "My children! My children!"

The eastern walls of the huts blazed pale orange. The hollow, dull rhythm died down as it receded into the alleyways. Shrouded figures, lying in the cool ditches like mummies, awoke, and cracked lips formed words of praise and offering to the one true God. Three dogs dipped their tongues into a dirty puddle. The whole night through the temperature hadn't sunk below thirty degrees.

Unfazed, the sun rose above the horizon and shone down on the living and the dead, the believers and the non-believers, the wretched and the wealthy. It shone down on corrugated sheet metal, plywood and cardboard, on salt cedars and filth and a thirty-meter-high wall of trash that separated the Salt Quarter and Empty Quarter from the remaining parts of the city. An enormous number of plastic bottles and gutted vehicles gleamed in the sunlight, piles of empty battery casings, pulverized tiles, rubbish, mountains of fecal sludge and the corpses of dead animals. The sun rose above the wall and illuminated the first of the houses in the Ville Nouvelle, free-standing, two-story Spanish-style buildings, as well as the crumbling minarets on the outskirts of town. Silently it lit up the runway of the military airport, the wings of a left-behind Mirage 5, the souk and the adjacent administration buildings of Targat. The sun's light glinted on the drooping metal roll-down gates of little shops and pressed through the blinds of the as yet unoccupied Central Commissariat, wandered up the alfalfa-grass-lined port street, gushed down the twenty-story Sheraton Hotel and shortly after six o'clock reached the sea, gently shielded by the coastal range. It was the morning of 23rd August 1972.

No wind blew, and no waves swelled. The sea stretched to the horizon as smooth as armor plate. A huge cruise ship with yellow smokestacks and strings of extinguished lights lay sleeping at anchor, empty champagne glasses on the railings.

Prosperity, as our friend with the blue plastic canister used to say, prosperity belongs to everyone. Just go out and take it.

2

The Central Commissariat

You know what happened to the Greeks? Homosexuality
destroyed them. Sure, Aristotle was a homo, we all know that,
so was Socrates. Do you know what happened to the Romans?
The last six Roman emperors were fags.

NIXON

POLIDORIO HAD AN IQ of 102, calculated by means of a
questionnaire for French school children aged twelve to
thirteen. They'd found the questionnaire in the Commissariat,
used as packing material for a box of forms printed in Marseilles,
and filled it out with a pencil, one question after the next, in
the allotted amount of time. Polidorio had been very drunk.
Canisades, too. It was the long night of the files.

Twice a year mountains of paper would be piled up in the
halls, cursorily inspected and then burned in the courtyard, an
onerous duty that often took until dawn and traditionally fell
to the most junior employees. Why some files were discarded
while others were kept, nobody could explain. Management
of the operation had been adopted from the French the way
one might reflexively adopt a particular way of addressing a
person, and the bureaucratic systems bore no relationship to
their actual use. Only a few of the accused could read or write,
trials were short.

In the middle of the night there had been an electrical outage at the Commissariat; it had taken Polidorio and Canisades hours to get hold of someone who had the Allen wrench needed to open the fuse box. For a while they continued working by candlelight, and under the influence of pot and alcohol their fatigue turned to euphoria. They staged a snowball fight in the courtyard using balled-up paper and a car chase through the hallways with rolling file cabinets. Canisades said he was Emerson Fittipaldi, Polidorio set a pile of scrap on fire with his cigarette, and then a bundle of special colonial-era credentials fell out of an overturned hanging file. They clamped the papers into a typewriter, entered made-up names and titles, and together they stumbled with them through the breaking daylight and into a bordello ("Bédeaux is the name, Special Prosecutor for the Virtue Committee…").

And before they left, of course, the fateful IQ test. In hindsight Polidorio had only hazy memories of most of the experiences of that fatal night. But the test result stuck with him. One hundred and two.

"Alcohol, stress, electrical outage!" yelled Canisades with a small-breasted black girl on each knee. "Is that an excuse? We'll just round it down to a hundred."

Canisades' test result had been significantly higher. Just how much higher was one of the things Polidorio couldn't remember. But his own number stood from then on as if carved in stone in his memory. Although he was sure he would have scored higher in a sober state of mind—not higher than Canisades, but definitely higher—his score always occurred to him now whenever he didn't understand something. When he struggled more than someone else to grasp something, when he laughed at a joke a split-second later than his colleagues.

Polidorio had always considered himself a rational and gifted person. When he looked back now he didn't know what grounds he had for this belief. He had made it through school, professional training and his exams with little difficulty, but then again that was it. Always middle-of-the-road, average. Which is what his test score also implied: average.

Realizing one is not special is something that hits most people at some point in their lives, not uncommonly at the end of school or at the beginning of professional training, and it hits the intelligent rather more often than the unintelligent. But not everyone struggles with the realization in the same way. Those who weren't sufficiently exposed as children to the ideals of personal merit, achievement, standing out, will perhaps accept the realization of pallid mediocrity as they would having too big a nose or thinning hair. Others, on the other hand, react to it with the stereotypical maneuvers, anything from dressing eccentrically or leading an eccentric lifestyle to ambitiously trying to find a self that they believe to be hidden inside them like a precious treasure, a sentiment granted even the last moron by the practice of psychoanalysis. And the sensitive ones spiral into depression.

A few days after Canisades had regaled the entire circle of work colleagues and friends with the glorious experiences of that night, Polidorio was standing in front of his locker, number 703, and saw that some prankster had used a pen to make a 1 out of the 7 and a 2 out of the 3.

For twenty-eight years he hadn't wasted a thought on the magnitude and measurability of his intelligence—and now sometimes he could think of nothing else.

3

Coffee and Migraines

Of course, a fool, what with sheer fright and fine sentiments,
is always safe.

JOSEPH CONRAD

"WHY SHOULD I CARE about that? You can tell that to
somebody, you can tell it to your briquettes for all I
care, but not me." Polidorio had poured himself a coffee and
stirred it with a pen. The blue blinds were closed except for
a tiny crack of white midday heat. "And you can't just show
up and drag someone in here. Hollerith machine! You don't
even know what that is. And I don't care. The only thing I care
about is: *Where* did it happen? It happened in Tindirma. Who
is responsible *there*? Right. So pack it up and get out of here.
No, don't talk. Stop blathering. You've been talking for an hour.
Now you need to listen."

But the fat man didn't listen. He just stood in front of
Polidorio's desk in a slovenly uniform, doing what everybody
did around here. If they weren't willing to co-operate they just
talked nonsense. If one quizzed them about it, they just changed
the subject to some other nonsense.

Polidorio hadn't offered him coffee or a chair, and spoke to
him rudely even though he was thirty years his elder and of

equal rank. These were usually dependable ways to offend such people. But the fat man seemed immune to them. Unfazed, he talked about approaching retirement, trips in an official vehicle, horticulture and a vitamin shortage. For the fourth and fifth and sixth time he went over the topic of filling his gas tank and his ideas about transporting prisoners, spoke about justice, coincidence and going the extra mile. He pointed at the windows on the opposite wall (desert, sea), at the door (the long route through the Salt Quarter), the defective ceiling fan (Allah), and stomped with his foot on the bundle lying on the floor (the root of all evil).

The root of all evil was a boy with his wrists and ankles bound named Amadou, whom the fat man had picked up in the desert between Targat and Tindirma, a fact that figured only tangentially in his flood of words.

Had he ever heard of responsibility, Polidorio wanted to know, and received as an answer that successful police work was simply a question of technology. He asked what technology had to do with the crime scene, and received as an answer how difficult it was to farm near the oasis. Polidorio asked what farming had to do with it, and the fat man went on about food shortages, sand drifts, water shortages and the resentment of the neighbors on one side, and the prosperity, electronic brains and highly organized police on the other. He cast another glance at the defective Hollerith machine, looked around the room with feigned delight and, as there was no chair to be had, sat down on the prisoner, all without interrupting his flood of words for even a second.

"Quiet now," said Polidorio. "Quiet. Listen to me." He let the palms of his hands hover above the surface of the desk for a moment before placing them on either side of the coffee cup, braced on the desk by his fingers. The fat man repeated his last sentence. There were two buttons missing from his pants. Beads of sweat hung from his fleshy earlobes and swayed in rhythm. Suddenly Polidorio had forgotten what he wanted to say. He felt his temples pulsing.

His gaze fell on hundreds of tiny bubbles that had frothed up in his coffee cup from the agitation of the pen and which now gathered to form a spinning carpet. As the rotation slowed, the bubbles dispersed out to the rim of the cup, where they piled up in a ring-shaped wall. Inside every bubble a tiny head was enclosed, a head that stared at him with squinting eyes, smaller heads inside the smaller bubbles, medium-sized heads in the medium-sized bubbles and large heads inside the larger bubbles. The audience moved in sync, with military precision, and for a few seconds seemed locked in a sort of rigor mortis. Then the heads suddenly expanded, and when Polidorio exhaled a quarter of his audience died.

Gasoline vouchers, desert sand, foot and mouth disease, gaggles of children, rebels, presidential palace. Polidorio knew what the fat man *wasn't* after. But he couldn't figure out what he was after. The transfer of a suspect to Targat made no sense. Perhaps, he thought, the fat man was just playing it safe and wanted to avoid any sort of personal problem falling into his lap. Or perhaps his company-time junket to the coast was an end in and of itself. Perhaps he had some business to take care of here. Maybe he wanted to see the port district. And surely it had to do with money. Everything had to do with money. He probably wanted to sell a few things. He certainly wouldn't be the first small-town sheriff to compensate for missed wages by dragging typewriters, blank paper or service revolvers to the souk. And if it didn't have to do with money, it had to do with family. Perhaps he had a son here he wanted to visit. Or a fat daughter of marriageable age. Maybe he wanted to visit a bordello. Maybe his fat daughter even worked in a bordello, and he wanted to sell her his service revolver. Anything was possible.

A dull alarm bell interrupted his thoughts. Polidorio pulled a large wad of cloth out of the bottom drawer of his desk and smacked his palm down on a specific spot, known only to him. The alarm went silent. He got a package of aspirin out of the same drawer and said irritably, "That's enough now. Get out of here. Go back to the oasis and take that with you."

He pressed two tablets out of the blister pack. He didn't have a headache, but if he didn't take medicine now he'd have one in exactly half an hour. Every day at four. Nobody had been able to explain the source of these recurring attacks. The last doctor had held the X-rays up to the light, said something about things looking normal, and had advised Polidorio to see a psychologist. The psychologist had recommended medications, and the pharmacist, who had never heard of the medications, sent him to a wise man. The wise man weighed ninety pounds, was lying in the street contorted and sold Polidorio a scrap of paper with incantations written on it that had to be put under the bed. Finally, his wife brought a package of generic aspirin back from France.

It wasn't mental. Polidorio refused to believe it was something mental. What kind of mind would trigger searing pain every day at the same time? There was nothing particular about four in the afternoon. It couldn't have anything to do with work, the pain came on days off as well. It started at four and stuck around until he fell asleep. Polidorio was young, he was athletically fit, and fed himself no differently than he had in Europe. Very near the Sheraton was a shop with imported goods; he didn't use local water even to brush his teeth. Was it the weather? If so, why didn't he have headaches twenty-four hours a day?

In the lonely hours of the night, when the blight of the heat pushed in on him through the mosquito netting, when the nameless sea pounded the nameless cliffs and the insects cavorted beneath his bed, he came to believe it was neither a mental nor a bodily ailment. It was the country itself. In France he had never had headaches. They had started after two days in Africa.

He took the tablets in his mouth and slurped them down with two sips of coffee, feeling the light pressure descend through his throat. It was his daily ritual, and it bothered him to have the uncontrollably blathering fat man sitting there watching him conduct it. While he put the package back in the drawer, he said, "Or does this look like the receiving office for provincial bullshit? Go back to your oasis. You kaffir."

Silence. Kaffir. He waited for the reaction, and the reaction came with just a single second's delay: the fat man suddenly opened his eyes wide, formed a small O with his mouth and lackadaisically waved a hand at shoulder height. Then he kept talking. Oasis, the condition of the roads, Hollerith machines.

It had been two months since Polidorio started his job here. And for two months he'd wanted nothing else but to return to Europe. Already on the day of his arrival he had realized that his knowledge of human nature didn't function among the foreign faces—a realization for which he had paid with his camera. His grandfather had been an Arab himself, but he had emigrated to Marseilles when he was young. Polidorio had a French passport and after his parents' divorce had grown up in Switzerland. He'd gone to school in Biel, then later studied in Paris. He spent his free time in cafés, in cinemas and on tennis courts. People liked him, but when there were arguments they called him *pied-noir*. If his serve had been better, he might have been able to become a tennis pro. As it was, he became a policeman.

Like so much in his life, it had been by chance. A friend of his had taken him along to the entrance exam. The friend was rejected, Polidorio was not. During his year of training, society had changed without him catching wind of it. He wasn't a political person. He didn't read the papers. The rioters in Paris in May and the lunatics at Nanterre University had interested him as little as the gasping of the other side. Justice and laws were pretty much the same thing as far as he was concerned. He didn't like the longhairs, but mostly for aesthetic reasons. He'd read ten pages of Sartre. It was easier, as his first girlfriend had written when she split up with him, to describe him by what he wasn't than by what he was.

His second girlfriend he married. That was in May 1969, and he didn't love her. She got pregnant immediately. The first year was hell. When he was offered a job in the former colonies because of his knowledge of Arabic, he took it straight away. Glossy photo books of picturesque deserts, primitive wooden sculptures on living-room shelves, idle chatter about roots. He didn't have a clue about Africa.

The thing that had struck him more than anything else were the strange smells at the airport. Then the loneliness of the first few weeks before his family arrived. A picture in the daily paper: Thévenet at Mont Ventouz. A postcard from a friend: snow-covered Alps. The stench, the horrible headaches. Polidorio had started stopping in the street when he heard somebody speak pure French without an asthmatic gurgle. The sight of tourists, their feeling of abandon, the bright blonde women. He had applied to return; the French state just laughed at him. With every week he became more sentimental. French tourists, French newspapers, French products. Even the bums and longhairs who always turned up in packs, hiking single-file out of the mountains into the valleys with a pound of pot in their bags, only to be handcuffed there by him—even they stirred emotion in him. They were idiots. But they were European idiots.

The fat man was still talking. Polidorio shoved the coffee cup on his desk to the side. He knew he was making a mistake. He gripped the far edge of the desk with both hands and pulled his upper body forward, peering down into the space in front of it.

"Twenty dollars, yeah?"

The tied-up boy seemed to have passed out beneath the weight of the fat man.

"The high commissioner is speaking to you!" the fat man yelled, and he smacked the prisoner on the ear with the flat of his hand.

"Twenty dollars and a basket of vegetables?" repeated Polidorio.

"What?"

"Yes, you!"

"Yes, what is it, boss?"

"A couple of dollars and a basket of vegetables. You mowed down four people in Tindirma for that?"

"What?" The bundle began to revive. "Four people where?"

"Four people in Tindirma. Four whites."

"I've never been to Tindirma in my life, boss. I swear!"

4

MS Kungsholm

Ellsberg showed the same childlike eagerness to share discoveries of a sexual nature as he did to share confidential nuclear technology. He once described his latest lover to the people at RAND the following way: "She had gaps between every tooth."

ANDREW HUNT

THERE ARE NOT MANY PEOPLE who can be described in a single sentence. Normally one needs several, and even for ordinary people an entire novel is often not enough. Helen Gliese, who was leaning on the rail of the MS *Kungsholm* in white shorts, a white blouse, a white sunhat and giant sunglasses, chewing gum with a half-open mouth, looking at the swarm of people on the nearing shore, could be described in two words: pretty and stupid. With these two words one could send a stranger to the port and be sure that he would pick up the correct person among hundreds of travelers.

The amazing thing about it, though, wasn't the brevity of the description. The amazing thing was that this description wasn't the slightest bit apt. Helen wasn't pretty. She was a collection of aesthetic commonplaces, an overabundance of personal hygiene and fashion effort, but she wasn't pretty in the classical sense of the word. She was someone best seen from afar. Some photos of her could have been used on the cover of a fashion magazine—giving an impression of smoothness, coolness, elegance of form. But as soon as the image came to life, one became immediately baffled. Helen's facial expressions were somehow off. The slow, monotonous sing-song of her voice produced the impression of an actress in a daytime TV series whose role is described in a note in the screenplay as rich and blasé, her arm and hand gestures were like a parody of a homosexual, and when one first met Helen, all of this, together with her excessive make-up and outlandish clothing, could delay for several minutes—or hours or days—the realization that what she actually said was logical and well thought out. Her thoughts were perfectly clear, and she formulated them effortlessly. Even more surprising was reading letters from her.

In other words, Helen was the exact opposite of stupid, and if not the opposite of pretty, at least far from the classical notion of beauty; none of which changed the fact that this description functioned fine for having her picked up at the port. Or would have functioned fine. It was Helen's first visit to Africa and nobody picked her up.

5

The Acts of a Crackpot

He urged us to start at once, at the same time announcing his intention of accompanying us so as to protect us against treachery. I was much touched by this act of kindness on the part of that wily old barbarian toward two utterly defenseless strangers.

H. RIDER HAGGARD

THE ACCUSED WAS NAMED Amadou Amadou. Every single piece of evidence went against him, and the sum of the evidence was a death sentence. Amadou was twenty-one or twenty-two, a gangly young man who lived or had lived with his parents, grandparents and a dozen brothers and sisters two blocks from the scene of the crime, an agrarian commune in the oasis of Tindirma.

The commune consisted mostly of Americans, a few French, Spanish and Germans, a Polish woman and a Lebanese man; all told, twice as many women as men. The majority of them had got to know each other in the mid-1960s in the coastal region around Targat and had stumbled accidentally on the property in the oasis twenty kilometers away, a two-story building with a bit of land that was available to rent cheaply. The dream was of a natural, self-determined life, of collective organization and so forth. None of the communards had any experience of this sort of concrete utopianism. At first they lived from a laboriously irrigated field and junk they bought from the locals and exported to the First World; later came the occasional dealings in illegal substances.

Initially viewed with distrust, the longhaired, talkative, directionless, bumbling communards won the goodwill of their new neighbors relatively quickly through their openness and helpfulness. They reached out their hands in a friendly and generous manner to those around them, and those around them reached back hesitantly at first and then affectionately. Foreign jewelry was marveled at, hair was touched, food was exchanged. It was the time of the big speeches, the long discussions and implied fraternity. Eventually came a few small fortifications and the first unrest. Over the summer, the number of uninvited guests who sought to extract financial gains from the commune became unmanageable. Medical, technical and sexual services were requested and at least in part granted. The consequence was a series of troublesome conflicts, called misunderstandings internally, whereupon they pulled back from the local people more and more, initially in a diffuse way and then programmatically, receding to a strictly business relationship, until finally an additional meter was added to the top of the one-and-a-half-meter wall already surrounding the property. By just two votes, a tiny majority was to thank for the fact that shards of glass weren't pressed into the fresh clay atop the new wall. All of this took place in the course of a few months.

The two most noticeable figures in the commune were a Scottish industrial scion named Edgar Fowler III and the French ex-soldier and drifter Jean Bekurtz. In one of their sober moments they had come up with the idea of the commune, recruited members with their infectious enthusiasm—among them a striking number of attractive women—and drafted a rough outline of what they called their philosophy.

But the desert quickly changed the outlook. Where initially one took up residence in the gray area of a discussion-friendly Marxism, the number of incense sticks in the household increased in a short amount of time. Between Kerouac and Castaneda, a half-meter of Trotsky molded away, and the idea of a constantly physically co-mingling mass of humanity ("It's just a metaphor") broke down due to the reluctance of the women, who were no longer inclined to acquiesce. At the time of our story, the commune had sunk to the level of a pathetic economic partnership of convenience—the prosperity of which seemed only negligibly better than it had been at the time of its founding.

In order to make the sequence of events and everything that follows understandable, a short explanation must be offered at this point of what we mean when we speak of "the oasis".

Archaeological examinations had uncovered no evidence of earlier settlements on the site. In 1850, Tindirma was still a collection of three mud huts around a meager reservoir on the slope of an isolated rock spire in the desert. Geologists speak of a cone of volcanic origin. The highest elevation is 250 meters above sea level, and provides a view that even on good days doesn't allow one to see anything more than sand all around, sand that had been blown into an endless field of crescent dunes by the constant wind from the coast. Only the western horizon offered even an inkling of moisture and green and blue.

Located at the crossing of two inconsequential caravan routes, the oasis first grew during the bloody battles surrounding the Massina Empire. Displaced Fula people with no belongings and, most importantly, with no livestock arrived here from the south, half naked and half starving, and negotiated the transition from a nomadic existence to farming. Three mud huts became fifty, pushing up the slope between scrubby acacias and doum palms.

Life is hard, and like many unwilling emigrants the Fula named the paltry patch of earth they cultivated after the place from which they'd fled: Nouveau Tindirma. In the space of a generation, the number of unfortunates there rose tenfold.

Historiography from that era does not exist in written or in credible oral form. The first documented image is a black and white photo from the 1920s of men with scarred faces. With deadened gazes and pressed into a dark rectangle, they are standing in the cargo bed of a Thornycroft BX, which is entering the freshly graded main street of a Tindirma that is barely recognizable; in the background is one of the first two-story buildings.

At the end of the 1930s two events profoundly transform Tindirma. The first is the arrival of a lost Swiss engineer, Lukas Imhof, whose car breaks down and who is hindered by the locals from repairing it. With practically no tools and just the help of a few Haratin, Imhof digs in the next few months a forty-meter-deep well next to the Kaafaahi cliffs, which henceforth provides the oasis with an abundance of water. Imhof is subsequently presented in ceremonial fashion with two refurbished spark plugs (family album, square photo).

The second is the mushrooming civil war in the south, which puts Tindirma in the most strategically advantageous location for smuggling arms and other resources. Only two or three families cultivate their millet fields any more; the rest bow out in favor of night work and flood the community with previously unknown prosperity and the routes south with dead bodies.

At about the same time, the first Arab merchant families relocate from Targat to Tindirma. Europeans with dark sunglasses and meticulously shaved necks drive through Tindirma in olive-green automobiles, and in 1938 the head office installs the first police station there. The appearance of state authority doesn't change everyday life much at first. Anyone who values a peaceful life and can afford it maintains a private army; the police find themselves fighting primarily for their own security.

The transition from lawless to half-civilized entity comes to fruition only with the displacement of the civil war in the south and west. The arms-saturated region becomes receptive to other goods. Former smuggling barons invest in infrastructure, the first bars and hotels sprout up. In the mid-1950s there's briefly a cinema. A paved road thrusts its way through the center of the oasis for several hundred meters, makes a weak feint at the coast and peters out in the sand. Two small mosques stretch their minaret fingers to the yellow sky. Religion exerts a moderate influence on the life of the municipality, strengthening the weak and the faithful and solidifying morals and civility through the clarity of godly thoughts, through education and shari'a law.

Parallel to the intrusion by state and religious organs, repeated attempts are made to change the name of the locale in order to erase the memory of its dark past, but neither the residents nor the Arabs nor the one or two cartographers who acknowledged the settlement up to the year 1972 manage to establish any other name than Tindirma.

On Wednesday, 23rd August 1972 the following occurred, according to witnesses: Amadou Amadou, intoxicated, drove a car, a light-blue rusted Toyota that did not belong to him, into the courtyard of the commune, which was near the souk. There, as five members of the commune concordantly reported, he initially offered to sell some unspecified service, then sub-sequently, over tea, made a speech about sexuality that was as explicit as it was anatomically incorrect (four witnesses), as well as starting to have a philosophical discussion about gender relations (one witness), then apparently made his way unnoticed into the kitchen where he helped himself to more alcohol, and finally, brandishing a firearm that suddenly appeared in his hand, stormed through the property searching for valuables. A stereo hi-fi system in the common room was the first thing to attract his interest, but he was unable to transport it alone. A female member of the commune, asked to carry the speakers to the car, had refused, as the stereo system wasn't fully paid off, at which point Amadou had shot her in the face. He then shot two other communards who arrived on the scene to try to disarm him (with words?). After further search of the property (now with the weapon held out in front of him like a dog pulling on a leash), he discovered a woven rattan suitcase that was stuffed with money (paper notes of unknown currency). Amadou had forgotten everything else and attempted to flee the house with the rattan suitcase. While attempting to do so he lost a sandal when it fell down a stairwell, shot a further communard hiding in a wardrobe, and took possession of a basket filled with fruit that had been standing in the kitchen pantry. Some thirty or forty witnesses, drawn by the gunfire, had seen Amadou as he fired into the air in order to disperse the crowd, jumped into the Toyota and drove off in the direction of the coast road. Halfway to the coast, in the middle of the desert, he ran out of gas and was arrested by the fat little village sheriff, who showed up with the suspect a short time later in Polidorio's office. Amadou was wearing just one sandal at the time of his arrest. The rattan suitcase with the money was nowhere to be found, but the basket of fruit sat on the passenger seat of the light-blue Toyota in the desert. The still-warm Mauser was in the glovebox. An empty magazine that fitted the weapon was later seized in the courtyard of the commune. A sandal was recovered in the stairwell, which was a mirror image of the one Amadou had on.

In his statements, Amadou didn't address any of the particulars of the allegations against him. He flatly denied the whole thing. This was not unusual. In a country where a man's word still held sway, there were in essence no confessions. The standard statement of all accused criminals in all investigations was that all allegations brought against them were fabricated

and that they felt their honor deeply insulted. If the suspect
or accused put in any effort to come up with their own version of events, as a rule they paid no attention to the details.
Amadou was no exception. Coherently integrating the facts at
hand into his fantasy version of events never crossed his mind.
How did the sandal end up in the staircase of the commune?
How did an empty magazine get into the yard? Why did forty
witnesses say they could positively identify Amadou? Amadou
shrugged his shoulders. He couldn't answer to save his life, and
he didn't understand why these questions were being asked of
him of all people. Wasn't it much more the duty of the police
to answer such questions? He pointed to some electric device
or other (telex, coffee machine) and begged to be hooked up
to the lie detector. He swore before the true and only God, he
stated that he could only say what happened *in reality*, and he
would be happy to do so at any time. He, Amadou Amadou,
had been taking a walk in the desert. The weather had been
lovely, and the walk took several hours. (It wasn't as unlikely as
it might at first sound. Many oasis residents still moonlighted
as smugglers.) While under way he had lost a sandal in a thorn
bush. Then, near the road, he had found an abandoned, light-
blue Toyota and had climbed into the unlocked vehicle because
there was a basket of mouth-watering fruit on the passenger
seat and he, Amadou, had toyed with the idea of eating some
of the fruit since he was very hungry. This was something they
could actually reproach him for, since the fruit did not belong
to him. He would swear to this. At that moment, however, he
was arrested and taken to Targat by a policeman who seemed
to materialize out of nowhere. He didn't know anything about
a pistol in the glovebox.

This statement he repeated on four consecutive days without
changing a word. Just once, on the evening of the fourth day
and in a state of severe fatigue, did Amadou remark that he

had tossed the rattan suitcase out of the window during the escape; he recanted this sentence after just a few minutes and later wouldn't admit to having said it at all. Didn't want to say anything more unless they let him finally sleep.

And the fact that the victims were foreigners made everything infinitely more complicated. Polidorio had led the interrogation only on the first day, on the second and third Canisades made half-hearted attempts to shift the case back to Tindirma; then the Interior Minister unexpectedly intervened, and the affair was transferred to the most senior member of the staff, Karimi.

A government official had already been in the United States for a few days and was negotiating alliances and development aid when the massacre received unusually extensive coverage in the American press. In Europe as well they busied themselves with the affair, even though no Europeans were among the victims. In the capital there were uncomfortable inquiries (the French ambassador, the American ambassador, a German news magazine), and the result of it all was that Karimi and a federal prosecutor had to be stationed in a hotel in Tindirma. Officially, in order to thoroughly reinvestigate; in reality, to provide the journalists gathered there with indiscreet information about the status of things and lurid examples of the insanity of the culprit. Because the victims may have all been a bunch of drugged-up hippies who ran an anti-imperialist pot business in the desert—but as soon as things got serious, the only thing that mattered to the First World was citizenship.

Amadou was barely aware of all of this. He kept pointing to the lie detector/coffee machine, swore on the life of his father and father's father, swore by the true and only God, called for the support of his family and king, and said that they could torture him and put screws into the soles of his feet but he would not budge one millimeter from the truth.

"Screws into the soles of the feet," said Karimi. "These are methods that would obviously not be utilized here. In all seriousness, if we had any interest in a confession from you, we would have long since got it. I hope this is clear to you. We don't need your feet for that. We don't need anything for that. It's just, who would care about it? Have you ever considered who would care about a statement from you? Have you looked at the evidence?"

Amadou shifted from side to side in his chair and grinned. Karimi turned to the lawyer: "Have you at least tried to explain this to him? A tenth of that evidence would send a man to the guillotine." He turned back to Amadou. "Nobody gives a shit whether you talk or not. Not even the most corrupt line judge in the world would let you off. You can keep your mouth shut or you can talk. The only difference is that if you talk your family will receive a tidy corpse. Think of your mother. No, correction—naturally that's not the only difference. The other one is that if you talk, you will be allowed to leave the room to take a piss."

The lawyer, who had sat by silently chewing his nails almost the entire time, protested meekly. Then he asked to be able to talk to his client privately. Karimi pointed to a sofa in the corner where normally the commissars sat while they smoked.

The lawyer could have gone into another room with Amadou. Or he could have asked Karimi, Canisades and Polidorio to stand outside the door. Instead he led Amadou over to the piece of furniture some seven or eight meters away and explained to him in a hushed tone—though still clearly audible to the police—that the evidence was overwhelming and the day very hot. With a raised index finger he added that everything had already been decided before the eyes of Allah. In an earthly court, on the other hand, one could in this case neither improve things nor aggravate them with a statement, only shorten the futile and dishonorable procedure. And a man of honor, like Amadou, and so on. The man wasn't exactly a star lawyer. He had the face of a farmer and was wearing a poorly fitting black suit with a mustard-colored handkerchief sticking out of the breast pocket like a desperate cry for help. It wasn't entirely clear to the Commissariat where the man had managed to get hold of Amadou's family. There was a strong suspicion that he was being paid in kind. Amadou had six or seven sisters.

"Oh, man," said Canisades with a glance at the desk. He lit up like a little child. "Oh, man. Oh, man."

Polidorio looked at his watch, took two aspirin out of his pocket and gulped them down dry. With his chin stretched upward he stared for a while at the ceiling fan. The accused still persisted in pantomiming his version: a walk in the desert, sandals, fruit basket, arrest. He squirmed around on the sofa, and as the lawyer repeated his argument for the third or fourth time in the manner of a primary-school teacher, Polidorio suddenly caught sight of a look from the accused that he hadn't seen before. What was that look? It was the desperate look of a not terribly intelligent man who in this moment, during the monotonous ripples of the flood of words from his lawyer, realized that his life was over, the look of a man who despite the overwhelming burden of evidence must have thought up until a few minutes ago that there was still a chance to avoid the guillotine, a look that was not only desperate but also seemed shocked, a look of a man, thought Polidorio, who—perhaps was innocent.

He paged through the files.

"Where are the fingerprints?"

"What fingerprints?"

"From the weapon."

Karimi unwrapped the foil from around a chocolate as he shook his head.

"We have forty eyewitnesses," said Canisades. "And Asiz is on vacation."

"Can't almost anyone do it?"

"Who is almost anyone? Can you?" bristled Karimi, who was determined to return by daylight to Tindirma, where he had an appointment with a reporter from *Life* magazine. "Asiz can't even do it. When he was a palace guard he spent a week pasting the place up. Then he took four hundred prints, and the only two that were recognizable were from the eight-year-old son of the janitor."

Polidorio sighed and looked over at the lawyer, who had stopped talking.

Amadou's head had sunk to half-mast.

6

Shakespeare

A wonderfully funny letter was sent to me signed by a fraternity in Boston, Massachusetts, medical school; the fraternity for doctors had voted me the body on which they would most like to operate.

DYANNE THORNE

HELEN WAS NEVER AWARE of the impression she made. She knew herself only from photos or the mirror. In her own estimation she looked good, even breathtaking in some of the photos. She had her life under control, without being particularly happy or unhappy, and had no troubles with men. At least no more so than her friends. Less, in fact. From the beginning of high school on she'd had seven or eight relationships, all with boys about her age, who were nice, well bred and athletic, boys for whom the intelligence of their girlfriends wasn't of particular importance and who rarely noticed Helen's.

Helen didn't let it bother her. If men wanted to consider themselves intellectually superior, she wasn't distraught. Most of the relationships didn't last long, but as fast as they ended new ones formed. A walk across campus in a midriff-baring T-shirt and Helen had three invitations to dinner. The only question that came up from time to time was why the genuinely interesting men never approached her. She couldn't explain it.

She suffered from depression only as often as anyone else, not more. From novels she knew that the most beautiful women were also the least happy. She read a lot.

The first blow to her self-confidence came when, as she was preparing for an exam, she recorded her voice with a tape recorder. Helen listened to the recording for exactly four seconds and subsequently didn't have the courage to press play a second time. An alien, a Tex Avery cartoon, a talking piece of chewing gum. She knew that one's own voice could sound strange, but the tones on the tape were more than strange. At first she had even thought it possible that the machine had some sort of technical defect.

The pimply chemistry professor who had lent her the tape recorder explained that resonant bones and cavities in the head were the reason that people perceived their own voices as fuller and more melodious than they really were, and that surprise was a reasonable reaction. He himself had the falsetto voice of a castrato and was unable to keep his gaze away from Helen's cleavage when he talked to her. She didn't participate in any further experiments of this sort and put it out of her mind. That was during her first year at Princeton.

Helen gained entrance effortlessly and was awarded a much-sought-after scholarship. But like many first-year students she reacted with fundamental insecurity to being replanted in a world full of strangers and cliquey rituals. In her dormitory she felt more lonely than she ever had in her entire life. She hurled herself into her studies, never broke off even the most boring small talk, and went to pains to find fixed appointments to fill most nights of the week.

Through an acquaintance who was studying English literature, Helen came into contact with an amateur drama club that put on classical plays, rarely anything modern, four or five times a year. Most of the members were students, but two housewives, a former professor who liked to get naked and a young railway trackman were also part of the group. The trackman was considered the secret star. He was twenty-four years old, had the face of a matinee idol, a body like a Greek statue and—his only fault—he could not commit any lines to memory. Not least because of him, Helen spent nearly three years working on dramas of the Elizabethan age.

At first she had only small roles, later she played Bianca in *The Taming of the Shrew* and the title role in *Dorothea Angermann*. She wasn't without talent, and she wouldn't have been opposed to playing the shining hero once; but the best roles, it seemed to her, were awarded on the basis of experience rather than talent. Whoever had been with the company longest ended up as Desdemona.

And then they put on *Cat on a Hot Tin Roof*. It wasn't so much that they put on the play as they mimicked the movie. The trackman shone as Paul Newman, looked jarringly similar to the role model and hobbled so coolly across the stage on his crutches that his interactions with the prompter came off as an artful part of the production. A stunning black-haired biology student in her senior year played Liz Taylor. Helen was Mae. The bigoted Mae with her bigoted family. They padded her waist to five times its size, powdered her hair gray, painted rosy cheeks beneath her high cheekbones, put her in a dress the shape and color of a potato, and to serve as the no-necked children they brought in the professor's grandchildren, who, because in reality they had necks, were wrapped with cervical collars. Their mouths were stuffed with foam rubber and instead of speaking, the children gave consonant-less groans, much to the delight of the audience.

The assistant professor who led the group recorded the premiere on an 8mm camera. It was the first time Helen had been filmed since her first day of primary school, and at the screening of the film she had to leave the room. She went to the bathroom, took a quick glance in the mirror and threw up. She walked stiffly back to the screening room and stared just to the side of the screen for the next hour and half and listened to the monotonous rattle of the projector. The next play on the schedule was Schnitzler's *La Ronde*, but before the suspense of who would play what roles was settled, she quit the theater group.

The assistant professor lamented this move. But other than him, nobody else seemed to take great note of it. Just as no one had taken note of what a thoroughly ridiculous and vacuous performance she had given on stage. In accordance with the role, of course—to be honest, in perfect accordance with the role—but played in such a convincing manner that one could scarcely believe it was even acting at all. Such facial expressions, such intonation! And nobody found it remarkable. During the final applause Helen took another look at the screen. The noise level and whistling doubled as Mae, in a grotesque cotton sack dress, took a step forward, stiltedly put her arms around two neckless monsters, and curled her mouth into an appallingly simpering smile. The last image on a rattling, spinning spool of film.

At the small party that followed, Helen drank too much wine, and her final act before she permanently quit the group was to whisper in the ear of the trackman that she was going to lay him that night. She rattled off her address and a time and left without awaiting his reaction. The fact that she had purposefully chosen such dramatic words in order to justify failure didn't make it any better.

But it was no failure. At one in the morning, fingernails scratched on wood in the dormitory. Paul Newman had in his hand a bouquet of flowers that looked as if he'd stolen them from the cemetery, and he seemed relieved when Helen carelessly threw them in the sink and uncorked a bottle of wine. At dawn he confessed with a gulp that he had a fiancée, earned in response a shrug of the shoulders, and the two of them never saw each other again.

In a white terrycloth bathrobe Helen crept down the hall of the dormitory, climbed two sets of stairs with a heavy head and knocked on the door of her best friend, Michelle Vanderbilt. Or perhaps not her best friend but her oldest friend. Michelle and Helen had known each other since elementary school, and since the first day of their friendship there endured a strong and constant imbalance of power between the two girls.

One of the earliest, most appalling and most exemplary memories: the matter of the canary. Perhaps in the third grade, perhaps even earlier. They were sitting on the floor among all sorts of playthings when they heard a horrible scream from the next room. Michelle's younger brother. Seconds later a small, yellow ball of feathers came hopping through the doorway to the children's room. The head hung limply, swinging to the side. Michelle jumped up in a panic, the ball of feathers flitted sideways as if caught in a gust of wind, rolled out into the hallway, getting dangerously close to the staircase. Helen blocked its way. The little brother ran hysterically back and forth. Mrs Vanderbilt slumped in a chair as if she had fainted, stretched out her hands as if to protect herself, and screamed at Michelle and Helen: "Help him! Help him!"

Eight-year-old Helen, who had no pets and who had also never seen the bird outside of its cage before, gingerly picked it up and straightened its little head with her finger. It dropped to the side again. She suggested putting the bird in bed, or splinting its neck with a matchstick. Nobody reacted. Finally she went into the Vanderbilts' living room and started looking through an encyclopedia. She jumped around from canary birds to medical emergencies, from broken neck and fracture to spinal cord injury. She suggested Michelle either call a doctor or call a friend who also had a bird.

In the end, Mrs Vanderbilt managed to get a veterinarian on the phone, who recommended putting the animal out of its misery. The lady of the house held the receiver out in the air, far from her ear, repeated the doctor's words loudly, and looked around, seeking help. But no member of the family was capable of doing what was necessary, and so finally Helen took pity on the miserable creature. She swept the bird gently into a plastic bag, put both her knees on the opening, and pounded with a volume of the *Encyclopedia Britannica* on the three-dimensional sack until it was two-dimensional. Afterward she buried the flattened result in the yard. Mrs Vanderbilt stood crying behind the curtains.

It was a mixture of fear and wonder that Michelle felt for her new friend that day, and that remained the predominant feeling she had about Helen in subsequent years. Occasionally (and especially during puberty), in addition to this feeling of awe, a range of other, alternating feelings came along: lack of comprehension, adoration, rage, jealousy, deliberate coldness, something like compassion… and then back to awe and genuine love—all increased in intensity by the fact that the object of these conflicting feelings never seemed to notice even the slightest difference.

And so the day after the film screening was a special day for Michelle. It was the first and only day on which she saw her friend seem weak. A picture of misery in a white bathrobe shuffled into her room in need of herbal tea and attention. Overwhelmed by the opportunity, Michelle stuck the knife in the wound and twisted it: it happened to everyone, she exclaimed, everyone was appalled by his or her own voice at first, even she, Michelle, had been put off when she recently randomly heard her own voice on a tape. Admittedly, there were also the gesticulations in Helen's case, and in conjunction with the facial expressions it was actually something that, if she was being honest… when through all the years, this look… and it was the meaning of friendship… but ultimately one got used to it. And for her, personally, now: really not a problem.

In a seminar room Michelle was no great rhetorician, but in private and in intimate conversation she could put together text blocks of formidable scale. Even when in her eyes it was only a trifle (lovesickness, failure, or the house cat being sick would have incited her more), she spoke for nearly two hours straight about what she later referred to as "the tape recorder affair".

Helen ignored the entire contents of the dispatch and noted only its length. One cannot speak about something for two hours, she told herself, that isn't a grave problem.

For a few months she used a dictaphone to practice speaking faster and more clearly, without success; simultaneously, in order to exorcize the stiltedness and sluggishness of her gesticulations, she sought out a form of exercise that, she assumed, would run counter to her idea of fun and to what her body might be suited for, and hit upon karate. She registered as one of two women for a course at the university and realized after four weeks that one can change a lot in life, but not certain physiological realities. Helen became stronger and more dexterous, but nothing about the nature of the way she moved changed. She was Mae in a keikogi, Mae doing yoko geri, Mae on the mat. It was a depressing time.

Despite the futility of her efforts, she did not give up on karate. When the course at the university was discontinued, she switched to a professional studio. She was the only woman there, and to her fell the unabated attention of all the other participants, almost exclusively police from a nearby academy.

By the time she finished her studies, she had two abortions behind her, held black belts in two martial arts disciplines, had dated three or four police officers, and had no idea what she should do with her life. Pronounced cheekbones and the first

lines around her mouth and eyes gave her face a certain severity, which wasn't something she'd wanted, but which was also
not entirely unbefitting. She wore make-up.

"Listen to your inner voice," advised Michelle, but in contrast to her friend, Helen could not seem to detect a voice anywhere inside her. A bourgeois existence felt alien to her, and if
she had been able to compare the nature and intensity of her
feelings with those of other people, something that for most
twenty-five-year-olds is either not possible or only possible in
a very limited way, she would have to have conceded that she
was emotionally cold. Situations others reveled in connoted no
more to her than an impressionistic postcard, a litter of kittens
or Grace Kelly's engagement, and an inattentive observer could
have taken her for altogether passionless. But her daydreams
were fraught with peculiar images. The fireman carrying two
stertorous children from a burning building that collapses behind
him... the pilot brandishing his cowboy hat as he sits astride an
atom bomb dropping into a valley... the crucified Spartacus,
lamented by Jean Simmons... *please die, my love, die now...* she
favored heroic subjects.

7

Lundgren

No Chinaman must figure in the story.

RONALD KNOX,
Ten Commandment List for Detective Novelists

AND NOW LUNDGREN had a problem. Lundgren was dead. When they pulled him by his welted shoes from a culvert in eastern Tindirma, the only thing about him that was still recognizable as European was the cut of his clothes. Children out playing had discovered the corpse, four men retrieved it. Nobody knew who the dead man was, nobody knew how he'd got to the oasis or what he wanted there, nobody missed him.

A fresh atrocity visited upon a white person, just three weeks after the massacre in the commune, caused quite a stir among the desert dwellers. With fingertips and wooden sticks they rummaged the pockets of his suit, found nothing of value—found nothing at all… and sealed the fate of his identity by dispatching the corpse back into the culvert.

An old Tuareg, who suffered from river blindness and had children lead him around using a broom handle, positioned himself at the scene of the crime for several days and, in exchange for a trifling baksheesh, a handful of pistachios or a nip of schnapps, told the gruesome story. He had topaz-blue eyes which no longer had pupils, and he squinted off into the distance, over the heads of his audience, and swore to have been out in the desert the day before the discovery of the body and to have been startled by a sinister sound. His underage attendants had chattered their teeth and trembled in fear; he, however, old fighter under Moussa ag Amastan, had easily recognized it as the sonic boom of an F-5. Correctly, for the children had immediately described to him a needle-thin vapor trail in the blue sky, out of the middle of which opened a golden parachute. This parachute and its shadow had circled each other across the face of the Kaafaahi cliffs like a pair of mating eagles; not long afterward a man in an expensive suit and on all fours had crept down from the mountain into the remains of some mud huts and disappeared, tugging the parachute behind him like a golden plow.

The parachute in particular aroused general pleasure among the listeners. In later versions the narrator also discovered a sports car, an intelligence operative and four men carrying steel rods, but after a few days everyone had heard the story, and it was no longer a money-earner. On to the next thing.

The truth was: there was no parachute. There were no steel rods. The truth was: nobody saw anything. In the entire oasis, there was just one single person who knew anything, and this person wasn't talking. It was the woman who had rented a room to Lundgren on the day of his arrival, and she said nothing because in the tiny room she rented out was an abandoned suitcase full of wonderful things.

Lundgren's arrival in the oasis was unspectacular. He had made his way to Targat by train. Once there, he had thrown on a djellaba, glued on a laughable beard and started off into the desert in a shared minicab without exchanging a word with his fellow passengers. A few kilometers before Tindirma the minicab broke down, and Lundgren, who believed himself to be in a hurry, hopped onto a donkey cart. He tipped the driver to take him down a particular alleyway. Then he had himself carted around in circles for a while and finally got out two streets from the aforementioned alleyway in front of a seedy bar. Above the bar was a seedy room that was normally rented out to seedy merchants. At the moment it was vacant, as a sign in Arabic and French proclaimed. Lundgren had a reservation at the local two-star hotel, but he was no amateur. He let himself be shown the little room.

The approximately one-hundred-year-old landlady led him up to the second floor. She had a face that consisted entirely of creases, with just two holes as eyes. She ground her jaw incessantly, and from each drooping corner of her mouth flowed a black froth. She opened a low door, behind it a washbasin, a mattress, no electricity. Cockroaches fled in single file along the baseboards. Lundgren smiled obligingly—affably—and paid for two weeks in advance. The vermin didn't bother him. A familiar thing: where there were Arabs, there were vermin. He unrolled a plastic tarp that with the help of the aged woman he spread over the bed, and he coated the overhanging edges of it with an ocher-brown sticky paste. Then he fogged the room using a hand-pumped bug-sprayer and closed the door. Whatever was alive, died.

The old woman was unimpressed. In the kitchen she offered Lundgren food, he declined gratefully. She pulled a bottle of home-distilled schnapps from beneath her apron, he contended not to drink alcohol on religious grounds. She proceeded to offer him in turn a coffee, a pure coffee, a rental car, a prostitute, and her granddaughter. A small girl, guaranteed not over ten! Her thin, cracked lips made smacking sounds to hint at the alluring freshness of her granddaughter. Lundgren looked at the aging woman pensively, pressed a small baksheesh into her palm, was handed a key to the room, and said his name was Herrlichkoffer but that she shouldn't speak to anyone about it. Then he righted the mustache stuck to his upper lip and strolled out to his death.

8

On the Gangway

If you look good and dress well, you don't need a purpose in life.

ROBERT PANTE

F OR A PASSENGER who wasn't just taking a shore leave in Targat but planned rather to disembark, Helen had astonishingly little luggage with her. A small calf-leather suitcase and somewhat smaller hard-cover case made out of black plastic. The chief steward saw the guests off. He paused at the platinum-blonde woman dressed all in white.

"Goodbye, Mrs…"

"Goodbye, Mr Kinsella."

The passengers were stalled on the gangway. Two sailors at the bottom tried to keep away the mass of people in gray djellabas, a swarm composed of porters, hotel agents and pickpockets. Cripples and merchants hung with their wares shouted agitatedly, a choir of children sang: "*Donnez-moi un stylo, donnez-moi un stylo!*"

They were the first words of French that Helen had heard since college. She pushed her sunglasses up on top of her hair and was wondering whether it would be sensible to look through her bags for a writing utensil when she felt at the same moment someone grab the handle of her suitcase. A little boy had dashed halfway up the gangway. He pulled at the case with a determined look on his face. Did he want to carry it? To steal it? Helen clutched at the handle. The boy—matted black hair, narrow shoulders—fought a mute and desperate battle, then the latch of the suitcase opened and its contents plummeted into the sea in a colorful sweep of lipsticks and salves and flasks and cotton balls, followed gracefully by the open suitcase itself, its two halves spread like wings. Helen stumbled backwards.

Mr Kinsella came running down immediately, and from below one of the sailors fought his way up through the passengers. The boy, being closed in on, slipped under the rope railing of the gangway and plopped into the narrow strip of sea between ship and pier. A drunk on the top deck clapped in applause, the boy laboriously doggy-paddled away.

"Welcome to Africa," said Mr Kinsella. He helped Helen to carry the remaining suitcase to the taxi stand and stood watching after her for a long time.

The taxi driver had just a left arm and shifted gears by turning his upper body while holding the steering wheel with his knees. "Mine," he said, wagging his right shoulder. It was his only contribution to the conversation. Along narrow, serpentine roads up the coastal range they climbed.

The Sheraton wasn't the only building atop the ridge, but it was the only one that with its twenty stories protruded high above the jungle.

It had been built in the 1950s and the architect had been unable to decide between functionality and the slapped-up folklore of gaudy mosaics, pointed arches and *muqarnas*: an eclectic catastrophe. Certainly it wasn't due to the lack of style alone that the hotel enjoyed such great popularity, but it played a role. Even in the off season one had to book far in advance.

My parents had rented a two-room apartment on the ninth floor, and when they sent me out, as they so often did, in order to be able to carry out secret things behind closed doors, I explored the sprawling grounds on my own. I had the pool attendant show me how he arranged the towels, contemplated the perplexing Droste cocoa advertisement in front of the restaurant, and helped a pretty young woman sort straws at the bar. With my first French words ("*numéro neuf cent dix-huit*") I ordered unlimited amounts of lemon ice cream and Coca-Cola and rode the elevator from the basement to the roof terrace and back again. The hotel employees loved me. I wore a white T-shirt with the Olympic rings on it and short lederhosen with red heart-shaped pockets.

What the secret things were that necessitated my parents closing the door on me day after day, I had no idea. I was seven years old. I knew only that it had nothing to do with sex. Sexual relations were taboo, because all life force was contained in the seed and the seed needed to remain in the body. That's what the great Sri Chinmoy taught. Today I believe the closed doors had something to do with the tiny plastic bags that were pinned inside my lederhosen with a safety needle during strolls through Targat. But I was neither very anxious to find out what it was about, nor unhappy with my fate. What I liked most was to stand on the roof terrace.

From the roof terrace of the Sheraton, one had on the ocean side a dizzying view over the bay of Targat and the little harbor. Numerous white bungalows that belonged to the hotel were scattered across the side of the ridge like sugar cubes. Rusty barges, sand-colored buildings and dirt lanes crowded around the half-circle of the sea, and every two weeks a gleaming white cruise ship bobbed up and down in the harbor, a giant ship, a floating temple that signified wealth and enjoyment to some and to others wealth and wealth alone. Toward the east, by contrast, one saw from the back side of the ridge way out into the interior of the country, over a jungle of green cauliflower, plantations and slums and on out to the endless desert, where, on clear days, the rock stack of Tindirma quivered on the horizon.

When from up there I looked out across five scoops of lemon ice cream at the curve of the globe, I was utterly happy. I was Rommel on the desert side and saved my men against the explicit orders of the Führer, I was Jacob Roggeveen at sea and discovered unknown Easter Islands, and when I was myself now and then I tried to spit on the heads of blond, brown or black ants that streamed out of the building fifty meters below me. The wind deflected my spit on the way down and for the most part I only ever hit a blue awning. To this day, I cannot answer with any certainty the question of whether on the last day of August in the year 1972 I was standing up there and noticed the American tourist and her one-armed taxi driver or whether a photograph has been superimposed on my memory. One thing, however, is certain: after Helen Gliese had picked up the key to her bungalow from the hotel reception, she immediately left the building accompanied by a young bellboy who was carrying her little calf-leather suitcase. The bellboy's head swayed as he walked, as if he were quietly singing, and when they crossed the road he absent-mindedly tried several times to take the hand of the platinum-blonde woman.

Helen's bungalow was halfway down to the sea. It had two rooms and a little kitchen, a terrace with ocean view and a yellow and blue arabesque mosaic above the door in which the numerals 581 were set in red stones. A photograph of the door, like the ones seen in many newspapers at the time, hangs above my writing desk.

9

Spasski and Moleskine

It is with trifling details of court life as insignificant as those
related in the last chapter that we should have to fill up the
history of the next four years.

STENDHAL

C ANISADES GOT ON BETTER with the locals. He was from
a small city in the north of the country; his forebears, who
had been relegated to civil servants after the war of independ-
ence, had once been part of the upper class. Like Polidorio,
he had studied in France. At the elite Paris boarding school he
had attended for two years, he claimed to have a Jewish mother,
which was not true. In Targat he boasted that he was the scion
of a French industrialist family, which was also not true. In other
respects Canisades was not a bad person. His easy, creative way
with his own biography seemed as innate to him as his elegant
manners and a charm that in middle Europe would have been
called smarmy but here opened hearts. He had taken up his
service in Targat shortly before Polidorio, but in contrast to
him had not had any trouble acclimating. Within two weeks he
knew half the city. He passed as easily in the hash dens along
the waterfront as in the villas of American intellectuals, and
incidentally performed his duty perfectly satisfactorily.

Only his attempts to integrate new colleagues into the social fabric of the city had not been crowned with success. Polidorio enjoyed letting himself be talked into all sorts of things by others, but he had no use for the groups that Canisades was so eager and indiscriminate in trying to get to know. The idea of choosing a high-society party over an evening with friends would never have occurred to him, and, as with everyone for whom social vanity is unfamiliar, Polidorio struggled to see it as the driving force in others.

What he most readily agreed to were the late-night bordello visits. Ever since Canisades had shown him how things worked on the long night of the files, the walk to the waterfront had become a beloved custom of his. Though it was difficult to say what it was that appealed to him about it. Certainly not the sexual gratification, the visits took place too infrequently for that.

The women who worked there came from appalling circumstances, none of them had ever been to school, and anyone who supposed that their empathy or physical talents compensated for their intellectual shortcomings would be disappointed.

Polidorio disdained them for what they did, felt ashamed for the deeds he undertook with them, and was too shy to request what he really wanted. It was more the atmosphere that drew him there, the subtle displacement of everyday life, the transgression against the order of things, something that he, by profession, had to stand against, and first and foremost the inexplicable excitement. He liked talking with the women, and it sent him into a peculiar state to know that he could do something with them if he wanted to. In this state of excitement, which gripped him reliably as soon as he started the walk to the waterfront, Polidorio constantly felt on the edge of some sort of abyss. Something deeply unsettling, yes, even demonic, that, as it does to many simple souls, appealed to him: are there perhaps hidden layers of my personality? Depths that threaten to engulf me? Though his idea of the demonic was barely more developed than the idea women's magazines had of psychoanalysis.

In return, and also to relieve his conscience, he provided his favorites with chemical treasures from the evidence room, official documents and tip-offs about raids, and even though he wasn't doing anything different from any other police officer who went to a bordello, he still felt what he was doing was a bit sinister, unfathomable and crazy. Perhaps the most sinister aspect, however, was that two-thirds of his take-home pay disappeared into this abyss. It goes without saying that Polidorio's wife lived humbly and knew nothing of all of this.

But on the evening of the day on which the two commissars had interrogated Amadou together, they did not go to the port district. Canisades had asked Polidorio to keep his schedule clear but hadn't revealed where he wanted to go, and Polidorio had with tempered enthusiasm acquiesced.

"Not to the god damn Americans," he said when he saw Canisades in his best suit. "Please, not to the god damn Americans." And Canisades said: "Don't make such a fuss."

In first gear the police car crept up the serpentine road of the coastal range and stopped among limousines and convertibles with white-wall tires across from a sumptuous villa from the 1940s. The villa belonged to one of the two American writers who lived in the city. It was surrounded by a high white wall with an oversized art deco portal in front of which tourists liked to have their pictures taken during the daytime. The portal consisted of two stylized columns of papyrus sheaves, before which were two androgynous youths with slender marble bodies, their feet hanging in the air mid-step as if they were running toward one another. The runner on the left was carrying a hammer and had a triangle in the crook of his arm; he was smiling. The one on the right had a whip and a trellis in his hand, and a deep buttock-like groove on his forehead expressed a dubious sculptural rage. Thirty years since the erection of the villa nobody knew any more how to explain the symbolic implications.

The clinks and laughter of a party wafted over the walls, and Polidorio asked with a sigh which of the two writers lived here.

"Just clench your butt cheeks." Canisades pulled on the cord that rang the doorbell.

"I really am interested."

"Then read one of their books."

"I tried. So who lives here?"

"There are mnemonic devices," said Canisades. "Those things look like chess figures."

As far as Polidorio could tell, there were a lot of Americans in Canisades' circle of acquaintances who had three things in common: they did something with art, something with drugs, and something devious when it came to sexuality. The two most prominent were the writers Canisades had dubbed Spasski and Moleskine in an effort to make it easier to distinguish them. Both were regarded as candidates for the Nobel Prize in Literature, Spasski for a long while already, Moleskine only recently and as more of a dark horse.

Spasski was from Vermont and didn't really like to see himself as American. In his eyes he was more the distinguished European type. He wore suits from Paris, enthused about technical advancements, and disdained his colleagues for their antiquated notebooks. Every day, with great discipline, he hammered out exactly four pages on a black portable typewriter, and evenings on the waterfront he tried to break the Sicilian defenses of local chess hustlers.

Why he poured such effort and passion into playing chess was not entirely clear. He pursued it in an amateurish manner and didn't seem to improve. In his last book there had been a scene in which the mysterious hero, having emerged from the underclass, demonstrated his razor-sharp intellect in passing by wiping out a Serbian grand master using a Sokolsky opening plus a queen sacrifice in the middlegame. A critic at the *New York Times* noted that he had already read the same scene, or one very similar to it, in two other books by the same author; fourteen days later the editorial office received a parcel from Africa that contained nothing but a decaying rat.

Moleskine on the other hand preferred more manly subject matter. He was a slender, asthenic type, suffered from the long-term effects of an uncured case of TB, and had a PhD in philosophy, which he liked to conceal from company. The best-known photo showed him in boxing gloves. The second-best-known showed him standing on the beach in Targat with his pants down, urinating on a copy of *The Queen's Gambit*, by his colleague Spasski.

He collected antique weapons and shortly after his arrival in Targat had founded a sort of homosexual paramilitary association. He had white pants and magnificent blue tunics tailored in Marseilles for a set of twelve-year-old boys, armed them with realistic-looking toy guns, and, with himself as commander-in-chief, staged paramilitary maneuvers in the nearby desert, during which they practiced endurance, withstanding physical and mental pain, working out in the torrid sun, and first and foremost the speedy removal of the little tunics. The two authors were alternately friendly and at odds with each other, and during each of the phases they reciprocally alienated the delicate, sunburnt boys who constituted their domestic help.

It was just such a boy, dressed only in a pair of short, yellow gym trunks, who opened the wrought-iron gate. The front garden was lit with torches and faded at the edges into darkness and tall trees. Polidorio trailed anxiously behind Canisades. They entered a hall with a giant staircase, tall doors facing the garden, men in suits, women in Yves Saint Laurent dresses. Among them more gym shorts, serving food and drinks on silver trays. No sign of the host.

Canisades greeted people all around, Polidorio followed behind him with his arms folded across his chest. Since there were no formal introductions or other old-fashioned courtesies, one was always left to guess whether one was facing a high-ranking deputy minister, a penniless intellectual or a random pervert. For someone like Polidorio, to whom hierarchical structures still meant something, this was tremendously stressful.

The buffet consisted of foods he had never seen before and the names of which he had never heard. On the walls hung paintings in a non-representational style, sawdust had been spread on the floor around the bar, and scurrying between the legs of those present was a little furry animal with a golden collar, an animal which Polidorio could not tell for the life of him whether it was a small dog, a large rat or something else entirely.

Canisades had quickly made his way over to a couple of acquaintances. Polidorio joined the group half-heartedly but did not participate in the conversation. He had taken a glass of champagne from one of the gym shorts, and his attention had been captivated by a woman dressed all in white standing a little ways away. Very slender, very blonde, large breasts, but something about her seemed off. Her gestures were odd. A handful of American officers stood around her, listened to her attentively and laughed a little too eagerly at every sentence she sluggishly recited.

"My colleague Polidorio," said Canisades, and a hand littered with liver spots extended toward the surprised commissar.

"A pleasure, a real pleasure! I wish my life were as exciting as yours. Why don't you ever turn up in your smart uniform? Are you afraid you'll turn my house into a disreputable site?"

Polidorio, who had missed the introductory sentences, shook his head shyly. The liver-spotted hand was apparently Spasski.

A large, bald-headed man. There was no denying that he was a charming character all the same. While Polidorio, still feeling flattered, tried to concoct a respectful response ("I read your most recent book," "This party is as scintillating as great literature," "I wish my life were as exciting as your books"), Spasski had already turned to someone else and was speaking exceedingly charmingly to that person.

Canisades subsequently introduced his colleague to two or three other groups, but Polidorio quickly had the feeling that he should free his friend from the dead weight that he himself represented. He wandered into the house and back into the garden, stopped here and there in order to look busy, and remained at loose ends. Everywhere the conversations were in full swing. There were none of the awkward silences, the occasional and not-so-disagreeable stumbles in communication, the contemplative pauses between questions and answers he was familiar with from other social situations. All the talk jumbled together maddeningly quickly. When he tried to enter he went unnoticed, sometimes demonstratively unnoticed, and when he himself added a sentence to topics he believed himself to know something about, people turned to him with such offended civility that he lost his train of thought. The assembled company was a single, vague indignity.

The entire evening he wandered around lost, avoiding only the group with the blonde woman, who seemed a bit odd to him. He became increasingly quiet and just listened. He observed.

If there is one characteristic that distinguishes an experienced criminal from a lay person, it is the quality of his perception. He knows immediately where he needs to look, he distinguishes the important from the unimportant, he recognizes the unreliability of human sight. Perception and observation are not natural talents, one can study them and practice... at least that was the nonsense Polidorio had been taught at the police academy, and often when he was bored in a social setting he tried in vain to do just that. He watched conversations and saw speakers exaggerate, listened to nonsense and non-sequiturs, tried for a moment to understand or at least to make a mental note, and only got more and more defensive and spiteful.

"Just to give a ballpark figure, we're talking about the vicinity of three five. Possibly three seven."

"A hundred years ago people would have said that, based on the data on increasing traffic volume in London, the city would be drowning in horse shit in 1972. That's no different than what Paccei is saying now, the idiot."

"Perhaps the most ingenious man in the southern hemisphere."

"As soon as an author comes up with some form of literary theory, it always boils down to elucidating a general goal that the author himself is best at accomplishing and has been practicing for years. This is not a theory. It's nothing more than what bunny rabbits learn when it gets dark in the great forest. And theories by people who *don't* write: ridiculous. So in that regard, there are no theories."

"So-called reality."

"And when somebody holds a door open for me, I'm immediately under pressure, I feel a sense of obligation. I start to run. But naturally I myself always hold the door. Does that make me a sadist? It just occurred to me this morning. The door-holding-sadist."

"Ah, Mr Cetrois. Good evening, good evening! On another secret mission? Where is your friend?"

"And by the most ingenious man in the southern hemisphere, I mean, I know 'Katanga' from him, you must hear it. He knows all the participants, he can describe the Belgian right down to the ends of her hair, he knows what everyone did, he knows where they live, how many children they have. And we're talking about the secret service here. He came straight from Cambridge. Law.

They laugh! They didn't take Lumumba seriously and they never learn. He's already got half the country behind him. I assure you, if there is ever a president of a united Africa… You mustn't let yourself be blinded by the crude rhetoric of the combatants. This is the pivotal moment, this is the blood beacon, and *he* is the man. Simply brilliant. And he's only twenty-nine. Dress warm. Dress warm! Helms has already planted his first agent in his office. You don't believe it, right? But he has."

The speaker had a light East European accent. The person facing him, a gray-haired man with a hat, suit and pocket square, didn't seem to agree. He didn't want to know anything about an African blood beacon, and had even less desire to hear about peaceful accord. The more desirable progress was, the more he demanded regression, regression though hardship, misery, sacrifice and revolution. And as a result there was no united Africa, the differences here weren't sufficiently pronounced. There was no clear upper and lower, essentially no upper at all, and no consciousness of upper and lower. Wherever one looked, nothing but societal formlessness, poorly understood structures and half-assed butchery. He corrected himself: pointless butchery. No, such utopias could expect to be realized only as part of the much larger project of the global state, for which one had to rely on Europe. America was too egomaniacal, Russia too broke, and the remainder of Asia had forever been apolitical and the secondary inheritors of Occidental political theories. He assumed by the turn of the millennium, at the latest: a global state, originating in Europe. At the phrase "turn of the millennium" the person opposite him broke out giggling, and it seemed to Polidorio, who was hearing the phrase for the first time, that it was highly unlikely that by that point there would still be human life on the planet. They continued to argue.

The blonde woman stood alone at the edge of the garden and looked out into the night. One had a view down the entire coastal range. The moonlit crests of waves landed gleaming on an invisible beach. A group gathered around Moleskine paged through one of Spasski's early works like frisky teenagers paging through a nudist catalog, a drunken fifteen-year-old in yellow gym shorts trailed along behind Polidorio with a giant syringe and several times took the liberty of jokingly pretending that he was going to ram it into his (and other guests') backsides.

At some stage Polidorio ended up standing next to the young diplomat being treated by the East European contingent as the future president of a united Africa. Gleaming white teeth in a black face, light suit, exceedingly winsome smile. He was in fact tremendously quick in the head, as Polidorio could tell with what was left of his drunken skills of perception, he had a sense of humor, he was ingenious. But what good was it to him? He was still a black. After his first use of hypotaxis Polidorio could no longer follow him.

As the tremulous host, braced by two footmen, stood up on a chair in the garden, all conversation fell silent. The footmen remained cautiously standing next to the chair, but Spasski shooed them away with an imperious gesture. The crowd pressed toward him in expectation of a meaningful performance, from somewhere came spontaneous applause, and Polidorio, who knew how much the acquaintance of this American artist meant to Canisades, drew closer with an eyebrow raised. When nothing more could be heard than the quiet clinking of ice cubes in glasses, Spasski raised his voice. Frailly, monotonously, almost purring, but still in its own way also penetrating, so that even in the furthest corners of the garden nobody had to strain to hear his words.

"It is considered virtuous to be far-sighted!" began Spasski, then pausing as if he were waiting until even the ice cubes had quieted down. "As one of the capabilities given only to man and not the animals, in order to worry about the future, to take preventative action. But the race that emerged from this anxiety, the aged European-American type, is exactly what we fled from to an unconcerned Africa, to a society, to a way of thinking, to an essence that is still in the blossom of its youth. I would like to drink to this blossom. I am glad that you all have come. Never should a murky future darken the luminous present. Look up." He himself looked up into the night with great pathos. Only a few party guests followed his example, most kept their gaze fixed on the grand gesture, an aged, scrawny arm trembling beneath the starry heaven. "Who among you would not at the moment of death be willing to buy back your life at the cost of the vast majority of humanity? Diderot. If I had to choose between the beauty of the moment and the survival of humanity—I want to state the following. If in the next ten years the lights go out here, as my friends in the Club of Rome never tire of telling me weekly via the newspaper; what is this, philosophically speaking? We could wipe away nine-tenths of humanity and then from those left another nine-tenths and there would still be scum. Indignation's not necessary. No, we know this. Nine-tenths. And then nothing in the world could stop us from flinging our arms around the neck of the Turin horse, sobbing. Because we are human. And that's the thing, and I mean it, dear friends, as solemnly as I say it, and anyone who knows me, knows it to be true. Let's come straight to the point. Liberate ourselves from the conceit of elucidation! Light does not belong in every darkness. We all know the feeling one senses. You toss a couple of copper coins to a starving child and see a glow of gratitude in the coal-black eyes, it shines brighter than a starry sky or any utopia the philosophers devise, and this feeling is, I reiterate, this *feeling*, this shame, this misery, this poorly veiled sense of superiority—and not rationality—believe you me. Humanity! Humanity. Mr Wallich was right to call the talk of the limits of growth a pile of irresponsible nonsense. We will still have electricity and be happy in 1980. We will still have electricity and be happy in 1990. And in 2000. And in 2010 we will all be dead but still have electricity. Carthage!"

His arm swung around like a gun barrel, pointed at a group of uniformed musicians, and the drum counted to four.

Targat's youngest commissar took leave of his colleagues using the pretext of having a headache. Beneath the portal of two marble runners Polidorio let out a deep breath.

Let a bomb fall on that place, he thought.

10

The Centrifuge

When I hear of Schrödinger's cat, I reach for my gun.

STEPHEN HAWKING

T HAT WAS HOWEVER exactly the problem with the camel jockeys. They wanted to fiddle around with the atom and didn't know how a centrifuge worked. Lundgren hadn't earned the best grades in physics; in his mind he was the type of person who was better with languages. He'd also been good at music, sports and in religion. But this much he had learned at school: a centrifuge was something that spun around fast. And an ultracentrifuge was something that spun around *really* fast. With one of those you could separate isotopes, for instance Uranium-235 from Uranium-238. A taller, narrower cylinder with great rotational energy, a device of middling complexity that to a design engineer posed primarily mechanical challenges. Challenges that a gifted auto mechanic could probably overcome. But not a camel jockey. The camel jockeys couldn't manage it; even the know-how needed for a rotating cylinder was beyond them.

If they had invested the time and effort and the money that they put into torture, human rights violations and fighting Israel, he thought, into educating their auto mechanics instead, they could have built their dim-witted centrifuges themselves. Virtually. Anyone should have been able to build the thing. Even he, Lundgren, could probably have managed it with a bit of practice and a little more attention in physics class. A rotating cylinder, for god's sake, what was the problem? But these people here couldn't manage it. Or didn't want to. Maybe they didn't want to. Lundgren looked at his watch. Pale-gray hands that glowed in the dark, a gift from his wife. He took a sip of mint tea and put the glass back down on the emerald-green surface of the table. On the opposite side of the street, directly across the way, stood a decaying two-story building. Green paint was flaking off it and a flagpole stood crookedly atop the roof, from which a dark-green scrap of fabric indicated the stillness of the air. The color of the revolution.

Lundgren had seen much misery in the world, and he had figured out at some point what the problem was with the Third World and its inhabitants. Among many other things they considered cerebral activities unmanly. Naturally nobody said it that way. But science stood in fuzzy opposition to the great ideals of pride, honor and razzmatazz. Science was for girlies. You could give a woman a hundred dollars and she would conjure up a sewing shop with eight employees. Give a man a hundred dollars: civil war. And the worst of all were the Arabs. What was in their blood was laziness, intrigue and fanaticism. But contemplation was for women, and women, this was also clear, were known to be too stupid for contemplation. A vicious circle. Lundgren brooded over it, and the longer he thought about it, about what he himself referred to as the vicious circle of the Arabic character, the less strange it seemed to him. Because in the end he was the same way.

What was science? A chicken-breasted crafts project. Run by self-important busybodies in shirts laid out by their mothers, tiny little men with coke-bottle glasses who could barely see as far as the laboratory door and who in condescending falsetto voices issued orders like: Go out into the world and clear away the filth, we've already calculated the important things and taken care of them. Physics was, philosophically speaking, a model to describe reality. But it was a false model. Physics was unsophisticated, because it had removed the most important thing, humans and their weaknesses. That's something the camel jockeys had realized: even the great Nobel Prize winners were incapable of withstanding the most basic use of force. Science bore no relation to reality, to *real* reality, the feedback was missing. Espionage had feedback. Espionage was complex, an almost artful process, and like all art it was deception and illusion. An art and a sport and in contrast to science, analogous to life, the magnificent, the great, the erasable, fragile *Gesamtkunstwerk* of human life, and the only thing that could drive one crazy was when the contact man didn't turn up. Probably hunkered down at his farm penetrating his favorite sheep having long since forgotten about separating isotopes.

When the contact man didn't turn up... and the sun. Already on the first evening Lundgren had bought himself a ridiculous straw hat. It barely protected him from the rays that had been emitted by the sun eight minutes prior as the byproduct of a nuclear fusion reaction, just to blaze unrelentingly down onto Lundgren's brow. But at the café he didn't dare to sit. Maintain an overview, safety. Basic rule. The electromagnetic rays burned through the straw hat, he looked at the green flag, he looked at the green building, and suddenly the word had disappeared.

A numb feeling like cotton padding clung to his tongue. The word was gone. It was as if he couldn't remember his own name. He couldn't remember the name of the thing. The thing that rotated. The reason he was here. Of course, centrifuge, centrifugal. That came right after centaur, central, the center of the solar system. Centrifuge, right. And before that? It kept getting worse. Before that he had thought of mint tea, mint a coin, tea. Mademoiselle, a coin of tea. And baby sheep. But why was he here again? Because of the... extreme centrifuge. The extremely fast speedifuge? After rubbing his temples copiously, Lundgren hit upon virtually. Virtual centrifuge. That wasn't the right word. Or was it? Was it the right word? And if that wasn't the right word, how was this going to end? Good day, my name is virtually Lundgren. I have the thing. Yes, thank you, no problem. It was getting ever more idiotic. It was the sun, the fucking sun. The fucking tea. The fucking centrifuge.

Two cigarettes and a half-cup of tea later, Lundgren was trembling like the leaves of a pea plant. As a man who was accustomed to meet all sides with distrust, particularly his own, the suspicion had plagued him from the beginning that he was being sent out as a decoy. Like a trainee sent out to get a left-handed screwdriver or off on a snipe hunt and everyone laughs at him afterward. The chicken-breasted. Point at him, look through their coke-bottle glasses and throw chalk. Only here it wouldn't be chalk they would throw but something worse. Favorite subject: torture.

It had not been without danger to look at the blueprints without being noticed (and it was also not easy). He'd needed to get hold of one of those illuminated devices. The text was encoded, or at least written in Arabic, which amounted to the same thing, but there were also engineering sketches. And even if Lundgren hadn't understood them, the images had made an ample cylindrical and secret impression on him. Over the course of hundreds of pages. It definitely wasn't just about centrifuges. Which made him uneasy. This was no snipe hunt. And it was too big for a left-handed screwdriver. He was on a real mission. He couldn't be fooled so easily.

And yet he still felt queasy. It wasn't the sort of mission where failure was an option. He was in no man's land, in the desert, and staring at him from the shadows across the street for the last two days was a toothless Arab. Continuously. Now and then he leaned forward to pray in some particular direction. Then he returned to staring at him again.

"He always sits there, he's crazy," the twelve-year-old server had informed him, but one couldn't trust her, either. Whenever he turned around she was casting fiery glances at him. A beast! That's the way it was in these latitudes. Dumb as a straw hat. But they could look good. Like animals. Virtually a national characteristic. The golden skin! The deep black eyes! It was in their blood. But who could one trust? That was the unsettling part of the job, one couldn't trust anyone. People were masks, the world but a façade, and behind it all were thoughts and secrets. And behind every secret another secret, like the shadow of a shadow.

Lundgren smiled inwardly, lost in thought. And then all of a sudden, on the afternoon of the second day: catastrophe. From out of nowhere the toothless old man suddenly had a little electronic device. He tried to hide it in his hand, but Lundgren saw it out of the corner of his eye. A tiny flash in the sun. The Arab moved the little box to his ear and in the same moment a jeep came driving down the street—and that was the signal. Lundgren jumped up. He ran inside the café, hid in the bathroom. He gripped the sides of the sink and urged the face in the mirror to stay calm. Then voices. Then footsteps: Lundgren dove through the window. Forty-two degrees in the shade. He hopped a wall in stride (110 meter hurdles in 14.9 seconds, a Swedish junior national record), veered through some startled chickens, turned left twice and reached the main road on which the café was situated, still flying. He felt for the weapon hidden beneath his armpit. He switched off the safety. Thought of his wife and peered around the corner.

He looked at the café through the sun-charged air, saw his notebook, his sunhat and his mint tea sitting alone at the table on the veranda. Before it an empty chair. Lundgren-shaped air had taken his place. On the other side of the street, in front of the green building, the stationary Arab, a transistor radio held to his ear. Music, the drone of singing. The jeep had driven past. Everything on Lundgren quivered. The twelve-year-old beauty queen waved at him friendly-shocked. Lundgren trotted back to his table like a sweaty piece of cheese. She smiled. He didn't look at her. She stuck out her underdeveloped breasts. He ignored it. First carry out the mission, then lay the girls. Old rule.

In the afternoon the street in front of the café began to come to life. Men hustled toward the center of town; something seemed to be going on there. Unintelligible calls, always the same word. Lundgren observed it all with a pained grimace on his face. A few hours later the masses surged back. The same calls.

On the third day Lundgren paid the toothless old man a baksheesh to sit somewhere else. The old man took the money and remained seated. On the fourth day Lundgren greeted him with the words: "Already fucked your sheep today?" The old man just held out his hand. A white ray of light shone down and Lundgren gave him an even bigger baksheesh and laughed and smiled and he couldn't stop smiling and noticed with what was left of his sanity that something inside him, maybe it was his brain, maybe it was the dysentery, maybe it was the sight of the nubile blackamoor princess, had pumped him full of euphoria. Euphoria was counterproductive. Euphoria was forbidden. He knew it. He knew everything. He was Lundgren.

11

Appeal

He who knows not where he's going,
Reaches his destination with every step.

FULANI SAYING

T HE NEXT DAY POLIDORIO had the file brought to him
again, a small stack of paper bound together with a thread,
and he spread the contents out in front of him on his desk. On
top was the transcript of the interrogation of Amadou that had
taken place in the Central Commissariat; Polidorio skimmed
through it quickly. He'd been present at two and knew that
Amadou had stuck to his story. The last transcript consisted of
one sentence: for statement see previous day.

The rest of the file was disorganized. Polidorio first looked
for the eyewitness reports. They were for the most part typed
out, though some were handwritten, and included indecipherable abbreviations and stenographic codes. Almost every typed
report was missing the name of the interviewer as well as the
date. Presumably Karimi had prepared the reports. Canisades
had been in Tindirma only once, shortly after Amadou's arrest,
Polidorio not at all. A series of idiotic phrases ("furthermore he
stated for the record", "stated the witness indignantly") certainly
suggested that someone with similar limitations to Karimi had

typed or worked on the statements. Among the papers were descriptions of the crime scene, sketched maps and timelines. But also hotel receipts, indecipherable scribbles, a briefing from the Interior Ministry about handling foreign journalists. Sums of money written on a paper napkin. A retrospective transcript of the crime scene inspection: undated. A begging letter from the mother of one of the victims: incomplete. A sketch-map of two of the bodies on a floor plan of a building: no commentary. The file was one big pile of junk.

An earlier summary of the events originated with Canisades, a crackpot assessment ("further murders in the foreigner milieu should be expected") filed at the police station in Tindirma. The presence of foreign observers had caused considerable agitation in the oasis. Polidorio knew from Karimi that it had come to blows between him and the local police because they not only persistently shoved their faces into every camera lens but also tried to hire themselves out as private security to the surviving communards.

There were no usable photos of the crime scene whatsoever, instead Polidorio found one paper-clipped to a blank sheet of paper, a picture of a plaque on the door of the commune. A handmade ceramic plaque adorned with green- and red-glazed flower tendrils:

> *Ici vivent, travaillent, aiment Bina Gilhodes,*
> *Edgar Fowler, Jean Bekurtz, Tareg Weintenne,*
> *Michelle Vanderbilt, Brenda Johnson, Brenda Liu,*
> *Kula & Abdul Fattah, Lena Sjöström, Freedom*
> *Muller, Akasha, Christine, Akhnilo James.*

The plaque must have been from the earliest days of the commune; just two of the murder victims were among those named. Of the rest, it seemed that only about half of them still lived in the commune, as a comparison to a list of current occupants compiled by Karimi revealed. This list included twenty-one people. Next to four names stood a cross; two others were bracketed with parentheses as if their presence in the commune at the time of the crime was unknown or perhaps they had put their youth behind them.

Polidorio groaned, tossed two aspirin in his mouth and started to read the individual witness reports. There were thirty-one in all, which by local standards—and not only local standards— was a grotesquely large number. Normally a single witness who told the truth would suffice, then one tried to get the suspect to agree with that account. In this particular case the level of public interest had prevented that.

The thirty-one witnesses were divided between five communards who were in the building at the time of the crime, and twenty-six passers-by who streamed onto the commune grounds after being attracted by the sound of the shots. The five communards described the rampage with varying precision but essentially consistently: Amadou's unexpected appearance, his rant on questions of sexuality, his plying himself with alcohol in the communal kitchen. The weapon, the attempt to carry out the stereo—the killing of the communard Sjöström. The discovery of the case of money. Three more murders, fruit basket, escape.

The statements by the passers-by, on the other hand, were short on substance and consisted for the most part of long-winded speculation about Amadou's motive and the political background. Nearly all alluded to a political background. It was a common way of talking. Mentioned as a motive: jealousy, revenge, injured familial honor, ardor, spirituality and disorientation. Not mentioned: greed. As for as the meager facts (shots on the grounds, rattan suitcase, escape), most of the statements were identical right down to the wording and consequently worthless. Either the people were just blathering on about things they'd heard or Karimi had coached them.

Three-quarters of the passers-by claimed to have noticed Amadou as he was first entering the complex. Polidorio had asked Asiz to show him the location of the commune on the map, the entrance was on a side street on the souk, no merchant to the left or right, lots of traffic. There was no way anyone had noticed somebody driving a car into an open gate fifteen minutes prior to pistol shots being heard inside. Even the number of shots: hundreds, dozens, lots, two.

Further discrepancies: not Amadou but a northern European had shot bullets into the air in front of the gate, and then had handed the weapon to Amadou (one witness, interviewed by "M.M."). A cloud had darkened the sky and facilitated Amadou's escape (one witness, interviewed by "Q.K."). Amadou had been wearing a gray wig "like a British judge in a movie" (one witness), had scattered large amounts of gold dust in order to cause a commotion (two witnesses), had been noticeably intoxicated (four witnesses) and had thrown up his arms upon leaving the building and with emotional words beseeched the aid of the one true God (one witness).

The investigation of the crime scene: a couple of shell casings, an empty magazine. Two bullets in the wall, one in the ceiling between the first and second floor. The four victims had each been struck by several bullets, all bullet wounds were from close range, one in the back, the rest frontal. Little doubt about the cause of death. No sign at all of another suspect. Signed by Karimi.

Other than the fact that the victims were white, there was nothing special about the case.

Polidorio put the file back together, stared for a long time at the notes he had made, then went to the boss and took two days' leave. He claimed to want to spend a little time with his recently arrived family, wrote a note asking Asiz to re-examine the fingerprints on the weapon, and got into his car.

12

Khamsin

At the interface of two media of different densities flowing with different velocities, wave-like oscillations will occur.

HELMHOLTZIAN THEOREM

T HERE WERE TWO overland routes to Tindirma. The shorter slanted through the Salt Quarter and the desert directly beyond, the other skirted the slums in a northerly arc several kilometers long and then veered off to the right just before the mountains. Polidorio didn't know either route, opted for the shorter of the two, and within five minutes had lost his way in the Salt Quarter.

As in every other large city, a belt of shanty towns surrounded Targat, and the willingness of authorities to repeatedly bulldoze the miserable huts off the slopes seemed to have about the same effect as the judicious pruning of a plant. After each wave of clearing, the growth came back even thicker, with roads and paths seeping into the area. Corrugated iron, canisters, debris. Everything, even the paths, seemed to be made from garbage and to grow out of garbage. In the middle of the broadest street holes cropped up in which entire families lived. Some were covered with plastic tarps and decorated with a stone crown. As Polidorio tried to turn around in a dead-end alleyway, barefoot children ran over and pressed the dirty palms of their hands against the passenger-side window. A girl on crutches blocked the way. Others joined her, in an instant a thick mob had welled up around the car. Cripples, adolescents, shrouded women. They screamed and pulled at the locked doors.

Polidorio attempted not to make eye contact with anyone. He clutched the steering wheel with both hands and pressed the car nightmarishly slowly through the crowd. Fists beat upon the roof. When a small hole opened up before the grille of the car, he stepped on the gas and escaped into the next side street. It seemed to him a marvel that this road was long, straight and empty of people. In the distance, between the huts, he saw the nearest edges of the desert.

He was about to lean back and relax when a noise made him wince. It seemed to come from inside the car. A look in the rear-view mirror: three smiling children. They were standing on the rear bumper, their fingers clawing the drip molding. The child in the middle had only one hand on the roof and in the other held a sickle with which he was whacking at the rear window. The speedometer said forty-five kilometers per hour. Polidorio immediately let up on the gas. Two of the stowaways jumped off, but not the child with the sickle.

In the sandy desert he drove in gentle s-curves and the picking sound stopped. The child was now holding the sickle sideways in his mouth and gripping the drip molding with both hands. A kilometer beyond the huts the boy finally jumped off. In the rear-view mirror Polidorio watched him tumble off into the dunes with his tool.

He let the car coast to a stop. The sweat had dripped all the way down to his shoes. He got a bottle of water out of the trunk. With the bottle in his right hand and waving his left wildly in the air, he climbed the tallest nearby dune and looked around. Off to the side up ahead he caught sight of a row of telegraph poles running at an angle in an east-west direction that probably marked the way to Tindirma. Otherwise just sand. He drank some of the water and shook the rest over his head and then skidded back down to his car.

He had been on the dirt road about three-quarters of an hour when he noticed something peculiar on the horizon. A small, yellow, dirty cloud that was slowly expanding. He watched it closely. After a few minutes it had overtaken the breadth of the horizon. He had never seen anything like it but knew immediately what it was. Up on the tops of the dunes, little flags of sand were already whipping around. The wind was picking up, the sky was turning dark brown. Finally there was a moment of stillness. Then the car was hit with such force that it was nearly thrown from the road. Polidorio stopped completely. A blast of sand was aimed at his windshield; he could barely make out the front of the hood. There was a crackling and pattering as if the car were on fire. Polidorio sat still for nearly an hour.

While he waited, it occurred to him that Amadou had been arrested somewhere near here, shortly after he had committed the four murders. Or perhaps had not committed them. The thought went through his head that in the conditions of this landscape, not only was a human life insignificant but, philosophically speaking, so were four human lives or even the entirety of human life. Polidorio wasn't sure how he had hit upon this idea. Sitting in his office, something of the like would not only not seem philosophical, it would seem banal. With fingers wet with sweat, he switched on the radio. No reception. The desert flew horizontally past him. When the road became dimly visible again Polidorio tried to drive on, but his wheels just spun. He put a towel around his head and opened the car door. A bucketful of sand flew into the car, he closed the door.

Once the wind had died down enough for him to get out of the car safely, piles of sand nestled aerodynamically around the shape of the car. A few meters in front of the car stood a sign that hadn't been there before. The top of it was sticking out of a dune as tall as a person, it was triangular and rusted and the writing was barely legible: *102*... the rest indecipherable.

The color of the sky changed to light ocher. Polidorio worked with his hands and forearms to clear the sand from the rear of the car and tried to get it rolling again with traction mats laid beneath the tires. He needed nearly half an hour to get it going and then another hour to reach Tindirma, and then, once there, another ten minutes of conversation with the members of the commune to figure out that they were credible. That they had told the truth. And that the crime couldn't have played out any differently from the way it was documented in the transcripts. One hundred and two.

13

At work

Well, what's there to say about capital punishment? I'm not against it. Revenge is all it is, but what's wrong with revenge?

RICHARD EUGENE HICKOCK

T HE CAMEL had one leg tied up. On three stilts it reeled around between the lanky men who were looking at its mouth and hooves. Lundgren wondered how many of the camel's legs one could tie up before it fell over. One was possible, two difficult, presumably three would be night-night. Physics wasn't his passion, as previously mentioned, but it also wasn't as if it didn't interest him at all. Lundgren was a naturally curious person, one who was thirsty for knowledge, undogmatic and cosmopolitan, but not bogged down in the swamp of liberalism. He could listen, he had a sense for what was going on in other people that bordered on eerie, a finely tuned power of observation. Always had. The girls in his school were the first to pick up on it. They liked him. The boys liked him too, even if they were a bit jealous of him because of the girls. Lundgren, shining middle point of the Moreno sociogram. El lobo. And he was the collegial type. Father a social democrat. When the teacher turned around during a test, Lundgren held his test booklet up so everyone could see it. In physics too, and biology.

Lundgren. He laughed. He would go to a camel market and pay ten dollars to tie up a second leg. Front right leg and back left. Or front right and back right. Ten dollars. Then he'd put his legs up and watch. What a crazy gag! Lundgren pictured the whole thing in his head. Hilarious. He would have told someone about it if he could have told someone about it. When he was finished with his mission here. First the mission, then the camel. Then the beauty queen. Or perhaps first the beauty queen, then the camel. He laughed so hard he cried. When he opened his eyes again, a man was sitting next to him at the table. A man in sunburnt clothing and checkered skin. Lundgren put up his professional façade again in fractions of a second. Kawock! There was a man sitting next to him. He looked at him out of the corner of his eye. He made sure to appear to be looking elsewhere. It was the man. The man, the man, the man.

The man ordered tea. Three minutes of silence. Then Lundgren couldn't stand it any longer and asked: "What's your name?"

The man was just putting his teacup to his mouth, stopped midway and said slowly: "Yes."

"What's your name?" repeated Lundgren quietly.

"Yes!" answered the man just as quietly.

"What's the story?"

"What?"

"Your name!"

"Huh?"

The checkered man looked worriedly down the street in order to get the lay of the land, gestured inconspicuously with his hand to bring the volume of the conversation down, and whispered barely audibly: "What's *your* name?"

"You first," said Lundgren.

"You started."

"What?"

"It was you who started."

"Fine," said Lundgren, mimicking the hand gesture of the other man. "Herrlichkoffer."

"What?"

"Herrlichkoffer. Not so loud. Or Lundgren. For you, Herrlichkoffer."

"For me, Herrlichkoffer."

"Yes! And now write your name here—here—here."

Lundgren pulled a memo pad out of his pocket and shoved it across the table. The checkered man wrote seven block letters on the paper. A short time later Lundgren headed to his pension. An indescribable feeling after all the excitement. All right! His brain transmitted the dispatch that the drilling for oil had been successful. A telephone would have been helpful just then. The desert is on fire, desert with one s. But there was no telephone. So the dispatch went only from Lundgren's brain to Lundgren's brain: *VC accomplished stop the desert is on fire stop C3 hit upon oil.*

No. Bullshit. UC, not VC! No mistakes now.

14

Black and White

I'm like everyone else. I'd rather watch a bad American film than a bad Norwegian film.

JEAN-LUC GODARD

C ANISADES SWITCHED ON the TV, put his feet up on the desk and stared for a long time at the black screen. The picture tube began to crackle, a snowy analog clock appeared. It was two minutes to six.

Canisades had spent the afternoon at the hospital trying to question the presumed victim of a mass rape, and was too tired to start the interview now. He also might as well have just skipped it. Three cousins of the victim had kept a bedside watch and made sure he was never able to see the girl. Only through the intervention of a female doctor had it been possible to conduct an interview through an improvised white curtain. The result was as unspectacular as it was predictable: no rape, just a fall down the stairs. Canisades had to have the doctor describe the nature of the injuries, the location of the hematomas, the hair pulled out by the bushel and the lacerations. He established the names of the cousins, two of whom would be charged with the rape and who took their leave of him impassively, almost cheerfully. The complaint had been filed by the eleven-year-old sister of the victim, who had seen the whole thing through a window and ran to the police, where she had the misfortune of encountering an uncorrupt official. Now the girl was sitting somewhere in the Central Commissariat, a straw doll and Targat's only female lawyer at her side, and was probably already beginning to realize that the nicer part of her life was over.

"You're watching TV?" Asiz tromped through the room chewing gum, tossed a file onto the desk, scratched his back and disappeared into the next room.

"What?" Canisades shouted after him.

"The file."

"What am I supposed to do with it?"

"The fingerprints."

"What fingerprints?"

"On the Mauser."

"What Mauser, are you stupid? The sentencing was this morning."

Nothing happened for five full seconds. Then Asiz's upper body leaned back into the room. He had stopped chewing. "Don't call me stupid, I'm just doing my job. I spent hours lifting prints off that Mauser. Don't leave me fucking notes in my locker if you don't want the fucking results."

He disappeared again. One could hear a door open in the next room.

"Polidorio, or who was it?" Canisades called after him.

"How should I know?"

"So what *are* the results?"

"Yeah, what indeed? Eh? You idiots, if I spent hours…"

The rest couldn't be heard.

One minute before six, dramatic string music started up. Canisades leaned toward the file, but with his feet on the desk in front of him he couldn't reach it. The music stopped, the camera zoomed out, and the snowy analog clock became part of a news studio. A very young, handsome man was sitting behind a teak table upon which, in perfect symmetry, sat a flower arrangement, a condenser microphone and a black telephone. The young man greeted the viewers in Arabic and French and then read the reports in French only.

A parade had been held in honor of the king's sixty-fourth birthday. There were men in white uniforms atop great white steeds, footmen in white togas decorated with peacock feathers. A high-ranking officer was appointed a provincial governor. A school had burned down. The newsreader read gravely, unctuously. As an image of a woman in a hijab standing in front of the blackened, writhing bodies of children appeared behind him, his voice cracked. With a suppressed sob, he ducked under the table, blew his nose, and then after a suitable pause read the output figures for the recently developed phosphorous mines in the north. In addition, one saw a woman in tight shorts with both legs stretched out horizontally in front of her. Beneath her a sand pit, behind her a track: Heide Rosendahl. The speaker faltered briefly and a clip showed a man with a white beach hat on his head and shoe polish on his face talking to a group of people in suits. Other men in tracksuits conducted exercises with machine guns on the flat roofs of the Olympic village. The Palestinian people's struggle for freedom would. The Munich police commissioner had. All hostages were. Subsequently an interview of several minutes with a religious dignitary who astutely analyzed the situation.

Canisades had folded both hands behind his head, opened his mouth wide and was moving his jaw back and forth with a cracking sound. Then he took his legs down from the desk and grabbed the file. The A4 sheet of paper with the fingerprints was sitting on top. Standard text, beneath that two square spaces each with a doughy print in the middle.

"Targat," said the newsreader.

Canisades looked up. The screen showed a picture of a white delivery van with grates over the windows that had been rammed up against a wall by a twelve-ton truck and burst open like a tin can. Amadou Amadou, sentenced to death in the morning for multiple homicide, had been sprung from custody during his transfer to the site of the execution. Turning to the photo, the newsreader indicated with both arms the intersecting directions of the two vehicles, explained the circumstances of the accident, and closed with a quote from the police general, who in turn stated that the escaped prisoner would be back in custody shortly and wished that Allah granted peace upon his soul because man would not. He stacked the pile of papers on the desk in front of him and cleared his throat. The camera zoomed back in on the analog clock. It was quarter-past six.

Canisades contemplated the squares. A right thumb from the weapon, clearly visible, and Amadou's right thumb, taken ten days ago at the station house. Identical.

BOOK TWO

The Desert

15

Tabula Rasa

At the distance of another ten days' journey from the
Garamantes, is another hill of salt, and water, and men live
around it who are called Atarantes; they are the only people we
know of who have not personal names. For the name Atarantes
belongs to them collectively, but to each one of them no name
is given.

HERODOTUS

A VIEW LIKE ON A THEATER STAGE, two dark wooden
planks right and left serving as improvised curtains. In the
narrow wedge between, the high, blue sky, nearly white, light
and painful on the retina. Below, the desert. In the desert three
men in white djellabas. At first the three men are indistinguish-
able, then they become a short one, a fat one and a nondescript
one. Their mouths are moving, their hands flit. The short one
speaks to the fat one, in his arms the fat one holds a rattan
suitcase that lights up in the sun. After a while the nondescript
one disappears from view. The fat one hits his own chin with
the flat of his hand and purses his lips. The short one laughs.
He strikes a comically exaggerated stance, with a fist extended
as if he wants to attack the fat one in the very next moment.
Then he really does attack the fat one and the fat one knocks
him to the ground. The rattan suitcase falls to the sand, a gush

of paper money flies out of it. The nondescript one re-enters the picture and talks to the other two. They bend down to gather the money. When the wind shifts, their voices become audible. They are talking about a man named Cetrois, assure one another that it wasn't their fault. That they are not to blame. Then they all stop still simultaneously and stare in the same direction. Only the hands of the fat one continue automatically to feel around for bills in the sand. The short one turns to the nondescript one and whispers something to him. The nondescript one holds up an imaginary bundle of money and then stuffs it into an imaginary pocket. The noise of a diesel motor sounds in the distance. Offstage a car door closes. A fourth man enters the picture, also wearing a white djellaba. His face and voice are not so different from the others, but his bearing seems more purposeful. He speaks broken French peppered with Arabic and English.

"Do you have it?" asks the fourth man, and the short one says that they smashed in someone's skull.

"Larbi smashed in someone's skull. With the carjack. It cracked like rotten wood."

"Do you have it?" repeats the fourth man, and the short one turns to the fat one, and the fat one says: "Cetrois took off with it into the desert."

"I thought you smashed in his skull?"

"Not Cetrois."

"Then who?"

"No idea."

"Where is Cetrois?"

"He won't get far."

"Where is he!" The fourth grabs the fat one by the collar.

The fat one, the short one and the nondescript one each raise one arm simultaneously and with some effort all synchronize the direction they are pointing.

"Why are you standing around?"

"He's on a moped!"

"I thought he was on foot?"

"Yeah, but he went into a barn. And came out again on a moped."

"Where's your car? And god damn it, what is with that shitty suitcase?" The fourth grabs the rattan suitcase out of the fat man's arms. The money starts to swirl out of it again.

"Well if I can just finish speaking!" says the short one.

The fourth man pulls out a pistol and points it at the short one, who steps sideways, shrieking. The fourth man kicks him so powerfully in the crotch that he flies out of the picture.

"You can see his trail," calls the nondescript man.

"Then show me the trail!" says the fourth.

The short man re-enters the picture, hunched. One arm across his stomach, the other held up as if in defense.

"We nearly had him," he laments. "We were right there. I had him right in front of the grille of the car! But then Cetrois went into the dunes and the Chevy got stuck in the god damn dunes. So we followed him on foot and Larbi was directly behind Cetrois—and as if we were climbing over a dune!" He held his hands at shoulder height and put a look of surprise on his face.

"There was money everywhere!" assisted the fat one.

"And I mean German money!" said the short one. "We'll split it four ways, obviously. Thirty-thirty-ten, just to mention an address, I mean, three times thirty and then… ten. We can make it twenty-eight or twenty-five…"

A shot rings out and the short man falls to the ground. For a moment he lies there motionless, then he starts to roll around, gazing at his unwounded body.

"Where is Cetrois? Show me the damn trail!" roars the fourth, standing over the short man and holding the pistol behind him, pointing at the horizon.

"There! There! There!" yells the nondescript one and runs out of the picture. The fourth follows him, as does the short one.

The fat man bends over the rattan suitcase and the fourth comes back immediately. He has turned the weapon around in his hand and hits the fat man on the head with the handle. He takes a fistful of notes and rubs them in the fat man's face. "Do you know who that is? That is Goethe. No, of course you don't know. Who is Goethe? Fucking Goethe is a fucking East German. This is fucking East German money, the lot of it's not worth twenty dollars. Show me the miserable trail, and if we don't catch him—pray! Pray!"

He walks out of the picture again with the fat one behind him.

The voice of the short man from offstage: "The one whose skull Larbi smashed in. You're not listening! Cetrois went into the barn and a minute later came out on a moped. We were three hundred meters behind him—no chance. So we went into the barn, too, maybe there was another moped? And there was this guy. So of course we asked him: where was he going? Where was he going?… Because we knew. And he didn't say, so then Larbi smashed in his skull with the carjack. And we couldn't get anywhere on foot… and since we knew you were on your way with the jeep… at any moment… don't make any accusations…"

Their voices become quieter. The opening and closing of car doors. Unintelligible. An engine starting and one more sentence shouted over the noise: "You asshole, what if he deploys the line!"

Then nothing more.

16

Possibilities of Awakening

"Fantômas."
"Qu'avez-vous dit?"
"J'ai dit Fantômas."
"Et qu'est-ce que cela signifie?"
"Rien... Tout!"

PIERRE SOUVESTRE, MARCEL ALLAIN

A T THE SAME MOMENT the men disappeared from the right side of the picture, the sun popped up behind the left wooden board like an actor in a light comedy. The clattering sound of the diesel engine traced a horizontal arc along the horizon.

The radiance. The silence. He tried to turn his head and felt pains he couldn't pinpoint. As if a fist were trying to push his eyes out of his head from the inside. He blinked. With his hand he felt around and, where he had expected to find a hole in his skull, found a giant lump. Dried blood and slime. They had smashed his head in. Why? He closed his eyes and opened them again: still the same thing, apparently reality. His first thought was: escape. He needed to flee. He didn't know why, but his body knew. Everything in his body wanted to get out of here.

That raised the panic-fueled question of where he should flee. That in turn raised the question of where he was. The view between the boards offered no information. Empty desert. He didn't know how he got here. He didn't know if they'd even smashed in his skull. He couldn't remember. And he also couldn't remember who the man was whose skull had been smashed in, even if he was that man. He didn't know his own name.

The first quarter-turn on his axis was so difficult that he couldn't tell whether he was in pain or his muscles had failed. He let himself lean back again and tried to lift his head. Sweating and wheezing, he looked around at the part of the room nearest to where he was lying against the wall. A hammer seemed to slam against the inside of his skull and made words appear rhythmically, like flashcards, in the rhythm of his heartbeat, *attic, timber wall, amnesia, pulley, titration flask* and *sand heap.*

The fact that such difficult words as titration flask and amnesia were still available in his memory came as some relief to him. The fact that nothing beyond these words entered his mind, nothing that could shed light on the situation, alarmed him. His own name did not surface. It wasn't on the tip of his tongue either, as he had believed a moment before. He lifted his head a little more.

What he saw was an attic perhaps seven or eight meters across and of indeterminate length. One end was completely swathed in darkness, while dusty light seeped into the other end from a window-like opening. Tables jutted up into the light surrounded by metal instruments and plastic canisters. On the tables small glass flasks, on the floor larger ones. The floor around the tables covered with sand. A laboratory? In an attic in the desert?

From a balcony up above, a pulley hung from a heavy iron chain and dangled down through a large, square hole in the floor.

He looked around for a long time, gazing at and coming up with the names for all the objects he seemed to recognize and then, after he had purposefully not thought about it for a while, he tried to apply the momentum to finding the flashcard with his identity on it.

There was no card.

He tried to remember what he could still remember. It wasn't as if he couldn't remember anything at all. He remembered four men beneath a high sky. He remembered how the men had talked, how they attacked each other. He remembered a rattan suitcase full of money. And that one man, whom they referred to as Cetrois, had fled into the desert on a moped. With something the others wanted. He remembered the glaring sun and the sentence: You asshole, what if he deploys the line. Words superimposed on engine noise. Employs the design... the sign... Klein. If his convoys make the coastline. If he's a decoy for Klein. Four men in white djellabas, a rattan suitcase, a jeep.

He struggled in vain to try to extend the little theater piece for four players back into the past. There was no beginning and no end and it floated like a tiny island in an ocean of nothingness. If he redeploys the carbine. Despoils the pipeline. Cetrois. The first faint characters on a blank piece of paper.

What else could he remember? It wasn't four men, at first only three. Stupid men. Pleased that they had smashed somebody's skull in with a carjack, and unable to distinguish East German money from real money. And a fourth who had a weapon and a jeep and who didn't seem as stupid. He remembered that the vehicle they drove off in had a diesel engine. He remembered that he had heard the whacks as the car doors closed and counted them: one, two, three, four. Four whacks to the skull. Four men had climbed into an invisible jeep through four doors and driven off. Unless one of them had closed the door twice because it hadn't closed properly the first time. In that case only three had driven off and one had been left behind to stand watch.

He remained quiet and listened for as long as he could. But the throb in his head couldn't take the stillness. If one had stayed behind as a watchman, that person knew where he was anyway. It didn't matter. He had to get away from here. His body wanted to flee, and his mind did too.

17

Possibilities of Descent

If someone is acting otherwise normal, he is fully criminally responsible. He could have no brain at all for all I care.

HANS-LUDWIG KRÖBER,
FORENSIC PSYCHIATRIST

FOR A SECOND TIME, he attempted to get up. This time his muscles obeyed him better, and he stood up with the amazement of a man expecting unbearable pain but feeling nothing more than throbbing in his head. The physical paralysis that he had sensed during the first attempt to get up turned out to be an object that was strapped to his back. He peeled off the strap and found himself looking at the barrel of a clunky machine gun. Breechblock and trigger, the unholy trinity of the piston, stock and magazine: an AK-47. At least that's what it said in awkward silver lettering on the stock: AK-47. But it wasn't factory lettering. And it wasn't an AK-47. The thing felt light and flimsy in his hand. It was actually a toy, cut from wood and painted black, carefully made and accurate down to the last detail.

He propped himself up on all fours and pushed himself upright. He closed his eyes, opened them again, and took a few halting steps across the floor. It was okay. At least that's what he told himself as he calmly tried to breathe: It's okay, it's okay, it's okay.

He peered out through the window-like opening at the front of the building. There was a drop-off of about five or six meters. He was standing in the gable window of a giant barn. There were stones below. To the left of the barn he saw a small hut on top of which laundry had been set out to dry. Beyond, the desert stretched to the horizon.

No stairs. No ladder.

He was sweating.

"My name is," he suddenly said loudly. "My name is. My name is." Each time he left his tongue in position after the final s in order to trigger an automatic reflex, but neither his tongue nor his lips had any idea what they were supposed to do.

He had to get down somehow. The only connection to the ground floor appeared to be the approximately three-by-three-meter hatch through which the pulley was hanging. The ground floor below was in complete darkness. He waited for his eyes to adjust to the darkness and thought he was able to make out some sort of corridor down in the depths. Somewhat lighter bands branched off from the corridor. He assumed these were partitions that divided the space into stalls or alcoves. The height of the partitions was tough to guess, as was the distance to the floor. The darkness seemed to have a similar effect to an optical illusion, allowing the floor to look alternately closer and further away. But he didn't know how far it was either way. Though the assumption was that it dropped off here exactly as much as it did on the exterior of the barn, which was five or six meters. With his foot he shoved a bit of sand over the edge of the hatch, heard nothing for a second, then a patter in the dark.

An oily chain ran from the pulley, over large wheels, to a beam, where it was hooked to a nail. He unhooked the chain and let the heavy pulley swing back and forth, and then re-secured the chain. He didn't trust himself to climb five or six meters down the oily chain. He stared at the attic, the hatch and the pulley for a long while and wondered for the first time how he had got up here. With the pulley? In that case someone would have to have taken him off it up here, dragged him into the corner and then found a way back down.

They probably had a ladder that they pulled away afterward. Perhaps he had climbed up here on his own and they smashed in his skull up here. Or: they had smashed his skull in down below, he had fled with his last ounce of strength into the attic, had pulled the ladder up and only then lost consciousness.

He looked around in the half-darkness but did not discover a ladder or anything else that might have been helpful. No rope. Only junk.

"My name is," he said. "My name is."

Would it be possible to attach a counterweight to the pulley and lower himself softly to the ground? He tried to recall the laws of physics involved. Force times force-distance, mass times mass-distance. But how long was the distance? There were two wheels, the chain ran from the top down to the lower wheel and then up and around the upper wheel. So, three—no, two sections. He needed a counterweight that weighed half as much as he did. Or a quarter? His heart raced. After he'd stared at the apparatus for a minute he was not even sure which end was supposed to hold the greater weight. And even if he made the right calculations, how was he supposed to know how much something weighed compared to him? If he used a weight that was too light he'd accelerate too quickly on the way down. If it was too heavy he'd be pulled up to the attic balcony.

He began to inspect the attic more closely. The devices on the tables, copper cauldrons and pipes. A metal tub sat on top of a stove made of stacked bricks. Apparently the sand strewn everywhere was for fire protection. He sniffed two plastic flasks that contained clear liquid. The pungent smell of high-proof alcohol.

The tables gave an impression of sturdiness. Maybe he could carefully push them through the hatch in the hope that they stacked up into a sort of platform. As he went to try to push one of the tables, something fell over, and there, beneath sand, dust and junk, the rungs of a ladder were visible. After all.

He uncovered the ladder, measured its length (five and a half strides) and came to the conclusion that if it was long enough at all, it would reach from the attic to the ground only in the most dire emergency. Gasping, he lifted the ladder at its middle and turned it like a clock hand toward the hole in the floor. The back of it caught on the beam where the pulley chain was secured. The chain came off the nail and the pulley slowly set in motion. With his head pulled down between his shoulders he watched, frozen, as gravity pulled the apparatus into the depths and it thudded down loudly below. The chain followed after it, rattling derisively as it unspooled over the upper wheel and clanked out of the picture. With a little more presence of mind he could have stopped it. And if he had dropped the ladder immediately. But now that he had the ladder, the loss of the pulley seemed bearable to him. What he was much more worried about was the noise. He didn't budge and held his breath. But it was quiet.

Carefully he tried to push the ladder over the edge of the hatch. When it was slightly past halfway into the abyss, the lever principle made itself obvious. He was unable to hold the shorter end against the floor and had to pull the ladder back up.

Lowering it vertically wouldn't work either. The ceiling of the attic was too low. After two more helpless attempts it seemed to him the only chance was to push the ladder over the edge with momentum and hope it landed sort of upright. As far as his calculations were concerned, it would have to remain within a few degrees of perpendicular if it was to reach up to the edge of the hatch. If it was even going to reach at all.

Like a lab animal in an experiment trying to practice the use of tools, he rocked the ladder back and forth over its balancing point. Trial and error, mind versus matter—and suddenly the matter developed a life of its own. He had pushed it too far past the tipping point and it accelerated, dragging him forward. He frantically clutched onto the last rung.

He slammed with frightening force onto his stomach, slid dangerously over the edge, and only kept from falling because his right foot had hooked around some object, probably a table leg. He couldn't breathe.

His right arm and an alarming amount of his upper body were hanging over the abyss. His right hand: just pain. His shoulder: even more pain. But with his last ounce of strength he held fast to the ladder with one hand and felt it dangling back and forth like a pendulum in the darkness below. Blood ran down the fingers of his right hand. The skin was ripped. He groaned and slid a few more centimeters forward into the abyss, and the pendulum grazed the floor and stood still. He wrestled the ladder straight upright.

Now it was standing up. There were about forty centimeters between the top edge of the stringer and the bottom of the attic floor. He shifted his left hand to the top of the stringer, waved his hurt right hand in the air and breathed deeply.

Of course, if this ladder was too short, what good was it? It was obviously not the ladder he had used to get upstairs. There must have been a second ladder that someone else had pulled down... He suddenly froze with fright. What if the other person *hadn't* climbed back down? What if he was hiding up here somewhere? He hadn't looked at every corner of the attic.

He peered around frantically, rolling his head here and there, and his gaze fixed on the window at the front of the building. And suddenly something occurred to him: there.

If he had pushed the ladder out of the window, it would have leaned against the outside wall of the barn. Maybe he had even come in that way. He tried determinedly to pull the ladder up again by the top rung. He could just barely lift it, and the effort pressed all the air out of his lungs. But when he tried to grab the second rung his body started to slide forward. He quickly lowered the ladder back down to the ground and lay there panting.

Two additional attempts were equally unsuccessful. He could have just let the ladder fall. But he'd already made one mistake and didn't want to make a second. He decided to wait and hold the stringer at least until a better idea occurred to him.

The first thing that crossed his mind was to somehow secure the ladder. Maybe he could take off his djellaba and try to loop it around the top rung and tie it to something.

He grabbed at his collar and realized that beneath the djellaba he was wearing a checkered suit. At least that explained why he was sweating so much. But why was he wearing a suit under his djellaba? While he was still considering how best to remove the piece of clothing while lying down, he heard a quiet burble. It was the burble of water. The squeak of a water spigot. And a human voice. Like someone talking quietly to himself. It came from outside the barn.

Muffled steps beneath the window at the front. A clacking sound and a gossamer thread of light entered the ground floor. As if someone had opened a door a crack. Rattling breath, then silence, then an earthquake of a coughing fit. The fit of coughing receded again and water burbled anew somewhere. He heard slurping and rattling breathing. The spigot squeaked as it was turned off.

He couldn't let go of the ladder now without attracting attention to himself. But he also couldn't lie there. Desperation left him willing to try something. With his left hand still holding the ladder, he turned himself on his stomach and swung his left leg into the abyss and felt around for the top rung. It was surprisingly close and he put his foot down, not on it but on the second rung. Then he carefully let go of the stringer. He could keep the ladder upright by pressing down on it with his foot. He swung his right foot over the edge and onto the second rung as well. He didn't have a plan for what he was doing, just an intention that came to him in a panic. He let his body down centimeter by centimeter, clamped a foot like a hook beneath the second rung and felt with the other for the third. When both feet were on the third rung, his hips were already below the level of the attic floor.

One hand on the edge of the hatch, one on the ladder, he wobbled down three more rungs. Then that was it. With the next step he would have to let go of the edge of the hatch. It was still several meters to the floor. He looked down. Twelve, fifteen rungs. The rattling sound was approaching from outside.

He straightened the ladder again, took a deep breath, then let go of the edge of the attic floor and climbed into the depths with ape-like speed. He managed four or five more rungs by alternately sticking his seat out idiotically and then jerking himself back close to the ladder, accompanied by unreal groans from his own mouth. Circus act: the clown, not the high-wire artist. Then the ladder began to tilt precariously and he managed just one more rung before his foot stepped into the void. As he was falling he pushed the ladder away and then crashed to the ground on his back. The ladder thudded down only a few centimeters to the side of him. Dust swirled up. Walls made of strips of wood, metal canisters, sand, a chain, a screeching sound. Light through an open door. In the door Poseidon, god of the sea, with a flowing beard and a trident.

Correction: a fellah with a pitchfork.

He had no time to consider what part of his body hurt the most. His bones seemed intact. He staggered to his feet, put an innocent look on his face and tapped two fingers on his forehead as a greeting: Good day.

The trident was lowered.

He thought he could make out an old, boozy face backlit above the beard, and he tried out a sentence that could be an excuse as well as an accusation: "I was up there." He pointed to the scene of the crime and wondered to himself how he was going to get past the trident.

Both men simultaneously took a step toward the other. Either the fellah was blind or he was badly cross-eyed. A white film covered one of his eyes, and the other stared somewhere into the dark of the barn. Then the trident swung in the direction of his gaze, and a ghastly rattle, very different from the earlier one, came from the throat of the fellah.

His opposite number turned to see what the fellah was looking at. Next to junk and machine parts, between the walls of a stall, lay a man in a white djellaba, his limbs oddly contorted. Atop his crushed head lay the pulley block with the heavy metal hook. The oily chain was coiled in blood and brain matter. The trident moved into the picture. It didn't seem like the right moment to explain amnesia to the man. A fresh body, four armed men in a jeep, a crazy-looking fellah with a pitchfork: the situation was confusing. He pushed aside the pitchfork and ran. Ran through the barn door, past the hut and into the desert. And ran.

18

Beneath Dunes

Not wasteland, but a great inverted forest
With all foliage underground.

SALINGER

T HE DIRECTION WAS DICTATED by the barn door:
straight ahead in a direct line away from the buildings.
He ran up a dune, stumbled, threw himself over the crown.
Slid fifteen meters down, sprinted across the trough of the
wave and stomped up the next lee side. The lee sides of the
dunes were steep; one sank up to the knees. The windward
side was flat and firm. Going the other direction would
have been easier, but it would also have been easier for his
pursuer.

He looked back: nobody was following him. Completely out
of breath already, he went more slowly. Some distance away
was a slanting row of poles, perhaps telegraph poles, a road.
He headed that way and heard a humming from somewhere.
At first it was like the buzz in one's own ears, but he didn't
indulge in any illusions. It was the noise of an approaching
diesel engine. More than likely they hadn't managed to catch
Cetrois and now they wanted him. Or they had caught Cetrois.
And wanted him in addition.

He ran. Twenty or thirty wave troughs away the jeep jumped over a dune, hung for a second with all four wheels in the air and dropped out of view, its engine wailing.

Crouching down, he took a sharp left into a serpentine wave trough, picked up a fist-sized rock in stride and let it go again. What did he want with it? To knock the revolver out of their hand with it? The afternoon sun burned on his face. He stood still. He panted. He retraced ten of his own footsteps and then turned to look back: absurd, the difference was immediately obvious. The engine noise rose and fell in the rhythm of the waves of sand. In a sudden fit of rash panic, he scrambled up a dune and then tumbled back down the same side and looked at the results. Then he ran back and forth through the entire trough and a small adjoining trough until they were covered on every side with trails.

Two flat slabs of rock stood in the sand next to each other as if in a toaster. In their slipstream a deep trench had formed. He threw his body into it, his head between the slabs of rock, and shoveled sand onto his legs and torso. He burrowed his arms sideways into the ground. It wasn't difficult to make little avalanches of sand pour down on himself from the slanted sides of the trench. Finally he rotated his head back and forth between the rock slabs. He felt his head wound open; the pain was phenomenal. Sand fell in his face from above and trickled into his ears. The sound of the diesel engine fell silent. All he could hear was his own wheezing. He held his breath and squinted. His torso seemed entirely covered. Beyond the sand on top of his body he saw the wave trough, the flank of the dune on the other side, and the telltale footprints all around. His field of vision was severely limited by the slabs of rock. On the other hand, his face was only visible if one stood directly in front of him. But it was still visible.

He breathed deeply, closed his eyes and rotated his head back and forth again. Another load of sand slid down over his forehead to his cheekbones, dusting his eyelids, cheeks and the corners of his mouth like powdered sugar. He had only a very rough impression as to how much of his face was still uncovered. Probably his chin and the tip of his nose. But he couldn't turn his head any more now. With a little puff he blew a few grains of sand out of his nose and waited.

An image of the just-seen dunes beneath the bright sun lingered on the insides of his eyelids. The dunes light and covered by the ripple pattern caused by the wind, a pattern that was reminiscent of the whorls of a giant brain, the sun a black ring with a light hole in the middle. Perhaps the last thing he would see in his life. If they discovered his hiding place, silently approached him and put a few bullets into the ground between the slabs, he wouldn't even have seen his murderers. The engine noise returned. Approached. Receded. It sounded as if they were turning. Suddenly he sensed light tremors. A fine mist of sand splashed onto the sand on his feet. He heard shouts. Apparently they were driving at high speed around the same trough he was lying in. He didn't flinch. He tried not to breathe. As the noises fell silent, he didn't know whether they had driven off or had got out to search for him on foot.

The silence went on for minutes.

Three minutes. Or ten. He could tell how uncertain his sense of time was and began to count his heartbeats. His heart was beating wildly. In his mind's eye he saw the sand over the left side of his chest hopping traitorously like it was on a drum. Hundred beats a minute. Approximately. After 150 beats he thought he heard a muffled squeak, but he wasn't sure. The sand in his ears itched horribly.

He continued to count in order to measure the time, to calm himself down and to concentrate: 199, 200. He couldn't rid himself of the idiotic notion that his exhalations would produce a pattern in the sand beneath his nose and give him away.

He counted to 300, 400, 500. At 3,200 the engine noise returned, but very faintly. This time they didn't get close to him. He counted to 6,000, he counted to 12,000. And did not move. The throbbing in the back of his head got stronger and stronger. His entire body pulsed. The whole time as he counted number after number he had the feeling that someone was standing directly over him with a pistol drawn, waiting out of spite. Waiting until he opened his eyes to blast him into a sandy grave with a smile. He counted to 15,000. It had been 12,000 heartbeats, so about 120 minutes, without any noise. He stuck out his bottom lip, blew air over his face and tried to blink. The narrow view between the rock slabs showed the trough churned up by car tracks and the dune on the far side of the trough beneath a glass-blue evening sky. On the crest of the dune stood something staring at him with two little button eyes. Piercing, emotionless, interested in an absurd way. A short-legged, furry animal, no bigger than a fennec. It had reddish-gold fur; two incisors stuck up from its tiny lower jaw. The animal looked around, squeaked and trotted off.

19

The Quarter Character

> Every one of the bastards that are out for legalizing marijuana
> are Jewish. What the Christ is the matter with the Jews? I suppose
> it is because most of them are psychiatrists.
>
> NIXON

H E HAD BARELY REACHED the dirt road beneath the
telegraph poles when he saw a dust cloud on the horizon.
He crept behind a dune until he could be sure it wasn't the jeep
approaching. It was a white Fiat 500, a leg hanging out of the
left side. He jumped up, ran back out to the road and waved
with both arms. Through the windshield he could make out two
occupants, light-skinned young men with long hair and bare
chests. They were snaking toward him and swerved around him,
gaping with wide eyes. And continued on at a walking pace.

He ran after the car and tried to yell his tale of woe into the
open passenger door window. The passenger had opened his
mouth, pulled his upper lip up to his nose and held his hand to
his ear like he was deaf. He yelled: "What? I said, What? You
are an amazing sprinter! But—what? What men? Slow down,
he's out of breath. Not too slow. Now come on, you must know
what kind of men! And now you're just wandering around
here? He says he's not just wandering around... no, he's *not* just

wandering around! You want a sip of beer? No offense, we're Christians. But at least he speaks English. Seriously, you're the first person who can speak English. All the kaffirs—pardon my French. But how do you see this working? I mean, look at the back seat. Yeah, isn't it about life and death for us all? Of course I understand that. But you have to understand us. The rule of the desert. Suppose you have a knife under your frock? Of course not! Nobody who wanted to slit someone's throat would admit in advance that he had a knife under his frock. But I say, better safe than sorry. And when someone is running around out here talking about not knowing who he is or where he's going and with his head all bashed in—I mean, what is the story, man? I'm not buying it. Are you buying it? Slow down. Sip of beer?"

They rolled along beside him in first gear. At one stage he reached for the held-out beer but it was pulled away. Finally, exhausted and completely out of breath, he stopped and watched as the Fiat quietly creaked away. Fifty meters. And then it, too, stopped. The driver got out, stretched and waved. Shimmering heat separated his arm from his body, his feet hovered twenty centimeters above the ground. Eventually the passenger also got out. He unzipped his pants, pissed in the sand and talked over his shoulder to driver. They laughed. Then they waved again.

Reason told him that they only wanted to make an ass of him. They would probably get back in and drive off as soon as he caught up with them. But oddly enough, something made him think for some reason that these were *friends* of his.

The expression on their faces was so oddly attentive and at the same time cheerful and open that he couldn't shake the feeling that they must be old friends or acquaintances of his who didn't understand the gravity of the situation. Either that or they were lunatics. But they didn't really look like lunatics. Hesitantly he approached the two of them. The hope and the wish that they might be his friends became so overwhelming that it spilled out of him.

"Do we know each other? We know each other!" he called.

"Yeah," said the passenger, pulling on a tie-dye T-shirt. "For ages. But are you serious? You don't know who you are?"

He nodded.

"And how long have you not known?"

"For a few hours."

"Do you not have a wallet?"

He hadn't thought of that. He reached under his djellaba and felt the back pocket of his suit. Unbelievable. A wallet. He lifted the djellaba so he could get the wallet out, and when he looked up again there was a switchblade knife pointed at his eye. The passenger took the wallet out of his hand.

"If we help you and take you with us, you have to help us out a bit, too. Gas and whatnot. That okay with you? Share the expenses a little?" He opened the wallet, which contained a bundle of notes and cards of various colors, took out the notes and threw the rest into the sand. His buddy smiled. He had giant pupils.

"Well, well, well. Looks good. I suggest we go get gas straight away, drop off some stuff. And then we'll come back. You wait here, okay? Maybe you can clean yourself up a bit in the meantime. You look like a pig."

"I think he's lost more than his memory, he seems to be having more and more trouble talking, too."

They turned his head this way and that at knifepoint and then the driver ordered him to crawl around on all fours and squeal like a pig. He crawled around on all fours and squealed like a pig. One of them asked why this was so easy for him, and the other asked whether the Arabs didn't consider pigs impure. They didn't have a lot of imagination. They gave him a kick in the side and finally went back to the car. The driver started the car, the passenger put one foot on the running board, held the knife and banknotes indecisively in his hand and looked around.

Out of fear that they might change their minds and hurt him badly or even kill him, he called out: "You can take the money!"

That was a mistake.

The passenger seized on it first. "We can take the money!" he said. He came back, beaming, picked up the wallet and watched the reaction of the man kneeling on the ground and pressing his hand against the pain in his side. He took the papers out of the wallet and studied them with the enthusiastic lack of understanding of a first grader who had just learned to read. A white card, a green card, a red card. Two rows of white American teeth and a whole bunch of gums were bared. As he read his smile slowly stiffened and then froze, his mouth still open. Appalled, he handed the red card to the driver and said: "Oh, my god."

The driver had a look at it, looked around baffled and then also said: "Oh, my god."

And then down toward the ground: "We didn't know! We are sorry. If only we had known who you were!"

"We wouldn't have attacked you!"

"Superman! We attacked Superman!"

"You said it, oh, my god. Superman!"

"The super brain with super strength!"

"And super squeals! Eh, man. We're doomed!"

They found themselves incredibly funny. They tried out another string of jokes with super dirty, super dummy and super piggy, and then the passenger pulled out a lighter and held it beneath the ID card. The blue flames moved very slowly up the tough paper. The last scrap fell from his hand, he waved his arm in the air and blew on his fingertips. Both the white and the green cards burned more readily. Then the order to crawl around on all fours and squeal in the direction of Mecca was repeated. Finally they got into the car and drove off.

With a lunge he grabbed the last smoldering scrap of the red ID paper, a tiny piece from which trembling bits of ash fell. He held it between the fingernails of his thumb and fore-finger, and, as if in the capriciousness of fortune there were a sort of logic and malice, it was the part of the card on which "Name:" stood.

Name, colon and a quarter of a letter, an upward squig-gle. Then the last ember consumed the squiggle. The letter had been rounded up and to the left, perhaps a C or an O. Dark-red ink on red paper. He looked at the horizon, where the dust cloud hung above the road. Then again at his sooty fingertips. The squiggle had turned into ash. But he had seen it. He now knew his name began with a C or an O. Or with an S. S was also possible. Whether it was his first or last name he did not know.

He walked along the road. For a long time no cars came past. He took off the djellaba, looked at the thin trail of blood on the back and then buried the piece of clothing in the sand. When the next dust cloud appeared on the hori-zon, he hid too late. A dark Mercedes drove past, honking. After that, as a precaution, he walked in the dunes, parallel to the road but at some distance from it. The going was dif-ficult, but the fear was killing him. At the top of each dune he kept a lookout. His wound throbbed, and he wrapped his undershirt around his head. He had long since inspected the rest of the contents of his suit: in the jacket he'd found a ring with seven keys, four safety keys, two normal ones, a car key. In addition, a used tissue and in the inside pocket a green pencil with a broken tip.

As he walked he recalled names with the first letters of C, O and S and was surprised how easily they came to him. Dozens of names came to mind with no effort at all, though not a single one seemed tied to any memories. Claude, Charles, Stéphane. Cambon, Carré, Serrault. Ogier. Sassard. Sainclair. Condorcet. Ozouf. Olivier. It was as if the names were written by an invisible hand and passed to him on an invisible tray. Perhaps they were names that everyone knew, not connected to any particular person. Or perhaps he had known a person connected to each name, which was why they all triggered the same reaction in him: nothing. He wondered how he even knew there was such a thing as memory loss. In what life had he learned that?

Then the letter Q occurred to him.

From the next cloud of dust on the horizon came the sound of a diesel engine. He threw himself onto his stomach in the sand. Quineau, Quenton. Schlumberger. Quatremère. Chevalier. The stream of names didn't stop.

Next the letter G occurred to him, and he had a fit of rage. He kneeled and wrote out the alphabet with his finger in the sand, to make sure he hadn't overlooked any more letters. C, G, Q and S. That was it. He staggered onward. If he annoys the hardline, he doesn't fall in line, delays the power line, if he destroys... The sun burned hot over the Sahara.

20

In the Land of the Ouz

Female Nines frequently mistype as Twos.

EWALD BERKERS

HELEN HELD THE PHONE to her ear for several minutes without saying a word. When all she could hear at the other end was sobbing, she asked: "Shall I come anyway?"

Around noon she found the car rental place that the receptionist at the Sheraton had described to her. At least that was the word she had used: car rental place. One could also have said junk yard. An oxcart and a rusty Honda pickup were the only vehicles in the yard, surrounded by piles of worn parts.

In a plywood hut sat a thirteen-year-old boy slumped in front of a shisha. The presence of a blonde woman temporarily revived him. He hopped up, made expansive gestures and spoke to her in a strange, quaint accent. What he was trying to get across, however, was less pleasing. The Honda was broken down and Helen did not wish to rent the oxcart (which included oxen and a driver), and the questions as to when a car would be available or how many cars they even owned the boy answered only with a shake of the head. Helen inquired about other car rentals in the area and learned that limousines could be hired at the airport. The likelihood of getting a car there without a reservation, however, was about nil.

"And what's wrong with that one?" Helen pointed out of the window.

Slow shaking of the head, coupled with raised eyebrows. The boy led Helen out, sat in the pickup and turned the ignition key. Clicks came from under the hood of the Honda.

"Mechanic coming. Probably. Two weeks."

Helen made another attempt to find out how many cars the place had, received just as little of an answer as before, and asked instead for tools. Beneath his table the boy had a set of crooked wrenches, pliers, a hammer, brushes. Helen carried it all out to the Honda. For a while the boy felt compelled to stand nearby slowly shaking his head, but in the end he couldn't bear to watch any more and went back inside his hut. A woman. A blonde woman! He wouldn't be able to tell anyone. He scrounged up charcoal, Nakhla tobacco and matches. Lit the shisha, and blew smoke out of the little window into the yard.

Now and then he heard American curses escape from under the propped-open hood, he heard banging on metal, the quiet click of the ignition switch in the midday heat, and then, as the coals in his shisha were already spent, engine noise. Shortly afterward the oil- and dirt-smeared woman came into the hut. She threw the tools on the table, took out her wallet and said in a tone so blasé as not to be outdone: "I need it for a week. How much?"

As far as Helen knew, there was a short, unsafe route and a long, safe route to the dirt road to Tindirma. She had time. For kilometers on end she followed the main road north to the foot of the mountains, where the city thinned out and a solitary sign marked the turn. The road went through dry vegetation for a few hundred meters. After sand dunes with salt-resistant plants there followed sand dunes with no salt-resistant plants, and the entrance to the desert was marked by a huge, geometric sculpture of two camels made out of clay bricks, the muzzles of which met high in the air above the dirt road.

Even if one had never seen the desert before, it got boring quickly. It was the time of the greatest midday heat, and Helen didn't encounter another vehicle. Here and there were car wrecks sunken in the sand like dead insects, eroded down to the bare metal and with their doors open like wings.

After two hours she reached a gas station with one single pump. The oasis of Tindirma was just beyond.

Helen tried exactly twice to exit the car in the oasis. Even though she had on jeans and a long-sleeve T-shirt, she caused a stampede both times. Men, boys and old men came running at her with their arms outstretched in front of them. She had a headscarf somewhere in the car but didn't want to wear it in the midday heat. She supposed the situation wasn't going to get any better. She gave up on her plan to have a look around on her own for the time being.

The little street with the commune wasn't hard to find from the souk. Helen recognized the plaque on the door from the description over the phone and she drove the Honda into the courtyard. A fluffy bearded man in a tie-dyed tunic opened the door. He repeated the name Helen Gliese, looked her in the eyes for twenty seconds and pushed his jaw from side to side before he let her in.

The building had been furnished in the same plush and padded style as normal Arab residences, and the first thing that struck Helen were the notes. Notes everywhere. Fluffy beard closed up behind her and barred the door with four locks, and at the same moment Michelle fell down the stairs into the inner courtyard with a scream. She flung her arms around Helen's neck and wouldn't stop sobbing. With his arms folded behind his back, fluffy beard stood nearby and watched the two women's greeting as if he were looking at a complicated car wreck. He was silent, Michelle sobbed, and over her shoulder Helen read the writing on one of the notes that was hanging next to the cloakroom: *The watcher is the watched.*

Michelle pushed her childhood friend an arm's length away and scanned her with a glazed look, then pulled her back to her, sobbing. She was so worked up that she couldn't say anything for a long time, and when she was able to speak again she said: "Asthma spray." She ran back up the stairs. Fluffy beard took his hands out from behind his back, raised them slowly to the height of his armpits, began to do stretching exercises and said: "It's not asthma. It's psychological."

He led Helen past a kitchen table where five or six communards were sitting, down a long, dark hallway, at the end of which stood a red upholstered bench. "Plant yourself there."

For a few minutes Helen stood alone in the half-darkness. Finally she sat down. Low voices could be heard, a water pipe, a pendulum clock. She tried to read the notes that she could decipher from her spot. Next to the bench was: *Everything is good, just not everywhere, not always, not for everyone.* Above that: *Turtles can tell more about roads than hares.* And more notes were stuck to the ceiling lamp, only one of which Helen could decipher: *If you want to build a ship, don't try to drum up men to procure wood, prepare tools, allocate duties and divide up the work, teach men to yearn for the vast, open ocean.*

Presumably these little notes had been there before the massacre (and certainly the first thing that occurs to one after such an event isn't redecorating).

Three women with long, straight hair stuck their heads one after the other out of the kitchen and then back again. A man walked crying through the hall. Fluffy beard showed up again and said: "We need to talk."

Helen didn't move.

He opened a black lacquered door at the end of the hall and looked over his shoulder. "Now!" he said.

He had a Scottish accent, and as a result of that fact and his bearing Helen concluded that this was Edgar Fowler, Ed Fowler III, the unofficial leader of the little commune. She waited a little while to see whether Michelle would show up, then followed him into the side room.

The room was lined with blankets, scarves and blue-gray mattresses. It smelled. In the middle was a small area that had been cleared; in it stood a child's playpen. Plastic blocks, colorful balls and rag dolls lay inside it, but instead of a child, an animal with slightly reddish, sand-colored fur crouched motionlessly in the middle of the playpen. One could have mistaken it for a plush toy if its whiskers hadn't quivered. Two incisors stuck up from its tiny lower jaw, and between its ears it was wearing something like a crown made out of white paper that was strapped to its head by a rubber band. It looked as if it could easily have stripped the rubber band off its head with its back paw if it felt like it. But apparently it didn't feel like it.

The animal took one sedate stroll around its playpen, sniffed its flank and stared at Helen with little, black button eyes. Although it was much smaller than the spaces between the slats, it didn't leave its cage.

Fowler sat down cross-legged on a mattress and waited until Helen, too, had sat down facing him. He gave her a look that was perhaps intended to be deep and fiery but which did not fail to make the opposite impression on Helen. Helen looked at the animal. The animal yawned.

"That's Gurdjieff. He understands everything you say."

"That thing?"

"That thing. It's an ouz."

"And if I speak French?"

"Does God understand you when you pray?"

"I don't pray."

"Sophism."

"What did you want to talk about?"

"We are talking."

"Oh yeah?"

"You're a Jew. Michelle says."

"Actually I'm not."

"Always looking for confrontation."

"This constitutes confrontation to you? What did you want to talk about?"

"Don't misunderstand me. I don't judge. I state. And what I state is: Negativity. Sophistry. Confrontation."

Helen sighed and shifted her gaze back to the animal again. It had followed the rapid exchange of words, followed as if watching a tennis match, attentive, serious, focused.

"Look at me," said Fowler with a menacing edge to his voice.

Helen looked at him and Fowler was silent. He moved his tongue inside his mouth and then slowly, meditatively closed his eyes.

"You didn't come here for no reason," he whispered. "But also not for the reason you think. You've heard about the murders. You are here to satisfy your curiosity. You are here because—"

"I'm Michelle's oldest friend."

"You can answer when I'm finished!" He opened his eyes angrily and waited a long time before he closed them again and continued with his speech. "I said: you didn't come for no reason. What you have heard triggered something in you. It has affected you more deeply than you know. You want to visit Michelle. So you say. You won't find her. What? You won't find her? You just saw her? Stay seated. The desert changes you. The nomads. When somebody has lived here for a long time they see with different eyes. The desert dweller is calm, he is the center. He doesn't approach things, things approach him. That is the coolness that you feel. It is not coolness. It is warmth. All-encompassing energy. The beginning of freedom." Fowler reached blindly for Helen's left breast and kneaded it lethargically. "What does freedom mean? Aha. Freedom doesn't mean to do and be allowed to do what you want. Freedom means doing the right thing."

He opened his eyes for a moment and blinked, as if checking on the effect of his words. Helen took this moment to hit him in the face. Fowler pulled his hand back slowly and majestically. He smiled grandly. Not at all offended. A question of knowing human nature. He had foreseen what would happen and he was still the master of the situation. He looked at Helen placidly and full of understanding, and Helen couldn't shake the feeling that the ouz was looking at her exactly the same way.

"You have your emotions under control. Have always had them under control. But that's how they get out of control. You are surprised how I know this. You are a nice piece of ass. You've heard that a lot. Nice piece of ass, nice piece of ass. From weak men. Men who didn't interest you. Deep inside you know: there is something else in store for you. You are a typical five, on the border of a six. Though with six I mean the co-operative type. You are not open. Stay seated."

Fowler stretched his hand out again, and Helen stood up and headed to the door. There she stopped and pointed at the playpen with her chin: "What's the rat got on its head anyway?"

Fowler ignored the word rat and gestured almost imperceptibly, stoicism and leniency beneath half-closed eyelids. He couldn't judge anyone, but there were the remains of condescension in his dismissive gesture. He had the strength and the talent to understand people, but not the strength to conceal his position. He still needed to work on that. He was a classic nine, straight out of the book.

Only as Helen took a few steps toward the cage did he jump up.

"Don't touch!"

"Why?"

"You aren't yet to that point."

Michelle was waiting in the hall with asthma spray and a tissue. Judging by her over-zealous disinterest, she had eavesdropped.

"Do you want to show me your room?" asked Helen. "If you have a room. Or the building."

21

Corn Plants

In any type of attack, it is essential to assail your opponent from behind.

DICTA BOELCKE

THE APPEARANCE of the old school friend on the premises of the commune forced Michelle to see the aphorisms, household altars, flower arrangements and batik images with a fresh set of eyes, and allowed a glut of long-forgotten ideas to well up inside her as she showed Helen around.

She apologized ceaselessly for the dirt and mess, scattered a pile of incense ash on the ground with a quick brush of her hand, and with her foot shoved under the bed a messy stack of notes, the symbols, arrows and zigzagging lines with which someone had decoded the secret messages of the *White Album* the night before. She called the godheads pretty carvings, the cards an amusement, and the stack of books with pentagrams on them relics of a long since departed member of the commune.

"I'm so happy that you're here," she said finally.

Helen looked at Michelle and frowned, and Michelle started to cry.

She had basically not changed. An innate sort of dreaminess, nebulousness, had always been particular to her, friendliness and kindliness. But these were traits that didn't amount to anything. Michelle made no decisions. And her childhood home, a solid education and the years in the commune had not been able to change that. She carelessly and aimlessly adopted strange ideas, mixed them with innocence and kindness of heart, and had the dubious luck to become part of a community where this was viewed more as appealing than as problematic. "Michelle is something else," was the most common verdict rendered behind her back when she had once again proved too clumsy or apathetic for tangible, worldly interests.

Tensions could thus arise, and Michelle took care of the problem by pursuing with even greater devotion the two things in the commune that didn't require any assertiveness and for which she had the most talent. First, farming: the fact that the fields of the commune still yielded a substantial crop was entirely thanks to Michelle. And second: that was something more complicated.

Second, namely, had to do with the fact that Jean Bekurtz, a longtime commune resident who had since gone into hiding (or gone missing in the desert), had brought back a set of tarot cards from one of his trips, a reissue of a northern Italian set from the sixteenth century, colorful wooden engravings, twenty-two cards, the Major Arcana. Bekurtz himself didn't believe in the agency of spiritual forces, or at least no longer did. He had bought two books on the subject along with the cards, but found them tedious reading and quickly lost interest. But the effect the wooden engravings had on the new member Michelle during a demonstration made him think: the way Michelle seemed at first more repelled than excited, how she nevertheless grabbed for the cards, how she contemplated them for a long time and asked questions about the positioning, made it abundantly clear to Bekurtz that he was not the right man for cartomancy. He taught her what he knew and gave her his tools of the trade without any sense of envy.

Michelle didn't find the books tedious. She devoured them. And after she had devoured them once, she devoured them a second time. Not for a single second did she have the impression that she was ingesting hidden secret lore, mysterious wisdom passed down for centuries from one adept to another. It was the opposite, as if she knew every word, every sentence, as if all of it had long since existed in her head, yes, even as if she had written the books herself.

Other members of the commune also became interested in the tarot cards, but nobody got into their secrets as effortlessly and quickly as Michelle, nobody told fortunes with such a lucky hand, nobody interpreted them so well and from so deep inside herself. When she picked up the deck and carefully shuffled, when she closed for eyes for a moment before she moved the top card slightly forward with her thumb and held the stack of cards above the finely woven carpet like a sensor, when her eyelids began to twitch from concentrating on a higher essence and function, even the most fervent doubter went silent.

Soon the odd person came to ask her for advice. Fowler was the only one who voiced concerns about these goings-on, but his objections were less about contact with the paranormal than about the threat to his hold on power (which was relatively transparent to all).

It didn't take long before Michelle was attending every important decision made by the commune with her cards in hand. While her own arguments during discussions often went unheard, her oracle came to dictate the outcome. At first it was consulted on only the most important group things, but soon enough there was nothing the cards didn't offer advice about. Anything that could be decided was at least in part decided by the cards, and nobody, not even Fowler, could say in retrospect that even one of these decisions had turned out to have been a mistake. The cards gave advice on matters great and small, the future, character and development, the weather and crop rotations, as well as the acceptance of new members, what color to paint a room and the location of a lost key.

Michelle's talent was extraordinary in every respect. But it was more than a talent, it was also a great burden. From the very first time she was shown the cards, some of the images had proved to exert such a power of suggestion over her that suggestion was too small a description.

The Moon was one of those images; but even worse than the Moon was the Hanged Man. Michelle had an allergy to cat hair, and the symptoms triggered by a glimpse of the Hanged Man—a tortured, boyish body hanging upside down by one leg in front of an autumnal landscape featuring mountains and the planet Neptune—were analogous to the allergy. As a result, at first she had liked to remove the Hanged Man and hide it, but after Bekurtz had once publicly expressed surprise that the deck had only twenty-one cards, Michelle developed a technique for shuffling that allowed her to shove the Hanged Man at the bottom of the deck and make sure it stayed there.

The consequence of these practices, which Michelle herself felt dishonest, was a certain imprecision in the interpretation of the cards, tiny cumulative mistakes that led to this or that inconsistency and then one day to catastrophe. Because this shuffling technique was the only way to explain how she failed to really predict the horrible threat looming over her community, Amadou's criminal intentions, the attack, the robbery, the quadruple murder, and had instead talked vaguely about great cataclysms (that in combination with the rest of the cards became abundantly clear). Since then Michelle had been a nervous wreck. Plagued by secret pangs of guilt, she became thin-skinned and short-tempered.

The only thing that assuaged her psyche was the fact that she hadn't been close to the four who'd been killed. That damped the pain a little, if only secretly. Because on the other hand it wasn't without its appeal to be grief-stricken and part of a great tragedy, marked for life. Almost like wearing a medal.

Michelle was happy when she and Helen finally arrived behind the house, where there was a small, lush green cornfield. These solid plants were beyond all ideological objections, respectable plants that one needn't be ashamed of.

"So what are you doing here—in Targat?" she asked.

"Work."

"Really? I thought—really? What kind of work?"

"For a company," said Helen. "Cosmetics. It's just that when I was disembarking I lost my sample case with all the materials—"

"You work for a cosmetics company? As a traveling saleswoman?"

"No, not a saleswoman. Something similar. I'm supposed to set something up here."

"For an American cosmetics company? You work for an American cosmetics company?"

"I'm just having a look around."

"Seriously?" said Michelle loudly.

She could barely keep calm. Her childhood friend, Helen, whom she had admired above all, the formidable Helen Glicse, with her incisive intelligence, cynical Helen, haughty Helen—a tiny cog in the machinery of bourgeois capitalist exploitation.

Her facial expression changed completely from one second to the next. It wasn't like Michelle to look down on someone, but her amazement was limitless and genuine. The raw power of that great destroyer Time had been confirmed once again: what became of people and their dreams and hopes? What became of that bright star, the intellectual star of Matarazzo

Junior High, the blonde, perky-breasted girl surrounded by all the boys?

She involuntarily compared herself. Michelle—and it had never before been so apparent to her—had dared to take the plunge into the unknown. Little Michelle, who had basically only been tolerated, Michelle Vanderbilt, whom Helen had never taken seriously, she had bid farewell to middle-of-the-road thoughts of security and realized her ideals. She had co-founded a commune in Africa, had broken out of her surroundings and transformed her being into a quest. She had stridden across the highest heights and been marked for life by tragic circumstances. Four people had been shot next to her! And in the depths of darkness, her soul had grown. How oddly her childhood friend came across by contrast, the way she stood there in front of a field of glorious, hand-planted corn in her somewhat impractical but stylish clothes—an employee of a cosmetics company! The irony of fate.

Helen ignored the thoroughly triumphant expression on Michelle's face and looked at a small, dried corn plant at the edge of the field that seemed to have taken leave of the great cycle of life and the pervasive energy. At the base of the plant was a nest of swarming, whitish maggots that was being attacked by ants. Little white orbs floated on the swarming, black current and were swallowed by a hole in the ground. Michelle, feeling ashamed at her own sense of satisfaction, followed Helen's gaze.

"Yeah, that's the way it goes," she gushed. "Sad, right? The white things crawl all around here. Once in a while I wipe the ants away with my finger, to help, but—it doesn't do any good. It's nature. It is how it is. And it's good that way. The maggots and all the other small animals and we humans, too, in the end we're just a part of a greater whole, a collective project."

"I suspect that if you could ask them, your theory would get more votes in the ant camp than the maggot camp."

"Most people don't even think about it, they see only a part. But as long as you don't have it, this yin and yang… everything belongs together, life and death, whether or not we are conscious of it. I don't fret over it. All is one. All makes sense."

"Auschwitz," said Helen.

But one couldn't trip Michelle up so easily. "Auschwitz," said Michelle gravely. "I know what you mean, and I understand. I understand it particularly when it comes to you and your family. And obviously it was wrong what the Germans did. There's no doubt about it: it was wrong!" She looked momentarily pensive. "Just as it is wrong to compare Jews to these maggots, as you—unconsciously, I assume, or unintentionally—just did. Even though you yourself… but what I want to say: Palestine. What you, I mean, what the Israelis are doing to the Palestinians, that's no different from Auschwitz—no, wait, let me finish—in essence it is worse, because you haven't learned from your own history, just as so many others fail to learn from their own history, but in this case it's particularly tragic because Jews, exactly like Palestinians, both under the influence of Mercury—I mean, in terms of the monstrous crimes being committed there, crimes against Palestinian women and children, against innocent people, against babies, intolerable crimes," said Michelle, looking with a furrowed brow at the massacre at the foot of the corn plant, "these intolerable crimes," she said, fighting back tears, "it's horrible, horrible, horrible."

"In your opinion," said Helen, using her foot to bury the nest with sand, flustering the maggots and the ants alike. She, too, seemed to have surrendered to the influence of Mercury.

22

A Gas Station in the Desert

GAS STATION ATTENDANT: Yes ma'am, what can I do for you
   today?
VARLA: Just your job, squirrel. Fill it up!

Faster, Pussycat! Kill! Kill!

BUT MICHELLE WAS UNABLE to convince her friend to stay. She knew that Helen might as well have been allergic to scenes like this, and as they said goodbye she tried to collectively explain her hysterical sobbing and her high spirits before that to an emotional state, a state produced by intense stress, suffering and joy. But Helen acted the way she always acted in such situations: coldly. What did she know about life? Would she ever know anything?

"I'd love to get together again," said Michelle, while two other sentences drowned in sniffles. Helen wrestled herself free of her friend's embrace, and as she did her gaze fell on a note stuck to the inside of the building's door: *Wherever you go, your destiny is waiting for you.*

"Don't get sentimental," she mumbled.

"We've eaten people like you!" called a voice from the kitchen.

Michelle protested weepily, but Helen didn't hear any more of the argument that ensued in the commune. She'd seen enough, her mission had been achieved.

She got in her car, breathed deeply and drove as fast as she could through the desert in the direction of her destiny, which at this point she assumed would be the hotel bar.

She bought two bottles of water at a gas station in the desert just outside Tindirma. She pulled a couple of coins out of her wallet and watched as a filthy eight-year-old smeared her windshield with brown soap suds. The station attendant filled the tank to the brim.

He took a twenty-dollar bill from Helen and while he disappeared into his shed to get change, a white VW bus with German license plates pulled slowly into the gas station and stopped on the other side of the pump with its engine still running. Yellow curtains in the windows, a young couple. Very young.

The driver took a quick look at Helen and looked away as soon as Helen met his gaze. He gripped the steering wheel with both hands. His girlfriend had spread a map out on the dashboard. She was clearly the more agile of the two, talked loudly, gestured while holding an open-faced sandwich, and honked the horn from the passenger seat in order to call the attendant. The eight-year-old had by now also smeared suds onto the side and back windows of Helen's car. She got out and lit a cigarette.

There was garbage all around the gas station. An Arabic-looking man was staggering down a dune through the garbage toward the station. His face was petrified, his eyes bloodshot. When he had made it beyond the garbage, he sank knee-deep in the sand for a few steps, then, once the footing was solid again, he swerved as he walked. He wasn't swerving like a drunk or someone lost in thought. It reminded Helen of lab rats at Princeton in an experiment where they kept trying to get at a reward even though they knew from extensive experience they would get an electric shock. The man lurched past the VW bus, circled the Honda uncertainly and then suddenly approached

Helen determinedly. "Help, help," he said hoarsely in English, bracing himself on the hood of the car. He was wearing a suit that was smeared with sand and black, sticky fluid. In the First World he'd be taken for a harmless vagabond, but in the middle of the Sahara he came across a little more threatening.

Helen pulled a coin out of her pocket and held it out to him. He didn't look at the coin. Some muck from his sleeve had stuck to the hood and he bent over to wipe it clean with a corner of his jacket.

"Leave it be. Take this."

"What?"

"Please, leave it."

He nodded, straightened up, and repeated: "Help, help."

"What do you want?"

"Take me with you."

"Where?"

"Anywhere."

"Sorry."

The man refused the coin again, his face contorted in pain, and as he turned his head Helen saw the large wound on the back of his head, crusted over with sand and blood. His eyes scanned the horizon. The German couple in the VW bus, who had watched the entire scene, were getting restless. The driver shook his head and gestured out of the side window with both hands as if fending something off. The passenger frowned as she read instructions on a canister of tear gas.

The attendant reappeared and gave Helen her change without a word, then got to work on the gas cap of the VW bus.

"What's going on?" Helen asked the wounded man.

"I don't know."

"You don't know what's going on?"

"I need to get out of here. Please."

"Do you believe in destiny or anything like that?"

"No."

"Well, that's something." She looked pensively at the man for a while. Then she opened the passenger door for him.

The couple in the VW bus couldn't contain themselves any longer. The man rolled down the window. "Attention, attention!" he yelled in bad English. "This is not Europe. No hitchhikers."

"Danger, danger!" his girlfriend assisted.

"Danger, danger," said Helen. "It doesn't have shit to do with you." And then to the man: "Come on."

They got into the Honda. He symbolically swatted the sand-crusted legs of his pants, then quickly hopped into the passenger seat, closed the door and stared out of the windshield like a bunny until Helen started the engine.

"You needn't be scared," he said once they'd been on the road a few minutes.

Helen took a drag on her cigarette and took another long look at him. Her passenger was half a head shorter than she was and sat with trembling arms next to her. She put her own muscular arm next to his and made a fist.

"I'm just saying," said the man.

"I'm going to Targat. I'll take you to the hospital there."

"I don't want to go to the hospital."

"Then to the doctor."

"Not to the doctor!"

"Why not?"

For a long time there was no answer. Finally he said uncertainly: "I don't know," and Helen let up on the gas and let the car coast.

"No!" the man screamed immediately. "Please! Please!"

"You don't know where you want to go. You don't know why you want to go somewhere. You need a doctor but don't want to go—and you don't know why. Come on. What do you know?"

Given the fact that he didn't know much, his explanation took a long time. Helen kept having to ask questions. The man spoke haltingly, painstakingly. Some words didn't want to come out, his upper body cringed. But he willingly expanded upon and corrected his statements, got upset at the inaccuracies that slipped in, tapped anxiously on his forehead, and kept spilling more and more details. Attic, case of money, Poseidon. Nothing that he said made sense, but this, as much as anything else, convinced Helen in the end that her strange passenger was telling the truth. Or at least trying to.

He left out just one detail. Despite all the composure and poise exuded by the American tourist behind the wheel, a man who'd been hit by a pulley block was perhaps one clue too many for an afternoon excursion into the desert. By contrast, he tried at length and mostly out loud to reconstruct the conversation he'd overheard the four men having, their unintelligible speech, their unintelligible rage, their unintelligible final sentence.

"If he's a decoy for Klein, if he employs the design, if he delays the pipeline... I can't figure it out."

"If he destroys the mine," said Helen, flicking the cigarette butt out of the window.

The two camels appeared in front of them, kissing across the road. The smell of wood fires and bunker fuel wafted over from Targat. The sky in the west was red and black.

23

Mercurochrome

If a thief is found breaking in and is struck so that he dies, there shall be no bloodguilt for him.

EXODUS 22: 1—2

THE LIGHT OF THE WORLD fell across a double bed in bars caused by the shades, parallel stripes of light. A second window stood open, the whoosh of the ocean and the smell of salt and iodine. The waves steady like breathing. He tossed and turned and saw a tuft of blonde hair an arm's length away from him.

He had gulped down four tablets, he knew that, and the rest of the tablets were sitting next to him on the nightstand in front of a glass of water. He knew that, too. His brow was covered in cold sweat. It was dark. He fought his way through a complicated labyrinth in order to be able to peer into a telescope. He was looking into the muzzle of a small-caliber gun, and a man with a trident was rushing at him. He gazed into his own face and heard a diesel engine. 581d. Attentively he followed as the mirror-image of a woman put a bandage on him. A vial of mercurochrome in her hand. How she held him under the shower. How he couldn't stand.

He gripped the sink with both hands while she disinfected the wound. He heard himself screaming in pain, a red blob on white porcelain. How she calmed him down. How she held him by the shoulders in front of her and drew a line on the sheets with the side of her hand: your half, my half. I'm putting tablets here. Do you see? Put your hands down. Breathe.

The parallel stripes of light shifted from the bed down to the floor and slid up the wall. He opened his eyes again and again through the course of the night and saw the stripes sometimes another half-meter away, sometimes in the same spot as before, without his sense of time ever seeming to keep up. Finally he got up and crept to the bathroom in the dark. Out of the corner of his eye he noticed that both halves of the bed were empty, but this did not particularly trouble him. The bathroom was full of sand. Beyond the largest pile of sand was a hole dug in the ground being watched over by an animal with two heads. One head in front, one in back. One dead, one living. The living head was sucking fluid out of the hole in the ground with a straw, a horrid bubbling noise. Telegraph poles began to move, upright yellow and blue bars flew past. He kept trying to get away from the bars of the cage, they kept surrounding him, before the calming sensation of yellow and blue striped wallpaper slowly supplanted them. This was no nightmare. Or at least only the nightmare of reality. A tourist bungalow early in the morning.

He was afraid to turn over in bed, afraid of the unexpected, and as he turned over he saw a kitchen. In front of the kitchen sink a naked woman. She was making coffee. The bubbling transformed into a fizzle.

With a look on his face as if he were staring at the sun he said: "We know each other from yesterday."

"Correct," answered the naked woman. She had perfectly polished fingernails. With her thumb and forefinger she swung a coffee filter into the sink.

"Your name is Helen," he said uncertainly.

"Yes. And if you don't know who you are, don't worry. You didn't know yesterday, either. Milk or sugar?"

But he didn't want milk or sugar. He didn't want to have breakfast. Just thinking about it made him feel sick, and he closed his eyes. When he next awoke the room was swathed in partial darkness. A shadow fell across the corner of the bed nearest him and dabbed his face with a wet cloth. Steam came from a porcelain bowl, voices trailed off out on the street, the woman popped a pill into his mouth. She was wearing a white dress with openwork arms now.

Once he saw her leave the bungalow in a bikini, carrying a beach bag over her shoulder. Once he heard her talking on the phone with the CIA. Once she had two heads. She came back from the hotel with two clumsy styrofoam trays. Both of them were wrapped in aluminum foil and when she took the foil off steam rose from the food as if it had come straight out of the oven. He couldn't eat.

"What have I told you?" he asked.

"Do you not know, or are you just not sure?"

"Not sure."

"You woke up in the attic of a building in the desert. You have cuts on your head, someone probably bashed your head in. You don't want to go to the police or the hospital. I'm Helen. I gave you a ride. This is my bungalow."

He looked at the woman and groaned. A face like something out of an American fashion magazine. He found it difficult to meet her gaze. He pulled the bedcovers over his head.

"Why don't I want to go to the police?" he asked with a muffled voice.

"You believe you have committed a capital offense."

That's what he had said.

"Supposedly you killed someone with a pulley block. Which I doubt."

He didn't ask why she doubted this. He remained under the covers, and the images came flooding back. The animal with the bubbling straw. He heard the woman talking on the phone and speaking about cosmetics. She went shopping, brought him drinks, sat on the edge of the bed and was gone again, a friendly hallucination. Then he was lying in the dark and heard no noise. No whoosh of the ocean. No breathing. Panic came and went in waves. He slept.

24

Swallows

PARSONS: The art of fighting without fighting? Show me some
of it.
LEE: Later.

Enter the Dragon

W HEN HE OPENED HIS EYES it was dawn. Beside him
a rumpled bedcover, he was alone. A nightstand full
of glasses and bottles. Two pictures on the wall. His body still
felt weak. He could feel sweat on his back and brow, but it was
more of a receding heat, the calming, slack feeling of the con-
valescent. Just a mild pain on the back of the head. He tried to
stand up and managed to grope his way a few steps from the
bed. Beyond the kitchen was another room.

"Helen?"

There were plates and utensils on the table, the door to the
terrace was open.

He stepped hesitantly out into the morning air, braced himself on the stone balustrade and looked out at the sea and sky.
Copper-colored pine trees clung to the long slope below. A light
fog hovered over the ocean, and the swells sent parallel lines
up the beach. To the right, stone steps led down to a second,
lower terrace, and from there an ocher path wound down to

the water. Helen was on the second terrace. Looking out at the ocean, her legs apart, her arms stretched out to either side, her platinum-blonde hair pulled back in a ponytail. For a few seconds she remained still, then her arms moved as if slowly pushing the air to the side. An arm rotated slowly forward, her knees slowly bent, and her upper body made a slow turn to the left. Her hands circled as if they were being dragged through thick honey. A floating step to the side, a shifting sideways of the body axis, a Kung Fu film in super-slow motion.

He looked up to the sky just to be sure, and two swallows flew by at normal speed. It wasn't his brain. She really was moving slowly. Somewhat relieved, he leaned on the balustrade and watched, not without emotion, her unathletic gymnastics.

Helen was wearing white sneakers and light-blue sweatpants. The elastic band cut deeply into her flesh and let a little bulge of naked skin stick out at her waistline. A sleeveless T-shirt, wet along the spine, clung to her upper body. He felt a peculiar feeling for this woman well up inside him, a possibly inappropriate and misdirected feeling, he told himself. She was the one who had saved him, she had put a roof over his head and taken care of him, she was his lifeline in a hopelessly sinking world. It wasn't gratitude. It was something else. It made his throat tight.

When she had been standing still for a while, he went down the stairs silently and wrapped his arms around her from behind. The heat, the moisture. He put his head on her sweaty back, felt her pulse on his cheek and looked out at the horizon.

She froze.

"I'm sorry," he said.

"Don't worry about it," said Helen, freeing herself from his embrace and heading up the stairs.

25

Swimming

And he took a piece of broken pottery with which to scrape
himself while he sat in the ashes.

JOB 2: 8

E VEN THOUGH HE STILL felt weak on his feet, he joined
her when she went to the beach. She had eaten breakfast
but he hadn't eaten anything more than half an apple.

The sun, still low in the sky, colored the path down to the
ocean orange. Bare-breasted women sat in a small group of
Europeans and it must have been thanks to the influence of
the group, the authority of the hotel facility, or hidden security
guards that there were at most two or three stray djellabas in
the tops of the surrounding trees. Helen spread two blankets
out on the sand. He fell to his back like a beetle, stayed prone
and mutely refused the suncream she offered. The fatigue
returned immediately.

"Nothing has come back to you?"

"No."

"But you can remember what ocean that is?"

"Yes."

"And also the name of this place here and of the country
where we are?"

"Yes."

"Your English is quite decent. French I can't judge. Can you speak Arabic?"

"Yes."

"What language do you think in?"

"French."

"Can you swim?"

While Helen walked across the sand and into the ocean, he gathered the towel beneath his head so he could watch her while lying down. The sun was almost directly above her. Glistening light made her contours dissolve in silhouette, her waist shrank to nothing.

He knew that he could swim. But he didn't know how he had learned to. He didn't even know how he knew he could. He could swim freestyle and breast stroke. The words and motions were immediately at his disposal.

Helen turned around and pushed her hair behind her ears with a charmingly affected gesture. A small wave splashed up on her, she smiled a little inscrutably, and he wondered whether a human brain could ever forget an image as captivating as this one; and whether he already had.

While he was still lying down, he felt a thought progress from deep inside him, a thought he now clearly realized had been stirring around in the dark for quite some time: what if he really did know her from before? If she knew him? If she was just putting on a show? He jumped up, ran down the beach, ran back and stumbled over two hotel guests. Helen only noticed him when he was already thigh-deep in the water, screaming. He didn't know anyone. No one knew him. He didn't know himself. He was lost.

"Breathe slowly. Easy. It's okay. You're going to be fine." Helen guided him up the beach by his shoulders, pressed him down to the blanket and held his arm tightly for a while.

"Calm down."

"I have to do something."

"What do you want to do? Don't hold your breath."

"I can't sit here."

"Then go to a doctor."

"I can't."

"Let us suppose that you didn't commit a capital crime."

"I'm definitely on the hook for something."

"But you're no murderer."

"How can you know that?"

"The pulley block fell by mistake. You said so yourself."

"And the other stuff?"

"What other stuff?"

"That I have something to do with these people. I'm probably one of them."

"You're paranoid. And you're no criminal."

"How can you know that?"

"I've experienced three days and three nights of you. Particularly the nights. You are not a criminal. If you really must know: you're a sweetheart. You couldn't hurt a fly. That's how you are now and my guess is that's how you were before, too. Your main personality traits don't change because of amnesia."

"How do you know that?"

"I just know."

He looked at her skeptically for a long time and then she finally stood up, bundled up the towels and nodded to him. It wasn't love. It was something worse.

BOOK THREE

The Mountains

26

The Devil

In pledging their faith they drink out of each other's hands;
and if they have no liquid, the parties take up some dust from
the ground and lick it.

HERODOTUS

C ARRYING A LITTLE PLASTIC BAG with a sunflower
printed on it, he went to do some shopping. The store
was right next to the Sheraton, 300 meters up the hill. He'd
gone there the day before together with Helen; this was his
first time alone. He had a hard time dealing with the strange
faces on the street. When they smiled he thought he'd been
recognized, and when they looked at him and didn't smile it
made him even more uneasy. A man in a trench coat stood out
to him when the man stopped just as he turned around to look
at him. The concierge at the Sheraton greeted him like an old
friend. A one-eyed woman held out a hand.

When he was nearly back at the bungalow with his full
shopping bag, he suddenly turned and, driven by agitation,
ran back to the hotel and asked the concierge if he had ever
seen him before.

"Yesterday," the concierge confirmed.

"But not before? You don't know me?"

"Bungalow 581d. With the mademoiselle. Who picked you up."

He walked through the alleyways with his head hanging. The despair was becoming overwhelming. Two men in dark suits who got out of a parked limousine followed him. He twice took wrong turns and didn't notice the men until they pulled a linen sack over his head. A cord tightened around his throat. He managed to claw the fingertips of both hands inside the cord, at the same time feeling his feet being raised. He kicked but forgot to scream. His shoulders banged against metal, then he had a brief sensation of weightlessness before a hard landing. The smell of rubber, the sound of a car trunk closing, muffled acoustics. An engine being started.

The ride in the car lasted barely five minutes. He was able to get the hood over his chin and mouth and up to the bridge of his nose, where it got stuck and pressed against his eyeballs.

He was still working at it when the trunk opened again. He made out two men who lifted him by his feet and elbows. A third one at the wheel. He had to lean his head way back to see them. Armed men. Black car. White-gravel walkway. Green lawn in front of a huge villa, around the lawn a wall too tall to see over, beyond it the sounds of a busy street, very nearby. They had put one of his arms behind his back but otherwise not bound or gagged him. They didn't seem to expect that he would shout for help, and the men didn't seem to have over-looked this possibility out of negligence. So he didn't shout. Blood dripped from his nose.

One of the men pushed the doorbell. A squawking voice asked who was there.

"Julius."

They entered an enormous entrance hall. Like something out of an American film, a tall, broad staircase with stone bannisters, plaster ornamentation and gold trim, magically flamboyant. A huge crystal mirror showed two burly men in black suits standing in an open door. Between them a wispy figure with one hand behind his back, blood coming out of his nose, and wearing a white hood that looked like a giant chef's hat pulled down to his eyes. A few young men and women of flesh and blood stood around a splashing fountain with others made of stone. The women wore airy dresses. Looked briefly at the door. Turned away.

The one who had just called himself Julius pushed him up the stairs and into a room. He cut the hood off him and shoved him into a leather armchair facing a heavy desk. On the desk golden writing utensils. The room was wrapped in a dark wainscoting. Oil paintings of naked women alongside the awkward circles and squares of modern art. Julius sat down on a chair in the corner. The desk chair, a cantilevered chair made of steel and blue suede, remained empty.

He opened his mouth to ask a question, but Julius lifted his weapon slightly and he stayed silent. He adjusted the bandage on his head. His wound throbbed. Voices and laughter could be heard out in the garden. A half-hour went by. Then a door opened in the wainscoting and a beaming white-haired man in shorts entered the room carrying a badminton racquet. Bloated flesh bulged out from under his sweaty T-shirt. His legs looked thinner than his arms, and his face could have come straight off a nineteenth-century physiognomic wall chart as an example of the sanguine type. Together with his clothes, his body, his motions and the surroundings, it conveyed the impression of someone upon whom nothing had been bestowed in life—and someone who hadn't been upset about this in the slightest.

The white-haired man sat down on the cantilevered chair, exchanged a brief glance with Julius and smiled. And was silent. He stretched out the silence for so long that its effect was nearly lost.

"You have a lot of nerve," he said. And then after another long pause: "We seem to have underestimated someone."

He had an indeterminable accent in his French.

"Two little sausages. Isn't that what I said? Two little sausages! We can be happy and give praise to the Most Merciful that we have the little sausages. And now *this*."

The white-haired man leaned toward him and tapped his bandage with the badminton racquet. There was an unpleasant noise from the wound.

"I want to ask you a question. Or maybe we should start at the beginning. Can we drop the formalities? Help jog my memory, little man. You don't mind if we speak frankly to one another, do you? Good. Do you have any idea what this is about?"

The white-haired man looked at him for a while, plucked two blades of grass and a chunk of dirt out of the strings of his racquet and then held the piece of sports equipment out behind him. Julius sprang up immediately and took it from him.

"Do you know what this is about?"

The difficult decision between a knowingly coy facial expression or an ignorantly confused one.

Ten seconds.

"No, you don't have a clue what this is about!" yelled the white-haired man. He leaned forward, pulled a charcoal-colored cardboard box out of a desk drawer and threw it across the desk. Half the size of a cigarette pack, the gold-embossed letters of some jeweler. It landed in his lap. He opened it hesitantly. A short gold chain lay inside along with a pendant that at first glance looked like a severed fingertip. The size of a fingertip, the color of a fingertip. But it was actually just a wax-colored piece of carved wood with two blood-red spots on the top of it. On the back, nearly worn down from long use, a demon's face had been carved. The red dots were the horns. He turned the amulet in his hands, perplexed.

"You are shocked now," said the white-haired man, leaning back, looking satisfied. "But one must consider that beforehand: he who attacks Rome must know Rome. Have you served?"

Julius playfully pointed his weapon at him. He struggled to find the right facial expression to reflect the feelings they must have expected him to have.

With a sudden motion the white-haired man reached across the desk and snatched the amulet out of his fingers and then threw it back at him. "Is it voodoo or what? Some sort of protection? From people like us perhaps? Now you're screwed. Despite your trying not to bat an eyelash. You're a bad actor."

The white-haired man lowered his head to be able to look up at his face.

"Looks like a little finger," he continued. "Like a real finger. And it came within a hair of being an actual finger. But it isn't one. And who do you have to thank for the fact that it isn't one?"

Julius blushed.

"Heart of gold!" called the white-haired man sarcastically. "Heart of gold! Julius has five kids. When you have five kids, you get soft in the head. Automatically. And he saved my life twice. You couldn't know that. Soft in the head, but twice saved my life. That's a pension plan. Loyalty, right or wrong, my country. If there is one trait that I value in people above all others, it's loyalty. The trait that's missing in you. And do you want to know what the result of that is? I'll tell you: I'm sitting there with the little shit on my knees and I say, the usual price, do we take the left index finger or the right? And Julius says: ouch. And then the mother shows up. Heavens! And what does the mother say? Come on, you must know: what does the mother say? Your wife. You talk with your wife after all, you're more of the sensitive type. So what does the fat cow say?"

Silence.

"I hope you will excuse me the expression fat cow. I don't want to offend anyone here; maybe she has other qualities. The fat cow. Though she's not a good lay either."

Without averting his eyes, the white-haired man turned to Julius. "Or is she a good lay, Julius? She's more of a middling fuck, or what did you think? Not really kept in good running order. But I guess your prick has better things to do. Like pissing on the word loyalty. Now the million-dollar question: What does the fat cow say about the idea of the finger? Piano player! He wants to be a piano player. Right before the main event she says he wants to be a piano player. Imagine that. Three years old and already a piano player. Unbelievable, right? Three years old, Beethoven. No problem I say, I just hope he doesn't want to be Johan Cruyff, Beethoven and Cruyff, that would be a rare combination after all. So I grab his toe and what does the fat cow say now?"

The white-haired man waited to see the effect of his words. He couldn't know that they were having no effect. At least not the effects they would have had on someone who had the capacity to remember.

"Come on, you know her, what do you think the fat cow said?"

He listened to the white-haired man's sermon with his head hanging, trying to feel something other than indifference. He had a family? He had a wife and child? They had been threatened? He just wasn't able to muster any feelings for people he couldn't remember. He tried to imagine recovering his memory and the great pain he would feel at the thought of his loved ones being physically abused, but it remained abstract, like anticipating a visit to the dentist two months down the road.

And anyway, the words fat cow and little shit reverberated in his mind, and he had to think of Helen. Slim, platinum-blonde Helen. The only thing the white-haired man's talking provoked in him was disgust. And fear for his own person. To get out of here whole. A few minutes earlier he had been prepared to say what he knew: that he didn't know anything. The sad speculation over amputated limbs made clear to him what sort of person he was dealing with. He tried to stay calm.

"Don't cry now. If you want to play with the big boys, you have to secure your rear. And even better than securing it is not having one. Look at me. You can take Gandhi, you can take Hitler, you can take anyone. Jesus. No, my dear. Wife and child: the worst rear of all. Anyone can march on them. You're as soft as cheese. Look at Julius: he used to be the best of the best, now he's a wreck. I say to him, Julius, I say, what do you think we should do? And Julius rips the amulet from around the little shit's neck and says: What do you think, boss? Isn't this enough? Delicious. And that's the situation now. The cow and the kid are being held. Just in case you were wondering. Or have you not been home at all in the last few days?" The white-haired man grabbed the amulet, had it perform a little dance routine as it crossed the edge of the desk, and said in a strange voice: "He thought he could hide from us. He thought so." And then again in a normal voice: "And now I must unfortunately ask you the question that Julius already asked: Is this enough?" He held up the demon. "Or do we need to deliver the cow and calf in slices?"

The amulet disappeared again into the cardboard box and the box into the drawer in the desk.

"Do you know what's next?"

He thought for a while, bit his lip and said: "A swap."

"A swap," said the white-haired man with a facial expression that alternated between jubilant and stunned. "A swap!" The white-haired man glanced at Julius, then stood up and reached his hand out across the desk in a friendly way.

He went to shake on it, but the white-haired man pulled him forward by the arm, grabbed a metal letter-opener with his left hand, and in a single motion rammed it through his hand and into the desk. Then he sat back in his chair and made clear with a wave of the hand that he should by no means attempt to remove the letter-opener from his flesh himself. Julius aimed his gun at him.

"Well, well, well!"

His hand was nailed down far enough toward the other side of the desk that he couldn't sit down or really stand up. It left him in an odd position, hovering half over the desk, making him look like someone trying to relieve himself outdoors.

"What is it you wish to trade, my friend, and for what?"

He gasped.

"You admit then that you have something you can trade?"

He whimpered.

"That belongs to me. You admit it?"

A minute went by. He feared for his life. What he really wanted to do was to shout it all out, but the last of his rationality held him back. Whatever it was the white-haired man wanted, he didn't have it. He assumed, and had good reason to assume, that it had to do with something that a man named Cetrois had disappeared with into the desert on a moped a few days before. He could have voiced this supposition, of course, but then he would also have had to say that it was a supposition that he didn't know anything more about and that he had lost his memory. Not without some logic, he concluded that in that instant he would become worthless to his counterpart. Even if they believed him. Especially then. And if they didn't believe him, which was likely, he would only make them angrier.

He couldn't tell the truth. But he also couldn't lie. In order to lie, he would have to have known what to lie about. So he bit down, holding his teeth together.

"It doesn't work that way," he groaned.

"Aha, it doesn't work that way?" The white-haired man took hold of the letter-opener as if it were the gear shift in a car and shifted once through all the gears.

"Maybe you think this is about your family. You think it's about something as trifling as your life. But that's not what it's about. It's about *justice*. Because there's one thing you can't forget: I paid for it. And I won't let some amateur like you screw it up."

"I'll fix it! I'll fix it!"

"How will you fix it?"

He cried. He looked up at the white-haired man's face and decided to poke a little further into the dark.

"I know who!"

"You know *who*?"

"I also know where."

"Where!" yelled the white-haired man.

"If I tell you, the outlook for me is shitty."

"The outlook for you is already shitty."

"I'll fix it, I can do it!" he yelled. Blood was bubbling up the metal blade. "You know me! And I know you! You have my family!"

The white-haired man stared at him silently.

"You can count on me," he whimpered. "My wife! My beloved son! Oh, my God, oh, my God, my son, my son!" Tears spilled from his eyes. He let his face fall to the desk in order to hide it. He wondered whether he had overplayed it.

Julius leaned forward and whispered something in the white-haired man's ear. The white-haired man leaned back in his chair. A minute went by. Another minute.

"Seventy-two hours," said the white-haired man. "Then the mine is my mine again. Seventy-two hours. Otherwise fingers, toes, ears."

He slowly pulled the letter-opener out of his hand.

27

The Runners Portal

I know a man who once stole a Ferris wheel.

DASHIELL HAMMETT

IT WAS A MILD LATE AFTERNOON beneath high cloud cover. He staggered out of the villa with his painful hand pressed to his chest. Nobody followed him. His knees were weak. He leaned against a wall above which sycamores towered. When he closed his eyes briefly, he heard quiet music.

The wall was part of an estate that was somewhat smaller and less showy than the one he had just left. Directly in front of him, a group of elegantly dressed men stood on the sidewalk before an art deco portal that had two strange marble statues of runners embedded in it. As he pushed his way past the men, a police car came driving up and stopped right next to him. Two men in civilian clothes got out of the car and headed for the portal.

"Karimi is an idiot," he heard one of them say. He stuck his bloody hand in his pocket and went past them with his head bowed. The entire way down through the serpentine streets to the Sheraton he kept asking himself what made the white-haired man so sure he wouldn't go to the police.

There was actually only one explanation: he was obviously entangled in serious crime and what he could expect from the authorities must have been even more nasty than what the white-haired man was threatening. But what could be worse than threatening his life and the lives of his family?

Only as he had nearly arrived at the bungalows did a second possibility occur to him. What if the white-haired man was himself with the police? A high-ranking representative of state authority. He turned to a few street merchants and motioned with his arm up at the coastal range and asked whether they knew who the giant villa belonged to, the one that was by far the most ostentatious of anything around, right next to the villa with the weird runners portal; he learned that the owner was a man named Adil Bassir. They pronounced the name with a certain reticence, awestruck. Finding out the man's line of business was much more difficult than finding out his name. When someone finally told him, it wasn't actually a line of business at all: King of Crooks.

28

In Atlas

Jesus said: Perhaps men think that I am come to cast peace
upon the world; and they do not know that I am come to cast
dissensions upon the earth, fire, sword, war. For there will be five
who are in a house; three shall be against two and two against
three, the father against the son and the son against the father,
and they shall stand as solitaries.

THE GOSPEL OF THOMAS

"THE TWENTY-TWO-YEAR-OLD suspect, whose blood-
besmirched clothing irrevocably placed him at the scene
of the crime—my God, whose blood-besmirched clothing...
irrevocably... the press here still has a ways to go. At any
rate the completely blood-soaked perpetrator drove a stolen
Toyota into the commune in which for years disreputable
foreign hippies... no, there's not much here. Overwhelming
evidence, confession... threat of the death penalty... Look
at this, he had the weapon with him. A Mauser, the bullets
of which matched to the holes exactly... to the holes, what
kind of expression is that? Hey, my colleague has holes in
him! Anyway, his fingerprints were found on the weapon. I
wouldn't worry too much if I were you." Helen lowered the
newspaper to look at the man lying on the sofa in his bloody
and dirt-crusted suit, legs up, a fresh bandage on his head,

the bandage on his hand already turning red again, an ice pack next to him.

He groaned.

"I called home again, by the way. A friend of my mother's knows about this sort of thing, and she said that as long as it went through cleanly and didn't hit anything, it's not a big problem. You just have to make sure it doesn't get infected. Although I would love to revisit the idea of going to a doctor."

"Read on."

"The pain is your problem, but I don't want to get in trouble because an unidentified man keels over in my bungalow from blood poisoning. The twenty-two-year-old murderer—he was only a suspect a minute ago—the twenty-two-year-old, who shed bitter tears of remorse during sentencing, managed to escape while being transported to the place of execution when the prison vehicle was involved in a credible accident... a credible accident, dear God, either there's something wrong with my French or they're totally crazy. Anyway, there's nothing here about memory loss. And it was also Tuesday. No, sorry. It would have been such a nice name for you: Amadou Amadou."

"How old do you think I am?"

"I'd say about thirty. Certainly not twenty-two. And I have to ask you again: why didn't you tell the guy about your amnesia?"

"What is so hard to understand?"

"If I'd been nailed to a desk with a letter-opener I'd have told him a thing or two."

"I had the feeling that I didn't know what he didn't know. He just didn't know that I didn't know. If I had told him, what would he have done with me?"

"But you could have told him about the four men in white djellabas. About the guy on a moped. And the thing that astounds me most of all: that he let you go."

"Maybe he thought I was the only one who could fix things? And he has my family."

"They're in a bad spot. Because you can't fix anything. Mine, Cetrois, Adil Bassir: you don't have the slightest idea what's going on. You don't want to go to the police. You can't wait around. The best thing in my opinion would be to see a doctor. Someone who could have a look and see what the story is with the amnesia."

"Do you not understand my argument somehow?"

"No. But you could consult a third party. I have money. I'm worried."

He looked at Helen pensively for a long time, then he said: "The mine. Show me the map again."

Helen handed him the map, stood up and filled the coffee press with water. "Forget it," she said. "If it's a mine as in a hole in the ground, what did the guy ride off with into the desert on the moped?"

"Maybe a deed of sale."

"The King of Crooks and *deeds of sale?*"

"Or I'm a mining engineer and I'm the one who developed the mine."

"How does that change things? It's all nonsense. What were the guy's actual words? Then I'll have it again? Then it will belong to me again?"

"Then it's mine. Seventy-two hours, then it's mine again."

"And you were speaking French the whole time?"

"What's the gray stuff here?"

"Granite."

"And the green?"

"Phosphorous, I think."

"What do you need that for? Is that what's in those luminescent paints?"

"It's dung. But it's hundreds of kilometers. Phosphorous is nonsense. Granite is nonsense. It's all nonsense."

"And the round bit here with the spike in it?"

"We're here."

"Yeah, but what about this? It's here and here and here."

"That's agriculture."

"Or maybe it's a tiny mine that's not on the map at all."

"What was the fourth thing again?" asked Helen. "You said before that you thought of four."

"Mien, as in facial expression."

"That still leaves me with only three."

"Mien, mine as in a hole in the ground, the kind of mine that explodes, and the stuff in a pencil."

"That's what it's called in French? *La mine*? I didn't know that," said Helen pensively. "But I can't imagine someone would make such a big deal over it, kidnapping and killing people, if it was about the pencil lead. Even if it was made of gold."

"How much would something like that be worth?"

"A couple hundred dollars maybe. A hundred. No idea. But not more than a wedding ring. And you said the guy is unbelievably rich? Landmines are the most obvious thing. Except that as far as I know, landmines aren't worth much either. They blow up and that's it."

"What if it were something bigger? Real weapon technology?"

"You know my opinion. First the doctor. Second Bassir. Because you can tell me all sorts of things about pit mines and landmines. But the most concrete thing you have to go on is still the guy in the villa."

"And what about this? Look, the little black box with the red dot inside. That's uranium."

"That's almost an entire finger's distance away." Helen put her finger down on the map to measure. Her finger was 300 kilometers long. "It's halfway to the Congo."

He thought for a long time and then asked, without looking Helen in the eyes: "Where'd you get it anyway? What are you doing running around with a map of natural resources?"

"It's an ordinary map," said Helen, turning the map over. "I never even looked at the back. And—why are you looking at me like that? What, am I a suspect now, too?"

"I'm sorry, but I have to ask again. Cosmetics?"

"Yes."

"Are you're a saleswoman?"

"Larouche is the second-largest cosmetics company in the US, and I'm supposed to—"

"And when you were disembarking the ship, your sample case, of all things, happened to fall overboard?"

"A boy yanked it out of my hand."

"And you don't have anything else… I mean… that could perhaps…"

"Legitimize me? Heavens. The replacement case won't arrive for a few more days."

"I know, I shouldn't—"

"Don't start again. Why don't you tell me what sausages are supposed to mean. *Two* little sausages."

"My friend and I. Cetrois."

"That's what I mean. What makes you so sure that it's a friend of yours? Because the enemy of your enemy is your friend?"

"It just makes the most sense."

"And even if he is your friend: the fact that he snatched the moped and left you behind in the barn, couldn't that have been the end of a friendship?"

"It could have been anything."

"Right. And nothing about it makes sense. Maybe Cetrois is a friend of the four men and is trying to cheat them? Maybe he is your friend after all and he smashed your skull, and the fat man was just taking credit for it?"

"This is getting really far-fetched now."

"Or there is no Cetrois. The three men made him up because they wanted to cover up their own deceit."

"They didn't seem that way… I heard them before the fourth one was even there. They seemed helpless and dimwitted."

"Fine. Let us suppose they're helpless and dimwitted, and helplessness and dimwittedness induces one to tell the truth, which I doubt. Then the only thing you can conclude from the sentence 'Cetrois took off with it into the desert' is: first, there is a Cetrois. And second, that he took off into the desert with something. But whether that has anything to do with you and Adil Bassir's mine is still completely up in the air."

"If he destroys the mine."

"Yes, but you heard: What if he deploys the line. And even if that is the case, how do you want to find this Cetrois in a city of a million people, and five million with the slums? Have you ever seen the phonebooks here? And I seriously doubt they have a population registry anywhere."

29

Tourist Information

I am certain that in summer he must have worn light prunella
shoes with mother-of-pearl buttons at the side.

DOSTOEVSKY

I N THE RIGHT WEATHER CONDITIONS and when the wind
came from the ocean, it was possible all the way up at the
bungalow to hear the soft lapping of the waves through the open
window. The bay, surrounded by mountains, focused the sound
and carried it into the ears of those who lay half asleep. The man
without memory had turned away from the window and closed
his eyes. Fatuous thoughts of eternity and exalted heights that
contrasted with his own unimportance swirled around his tired
night-time brain, and he awoke with pain in his entire body. There
was a shadow in the middle of the room. At first he thought it
was an illusion. But the shadow moved: a woman in jeans and
a tight T-shirt, barefoot. She was standing in front of the chair
where he had laid his clothes the preceding evening. She was in
the process of turning out the pockets of his suit. She felt the
waistband and then noiselessly placed the pants down on the chair
again. Next she examined the jacket, from which clumps of sand
fell. She checked the inside pocket, the two other pockets, and
ran her thumb and forefinger along the seams. She picked up a

brown loafer, pulled out the liner and looked inside the empty shoe. Shook the heel, put the shoe back down and reached for the second one. Before she could turn around and look at the bed he closed his eyes. But he couldn't hold out for long.

"Did you hit pay dirt?" he asked.

"Only a pencil stub," answered Helen without the slightest hint of guiltiness.

"I know." He sat up in bed.

"And a keychain."

"Yeah."

"Does the name mean anything to you?"

She held his jacket up by both shoulders. A little white square of cloth was sewn inside the collar. On it, in dark-gray thread: CARL GROSS.

"Isn't it the name of the maker?"

"I think so, too. Though I've never heard of that company."

Helen retrieved a razorblade from the bathroom and cut the tag out while sitting on the corner of the bed. On the back the threads were neat, long, dark-gray parallels, machine-sewn, very obviously the manufacturer's name. Helen pressed the tag to his forehead.

"Would you object to my calling you that anyway? Because, somehow I just have to call you something. Carl."

"Carl?"

"Carl."

"There must be something else," he said, fishing a little reddish snippet of paper with blackened edges from out of the pocket of the suit pants. *Name, colon.* Nothing else.

During breakfast, Helen leaned her head in her left hand, her cigarette sticking straight up, and made a game of addressing him as Carl in every sentence. "Sugar with your coffee, Carl? Why did you burn your ID, Carl? There was no talk of hippies yesterday. Carl."

"What did I say?"

"Guys."

Helen brought a yellow blazer and salmon-colored Bermuda shorts out of the bedroom. It took her two cups of coffee and four cigarettes before she had convinced Carl to at least try on her clothes. They fitted him like a glove.

"You can take your things to the hotel later."

"I look like a canary."

"They'll be ready by tomorrow."

Afterward Helen drove the Honda to the American consulate, where, she said, she needed to get a little information, while Carl took a walk up to the Sheraton. After he had dropped off his clothes at the hotel cleaners (and used the opportunity to present himself for the first time as "Carl Gross, number 581d"), he asked the hotel employee whether he knew on the off chance a Cetrois, Monsieur Cetrois. Yes, a native of Targat. No, not a hotel guest. Probably not.

But the man didn't know any Cetrois and summoned a second employee, who likewise didn't know anything. The first employee called a third employee and the second a fourth, and before it could become a scene, Carl gave the men a baksheesh from a bundle of small bills Helen had given him, thanked them and left.

Against the explicit advice of his friend, he headed down toward Targat. He saw friendly faces, he saw unfriendly faces, he read street signs and company plaques. A lawyer named Croisenois. On a stone was written: *In memoriam Charles Boileau.* He tentatively asked a passer-by, but the nearer he got to the center of town the more frequently he himself was spoken to. With the yellow blazer and Bermuda shorts he looked like a very eccentric, very rich tourist, and in the streets around the souk he couldn't take five steps without men rushing up to him with the most affectionately familiar words and gestures.

Helpful young layabouts, charlatans, merchants greeted him with handshakes. What they wanted from him was written on most of their faces, but he was plagued by the suspicion that they might know him from a previous life.

But asking the men questions was futile. With an eager "How are you?" they put a heavy arm around the shoulders of their dear old friend and tried to steer him into little shops where they or their cousins indiscriminately hawked spices, sandals, thuya-wood boxes, colorful cloth, plastic spoons and sunglasses.

In order to abbreviate the process, he suddenly changed his strategy. In a slightly less lively street he put a look on his face as if lost in thought, then went up to people giving every indication that he was happy to run into them again, and asked where they had last seen each other or whether Monsieur Cetrois had already been there that morning. He acted as if he were meeting his friend, his enemy, his brother-in-law, his debtor. He acted as if he had seen him only fifteen minutes ago, or gave the impression that Monsieur Cetrois lived right around here, just forgot his address. He described an average Arab, a Frenchman, a black man. But nobody seemed to have ever heard of a man by this name. The only result of his research was a cluster of street kids who trailed along behind him and promised to produce a Monsieur Cetrois of any description, tall, slim, short, bearded, fat, light-skinned, black, rich, stinky or wiry, for a couple of copper coins or a ride on a bumper car. In the end he sat down at a street café, exhausted.

He had already drunk half of his mint tea when his gaze fell on the sign above the entrance to the next-door building: *Central Commissariat.*

His fear of the police was unshakably strong, but at the same time he had to fight the gravitational pull the building seemed to have on him: where if not there would one find information about missing persons?

He saw two policemen step out of the door, talking, not more than twenty meters away. One of them clearly had a weapon bulging underneath his clothes and he let his eyes glide over the crowd while he ran his fingers through his hair. He froze with his finger still in his hair, nudged his partner's arm, and gestured with his chin in the direction of the café where the lone guest sat there in a yellow blazer... or had been sitting there until two seconds ago.

Carl had awkwardly turned his back to them, slipped a note under his tea glass and run off. He could easily shake the police in the maze of narrow streets. If they even followed him. He hadn't dared to turn around and look for them, he'd already had sufficient excitement for the day. He made for the Sheraton, going back along the harbor and then up the coast road.

Rich Americans in white clothes posed in front of the ocean. Golden stewards leaned against sleek yachts, and the entrance to the seafood restaurant looked like a Greek temple made of plastic. He felt empty and numb. The sight of a cruise ship heading out to sea with steam rising from its smokestacks prompted the thought of emigrating. He had no past, and if he had one there were signs that violence, crime and legal problems played starring roles in it. The will to resume his previous life was not nearly as strong as his desire for peace and safety. Emigrating to France or America, starting an unencumbered life, slowly finding one's way at the side of a platinum-blonde woman. Wasn't that possible?

"Cetrois!" someone called behind him. "Cetrois? Who are you looking for? Cetrois?"

A man in blue coveralls stood in the sliding gate of an auto repair shop, in front of which lay piles of car parts. With a conspiratorial gesture he waved Carl over, took him into the shop and pulled down the gate behind them. A second, very burly man was waiting in the half-darkness and swiftly kicked Carl in the gut.

He slumped forward and felt someone grip his throat from behind. They asked no questions. They seemed to assume that he knew what they wanted from him. That is, if they even wanted something from him and this whole thing wasn't just the price to be paid by a man wearing women's clothing, which in a traditional society provoked understandable aggression. The questions he gasped while being kicked, who were they, were answered with further kicks. He tasted blood. They pulled him into the back of the workshop and the burly one pushed him against a workbench with a large wooden box on it. Inside the box, which was open on one side, was a hypermodern-looking, gleaming chrome machine. They hit his head against the machine.

"How's that? How's that?" yelled the burly man.

The machine wobbled and Carl slumped to the floor, dazed. They jumped on top of him, choked him, and didn't stop until a noise from the sliding gate startled them.

A narrow but slowly widening wedge of sunlight flooded across the floor, the workbench, the gleaming chrome machine and the less than traditional three-man wrestling match. For a few seconds silence hung in the air. Then, in a droning woman's voice with a strong American accent: "Excuse me, can you tell me where to find the tourist information?"

The smaller man jumped up and ran to the door with his arms stretched out in order to block the view of what was happening behind him. The other man held Carl down by his throat. Through a veil of sweat and tears Carl couldn't see anything more than two shadows silhouetted against a rectangle of light. He heard quiet words, then a nasty crack, and one of the shadows sank to the ground. The second shadow came marching into the workshop with swaying hips and stopped in the darkness. The burly man let go of Carl's throat and headed slowly, carefully, toward the shadow, kneading his fists.

This time Carl saw the blow with the side of the hand that shattered the man's larynx with a crack. Ninety kilos writhed on the floor. Without hesitation, without smiling, without a word, Helen hustled over to Carl with a quick, businesslike sideways glance at the machine. She lifted one end of the wooden box from the workbench, braced it with her shoulder and had Carl pick up the other end.

Carrying the heavy box, they stepped over an unconscious man in the middle of the workshop and a conscious man by the door who was holding his throat with both hands and gasping. Helen's pickup was outside. Together they centered the machine in the bed of the truck and drove speedily away.

"That's not the thing, is it?" asked Helen when they were inside the bungalow with the gleaming chrome machine on the table in front of them. Standing on its base the device was nearly a meter high, had a slim, cylindrical middle section, pipes running around the outside, a central gauge and, on top, a filler neck. It appeared to need electricity but had no cord to plug it in with, just a two-holed panel plug on the side.

"What thing?"

"The mine."

"The mine? This? You took it because you thought—"

"It stood out so prominently in the room. And you and the men directly beside it—I thought you had found it."

"You thought *this* was a mine?"

"What do I know," said Helen irritably. She turned a bolt on the filler neck. "So what were you after there in the workshop?"

"What about you?"

"I saw you, you performer, how you went in there. So what is this thing?"

A close examination of the machine brought no additional clarity. There was technical data on a small metal plate in the base—*2500 wat, 12 amper*—and above that a small amount of text in a language they didn't know.

"Norwegian or Danish," Carl guessed.

"Polish. *Warszawa*, that's Polish. And those were Adil Bassir's men?"

"I don't know. I don't think so. The ultimatum hasn't run out yet."

"Or the ones from the desert?"

"Nope."

"Speaking of the desert," said Helen, "there are no natural resources here. But there is a goldmine."

30

Hakim of the Mountains

Why shouldn't it be possible to make gold? We now know from atomic physics that everything is possible. Until recently we didn't think everything was possible.

SCROOGE McDUCK

I N THE YELLOW HAZE, the yellow mountains. Helen had been assured at the American consulate that there were no natural resources in this area. The friendly officials at the consulate also knew nothing of any pit, excavation or mine of any kind whatsoever.

Helen had already left the consulate when a young man with a scrubber and bucket approached her in the parking lot. He had evidently followed her conversation with the officials from some distance. His English was very bad, and he had apparently not understood everything correctly. But, standing beneath the giant American flag at the entry gate, he excitedly reported that *of course* there was a mine in the north. Or there had been.

Innocently staring into Helen's eyes, he waited until Helen had got out her wallet, then told her of an old goldmine on the arterial road to Tindirma. Admittedly, it wasn't a real mine, as he was forced to admit after several minutes of flowery speech; it had actually been a restaurant run long ago by a Nigerian or Ghanaian, it had been called the Goldmine and contrary to its name had been anything but a goldmine, which is why it no longer existed. There was nothing left but the remains of the building. But you couldn't miss it, he said, it was only a kilometer beyond the huge brick camels in the desert, and there was nothing else around, just the ruins, right before the little road split off into the mountains.

"And that would presumably all be a bunch of nonsense," Helen said to Carl, "if it weren't coincidentally also the place where I picked you up. Or at least, close to it."

They drove off.

The camels kissed their eternal kiss in the shimmering afternoon heat. The wind blew yellow dust from their backs.

The little road that split off to the mountains was easy to find, but one could hardly call what was left of the building a ruin. A couple of boards between the rocks, a dented bucket. After searching for a long time Carl located the four posts that must at one time have been the corners of the building and even a little sign with peeling Arabic writing on it: part of the word Goldmine. That was it.

Carl, who had put great hope into this lead, and who kicked a rock so hard out of frustration that he thought he had broken his foot, wanted to return to Targat immediately. Helen was opposed.

"If you have an inn and you call it the Old Mill, then normally that means there had been a mill there at one time. Even if it had been destroyed hundreds of years before and nobody remembered it. Right? Why would someone call his restaurant the Goldmine? Let's at least try." She pointed to a trail that snaked up into the mountains, and Carl, who wanted to avoid another disappointment but who was also angry at himself for not hitting upon that same thought, begrudgingly climbed back into the car.

The mountains were lined up next to each other, barren and uniform. Stray hunks of rock had fallen down the bare faces. Here a small rock, there a large one. Yellow and gray and brown monoliths dotted the slopes like a mediocre art exhibition. The Honda crept up the incline at a walking pace.

Helen braked after a bend because she thought she had seen something move up above, in the mountains. She backed up a little and through a narrow crack in the rocks a man in colorful athletic wear became visible thirty or forty meters above the trail. He was looking down at the ground. A handkerchief tied at each corner decorated his hairless skull. A piece of equipment seesawed on his shoulder, and every time he leaned down a pole rose behind him. The gadget consisted of a long fishing pole with a large mesh net on the top. The net was covered by a round piece of wood that was opened and closed using a cable that ran down to the handle of the pole. The man briefly looked down at the Honda and then ambled on.

Helen leaned out of the window.

"Do they bite?" she called out in English. The sound broke against the rocks and echoed back. The man took an uneasy step to the side so he could see them better. With his thumb he pointed over his shoulder at the gadget and called: "My own invention!"

"Do you know this area? We are looking for a—"

"Levi Doptera! Me!" bellowed the man.

"A pleasure, Helen Gliese!" called Helen. She turned off the engine. "For a mine. There's supposed to be a mine around here somewhere."

"A shrine?"

"Mine. A goldmine."

"Do you need money?"

"We're looking for a mineshaft."

"I have gobs of money," called the man, waving.

"Say yes," said Carl.

"No!" bellowed Helen. "You didn't happen to see anything, did you? An abandoned mineshaft?"

"Excellent!"

"What is he talking about?" asked Carl.

"I don't know," said Helen. And then loudly out of the window: "What is excellent?"

"I'm also searching!" bellowed the man. "Levi Doptera."

"Fantastic!" called Helen. "But you haven't seen anything like a mine?"

"Where there are mountains, people dig! Don't let yourself get discouraged. My experience."

"Let's keep going," whispered Carl. "He's nuts."

"Thank you for the wise words!" called Helen. "Shall we bring you a nugget?"

"No, no!" The man laughed and the net whipped around.

"Suit yourself. Jackass."

The trail became narrower and steeper and ended among crumbling rocks a few kilometers on, in the middle of nothing.

Carl and Helen got out and looked around. Bleak mountain faces to the right and left, lizards in the sun. Dusty thistle plants.

At that point Helen declared the venture a lost cause, but Carl had already clambered fifty or a hundred meters up the slope and was continuing up, looking for signs of human activity. Helen called after him for a while, then sat down in the car and watched the scrambling figure through the windshield. After a while he reached the crest, took a quick look around and then disappeared over the far side with a shrug. Ten minutes went by. Half an hour. Helen slumped in the driver's seat, both car doors wide open. A mountain peak cast the first shadow into the ravine behind Helen. She took off the emergency brake and let the car roll slowly into the shade. After she set the brake again, she saw a man waving from way up on the rocks. Carl was waving, and he must have been waving for some time. Helen yelled something to him, he didn't answer and just continued to gesture with his arms.

With a sighing glance at her strappy sandals, she started warily up the mountain.

"Psst," said Carl when she arrived at the top. He pulled her past a boulder, crawled a little ways on all fours and pointed down into a ravine. About halfway up the opposite mountain face was a tiny cabin. A windmill spun above it, barrels were stacked in a pyramid nearby, and just above the cabin a huge tunnel had been cut into the slope. Heaps of waste rock ran down the slope on either side like a calcified waterfall.

"Soldiers," said Carl.

"Inside the cabin?"

"There." He pointed in a completely different direction. "They were marching in formation and moving very oddly. I didn't realize they weren't adults until someone showed up who was twice as tall as all of the rest."

"Children?"

"But they have guns and uniforms and everything. They've been gone about ten minutes now."

"But they weren't near the cabin?"

"No. There's nothing happening at the cabin. But if that's not a mine, I don't know what is."

They observed the ravine and the cabin for a while and then decided to walk down on a path cut into the steep slope. As they were crossing the floor of the ravine a shot rang out in their ears. Carl immediately threw himself to the ground. Helen took cover behind some boulders. The sound echoed back off the rock walls. Neither of them had seen where the shot came from.

It was silent for a while. Then they heard someone yelling in poor English: "America! Shitty Americans!"

On a plateau above them, a man was now standing and swinging a Winchester above his head like a leg of lamb. The weapon fell from his hand. He laughed. He picked it up again, fiddled with the breech and then held it out in front of him with one hand, pointing into the air. He pressed his head to the outstretched arm and put the index finger of his other hand in the opposite ear and pulled the trigger. The shot rang out like before. The man hopped around, shouting: "Shitty Americans!"

"This country is beginning to get on my nerves," said Helen.

She yelled to the man in French from her hiding spot, saying that she was lost. That she didn't know how to get back to the road and that she could use a sip of water.

In answer the man started swinging the gun around again and it fell out of his hands once more. He was drunk.

Helen climbed up nearly to the edge of the plateau. She was wearing shorts, her blouse was drenched in sweat, and with her hands raised she spoke quietly with the cabin owner.

"American!" he repeated haltingly a couple more times, staring with wide eyes down into Helen's blouse. Then he yelled in Carl's direction: "I can see you! I see you! I want to see both of you!"

He made an ambiguous gesture and fell over backwards. Using the rifle as a crutch, he tried to get up again. He had light, waxy skin with tiny wrinkles. He could have been thirty or seventy.

Carl and Helen, who had by then both climbed onto the plateau, grabbed the reeling man under his arms and guided him to his cabin. It wasn't much roomier than a large car, and its interior resembled the state of mind of its owner: disorderly.

He fell immediately to the floor, trying to gesture to his guests to have a seat, and listened with a childlike expression as they repeated their questions four or five or six times.

No, these days he wasn't digging, he said, gesturing to a bandage on his calf out of which mud and withered herbs pressed. He couldn't say with any certainty how long it had been since he last dug, but, as was common knowledge, he was Hakim III, son of Hakim II, grandson of Hakim of the Mountains. And of course, the legendary gold that his grandfather had pulled from the dust with his own hands a hundred years ago on the exact spot where this cabin now stands, thanks to Allah and with the intention of marrying Leila, the flowery, gazelle-like, dark-eyed Leila with the dainty ears, his mother—please forgive me—grandmother... what was the question again? Ah, right. He went crazy, crazy with greed. Instead of having the gold made into bridal jewelry for Leila, the ravishing, small-eared Leila, and happily living out his predetermined life, Hakim, shame on him, had invested all his wealth in hammers and chisels and drills and begun to mine the cursed rock.

Hakim of the Mountains had taken his first swing with the hammer at nineteen, and dug until his hand withered at the blessed age of sixty-eight. Liver. And not a speck of gold in forty years! As a result, the rumors wouldn't subside that even the first gold had been... but those were just rumors. And Hakim II, the loyal son, began to dig when he was twenty and dug until the chisel slipped from his hand at the age of sixty-four. Heart. He, too, never found a speck. And finally Hakim III, the grandson, truest of true. The man with no doubts. He began to dig when he was thirteen.

"And what became of him?" asked Helen.

"He is still digging," he said, pounding himself proudly on the chest. And would dig until the end of his days, following the example of his ancestors, and when he died it wouldn't be his heart or his liver but black bile, and he would shoot himself in this exact spot, in front of the tunnel he had dug with his own hands, his life's work and the life's work of his forefathers, he would simply blast away his brain and become a speck of dust among these mountains of dust. He put the muzzle of the Winchester in his mouth, puffed out his cheeks and rolled his bloodshot eyes.

"Do you want to see the tunnel now?"

They did. It was much cooler for the first few meters under-ground. Then it quickly got hot the deeper they went. And stuffy. Hakim tottered ahead with a carbide lamp and kept telling Carl and Helen to stay close behind him: "You'll never find your way out of here without me."

Long, shoulder-width tunnels crisscrossed the rock. Only near the entrance was there a somewhat larger main tunnel that seemed to be a natural cavern that had been widened here and there with a hammer and chisel. With a click of his tongue Hakim drew their attention to a system of markings at chest height that mapped the tunnel system using soot-black handprints. Near the main entrance lots of right hands about half a meter apart; tunnels that branched off had other mark-ings. A left hand, a left hand with just four fingers, the palm of a hand with thumb and forefinger. The deeper they went, the fewer fingers were used in the markings.

When the markings were reduced to a left palm and a thumb print, they found themselves in a low, cave-like space with three or four tunnels branching off from it. Hakim shone his dim light around and explained which tunnel had been dug in which year by which ancestor. From time to time he tapped his own chest proudly and raised his eyebrows know-ingly, and Carl, who was listening attentively, couldn't help thinking that the speaker had begun digging as a young man and continued as an adult and an old man, and that he was the grandfather, father and grandson in one person. While he was still speaking, a ghastly moan came up from the depths. Carl looked at Helen, Helen looked at the old man, and the old man acted as if he hadn't heard anything. He was talking about how Hakim the second, or the third, had tried in vain to use a jackhammer down here, imitating the rattling of the machine with his cheeks puffed out, but couldn't drown out the eerie noise that had briefly stopped and then continued an octave lower.

"What—is—that?" asked Helen, and Hakim put a hand to his ear.

It was silent.

"Something is groaning," she insisted, and the old man's face lit up.

"Ah! Something groaning? I'll show you."

He rushed down the steepest tunnel with his lantern. Carl and Helen stayed still and called after him that they'd seen enough and didn't want to see any more of the tunnels. The only answer they got was the sound of his receding footsteps. The cave-like space darkened with his every step.

"Hey!" yelled Helen. "Hey!"

"You'll never find your way out without me," came the voice from the depths; holding each other's hands, Carl and Helen hurried after him. The tunnel was so small that they had to squat down and waddle. Carl was nearer to the old man. Helen tried in vain to pass him and whispered in his ear in English, "If something happens, get the lamp first and then the old man. Without the lamp we're screwed."

On the wall was a palm with only a pinkie finger. After a few sharp turns the tunnel widened and opened into a large, reverberating dark space, a craggy grotto that was so gigantic that the light of the carbide lamp didn't reach the far edges. The ceiling was pitch-black and was buttressed by natural columns and anthropomorphic rock formations above a muddy pool several meters across.

Carl cleared his throat and the noise rang out again, frighteningly close and directly in front of them.

From a distance, it was possible to mistake the sound for a hidden draft or something of that sort, but now it was clear: there was something living, waiting in the nearby darkness.

Hakim hopped over a few boulders and used his lamp to light the far side of the pool. A goat stood there on four shaky legs. Or at least something that must at one time have shared some similarities with a goat. Its coat had completely fallen out. There was a white film over its eyes. The animal turned its head horribly slowly toward the visitors and wheezed asthmatically. Around its neck was a heavy metal chain that was secured somewhere in the pool. A half-circle of filth and vomit along the bank offered an estimate of the length of the chain.

Hakim took a bundle of grass from his pocket and threw it to the goat. It cringed and then sniffed around on the ground for the greenery.

Beaming, Hakim pointed back and forth between the animal and his toothless mouth, smacked his lips and pressed the tips of his fingers to his lips. "My grandfather discovered it! Six or seven months and the meat is softer than soft, so tender. Tasty, tasty. It only works in the dark."

That night Carl had nightmares again. He was lying on the beach not far from the hotel and beside him, on a bath towel, lounged a giant, fat goat with white, blinded eyes. When he looked into its eyes he immediately realized that it wasn't the first time he had encountered them, and the voice of the dream revealed this was in reality a sphinx whose riddle it was necessary to solve.

He thought for a long time and then asked: "How might you be doing?" and the goat answered: "Fine." He only realized at that moment with a fright that the animal could talk. Smiling, it rubbed its face with its hooves and beneath them Helen's face appeared. Her *mien*. Carl sat up, aghast. A magnificent, bright-blue day out of the window. He was alone in bed. Was he still dreaming? Or something else? He heard human voices and got up to look out.

Helen was standing in front of the bungalow with a hotel employee. They were talking quietly. Helen laughed in a friendly tone, waved goodbye to the employee and went with two shopping bags under her arms to a white column between two oleander bushes in the front garden. She opened a compartment in the column with a small key, pulled out a stack of mail and leafed through it.

"Sleep well?" she asked. "I'm surprised they haven't written to me, I'm really surprised."

She sorted the mail into several stacks on the kitchen table. Though mail wasn't really the right word. The contents of the mailbox consisted of two flyers for local restaurants ("quality Arabian cuisine", "finest French dishes"), a letter from the hotel containing the code of conduct and a telephone number for emergencies (water leaks, electrical outages, Africans on the grounds), and a colorfully illustrated pamphlet in plastic wrap for Poseidon scuba-diving school ("the diving school with the trident", "we and our cutter", "get to know the fascinating world beneath the waves from a new perspective") with a handwritten note on it that said: *Please return pamphlet to mailbox upon departure.* In addition, two crumpled tissues, an empty envelope, an empty chocolate-bar wrapper and finally a strip of paper that had been typed out on a typewriter with many crossed-out mistakes that Helen read while biting her lips and then handed to Carl without a word:

++++++Psychologist's Office++++++
J. Carthusian Cockcroft, M.D., Corniche 27
Tel: 2791, Languages: Frnch, Engl, no
Arabic—Office houers: Mon-Thur 8-12 and
By appointment; state-of-the-art
methods—introductory rates thanks to our
++++++GRAND OPENING+++++++

"What's that about? Is this normal?" Carl turned the slip of paper around in his fingers.

"Maybe it is here."

"But you don't seriously think I'm going to go?"

Helen put the contents of the shopping bags in the refrigerator, fruit basket, sink and on the table and began to cut up a pineapple. Carl followed her undecidedly.

"Introductory rates. It's quackery."

"You can't ask me."

"But I am asking you."

"The density of psychologists probably isn't as high here as in Manhattan. That's why the ads look a bit different. But if you won't go to the hospital and or anywhere else—"

"Did you notice? Houers, with an e."

"Memory loss *and* persecution complex. You should definitely see a psychologist."

"You don't find it strange?"

"Maybe if it said 'landmine' or 'women and children half price'—but you don't need to get all worked up about a typo. It's probably a practice aimed at tourists who've had a bit too much sun—"

Helen broke off her sentence when she saw his unhappy face.

"I'm scared," Carl said softly. The paper trembled in his hand and the trembling worked its way up his arm and through his body. Helen put down the pineapple and approached him with the dripping knife. She wrapped her arms around Carl, the knife poking like a steel shark's fin from his back, and said: "Just try it. And if it's quackery you've only wasted a little time."

"No way," said Carl. "No way am I going there."

31

The Tyrant of Acragas

If the human brain were so simple that we could understand it,
we would be so simple that we couldn't.

EMERSON PUGH

"WHAT'S YOUR NAME?"
  "I don't know."
  "What language do you speak?"
  "French."
  "What city are we in?"
  "Targat."
  "What's the date?"
  "1972."
  "More precisely?"
  "September seventh. Eighth."
  "How do you know that?"
  "From the newspaper."
  "When did you read a paper?"
  "Yesterday?"
  "Did you know what day it was when you woke up in the barn?"
  "No."
  "When you saw the date on the newspaper, did it surprise
you? Or did it seem to be about what you expected?"

"About what I expected."

"How old are you?"

"Pfff." Carl looked at Dr Cockcroft. Dr Cockcroft had a voluminous full beard and slightly long hair that must have been blond not long ago. Eyes, nose, mouth were squeezed together in the bottom half of his face beneath the weight of his block-like forehead. He could as well have been a composer, or an astrophysicist. His hands were gigantic and his nails were chewed all the way down to the skins. He sat opposite Carl in a large, flowery, plush chair, a bit tense and decidedly unfashionable. On the small table between them sat the browned remains of an apple, Dr Cockcroft's notebook and a Montblanc fountain pen. A TV was showing a football match with no sound. The blinds were pulled shut.

"What would you guess?" asked Dr Cockcroft.

"Thirty?"

"Do you have a family?"

"I don't know."

"Do you remember any pets?"

"No."

"The president of the United States?"

"Nixon."

"France?"

"Pompidou."

"How many fingers am I holding up?"

"Eight."

"Put your fingers in the same position as mine. Right. And now a mirror image, with the other hand? Okay. Take that piece of paper there and write something."

"What should I write?"

"Anything. Write: Dr Cockcroft has four fingers on each hand. Good. And now draw a square. And now a circle around the square? If that is a circle for you, then please draw an egg. Can you draw a three-dimensional cube? Does seeing it cause you any difficulty?"

"No."

"Without checking, how many feet do you have?"

"What?"

"How many feet do you have?"

"Is that a serious question?"

"Just answer."

"Two," said Carl, looking at his feet.

Dr Cockcroft took notes. "Which of the following words does not belong in the series: person—sheepdog—fish?"

"Fish… no, person. Person doesn't belong."

"What type of music do you like?"

"I don't know."

"If I was going to play something, what would you like to hear? Arabic music? European? Rock?"

"Not classical."

"Can you name any groups? Bands?"

"The Beatles. The Kinks. Marshal Mellow."

"Can you sing a Beatles song?"

"I don't think so."

"Hum a melody."

Carl faintheartedly hummed a few notes and then, surprising even himself, said: "Yellow Submarine."

"Can you remember what the sign behind you says?"

"Exit."

"What's your wife's name?"

"No idea."

"The woman who brought you here?"

"That's not my wife."

"The woman waiting for you outside?"

"Right."

Dr Cockcroft gnawed on his left thumbnail. He looked at his notes and crossed something out. "And what is the name of the woman who isn't your wife?"

"Helen."

"Where do you live?"

"Two or three streets from here. In a bungalow."

"With this woman?"

Carl thought for a while and then said: "Why do you want to know that?"

"Do you live with her?"

"The bungalow belongs to her. She's on vacation. We met by chance."

"After you were released from the hospital?"

"I wasn't in the hospital. She put on the bandages."

"Why didn't you go to the hospital?"

"As I already said, I was attacked and… I didn't think it was so bad."

"Not so bad." With his tongue Dr Cockcroft pushed a bitten-off sliver of fingernail out between his lips and then blew it away. He nodded. "I can have a look at it later, if you'd like. And what about your hand?"

"I cut myself," said Carl, hiding the clumsily bandaged hand beside his thigh.

Dr Cockcroft glanced at his notes and sighed. "Right," he said, "count backwards from one hundred by sevens."

"One hundred," said Carl, and he proceeded to count until he reached seventy and a grumbling noise from the doctor convinced him that he had done enough. Dr Cockcroft had written as he counted, and based on the way his hand moved next, he was drawing a double line beneath the notes. He sucked in the left corner of his mouth, he sucked in the right corner of his mouth. Then he flipped back a few pages and said:

"Now please tell me the whole thing again, backwards. Everything that you told me, step by step, from the moment you arrived at the bungalow."

"Everything?"

"Everything. Backwards."

Carl's gaze fell on an iridescent-blue beetle that was crawling up the table leg right in front of his foot. "Right. Helen and I arrived at the bungalow. Before that we drove through Targat. Before that through the desert. Before that I spoke to Helen at the gas station. Where there was also a white VW bus with German tourists in it. Before that I had walked along beside the road. Before that they stole my wallet. The hippies. Before that I was buried in sand. The men in the jeep had driven around near me. Four men in white djellabas. Before that I'd dug myself into the sand. Before that I was running through the dunes. Before that I went out of the barn door..."

Dr Cockcroft tapped his closed fountain pen on his notes, step after step, and said: "Good, good. Well done. That's enough. Do you drink alcohol?"

"I don't think so."

"No. I mean, do you want a drink?"

Dr Cockcroft went over to a small bar, poured himself a glass of bourbon and looked back over his shoulder. "Something else?"

Carl had leaned forward a bit. He thought he could make out an upside-down word in the notebook: Banser or Ganser. Beneath it a large question mark.

"No thanks."

The psychiatrist sat back down in his chair, wheezing, took a sip of his drink, put down the nearly empty glass on the table and awkwardly pulled a giant handkerchief from his pants pocket. He took off his watch, set it down next to the glass and pen and pointed to the three objects. Then he covered them grandly with the handkerchief.

"What do a car and a boat have in common?"

"They are means of transport."

"Anything else?"

"You can sit in them?"

"And?"

"And?" In his mind's eye he saw Helen's rusty pickup and the cutter in the Poseidon dive school pamphlet. Both had something to do with Helen. No, that was nonsense. He shrugged his shoulders.

"Good," said Dr Cockcroft. "Now I'll tell you a story. Try to remember as much as you can. The tyrant of Acragas, a man named Phalaris, had a bronze bull made by the sculptor Perillos. The bull was hollow and large enough to hold a prisoner. Set a fire beneath the sculpture and the screams of the person inside were supposed to have sounded like the bellowing of a real bull. The first person roasted for test purposes was the sculptor himself. Now tell me the story in your own words."

"The whole story?"

"The whole story."

"So, a man named… something had a bull made. Out of bronze. To torture people. With fire. And the sculptor was the first one to die."

"How would you interpret that?"

"Interpret it?"

"What is the moral of the story?"

"What moral?"

"Is there a moral to the story? Some sort of point?"

Carl looked uneasily at the beetle, which had by this point reached the top of the table leg and was feeling its way carefully up over the edge of the table.

"Think about it. What does the story boil down to?"

"Art and politics don't go together?"

"More specifically?"

"Art is immoral?"

"That's what you think the point of the story is?"

"I don't know," said Carl irritably. "The tyrant is an idiot. The sculptor is an idiot. One idiot kills the other. I can't see much of a point."

Dr Cockcroft nodded a bit sadly, leaned back and asked: "What is underneath the handkerchief?"

"A watch, a glass and a white bunny."

The doctor's face remained expressionless. "Under the handkerchief?"

"A fountain pen," Carl corrected.

"Do you feel a strong desire to move?"

"Move how?"

"You described your first memory as 'I'm running through the desert.'"

"My first memory was of the barn."

"And then you ran," said Dr Cockcroft while laboriously trying to put his watch back on. "You used the word 'escape'."

"Because someone was chasing me."

"Does this desire to move still exist?"

"I'm not being followed any more."

"Is it possible that the people chasing you will return?"

"What are you getting at?"

"Give me an assessment: what do you think the chances are that the people following you will return?"

"They didn't just disappear into thin air. And I didn't dream them up. If that's what you think." Carl held up his wounded right hand—and realized too late his mistake.

Dr Cockcroft poured himself another bourbon at the bar. This time he brought the bottle back with him.

"Let's return to the barn," he said, sitting back down in the plush chair. "You described flasks and cauldrons and pipes. What did these things remind you of?"

"I had never seen them before."

"But didn't you have any thoughts about the function of the equipment? What it all could be?"

"A lab."

"More specifically?"

"Why are you asking this?"

"Why aren't you answering?"

"Because you don't know the answer either."

"Answer anyway."

"Why? If I say it looked like a fertilizer factory, or if I say it was a physics lab, what are you going to do—drive there and have a look?"

Dr Cockcroft was silent, and Carl, who was trying in vain to suppress his increasing mistrust, said: "I don't understand what you are testing here."

"Just answer my questions. What could it have been?"

"You tell me."

"The way you describe it, and given the fact that you detected, and I quote, a slight smell of alcohol when you woke up, could it perhaps have been a distillery?"

Carl shook his head. "Could be," he said, seemingly offended. "Could be."

"Do you know how alcohol is made?"

"From fruit. Through fermentation."

"More specifically?"

"Once it's fermented, you heat it up… you heat something and then filter off the alcohol. Or the water out of the alcohol. And then… I think you have to dilute it again at the end."

"Should we take a short break? You look tired."

"No," said Carl resolutely. "No need."

"Or shall I take a look at your head wound?" Dr Cockcroft poured himself another bourbon. "I'm only a psychiatrist, but you pick up a lot during your studies."

With his glass in one hand, he began to unwind the bandages on Carl's head.

"Just stay seated. I'm going to open this very carefully... Okay. Aha, aha. It's all nicely scabbed over. But cleaned up first and stitched together, eh? Looks almost professional. Hold this glass for a moment. How does it feel when I press here? Ouch. Right. Of course that hurts. And here? Overall it looks very stable. A bruise, maybe a small fracture, but not too bad. I'll close it up again. The problem is when you have hemorrhaging in the brain. But when that happens you're dead within forty-eight hours. So in retrospect that can be ruled out in this case."

With cautious if also a bit awkward and drunken handiwork, Dr Cockcroft tried to put the bandages back in their previous form while lecturing about intracranial hemorrhaging until finally turning back to his bourbon.

"I wouldn't worry about it too much," he said. "Even if it offends our vanity: we shouldn't overestimate the complexity of brains like ours. Have you ever seen a computer? What you call an electronic brain? No, of course not. I happen to know a little about them from my time at MIT... does the Dreyfus Affair mean anything to you?"

Dr Cockcroft froze, both hands still hanging in the air in front of him holding the quotation marks he'd signed in the air around the phrase "electronic brain". He leaned forward and looked at the iridescent-blue life form crawling along on dark tarsi in front of him. He held his finger down to the table top and waited until the beetle had scaled the impediment, then flicked it onto the carpet. The insect immediately began to paddle across the woven sisal fibers to the table and once again started to scale it.

"Sisyphus. Or Sophocles. What's it called again?"

"Sisyphean," said Carl.

Dr Cockcroft sat there with his head lolling. A hidden smile pushed his beard out into puffy hamster cheeks.

"A strange country. With strange insects. But what I actually wanted to say: that during my studies I was really into cybernetics. Without actually knowing anything about it, of course. I was from a human sciences background. But I found the computer fascinating. And the people there, and, to be frank, I was in love with a girl, a supposedly highly gifted engineer. Just let me know if I'm digressing too far... In any event, I watched her battle a computer once. And that was my first glimpse at the inner life of such a machine. A dusty diorama of green and brown circuit boards surrounded by a circulatory system of colorful cables. A foot on the overturned box, she ripped cables out of their mounts with a screwdriver. She broke squares out of the crystalline structure, soldered something on somewhere, wrestled it back onto its trembling legs. It didn't take even thirty seconds and the computer was up and running again."

Dr Cockcroft stuck his arm out, flicked the beetle off the table a second time and then tried to catch the uncomprehending gaze of his patient. "What I'm trying to say: that is the way one should think of our brains, or just about. Inevitably we think of our own organ as highly complex because, rightly or wrongly, we wish to think of the expressions of this organ as complex and rarefied. But it's just not borne out on a strictly physical basis, and one can expect good outcomes with screwdrivers and pliers. To put it more succinctly: I wouldn't worry about the hole in your head too much. The most dangerous thing is cerebral hemorrhaging and—"

"What is the Dreyfus Affair?"

"Aha, you noticed that? You're as observant as a lynx."

Dr Cockcroft looked around somewhat mystified at the three disparate entities surrounding him: the beetle that had now for the third time scurried back up the table leg, the inquiring patient and the reddish skin-covered gripping device made of bones, sinews, nerves and muscles that was trembling while holding a glass of bourbon. It guided the bourbon up to his mouth.

"Dreyfus has nothing to do with us!" he said positively. "Just that the computer that I was talking about was of course a chess computer. Richard Greenblatt. Probably doesn't mean anything to you. But he started it about five or six years ago. He and a few other people tried to teach the machine how to play chess. Useless, but that's the way computer scientists are. And Dreyfus—Hubert Dreyfus—was a philosopher at MIT. He was of the Heidegger school and didn't really know much about electronics. Had written books for years about why there was no such thing as artificial intelligence, why there never would be, and why any eight-year-old played chess better than a punched-card system. Of course he annoyed his colleagues in the computer science department with all of that, and at some point Greenblatt invited the good Hubert to play against his computer. As far as I can remember the machine went by the *nom de guerre* of Mac Hack. And Mac Hack wiped the floor with the philosophy department. As a result Dreyfus achieved a dubious sort of immortality as the first human who was stupider than a couple of copper wires. Not quite as great as the first man on the moon, but still. I've heard that his subsequent books criticizing the machine world have got a touch more adamant…"

Dr Cockcroft went on that way for some time. Carl, who didn't know why the doctor was telling him all of this, and, most importantly, whether the peculiar memories of this man's university days were part of the examination or not (and if they were, what the aim of them was), fought in vain against the impression that the psychiatrist was trying to bait him into some kind of trap in a way that was as intricate as it was slippery.

"What does this have to do with me?" he finally interrupted.

"Nothing!" Dr Cockcroft said cheerily, taking a big sip of bourbon and setting the glass down on the table with verve. He opened his eyes wide and looked at the patient.

"Was that on purpose?" asked Carl.

"What?"

"That." He pointed to the bourbon.

Dr Cockcroft squinted one eye, left the other wide open and peered down through the amber liquid at the beetle. A knuckle tapped Morse code on the table and the insect, trapped beneath the recessed bottom of the glass, scrambled around in tiny panicked circles. A lifting of the glass prison —"Pardon me!"—and the six-legged creature rushed across the table top, flopped over the edge and whisked itself under a stack of newspapers.

"So why are you telling me all of this?" asked Carl.

"Why am I telling you? Because I find it all highly interesting! And because I believe we are heading into a golden era." With his two index fingers he tapped on his right and left temples while his eyebrows danced up and down. "Sooner or later two integrated circuits and a couple of colorful wires will replace that thing we carry around in our heads and allow to torture us. Gorgeous female students will free you from misery with a kick, a hammer and a pair of pliers, and as for the question of immortality... but I see that this doesn't particularly interest you. That's fine. It's all just a pleasant dream of things to come. Right now, however, we need to dive back into the whorls of your brain by conventional means, no matter how painful."

He picked up his notebook again, flipped through a few pages and suddenly froze: "It occurs to me, did you mention why you are here? I don't mean because of the amnesia. Initially you didn't want to see a doctor. And now—did something happen in the meantime?"

Carl shook his head. "Except that I found your flyer. And I wasn't doing well. I'm anxious and getting more and more anxious. I can barely sleep. I have horrible dreams."

"I see."

"Last night I basically didn't sleep at all. One continuous nightmare."

"That's understandable. So back to the question—"

"Shall I tell you what I dreamed about?"

"No, you don't need to. We can move on."

"It's of no interest to you?"

"You think, because I'm a psychiatrist." Dr Cockcroft chewed on the last of his thumbnails. "If it would help you feel better, then go ahead."

Carl hesitated momentarily and then described his dream about the giant goat. The goat that had taken on Helen's facial mien. "That is, Helen's *face*," he corrected himself. Carl became more and more insecure as he went on, since he realized that he couldn't express even the basics of what had been so horrifying about the dream. In the cold light of day it all seemed quite harmless.

"And now you want me to come up with a meaning?" asked Dr Cockcroft. "What do you want to hear? That you are apparently afraid of the American tourist who has taken you in, nursed you back to health, set you up with money, bandaged you and sent you to me? That the woman's face is as unfamiliar to you as any other face? That you've fallen into the claws of a cleverly masked con woman?" He grabbed his beard with both hands and pulled on it, as if proving its authenticity. "A spy on a secret mission? Your longtime wife who is using the situation to play out an exquisite joke? I may be a psychiatrist but I'm no friend of the Viennese sewer. If you want my modest opinion: dreams are fireworks in our brains. They have no meaning. That is also the position of the scientific community."

"That's not very comforting," said Carl after a long pause.

"None of the findings of modern brain research are very comforting," answered Dr Cockcroft excitedly. "What is the story with the word *mien*?"

"What?"

"You immediately went back and used *face* instead. Right? So, back to the American tourist. Helen. The one you apparently have difficulty trusting. Do you have an intimate relationship?"

"What?"

"Do you have sexual relations with each other?"

"What business is it of yours?"

"I'm a doctor. Are you living together?"

"What does that have to do with my amnesia?"

"Are you unable to remember intimacies?"

"No. Because there haven't been any."

Dr Cockcroft nodded, rapped the end of his fountain pen against his neck and looked Carl in the face for a long time. "One last question. Try to answer without counter-questions for once. Are you entirely sure that you don't know who you are?"

"Why else would I be here?"

"I'm not asking without cause."

"Yes!" said Carl desperately.

32

Dissociation

His face bore the artless expression of a man who meditates and makes no effort to conceal it.

KAFKA

"YOUR CLINICAL PICTURE IS, let me put this gently, unusual. I know that one should be conservative in any diagnosis, but we don't have the time for the appropriate level of restraint. First of all, we're not in a clinical setting, which is where you actually belong. Second, I would venture to say that there's not an adequate clinical facility for you anywhere within five hundred kilometers. And third, you have a rather tenuous livelihood and moreover seem to be involved in things that could hinder any further treatment. Provided, of course, that what you say is true. Finally, I'm also no specialist in the area of amnesia, I'm more of a run-of-the-mill psychiatrist. I know a bit, but certainly not all. I'm going to take a shot in the dark, if you don't mind. And in the hope that you will help me."

He flipped through his notebook. "You don't have any major functional deficits, you realize that yourself. You are well oriented chronologically and spatially. Your real-world knowledge is intact and seems to be at a middle-school level. You can remember all the occurrences since your—let's call it an accident—and when it comes to anterograde amnesia, which would be typical of craniocerebral injury, you seem to have none whatsoever. The shortcomings in your memory apply exclusively to the past. And within that, to things tied to autobiographical information. Which is not unusual. Functional knowledge and procedural faculties often remain unaffected, the autobiographical content disappears in accordance with Ribot's law: last in—first out. One forgets the most recent periods of time before the trauma, days, weeks or years. There are known cases where the last thing the patients remember are their seventh birthdays. There are also cases where they believe themselves to be seven still. Something is really shot in cases like that. What is, however, extremely rare, and I mean extremely rare as in essentially zero cases, is when the missing period of times encompasses one's entire span of life and one's identity. Someone not knowing their name. That's the way amnesia is usually depicted in fiction or film. You get hit on the head and your identity is gone. You get hit again and it's back. Asterix and Obelix."

Dr Cockcroft leaned back in his chair, put his hands together with the fingers intertwined and smiled weakly.

"So?"

"So, I want to be honest with you. Your condition has characteristics of something non-existent."

A mob of people had gathered around the referee in the penalty area, players in dark uniforms protested. The players in white uniforms pushed those in the dark ones. The line judge ran out across the field.

"What are you trying to say?" asked Carl. "That I'm faking it?"

"I didn't say that." Dr Cockcroft pulled his gaze away from the television. "I said your condition has characteristics of something non-existent. Which means one can doubt certain things. One thing I don't doubt is that you... how should I put it? That you have some sort of serious damage. I just can't say what sort. Of course faking sounds very negative at first blush, but it doesn't typically mean that someone is affecting brain damage for laughs. It can also be out of necessity. In a desperately stressful situation, for instance. Modern science has encountered feigned memory loss that happens subconsciously. Ganser, for example… Although it's not relevant to your case. And that's where the problem lies. They don't fit your case, either: dementia in old age. Total senility. Korsakow. Quite apart from more dubious things like hysterical dissociation."

"What's Korsakow?"

"Alcohol. But you're clearly too together for that to be it. It would have been perfect with a barn full of distilling equipment in the background. But a true Korsakow has completely destroyed the brain through drinking. They can't even put together a sentence with a clause. No, sorry, that's not it."

"Which means?"

"It means that I can rule out a few things by process of elimination. And, as I said, you can be sure that I'm no specialist. But I can quote from the classical medical school textbook: global amnesia is so rare that you are a thousand times more likely to encounter a fake version of it."

"But it does exist."

"It appears to exist."

"What is Ganser?"

"Ganser was a German doctor. He first discovered it among prisoners. Initially he called it *Vorbeireden*, or paralogical, talking past someone. Can you picture anything about a disease referred to as talking past someone? Yes, of course. And what do you picture?"

"That somebody's answers have nothing to do with the questions. Like you and me."

"If you ask somebody with Ganser syndrome what two plus two is, he will answer five. He doesn't answer forty-eight, but he also doesn't answer four. Always just a little off. How many ears to do you have? You feel around and then guess two. Questions about identity: apparently impossible to answer. It lasts three days, followed by a full recovery, and no memories whatsoever of the three days of apparent dementia. Which is what the condition is called: pseudo-dementia."

"And you've ruled that out in me?"

"I could be convinced by some of your answers. But others, on the other hand—"

"But if this is all pseudo-dementia, do other people who get it also have their skulls smashed in beforehand?"

"That is a very good question. A really very good question. I was just about to get to that. Of course a blow to the head is not a precondition for Ganser syndrome. But a blow to the head isn't a precondition for any other possible causes of loss of identity, either. It takes a psychologically traumatic event."

"And what are the other possible causes?"

"You're grasping at straws, which is understandable. I would probably do the same thing in your situation. But there's no point."

"What was the other thing you mentioned before? Hysterical dissociation?"

"Dissociation. No. You don't have that."

"But what is it?"

"It emerged at the turn of the century. A roving spirit. Called *a fugue state*. It's questionable whether it's an actual condition. It is disputed within the profession."

"But it makes you lose your identity?"

"Some say so, others disagree. Like I said. But there are very few case studies and no reliable ones. It's the same with Ganser syndrome. Things having to do with identity loss are all very controversial. If you want my opinion—"

"And the symptoms?"

"Of which one now?"

"Fugue state."

"Fugue state," said Dr Cockcroft, "happens within a discrete and usually limited time frame, which you have already exceeded. And it also involves the complete loss of a sense of self and an overwhelming desire to stay on the move. Something you, too, showed a modest amount of. And all triggered by a psychologically traumatic event. Torture, childhood abuse—whatever the current fashion is. But you are far too rational and collected for that. Your story is altogether too lucid and linear. Just your imaginary or not imaginary pursuer—"

"They are not imaginary."

"That's a complicating factor. An imaginary pursuer would be useful for a nice little personality disorder... but unfortunately real pursuers don't fit in a dissociation narrative."

"Four men following me and smashing my head in doesn't count as traumatizing?"

"Having one's head smashed in doesn't constitute trauma in this instance. It must involve psychological distress. I don't mean to trivialize it, but I'm afraid that to lose one's memory it takes a bit more than four halfwits in white frocks swinging a carjack."

"Swinging a carjack and threatening to kill me."

"No." Dr Cockcroft lowered his chin into his hands, which were resting on his chest, looked deep into his patient's eyes and shook his head. "No, no, no. Can you imagine how many traumatized people we'd have running around if that were the case?"

"What about before? Not the blow to the head. Whatever came before it, that I can't remember? Couldn't something... a prolonged event, beforehand, have happened? Involving psychological distress—that was the cause; and the blow to the head and all the rest came afterward?"

"You would make a great detective. Truly. But they don't talk about the roving spirit aspect of a fugue state for nothing. A person in a fugue state is empty inside: he roams around because he roams around. He sees a pretty river and thinks to himself, I'll follow this pretty river, and he'll walk for a hundred kilometers, and sometimes he'll be stopped and if he's asked why, he can't answer. He has completely forgotten what made him set out. He's filled with indifference. First. Second: if your pursuers are in fact real, that is a nice starting point for psychological distress, as you correctly figured out in your role as Sherlock Holmes just now." Dr Cockcroft closed his eyes for a moment as if he were trying to picture the four men. "In that case you were abused and put under such extreme pressure by these guys out there in the desert that you were deeply traumatized. Then we don't even need the gratuitous blow to the head, that's just an extra, the icing on the cake, so to speak. But. And here comes a major but. Trauma so severe that it causes your entire identity to disappear would, among other things, also erase your pursuers. In fact, first and foremost them. Do you understand? The thing that traumatizes you is the first thing to disappear. That's the whole point. If everything is erased, then so is the memory of the traumatic event. In particular, four men and a carjack. You can call me Watson."

Carl looked at the psychiatrist. He looked at the bare walls, the notebook and the table. He rubbed his eyes with his hands, thinking. He listened to Dr Cockcroft pour himself another bourbon. Something about the psychiatrist's argument struck him as illogical. It bothered him more and more that Dr Cockcroft seemed almost more interested in the sequence of events in the desert than in the phenomena in his psyche. Or was he fooling himself? He tried to picture the doctor in a white djellaba.

"I'm sorry," said Dr Cockcroft. "You wanted a diagnosis from me. That's it."

That of the poor, unsteady doctor. The stark furniture. The soccer match.

"You are sure," said Dr Cockcroft, leaning forward, "that you're not keeping anything from me?"

"And you are sure that you're a psychiatrist?"

"Do you have any doubt about that?"

"If you think I'm faking, if you are sure—then I am just as sure that you are no doctor."

Dr Cockcroft didn't answer.

"Why for example do you keep asking questions that have nothing to do with amnesia? Why does this place look like… like…"

"What questions?"

"Take the question about alcohol, what's that about?"

"Have you already forgotten?"

"No. And I also haven't forgotten that you said: a Korsakow can't even put together a sentence with a clause. The brain is completely destroyed. So why all the questions? What's the point, when it's self-evident that I—"

"Can't you figure it out?"

"No, I can't!" Carl leaped up and then sat back down again. "I can't. Or have binge drinkers started to make their own stuff?"

Dr Cockcroft's conciliatory hand gesture signaled that he was at least willing to take his patient's agitation seriously.

"Trust," he said. "Please stay calm. Trust is the most important thing. The reason I'm questioning you so thoroughly is because we're trying to figure out your identity, in case you've forgotten. And when someone wakes up covered in blood, with a smashed skull, out in the desert, surrounded by equipment for distilling alcohol, there is the suspicion that he himself could be the bootlegger and it could be his own distillery—actually a likely scenario, wouldn't you say?" Dr Cockcroft held his fingers out in the shape of an imaginary funnel, then drew his fingertips together. "Only now we can eliminate that possibility. You don't know any more about alcohol and its production than anybody else does. And that's not a lot."

"And what about sex?"

"Pardon me?"

"Why did you want to know whether I'd had sex with Helen—"

"Routine," said Dr Cockcroft. "Purely routine. A test to see whether you were prepared to answer honestly."

"I don't believe you."

"Why not?"

"No serious doctor would ask that. He would ask something else."

"What do you know about what a serious doctor would ask?"

"Hasn't my functional knowledge remained unaffected?"

"Good that you remember that. Less good that you—"

"You're not a doctor."

"You really have doubts? And since what point, if I may ask?"

"As soon as I came in here. The whole time. As soon as I saw your flyer."

"What flyer?"

"Introductory rates."

"What about that gives you pause?"

"No normal doctor would write *introductory rates. Thanks to our grand opening.* And this isn't how a doctor's office looks. Why is the TV on? Where are your... devices? And you don't have any medical books. You don't have a lab coat on. You—"

"A lab coat!" For a moment, Dr Cockcroft seemed incensed. "And if I had a lab coat on you would believe my diagnosis? I'm sorry, but psychiatrists don't wear... though I do own one, actually. It must be upstairs. My library of medical books is upstairs, too. And as for the TV, I'm sorry, but the power switch is broken. You have to unplug the cord, and that's tricky. And as you no doubt remember, when you showed up here it definitely wasn't during my office hours."

Dr Cockcroft kicked at the TV. A newsreader flickered eerily, disappeared into wavy lines and lost his head. The picture slowly took shape in the middle of the picture tube again except for a piece of his head, which remained stuck in the corner of the screen.

"I can tell you something else," said Dr Cockcroft. "I don't know whether I will win back your trust or lose it for good—but you are of course correct. It doesn't look like a doctor's office in here. You probably have no idea how one earns a living here. Patients like you are the exception. To be frank: you are my first patient, my first proper patient."

The TV newsreader straightened up a stack of paper on his desk and Dr Cockcroft tipped back the last of his whiskey.

"But this is Africa. How many psychiatrists would you guess practice here? There's supposed to be another one in Cape Town. You can't do any business with the natives. They have their own methods. A bit of drumming, a bit of singing: for the most part that's sufficient for their so-called problems. The African soul is still in its infancy. There's no comparison to the web of neuroses in an average American housewife. And if you want to know how I make my money: ugly mothers in giant sunglasses. Wide-hipped teenagers from reputable families. Tourists. That's what this place is gauged for. A little holidaymaking, a little stress on the beach, a little sexual misconduct here or there—I work more or less in conjunction with the leisure industry. If that answers your question. My practice belongs to the hotel. And every two weeks we offer introductory prices for our grand opening—it's been a successful strategy."

"But you are… a real psychologist?"

"Psychiatrist. Studied at Princeton," said Dr Cockcroft, rattling off a series of hospitals and universities that naturally meant nothing to Carl.

"And do you have a diploma? Something that proves you are a doctor?"

"Perhaps a lab coat?"

Carl didn't want to nod or shake his head.

"You want to see my lab coat?" Dr Cockcroft rephrased the question. He smiled. Not an insecure smile, more of a watchful, cunning smile, as if he had asked: You want to see your mother's vagina?

"Yes," said Carl.

"It's upstairs. As I said. I think. It's also possible that it's at the cleaners."

"Or a diploma. Or medical books."

"The books are upstairs. You want to have a look?" (Do you want to enter the vagina?)

Carl wrapped his hands around his head and, with the healthy hand, massaged his scalp. Dr Cockcroft watched his patient placidly.

"In all seriousness," said Carl, "would you mind going up there with me and—"

"If you'd like. If I can win back your trust that way. Therapy is useless without trust between the doctor and patient... no, it's no trouble." Pushing on the arms of his chair, Dr Cockcroft raised himself a few centimeters. "I'd be happy to show you my beautiful lab coat. Is that what you would like?"

His entire demeanor oozed such a willingness to co-operate that the walk to the next floor seemed unnecessary. Carl couldn't insist on it without looking like an idiot. He sensed that, but he also sensed that that might also be the secret purpose of this cordial co-operativeness, and so he said: "Yes. Yes, that's what I would like."

33

The Library

ED: "Night has fallen. And there's nothin' we can do about it."

JOHN BOORMAN,
Deliverance

A WIDE WOODEN STAIRCASE led to the second floor. It opened onto a long, dark corridor with four or five doors off the right and left sides. Carl followed two steps behind Dr Cockcroft; he could smell what had become a strong scent of alcohol billowing out behind him.

"My library," said the doctor. He had stopped in front of a door, opened it grandly and flipped on the light. The glow of a dim bulb illuminated a minuscule room. A broken sink lay in the middle of floor surrounded by dust and crumbled bricks, and two pipes stuck out of the wall.

"Whoops!" said Dr Cockcroft. He closed the door nonchalantly, went a few more steps down the hall and reached for the handle of the next door.

"My library!" he said. He pulled on the handle. He yanked at it. The door was locked.

"Really not a good idea to call on me so late in the day," he said, shaking his head.

He turned around and, less confidently, tried a door on the

other side of the hall. This time he didn't make any pronounce-ment about what waited behind the door. Four fluorescent bulbs flickered on and lit up a room that was almost completely empty. The walls were bright white, paint-splashed newspaper lined the floor, it smelled of solvent. A white plastic bucket lay to the side, tipped over. A table, also covered with newspaper, stood in the middle of the room on four slim, round legs that ended in pointed brass feet. One of the feet was broken and the leg was resting on one thin and one thick book.

"Your library?" asked Carl.

Dr Cockcroft smacked himself on the forehead like a slap-stick actor and said: "Totally forgot! The workmen were here today."

He leaned down to the two books, took a quick look at them and then picked them up and handed them to Carl with a triumphant smile. A narrow volume wrapped in gray paper and a voluminous tome bound in blue linen.

"Specialist literature from the motherland of psychoanalysis!"

"In German?"

"And before you ask: I can't read them. They're not mine. They belonged to my missing predecessor..."

Carl took the thin book and turned it around in his hand. On the gray paper cover was written in pencil: *Albert Eulenburg SUM I.*

"... from whom I took over the practice. The practice, the patients and the library. All he took with him was, understand-ably, his wife. And no!" He waved his hands drunkenly in the space between him and Carl. "Don't get your hopes up! He went back to Europe. Probably. He was Austrian. And anyway, if you were a psychiatrist, we'd have noticed that, don't you think?"

"Yeah," said Carl, although he was thinking no, and he opened the thin book. The first thing to catch his gaze was a poem in gothic lettering.

Ich habe so viele Gedanken
Und pervers bin ich außerdem;
Ich bin in der Tat für alle
Ein ungelöstes Problem!

"Can you figure it out?" asked Dr Cockcroft.

"Sorry?"

"Can you read it?"

"Yes," said Carl, mystified. He flipped through a few pages. Non-fiction with lots of long, difficult sentences. The poem was the exception. There were no illustrations. And all of it in gothic lettering.

"You didn't say that you spoke German."

"I didn't know myself. I can only... sort of."

"Those weird letters. What does it say?"

"It's about women."

"And does it evoke any feelings in you? The language, I mean."

Carl stared at the book and mutely moved his lips.

"No. It's too complicated for me. I understand most of the words, but not the meaning. It's not my native language."

"What do you understand?"

"That women aren't cruel. When it comes to sex. That's just something men imagine."

"That corresponds to the stand taken by science," said Dr Cockcroft pensively. He took the book from Carl's hand to have a look at the puzzling script. As he was doing so he suddenly froze as if he had spotted a rat in a dark corner of the room, then went over to the corner. He triumphantly held up a white lab coat and brandished it the way a soldier would a conquered flag. It could have been a lab coat; covered with splatters of paint, however, it bore a bit more resemblance to a painter's smock.

Carl picked up the other book and began to flip through it energetically once he had convinced himself that the doctor, who was flapping around in the lab coat, tangled in the sleeves, wasn't going to let him out of his sight. It was another German book, a dictionary published by Brockhaus in 1953 in Wiesbaden, the volume covering letters A to M.

Mindererus, mindset, mindsight, mindstuff... mine. He skimmed quickly through the entry once, twice, and tried to memorize the contents.

MINE [French], *Mil.*: a cavity in the earth, or a container, holding an explosive charge. 1) *Landmines* are used to destroy enemy personnel, material or works and are ignited by contact or by electrical means. *Minefields* are entire spaces occupied or commanded by mines either on land or in the water, particularly as defense against vehicles or watercraft. 2) *Wurfmines* are the munitions used by a *Minenwerfer*, or *mine thrower*, a muzzle-loading trench mortar. 3) *naval mines* are explosive charges contained in cases and placed in the water to destroy or impede enemy vessels, called *buoyant mines* when held in place beneath the surface by cables and anchors, or *ground mines* when fixed to the bottom. Enemy naval mines are cleared by military ships called *minesweepers*. 4) *Luftminen* are aerial bombs with steering mechanisms. 5) a pit or excavation in the earth, from which ores, precious stones, coal or other mineral substances are taken by digging or by any of various other mining methods.

MINE: 1) ancient Greek coins, = 1/60 of a Talent = 100 Drachmas. 2) an ancient Greek measure of weight.

MINE: 1) Isadora, actually Minescu, Romanian-French surveyor and biologist, * Mamaia 1837 † 1890, visited on behalf of—Pélissiers North Africa in search of—Ouz, completed first-rate cartographic material and authored a travel report, *On the Golden Sources*, Marseilles 1866, 2 volumes. 2) Aimable-Jean-Jacques, son of 1), playwright,* Algiers 1874, portrays the vacuousness of cosmopolitan society in humorous, finely detailed sketches, later turned to adventure novels with trivial elements. Chief works: *Mama's Big Voyage* (1901), *Mama's Next Big Voyage* (1903), *Sons of the Sands* (1934), *The Invisible Fata Morgana* (1940) and *The Shadow of Yellow Death* (1942). He received the 1951 Prix Goncourt for the novel *Beach With No Sea*. 3) Wilhelm,* 1915, German astronomer.

"Pencil lead is missing," said Carl.

"Sorry?" Dr Cockcroft looked at him through a sleeve.

"There's an ancient Greek coin called a mine?"

"What exactly is the question?"

"Do you know whether there was an ancient Greek coin called a mine in French?"

"I'm afraid I don't know. What do you find interesting about mines?"

"Nothing… I'm just wondering if the name is the same in French."

"You ask strange things."

"And do you have O? The letter O? The other volume?"

"Astonishing, this curiosity. No, sorry. As I mentioned, this is all I received from my predecessor."

A razor-thin sliver of moon hung between rocket-shaped minarets when the two men stepped out of the building around midnight. The air was warm and dry. Dr Cockcroft had given up on the sleeves and thrown the lab coat carelessly over his shoulder. He didn't look like either a doctor or a painter, more like a mad scientist in a movie; he slapped his patient on the shoulder jovially, told him to come back anytime and mumbled something about a secret desert disease that would probably soon be known as Cockcroft Syndrome.

"What was the name of your predecessor?" asked Carl.

"Sorry?"

"What was his name?"

"No, no. Believe me… you're no Austrian. And besides, he was supposed to have been short and wiry. You're more average height and wiry. Geiser. Or Geisel. Ortwin Geisel."

He waved goodbye with stiff cordiality as Carl crossed the street with his head down. On the other side, Carl stepped into the shadow of an entryway and turned around. He saw Cockcroft disappear unsteadily into the building. After a few minutes the light in the practice went out. A few moments later Carl could make out a bearded silhouette through one of the blinds on the second floor. He waited a while longer, hurried across the street and pulled a ring of keys from his pocket. Carl had four safety keys. He quietly tried one after the other. None fitted.

It was more of a relief than a disappointment.

Helen, who was waiting in the bungalow, put an arm around his shoulder. Carl took it for a gesture of tenderness initially, then he noticed that there was no tenderness in her facial expression. She was supporting him. He was unsteady on his feet.

"So?" she asked.

"Don't know," he said.

"Did you have trouble trusting him?"

"That's the same thing he asked."

"Whether you found it difficult to trust him?"

"Whether I found it difficult to trust you."

"So? Do you?"

Carl didn't answer.

"Did he at least seem halfway competent?" asked Helen as they lay next to each other in darkness on the bed. "Or more like his flyer?"

Once again he didn't answer for a long time. "He's definitely not a charlatan," he said after Helen's breathing had already become smooth. "A charlatan would have put more effort into seeming like a real doctor."

34

The Banana

God made some men small, and some men large; but Colt made them all equal.

AMERICAN SAYING

THE WOMAN, the trusted woman, trying to put one over on you... your longtime wife who is using the situation to play out an exquisite joke... How had Dr Cockcroft formulated it exactly? Of course it was nonsense. Carl knew that it was nonsense. But the words kept welling up in the boundless vacuum of his mind and floating around like iridescent bubbles in the dulled spheres of his consciousness.

Their first chance encounter, a gas station in the desert. An American tourist in shorts, a friendly bungalow. His not-wife, his longtime not-wife, Helen, whom he had no reason to mistrust, who had taken such tender care of him. She had looked through his things. So he didn't feel bad going through hers.

First he went through her suitcase, then he rummaged through the entire bungalow. She had carelessly thrown her underwear and a couple of sweaters in the armoire, the rest was still in the suitcase or within a meter of it. Two blazers, socks, a silk evening gown. A yellow outfit, a white outfit, an empty notebook. A tiny dressing case, needle and thread. No make-up, no body-care products. An American newspaper, apparently unread. A clipping from a local paper denying French atomic espionage without mentioning who had made the claim and why. A clipping from an English-language paper with the results of the American baseball league. On the back of it an article on Harold Pinter. A pair of reading glasses with one of the arms held to the frame by adhesive tape, a pair of handcuffs and another larger pair of handcuffs, maybe ankle cuffs if that was the right word, a baton, a robe and two pairs of jeans. A beach-ball racquet and a hard rubber ball. And at the very bottom of the suitcase a solid wood case about the size of a large cigar box, that could not be opened with his sturdy fingernails. Inside was apparently a heavy, asymmetrical object. Carl had just tossed a stray bright-green bikini that had been wrapped around the box back into the suitcase when he heard a noise behind him.

"Is this payback?" The owner of the bikini was leaning against the doorway with her arms crossed, smiling. Next to her was a bag of groceries.

Carl didn't have time to replace the look of disgust on his face with a mien of surprised innocence.

"What are you, a cop?" he yelled. He held up a pair of hand-cuffs and the baton and glared angrily at his definitely-not-wife. He looked like a little boy who wanted to know the truth about all sorts of secrets. Carl couldn't read her face, couldn't read her gestures either, and then Helen got explicit and explained that some bees liked to pollinate their flowers with handcuffs, and that the long rubber device that he had in his hand wasn't a "baton". She spoke of freedom in America and used the word modern.

At first Carl was silent. Then he saw himself with the dubious objects in each hand and carefully laid them back in the suitcase. With an unsteady look, he said: "And I can't get that wooden case open."

"A .357."

"What?"

"A .357 Magnum," said Helen, smiling in her eccentric way.

"I don't believe it."

Helen shrugged as she tossed the box into the suitcase, slammed it closed, pushed Carl out of the bedroom and sat down at the breakfast table.

"I don't believe it," Carl repeated. He turned his chair around. Helen poured herself a cup of coffee, grabbed a banana from the fruit bowl, pointed it at him and said: "I wouldn't go unarmed among you lot."

35

Risa, Known as Khach-Khach

These bullets are not meant to kill. They are mainly used to create serious wounds, and to incapacitate the enemy. After all, seriously wounded soldiers take the enemy more time and money to treat than dead soldiers.

DOCUMENTARY ABOUT THE BELGIAN
ARMS MANUFACTURER F. N. HERSTAL

T HE MAN WHO WAS SITTING alone all the way at the back of the dark bar was named Risa, but he was known as Khach-Khach. He had a nervous, observant face with three vertical scars running from his forehead to his chin. He was about twenty. He was left-handed.

At the age of six he had watched as his parents, grandparents, four sisters, a brother-in-law and all of his relatives, as well as two other Tuareg families, a handful of rebels and several bystanders had been laid down in a row in the desert sand and staked. Then a tank rolled over their bodies so they exploded like tubes of toothpaste. Until he was ten he lived in a prison camp north-east of the Empty Quarter. He spent two summers at an army school where a fat Spaniard offered free classes. Risa was the most intelligent student the school had ever seen. He learned to read and do math and landed an apprentice-ship with a tanner. The tanner's workshop sat in the shadow of the mountains of garbage, and one day a giant black man in colorful clothes and lots of gold jewelry on his fingers came to the door. The tanner kneeled on the dirt floor in front of him, then gathered up all the money he had and placed it at his feet. The black man took the money and he also took Risa. He housed Risa in the basement of his magnificent villa. He bought him clothes and gave him food. For a year Risa learned how to deal with businessmen and weapons. He served as a courier and took care of the accounting. He killed a man for the first time at age thirteen.

These days he lived on a small island off the coast. Twice a week he came to the mainland to do business. A fat gold ring, inherited from his mentor, glittered on his right hand. Risa was flipping through a feature on underwear in the American edition of *Vogue* magazine and didn't look up when a somewhat insecure-seeming man addressed him.

"I heard you were selling something?" asked the man.

"N-n."

"You're not selling anything?"

"Fuck off."

Carl looked undecidedly at an empty chair at the table. He didn't dare sit down.

"Someone told me you were selling something."

"Drugs are back there."

"Not drugs."

Risa lifted his scarred face, gave Carl a quick once-over and looked toward the exit just as a boy disappeared out of it. He looked at the bartender. The bartender shrugged his shoulders.

"Just some information," said Carl awkwardly.

"What do I have to do with it?"

"Someone said you were the right person."

"I'm not the right person."

"I thought—"

"You thought what?"

"Or perhaps you know someone who knows."

"Who knows *what*?"

"Someone who can give me some information."

Risa waited a moment to see whether the strange apparition in a yellow blazer and salmon-colored Bermuda shorts would dissipate into thin air on its own, then he said: "I can give you information on how you can get out of here alive in the next ten seconds."

"Please." Carl reached for the back of the empty chair and pulled it a few centimeters in his direction. "I've been out all day. Somebody told me that you—"

"Who?"

"A boy."

"What boy?"

"I don't know… a boy. He brought me here."

"How did you know him?"

"I didn't know him. Somebody referred me to him."

"Who?"

"I didn't know him either."

"Are you from Westinghouse?"

"No."

"From El-Fellah?"

"No."

"You come in here alone, nobody sent you, and all you want is some 'information'?"

"Research."

"Then fuck off."

Risa turned back to the colorful photos. Underwear, under-wear, lipstick. Five women on a platform. Two women on a sofa. Cigarettes. When he looked up again and saw the man still standing there, he suddenly swung his fist up and stopped it just below Carl's chin. Carl didn't flinch. It was impossible to read Risa, whether he was boiling with anger or just amusing himself, and the lack of transparency in his facial expression convinced Carl that this was the man he was looking for.

"Can I get you something to drink?"

Evening wear and coats, underwear, a woman with two Great Danes. A woman in black boots. A woman in white boots. Risa didn't answer.

"I really don't want to buy anything," said Carl.

"Where do see anything to buy?"

"I know. I just wanted—"

"You wanted to get me something to drink?"

"Love to," said Carl, ignoring the sarcastic look of his counterpart. He called out something to the bartender. The bartender stood with his arms crossed and didn't move.

Beach fashions, beach fashions, bathing suits. A woman crouched down naked, wearing only a pair of sunglasses. Risa looked up quickly and casually, flipped through a few more pages and held two fingers in the air. The bartender filled two marmalade jars with a clear fluid and brought them to the table. Carl waited a few seconds, pulled the chair out and sat down. A ten-watt bulb over the table diffused the darkness.

It had taken him almost the entire morning to find his way here. First he had asked on the street what part of town he should go to in order to have some fun. People sent him to the harbor. There he cautiously asked about weapons. One person had sent him to the next. The more concrete his questions became, the more vague the answers became. Finally Carl had let a boy lead him five or six blocks into a shanty town and he'd landed in this hole. The boy demanded a dollar for his services, three times as much as all the rest, which is why Carl chose him.

Risa moved the jar to his lips, closed his eyes and smelled the woody aroma of the home-made liquor. "If you don't want to buy anything, why all the commotion?"

"Like I said—"

"You think you can fool me," said Risa. "But you can't fool me."

Carl was silent.

"You want to buy something."

"No, I—"

"Then sell something."

"No."

"Buy or sell." Risa's voice had taken on a threatening overtone.

"So you are selling something?"

"No."

"Okay, fine," said Carl, thinking for a moment. "Let's suppose I wanted to buy something. Or let's suppose I wanted to buy something and was to ask someone who wasn't selling anything and had nothing to do with that sort of thing where one might get hold of something."

"Let's suppose you're a poof." Risa leaned over the table and moved Carl's chin from side to side with two fingers.

"Good," said Carl, ready to compromise. "Let's suppose I'm a poof. And as a poof, naturally I have no clue about this particular subject area and need some information. Like how much it costs."

"How much what costs?"

"Mines, for instance."

"What kind of mines?"

"A mine. Any kind."

"Any kind? You want to know how much any kind of mine costs? So you came here?"

"The most expensive kind."

"The most expensive? One with a lot of bang, or what?"

"Yeah. But the main thing is that it's expensive."

"No," said Risa. "No, no, no, no! With a lot of bang, or expensive?"

"It's about the price."

"You want to buy some kind of mine—and the main thing is that it's expensive?"

"I don't want to buy it."

Risa tilted his chair back and forth. He tapped the flat of his hand on the bandages on Carl's head. "What's the story? Did you have your brain removed?"

"In a way."

"In a… so you admit that you have some damage?"

"Yes."

"You're not going to put one over on me."

"I wasn't planning to."

"The last cop who tried that—"

"I'm not a cop."

Risa drank a sip and put the jar down in front of him. He rolled up the magazine and put it in the right pocket of his jacket. Simultaneously he reached inconspicuously into the left pocket. Two guests who were sitting further back in the darkness of the bar jumped up and ran to the exit. The bartender ducked beneath the bar. A chair fell over.

"Let us suppose," said Risa quietly, "that I really had heard something about the thing that you are talking about. Weapons." The corners of his mouth stretched out to reveal two rows of gleaming white teeth, very slowly, just the way he'd seen Burt Lancaster do it. "And let us also suppose that you really have no interest in it. That you don't want to sell me anything, that you don't need any weapons, and that you're not a cop. Let us suppose that you really are just—how did you put it—doing research."

"Right," said Carl fearfully.

"Journalistic research. What for? So you can publish pacifist articles crusading against landmines in the leading journals of Europe's intelligentsia and make the world a tiny bit nicer and more morally upstanding?"

Carl tried to read the facial expression of his counterpart and decided to subtly nod.

"Let us suppose that I believed you. I don't believe you. But let's suppose I did. Wouldn't even the stupidest journalist first pose other questions?"

"What sort of questions?"

"Questions about the source, the availability, the range? And if it's about the price, wouldn't you have to specify the type?"

"What type?"

"What *type*?" Risa took both hands out of his pockets and put them on the table in front of him. "You asked about a mine! That's like asking: How much is a fruit?"

"But I told you: the most expensive fruit."

"And that's it? The most expensive fruit? That's what people in Europe are interested in?"

"I never said anything about Europe."

"And that's it? You want to know how much the most expensive mine is? Why are you asking me of all people? Anyone could answer that."

"But nobody else answered."

"Any idiot on the street can answer that."

"The problem is that none of the idiots that I asked answered. No more than you. Because they all think that I want something. Or that I'm acting like I want something. But I don't want anything and nobody will tell me."

"Because everyone knows."

"I don't know."

"Because you are an idiot. Look at this!" Risa grabbed the lapel of Carl's yellow blazer. "I wouldn't even tell you your name when you're dressed in this clown outfit. Put on some decent clothes. It's not good for your health to look like that. And it's also not good for your health to be so clueless. Got it? And you're clueless. You have absolutely no clue."

"True. I have absolutely no clue. And you're the expert, which is why I'm here."

"I'm no expert."

"No. Okay."

"Who said I was an expert?"

"Nobody said it. Sorry. Of course you're no expert. But unlike me, you at least know there are different types of mines that cost different amounts. Probably. And you probably also know how much they cost because everyone on the street knows. I'm not after anything more than that."

"My glass is empty," said Risa after a long pause. Carl pushed his own glass, which he hadn't touched, across the table to him. Risa drank it down in one gulp and said: "It's empty again."

Carl tried to motion to the bartender and once again the bartender moved only when Risa confirmed it with a nod of his head.

"All right," said Risa. "You want to know something. And I'll tell you something. Since it is common knowledge on the street. You want the Rolls-Royce of mines. Yugoslavian-made?"

"Yes."

"Or British?"

"Sure. It doesn't matter."

"Or American?"

"Yes, American."

"So you want American ones? The Yugoslavian aren't good enough?"

"It's just about the price. The most expensive."

"The most expensive?" Risa stared angrily at Carl. He jumped up and then sat down again. The scars on his face glowed light pink. Carl, who was unable to hold his gaze, made the mistake of looking away. In the next second he was lying on his back on the floor next to the bar. The scar-faced man was kneeling on his chest, glass broke, and the bartender stood over him holding a broken bottle.

"The! Most! Expensive!" screamed Risa. "Do you really think you can fool me? Do you think I don't know who you are? I knew as soon as you came in the door! I recognize a cop! And you're no cop! What is going through your head, you fucking faggot?" He tightened the shirt collar around Carl's neck. Carl gasped and tried to resist as little as possible. "Do you think you can trick somebody when you don't even know the difference between a British and Yugoslavian mine? Don't treat me like a fool. Because I'm not stupid! Your face stinks. I know you. I know people like you. Should I tell you what you are? You're an intellectual. A fucking intellectual, one of those idiotic communists who's read too much of that French turtleneck shit and now wants to blow something up. Fucking nutjob. I know nutjobs. And you're a nutjob. A hobby terrorist." He loosened his grip and continued somewhat more calmly: "But at least you've got balls. And now you want a mine with a big bang, and I'll tell you something. If you want to start your own little, private campaign of revenge against imperialism in this shitty little town, if you want to blow something up, I mean, if you have nothing more in mind than to start some sick shit here and blow hundreds of Arabs into the sky and drown this place in a sea of flames, *you—have—my—support.*"

Risa's expression slowly relaxed. He took his weight off Carl, brushed the dust off his knees and sat back down at the table. "But don't lie to me. For god's sake don't lie to me. And sit down. Sit down. You're lucky that 'boy' sent you to me and not to some lunatic. If there's one thing I can't stand, it's when somebody lies to me. Got it? Sit down."

Carl buttoned his shirt again, repositioned the bandages on his head and sat down. He was silent.

"It's just that I don't deal in weapons. So unfortunately I can't be of help in this particular area. But what I'm wondering is—purely hypothetically, because you don't want anything and I'm not selling anything—but if someone really needed a mine, why wouldn't you do what everyone else does and go to where they are and just take one? You know where the south is? Where the sun is. You go down there and you'll find as many Claymores as you want."

He pointed with a nod of the head at a man sitting a few tables away who was leaning over and slurping soup out of a bowl with his mouth. The man had no arms.

"Maybe that's why," said Carl. "That's the best kind available?"

"Claymore? No."

"Okay, fine. Let's suppose somebody gets lucky and gets hold of the best kind there is. And he wants to sell it. How much would he want?"

"Two hundred."

"Dollars?"

"For you, a hundred and fifty."

"And what kind is that?"

"Anti-tank mine. Hollow charge, magnetic."

"And that's the most expensive there is?"

Risa was beginning to get agitated again. He looked around the bar. "What the hell are you planning? Isn't a hundred and fifty enough?"

"I thought there were more valuable ones."

"Valuable? A valuable mine?"

Risa put his face right up to Carl's and stared at him. Up to now he hadn't given it all too much thought. This guy was an idiot. A commie. Or an auxiliary policeman. In any event too stupid to be dangerous. But there was something off about him. What in god's name did he want to blow up?

"Are you sure you need a mine and not an atom bomb?"

"I can't say what I need. I really just need information… about cost."

"So now you are satisfied."

"I guess the manufacturers don't exactly get rich, eh?"

"What manufacturers?"

"Of mines."

"There's not a single manufacturer of mines on the entire fucking continent. What does it matter to you?"

"Just a question. I thought there would have to be something else. But a hundred and fifty—"

"Oh, man," said Risa, putting a hand on Carl's shoulder. He spoke very quietly, nearly whispering. "I want to tell you something, my friend. Because you are my friend. We're drinking superb liquor together here. And your brain is apparently no bigger than a pea. And I'm telling you: I, Risa, known as Khach-Khach, do not deal in weapons. There is nothing to buy. But if you want to buy a mine, do not pay more than *ten* dollars. Understand? You can get them for five. Or even less. Anti-tank, personnel, doesn't matter. Only the new Claymores with remote ignition—ten for those. Twenty max. If you're stupid. It's not a Claymore anyway, it just says Claymore on it, but they work just as well, and you can blow an entire bus sky-high with one, everything else is a rip-off. Got it? Can you get all this through your amputated brain up there?"

Carl slumped a bit.

Risa emptied his glass.

"And if you have other crazy questions you want answered, my friend: each answer costs a glass. Or five dollars. That's how much this stuff costs."

He looked at Carl, Carl looked at the bartender.

"Fine," said Carl, "I have one more question. Do you happen to know if there are any mining sites anywhere in the area?"

Risa was silent. He crossed his arms on his chest and pointed with his pinkie at the table in front of him.

Carl pulled his money out of his pocket and laid the notes out in a row. He set aside what he already owed; three five-dollar notes were left. He pushed one forward.

"Do you know if there are any mines around here?" he repeated.

"What kind of mine?"

"Any kind of mine."

"Any kind of mine?" Risa's voice began to rise. "You want to know if there are any mines around here? And why do you want to know that? Are you planning to blow up *any kind* of mine, the existence of which you know nothing about, with the mine of *any kind* that you do not wish to buy?"

"There's no connection. The one has nothing to do with the other."

"Other than the fact that they are both called mine."

"Yes, but that's a coincidence."

"That's a coincidence? What's a coincidence?"

"That they are both called the same thing. I only asked—"

"Since when is it coincidence what something is called? *Mine* and *mine*. You think that's coincidence? Maybe you're not a fucking intellectual after all, eh?"

"I never said anything about being an intellectual. You said that."

Risa grinned as if he had a knife between his teeth. He leaned back, put both of his hands on the edge of the table and said: "Why do you think a mine is called a mine?"

It was a question Carl had never thought about.

"Think about it," said Risa. "If you come up with the answer on your own you'll save five dollars. Why is the one called a mine and the other as well?"

"Because you use explosives to dig out a mine, I would guess. You blow up the stone with mines. Which is why a mine is also called a mine."

"That's your guess. But you're wrong. How long have mines been around? Since the Bronze Age. And how long have explosives been around?"

"So the other way around," said Carl. "Mines were already called mines, and when explosives were invented they were used in mines. And the name got transferred over somehow."

"Ah, transferred over. Somehow! It's not that easy. When something can explode, where is it used first? Not in a mine. On a battlefield. Do you want to keep guessing, or is the next note planning to make a trip my way?" Risa visibly enjoyed playing the teacher.

Carl thought for a while. Several minutes went by. With his index finger he slid the middle five-dollar note forward.

"So you don't know." Looking satisfied, Risa motioned for the bartender to fill the glasses again. "Battlefield is correct. War. In this case: siege. It has to do with siege warfare. When they used to lay siege to forts, and I'm talking here about the Middle Ages… when they tried to break through fortifications, how did they do it? First they built a trench. And then they zigzagged their way up to the walls so they couldn't get shot at. And when they were close enough, down they went, under the ground. And who dug underground? Experts, of course, people who worked in mines. Miners. They dug tunnels, braced everything with wood, and when they were underneath the fortifications they set fire to the wood and ran out, and the tunnels collapsed and the walls above them fell over. That's why a mine is called a mine. Explosives only entered the process much later. Because of the extra bang. But it worked without it."

"Aha."

"And to answer your question—no, I don't know anything about any mines around here. The mountains are worthless. Do you want to blow your last five dollars, too, or is that it for today?"

Carl thought for a long time, tapped the leftover note and said: "Please don't smack me. But do you happen to know if there are any old fortresses around here?"

BOOK FOUR

The Oasis

36

At the General's

On the country of the Nasamonians borders that of the Psylli, who were swept away under the following circumstances. The south wind had blown for a long time and dried up all the tanks in which their water was stored. Now the whole region within the Syrtis is utterly devoid of springs. Accordingly, the Psylli took counsel among themselves, and by common consent made war upon the south wind—so at least the Libyans say, I do but repeat their words—they went forth and reached the desert; but there the south wind rose and buried them under heaps of sand: whereupon, the Psylli being destroyed, their lands passed to the Nasamonians.

HERODOTUS

C ANISADES OPENED THE DOOR to the presidium adequately humbly but also quickly. Beneath lavishly framed verses of the Koran painted in red and gold sat a 200-kilo man, the police superintendent. His pear-shaped face recurred in stunning fashion in the shape of his body: the architect's model and the finished product. Narrow little eyeholes beneath meager eyebrows, small nose and a mouth with a fleshy bottom lip that drooped from the gravitational pull on it, permanently revealing a row of tiny mouse teeth. Two prodigious sagging breasts arched beneath his shirt, his stomach kept him from sitting upright, and a police officer who had seen the superintendent in the shower at the casino knew to report that he'd seen *nothing* at all. That notwithstanding, a color photo stood on his desk showing the superintendent with his rail-thin wife and eight pear children.

Wheezing, he directed Canisades to a chair and then allowed his famous superintendent's minute of silence to follow. Canisades counted to himself. Fifty-six, fifty-seven, fifty-eight. At fifty-nine the superintendent pulled three folded pieces of paper out of a file and threw them onto the desk in front of him with a facial expression that made clear he was not a member of the world-spanning sect of friendly, jovial fat men. He belonged to the other category.

"And don't deny it! Asiz found them in your desk."

Canisades didn't deny it. He recognized the papers at first glance, even if he had no idea what the allegation was that was tied to them. A couple of silly forms from the colonial era—that was the reason the superintendent had called him in? Still, after fifty-nine seconds of silence it seemed advisable to him to go immediately on the defensive. "I can explain, I apologize. Polidorio and I, the night of the forms, the long night of the files…"

"Special Prosecutor for the Virtue Committee! Have you lost your mind? Who thought up this idiocy?"

"Both of us," said Canisades. "Polidorio."

"And who else was there?"

"Just Polidorio."

"Don't tell me lies! There are three credentials."

Legitimate question. Although the correct answer would have been: there had originally been four.

"It was a joke," Canisades took a run at the difficult truth, "and we didn't do anything with them. We showed them to the prostitutes, nothing more."

"The… prostitutes. Aha." The superintendent wrote down some notes. He had a poor short-term memory and couldn't stand it when conversations digressed. When questions and follow-up questions came to him during a conversation he wrote them down so he could work through them point by point.

"You are the lowest-grade officers here," he said threateningly, and Canisades continued on rashly: "Really just a joke. We were overworked and tired, the mountains of paper... and they fell out of a hanging file. Along with a bunch of other things. We did a lot of other things, too. Had to. Just to stay awake. There had been another electrical outage—"

"What other things?" The superintendent's body sloshed forward.

"Other things... various kinds of nonsense. We had to hang in there until dawn and—"

"What other things!"

"Drank, told jokes... had a snowball fight with paper." Canisades left out the race they'd had with the rolling file cabinets as a precaution. "And then, by chance, this stuff from the Virtue Committee. We also took an IQ test. And we were sitting in the dark the whole time because the key for the fuse box—"

"What kind of IQ test? Since when do we give IQ tests here?"

"They were floating around, too. A test that measures intelligence like with a ruler."

"Result?"

"Me, 130, Polidorio, 102."

"Result! Are you intelligent or not?"

"Well, um," said Canisades, "kind of average. Nothing special."

"Kind of average! Do you know what I can do with you and your average?"

He looked angrily at the desk in front of him. He had lost his train of thought, but before Canisades was able to throw the next smoke bomb, the superintendent said: "And what kind of crazy names are these? Adolphe Aun!"

"Polidorio thought it up."

"Is that German?"

"No idea."

"And this, Didier… and Bertrand, are you serious? Are you gay? Are the two of you a gay couple?"

"Sorry, boss."

"You're sorry, you're sorry!" The superintendent's expression suddenly changed, and he ripped the credential into shreds with a placid look on his face. "You are going to do me a favor now. Will you do it?"

So that's what it came down to.

"Of course."

"What do you know about this Amadou? The murderer who escaped from the transporter."

"Karimi is handling that."

"I'm aware. Your assessment."

"Pfff." Canisades wracked his brain. It seemed advisable to cautiously distance himself from his colleague. "Karimi is doing what he always does. He's requisitioned a second bulldozer to squeeze the Salt Quarter."

"Assessment!"

"It's more for his personal enjoyment. At least that's what I would say. This Amadou is too nuts to stay in hiding anywhere for more than five minutes."

Canisades had apparently scored with that assessment, and the superintendent continued in a somewhat more friendly manner: "Amadou is too nuts, *indeed*. But that is exactly the problem. Because he's nuts, he doesn't know how nuts he himself actually is. He'd never have escaped the transporter on his own. And he was also nuts enough not to realize he had a helper. In other words, he didn't only escape our constables, but also our… his… anyway. For forty-eight hours now we've had no idea of his whereabouts. Amadou is untraceable. And what I want and what Karimi doesn't understand, is… that Amadou remains untraceable, capiche?"

The two slits in the flesh of his face narrowed even more. Canisades nodded, put his index finger to his head and then lifted and pressed down his thumb.

"No, no, no!" yelled the superintendent. "Untraceable in the sense of *untraceable*. Am I speaking Chinese or something? Karimi doesn't get it, and you don't get it, either? The poor young man can't help… it's not his fault. He grew up in the most pitiable circumstances, life treated him harshly, he never did anything wrong. It's really not so difficult to understand! He lived in peace in Tindirma until those hippies moved in and provoked him. For a long time Amadou watched calmly… but at some point he'd had enough. Like any normal person. And he overreacted a little. That's one way to put it. It's just that he's a good guy, actually. Amadou. Capiche?"

"You mean—"

"I mean he hasn't done anything to us. It's simple. And we're not going to do anything to him. And you are responsible for that now."

"And Karimi?"

"Karimi is going to give up the case. Has already given it up. And I expect… do you at least understand what I expect from you?"

"To do nothing."

"I guess the intelligence test paid off."

"Do I need to know anything else?"

"No." The superintendent clapped his fat hands together. "You don't. Although I can also tell you that it doesn't matter. There's no particularly mysterious rationale. But it did emerge a few days ago that Amadou is the grandson of the Secretary of the Interior's cleaning woman. Or the Under-Secretary of the Interior, or whatever. It doesn't matter to us. A top dog… and when someone gives me a directive, I stick to it. Capiche? Not like Karimi, the stupid cur. That's why we need someone who can also stick to it. Then the whole thing is simple. You take a few men and set out on the search for Amadou. Who in reality isn't nuts at all, of course, but rather cunning like all of those herdsmen. And how do you look for someone like that? You drive around the area and storm into a few buildings. Capiche? And most importantly you make sure that you drag along a load of press people. The two Americans are still in the Sheraton, the Brit as well—you know him, right? And they should be sure to film the raids. And then you arrest someone at some point, or round up a dozen straight away, and hold onto them until the press whores have had enough. Leave the rest to me. The only thing you have to worry about is to make sure that Amadou isn't hiding in the Salt Quarter. Because that's where he grew up. He knows the area like the back of his hand, which is why every half-assed policeman, including Karimi, would assume he's there. But because Amadou is such a cunning fellow, as we just realized, that's exactly the place he's *not* hiding. Capiche?"

"Capiche."

"Another reason: after Karimi went into the Salt Quarter with his bulldozers yesterday, there was another little uprising. That's no good. You know what I mean. More people died there than Amadou had on his conscience. Which for you means: the entire quarter and beyond into the desert, toward Tindirma, the Empty Quarter, the Salt Quarter, the entire area is off limits. Do we understand each other?"

Canisades nodded solicitously. He couldn't imagine where the protection for the moronic Amadou had suddenly come from. The thing about having a relative who knew the Secretary of the Interior was obviously nonsense. A filthy goat herder from Tindirma didn't have any connections to the Secretary of the Interior or his cleaning woman. If he did, he would have said so at the first police interrogation, he would have screamed it in the interrogators' faces instead of insisting on his innocence for so long. Amadou's family probably got hold of a little money somewhere. And it was flowing where exactly? Not to Karimi, apparently. Directly to the superintendent? Or maybe it really was someone in the Interior Ministry? Canisades was just annoyed that it had bypassed him. The usual protocol provided for the involvement of all the investigators, and he had been the first one assigned the case. Instead, he had been confronted with the embarrassing papers. He had more than a little desire to capture Amadou and chop off his head. It couldn't be too difficult. If it had been necessary to take the search away from someone as useless as Karimi, Amadou was probably sitting drunk and naked in the middle of the road to Tindirma singing off-color songs.

Canisades decided the time had come to look questioningly at the ripped pieces of paper.

"Childish bullshit," said the superintendent, brushing the paper into the waste basket and shooing Canisades out with a wave of his hand. Just before the commissar had closed the door behind himself, the superintendent called him back. The superintendent had his notebook in his hand and tapped on something he had jotted down.

"And that works?"

"What?"

"The Virtue Committee. The prostitutes. I'm a family man, as you know, and very pious. I only ask because I have an uncle… so it works?"

"As I said, we were there just the one time. Or I was."

"Please answer! Do the little whores do it for free or what?"

"They do it for free anyway with anyone of the rank of officer and above."

"What?"

"They always do it for free." Canisades took two steps back into the room. "It's normal. We're the police, after all."

"So why the nonsense with the credentials?"

"Like I said, I didn't try it out. But Polidorio said they did a better job. They did things they otherwise wouldn't do."

The superintendent stood partly up out of his chair, shoved his fist between his fat ass-cheeks and looked at Canisades.

"Yeah, that sort of thing."

"And this? Like this?"

"Yeah, that too."

"And this way?"

"Everything. According to Polidorio."

"Seriously?" Shaking his head in disbelief, the superintendent looked at Canisades, and then at his notebook with equal disbelief. "The little whores!" Then he waved his visitor away without looking up, jotting down notes and underlining them.

A short while later the superintendent was called out of his office by a worker who had come to fix two windows, and Canisades, who had been waiting in front of the mailboxes in the hall, slipped into the office and grabbed the scraps of paper from the waste basket and put them in his pocket. One could never be too safe.

Afterward he called the Sheraton and had himself connected to Mr White, the British journalist, in order to ask him whether he would like to take photos of the imminent arrest of Amadou. And as he was still on the phone the superintendent waddled by again and placed a note on the phone. Canisades covered the mouthpiece of the phone.

"Forgot. You have to do this, too," whispered the superintendent. "Because you kept interrupting me. But there's some fellah whose two sons are missing. Apparently murdered. In the desert. One shot, the other beaten to death. It's all in the note. The road to Tindirma, the old barn where they used to distill liquor. Just stop by there first. Then Amadou. Capiche?"

37

The High Priestess

I have no feeling for feminine virtues, for a woman's happiness. Only that which is wild, great, shining appeals to me.

KAROLINE VON GÜNDERRODE

"NOT A MINE, because there's no mine here. Not landmines, because no reasonable person on earth would kidnap a family and threaten them with death over ten or twenty dollars. And to round out the improbable, a fortress beneath which mines were dug is also out," said Helen with a crooked smile. "Because there are none. Assuming the guy with the scars didn't tell you any bullshit, which seems to be the case. So the only thing left is a mine as in pencil lead."

"Or the coin. Or the book."

"Isadora Mine? And her son Aimable-Jean-Jacques? No. I don't buy that."

"What if it's not the book but something hidden in the book?"

"I still don't buy it," said Helen. "Not because a book can't be valuable. But because Bassir said *mine*. Seventy-two hours and I'll have the mine back. A barely literate idiot who spent hours twisting a letter-opener in your hand wouldn't say mine if he meant a book. He would say book. Same with the coins.

He would say coins if he meant coins. Maybe we'd be better off concentrating on Cetrois."

"How can we do that if we don't even know where to look?"

Helen stood up with a shrug, went over to the phone and arranged a long-distance call to America. While she was waiting to be connected, Carl gathered up all the things he'd had with him in the desert and placed them on the table in front of him. The empty wallet. The crumpled tissue. The ring of keys. The pencil.

The pencil was six-sided and coated in a shiny green lacquer. Embossed in gold print at the top of it was 2B. The tip was broken; a thin sliver of wood was peeling away.

"Forget it," said Helen.

"Just a moment," said the telephone operator.

Carl put down the pencil and picked up the wallet, examining the empty compartments but finding only grains of sand. He put it back down next to the pencil. He unfolded the tissue out of which sand also trickled, stared at it, then balled it up again. A few minutes went by. Then he stood up, grabbed a breadknife from the kitchen and began to cut the pencil. Helen watched him, shaking her head. As the stub got shorter he pressed it down with the heel of his hand and kept sawing at it with the knife until there was nothing more left than a pile of thin wood shavings and crumbs of graphite that he stared at pensively but which held no secrets.

"Don't be an idiot," said Helen when she saw him tap his finger in the graphite dust and then taste it with the tip of his tongue.

Suddenly the phone line was dead. Helen banged on the cradle and after the operator also didn't respond for several minutes she got up and said to Carl: "I have to buy something else. You want to come with me?"

But Carl didn't want to go. He sat leaning over the table, his head in his hands. He reached for the tissue again and tried for a second time to unfold it without ripping it to shreds, and held it up to the light as if he might have overlooked some secret markings.

Helen closed the door behind her with a sigh.

When she returned with two heavy bags of groceries in her arms, she thought she heard voices. She carefully put down the bags, walked quietly around the bungalow, crouched behind an overgrown bougainvillea and pushed aside a blooming bough so she could peer at the terrace.

Just a few meters away, Carl was sitting on the ground with his legs crossed, staring intently at something in front of his lower leg. Facing him, turned away from Helen, a long-haired, broad-shouldered woman. Or a long-haired man? Both of them had their heads lowered, and a voice well known to Helen said: "That is the Tower. And now the Hermit. And this is the Chariot, the Star... I always find the Star a beautiful card. The star in the unconscious, I'll explain in a minute what that means. And on the five, that is... the Hanged Man," said Michelle, quickly removing the card and replacing it with another.

A questioning look crossed Carl's face. Apparently he didn't agree with the switch, and Michelle, who tried to hold the gaze of his coal-black eyes, felt a wave of painful empathy wash over her. She knew what that meant. It meant that she had to be on her guard.

From the moment this handsome man agreed without hesitation to have his fortune told, from the moment he asked her with unsure gestures to join him on the terrace and offered her a coffee, no, to be honest, from the moment he opened the door to bungalow 581d with a bloodstained bandage on his head and a broken cigarette dangling from the corner of his mouth, she'd been overwhelmed by the unspeakable sadness in his features.

In fact, overwhelmed to such a degree that Michelle Vanderbilt had decided at that moment not to let his life affect hers. She made decisions like that in fractions of a second. Even if not everyone would believe it and even though on the surface, as she well knew, she often seemed the opposite: Michelle was a very resolute person. Strength of will and decisiveness she had inherited from her Italian grandmother; on the other hand, and in apparent contradiction to those traits, she had inherited an exuberant temperament, spontaneity and a typical Italian warmth from her, as well. Cerebral and carnal at the same time. And when the situation demanded it, Michelle was resolute. And made decisions. And from extensive experience she also knew that the best way to navigate the jungle of complexity was with intuition. And her intuition told her from the first moment: be careful. Be careful in the face of a handsome, suffering man with a bandage straight out of a painting and sad eyes, be careful, Michelle Vanderbilt!

As a result of a short telephone call that she'd had with Helen just after her visit to the commune, she also knew who this man was. This was the man who had suffered some sort of memory loss. What did that mean?

First of all, it meant that Helen, with her characteristic lack of discrimination, had probably entered a sexual relationship with him, which the man with the provisional name of Carl denied for the time being. Or at least had denied it a few minutes before. Second, it meant that compared to the pain Michelle was dealing with, the prodigious pain of having recently lost four friends in a massacre, an amnesiac, who had lost nothing more than his identity, should be a comparatively happy man. And third, this comparatively happy man could or would, if he wished, take advantage of this difference in their respective levels of pain to his benefit. If Michelle allowed it. But she would not allow it. This decision was made in the first instant. And when a decision had been made, nothing was going to change it.

"Because otherwise it means, in this combination, ultimately, if you take it literally, with the Tower here, and Death," said Michelle as she hurriedly laid out the rest of the cards and then stared with wide eyes at the resultant combination, "with Death in the near future... which is normally a transformative process, Death as metamorphosis, as transition... although we... if we, I mean..."

Michelle watched, bewildered, as Carl took the Hanged Man from her hand and put it back down in its original place.

"That's the Hanged Man," she said, "normally I take it out because if we leave it lying there, when things stay like this, it could also mean that someone really will die... or something... no, somebody... because, when we asked, when we said just now what it was about, and it was about you, right? That means *you*..."

"And if you just remove it from the deck nobody dies?"

"I didn't say anything about dying! Not necessarily, but hang on... let me think. Just a moment, please. Like I said at the start: they are patterns that are more like force fields, and you can never say it's like this or it's like that. It's just that this card, I mean, Death... and the Fool and the Devil, and Justice here, in this order, the way they are laid out... I've never seen anything like it."

Michelle ran her hands through her hair. She tried to buy time. Looking like a child who was about to start crying, she contemplated the problematic combination. But the cards left little doubt.

Michelle felt it, and she could feel that Carl also felt it.

"Anyway, everyone has to die. It's not like it says when, right?"

"It is the near future, nearly present. I mean—"

"And what if I'm already dead?"

"Let's start again from the beginning," said Michelle, her voice trembling. "I want to try to see the whole thing again. There we have the Star, which I always think is good, a good card, that means that you were full of hope at the start... and that's true. You talked about how you woke up in the barn—"

"And what if I'm already dead?"

Helen couldn't see Michelle's expression from behind, but she saw her friend's body stiffen, one hand over the cards, the other on the back of her head, the elbow pointing to the sky.

A full ten seconds went by. Then Michelle realized what Carl was getting at. Helen suppressed a groan.

"If you're already dead!" Michelle shouted excitedly. "Of course! If you're... you really, you're really a special person," she said, tapping her forefinger excitedly on the Hanged Man, which lay directly next to the Tower (that was nearly a ladder, a ladder in a barn!) and Death followed shortly thereafter: Carl's memory loss. The death of his previous identity.

Michelle shook her head, stunned. "It's sometimes crazy how precisely the cards know things! And that you figured it out... I'm not just saying this to flatter you. But I'll be honest, I knew from the moment you opened the door that you were a very special person. A *very* special person. And you have a great gift for the cards. The Tower, the Hermit and the Chariot... didn't you also say something about a car with four people in it? Because these are the external influences. Though the Chariot could mean a search, the search you are on... the search for your identity. And the Hanged Man, I usually remove that, like I said, but it actually only means a reversal, a reimagining of one's own situation, and the fact that you are in essence the Hanged Man yourself since you're dangling from the ladder... it's just crazy." Her index finger moved with new confidence to the right, into the future. The death of identity, the Fool, the High Priestess and at the end,

Justice. The cards no longer had an obvious connection; now concentration was needed.

Michelle concentrated and said: "The Fool on the seven, that is the self, as you yourself see it… and Justice, that's the outcome. What does it mean? It means the end of a period of suffering. A new beginning, I would say… though the card is turned the wrong way, so it could mean the opposite, I mean, if we don't turn it around, and you… no? There are differing schools of thought, I usually turn them around."

Michelle looked up at Carl with the trusting look of a child, but he shook his head obstinately.

"Well, if you don't want to… so, Justice could also signal the beginning of a period of suffering when it is turned this way, but really it only means the *possibility* of pain, that is, if you do something wrong. It always depends on you. Tarot shows the outcomes, but you choose which one, I mean… what exactly it means to have the High Priestess on eight and pain…"

"The High Priestess of pain, obviously that's me," said Helen stepping through the bougainvillea onto the terrace and walking past the pair of them into the bungalow. Carl looked up embarrassed, and Michelle sank her head like a little kid who'd been caught playing doctor. She knew what Helen thought of the cards, of divinatory knowledge and spirituality, and it hit her at that exact moment: these were exactly the characteristics of the High Priestess, cleverness and cautiousness—that could transform negatively into rationalism and intellectualism. If the card was upside down. And it was upside down.

38

Battle of the Chieftains

"Allusions, there are allusions in this book," I thought, "I want my money back."

MAREK HAHN

As it happened, directly following and probably provoked by Helen's visit to the commune, Michelle had decided to leave this gruesome and violent continent behind for ever. She had scraped together some money from friends to buy a return ticket to America; now she hoped Helen would throw some in as well. Unlike Helen, Michelle had never been interested in material things, and the luggage she had with her consisted almost entirely of spiritual items: an amulet with the tooth of an ouz that Ed Fowler had given her as a parting gift, the tarot cards, her favorite books and in addition, as would soon be revealed, a stack of comic books that Michelle had wrapped in a handkerchief and took with her as they all left together for the beach early that morning.

There was little going on there at that hour. A shroud of mist hid the sun. Helen and Carl sat down on a large towel and talked as Michelle lay down on her stomach a little way away and immersed herself in the colorful stories. There was something in her bearing that seemed to be trying to pre-emptively head off any criticism of the quality of her reading materials. After she'd flipped through a few pages she noticed out of the corner of her eye that Helen had got up and headed back up to the bungalow. Carl stayed behind, lost in thought, and barely acknowledged Michelle's friendly gaze. Michelle tried to focus on her reading again. The sand slowly filled with other people. Helen returned after about a quarter of an hour with a piece of paper in her hand and sat down right next to Carl.

"Listen up. There's no Cetrois," she said in a muted voice. Carl took the note out of her hand and looked at it.

"There's nothing. There's nobody with that name. The name doesn't exist. I called France, America, I called London, friends in Spain and Canada, I asked people to look in their phonebooks. Not a single match. No Cetrois. No Cetroix, no Sitrois, no Setrois... nothing."

Carl squinted at the list of crossed-out place names: Paris, London, Seville, Marseilles, New York, Montreal. Beneath them were a dozen different spellings of the name, likewise crossed out.

"You have friends everywhere," he mumbled, impressed.

What he found most impressive was the fact that someone could call all those places from the little holiday bungalow and how quickly Helen had managed to get all the research done. Though something about the list still bothered him, seemed mistaken. But what was it? Was it the alternative spellings of the name? Or Helen's handwriting, using all capital letters except for the letter n? He thought for a long time about what it was, but he couldn't put his finger on it. (And when he hit upon it three days later, it was already too late.)

While Helen stretched out in the sun again with a sigh, putting an arm across her eyes to block the sunlight, and talked about francophone Canada and her friend in Paris, Michelle studied the backgrounds of the images in her book with a look of devotion on her face. She'd probably read the thing twenty times before, but there were always new, wonderful details to be found in the backgrounds. Now and then she took a shy glance at the other two, and when their conversation had ebbed and Carl seemingly coincidentally caught her eye, she offered him one of her books. Carl opened it absent-mindedly. It was called *Asterix and the Big Fight.*

On the first page was a map of France with a Roman flag staked in the ground and a large magnifying glass above Brittany; beneath that, a Gallic village surrounded by four Roman camps. It seemed familiar to Carl. Likewise the personal descriptions on the next page seemed familiar.

While he tried to make sense of the sometimes oval, sometimes round speech bubbles, he heard two women's voices behind him, one familiar and one unfamiliar. He didn't turn around. He saw that Helen had her face pressed into her towel and her arms wrapped around her head as if she were trying to block her ears.

The unknown voice spoke in a strong German accent about Duisburg, coal-mining and culture; the voice he recognized, which belonged to Michelle, chipped in adjectives.

The first panels showed the contrast between the Gauls, adapted to Roman civilization and somewhat ridiculous, on the one hand; and on the other, the traditional, boar-hunting good guys. A druid lost his power to brew magic potion along with his memory after a blow to the head; a second druid named Amnesix, who ran a sort of psychology practice in the forest and who tried to blame his counterpart's condition on a stone monolith, also lost his memory.

"Reality is a mirror," said Michelle's voice, "through which you reach your hand."

Both druids suddenly knew nothing and nobody. People put kettles and herbs in front of them in the hope that they'd be able to unconsciously remember their magic formulas, but all the potions they brewed produced nothing but facial discoloring and small explosions and caused a Roman legionnaire who served as a guinea pig to float away like a helium balloon. A fat Gaul thought he could dispatch the memory loss with a second blow to the head with a monolith; a light-bulb went on above his head. A little Gaul spoke three angry exclamation marks.

"... Akasha was the only one. But my four best friends, they're in a better world now, I'm positive of that. When you've lived in the desert for a long time, your perspective changes."

In the end the surprising cure, a sickly green drink brewed beneath bubbling captions which caused hair to stand on end and eyes to redden and steam to shoot from the druids' ears, was recognizable even to uninitiated readers. The final panel was a party, a bonfire and a gagged troubadour, and even this seemed vaguely familiar to Carl. He was baffled. But the thing that baffled him the most was the druid Amnesix's secretary. Very slim, very pretty and very blonde, she seemed to Carl the spitting image of Helen. He took a quick glance at the original, then looked from Helen over to Michelle, and there was another person as well. A pale, female person.

With a sociability she had likewise inherited from her Italian grandmother, Michelle had a few minutes before she made the acquaintance of a German tourist who quickly proved to be surprisingly wise. The German woman was wearing a green and yellow striped bathing suit, spoke broken English and worked as something she described as "a woman for everything". Michelle showed her the tarot cards, she talked about growing crops and the weather, and the German complained about politics. Not that she had any time for the Israelis, but what had happened in Munich, it was awful! Of course one could understand the Palestinians' despair, could understand why they attacked the Jews abroad, after all, what other chance did they have to get the attention of the global public? Which is why the killings were a consequence of international politics, of the attitude of the community of nations—but still! There were innocent people among the victims. Was there anything more cynical than "the games must go on"? The two women shed a few tears. A breeze kicked up. Michelle couldn't remember the last time she'd had such a good conversation. It felt pleasant to lean on the shoulder of the German, who smelled a bit of mayonnaise, to surrender her feelings to her while looking out at the ocean beyond which lay America, which, Michelle had just learned, was also run by Jews. At least economically speaking. This German knew all sorts of things. With a finger placed pensively on her lower lip, Michelle suggested asking the tarot cards about the Palestinian conflict.

She spoke in a low voice, but the people on the other towel weren't paying attention to the two women anyway. Carl had just asked Helen some question, Helen had answered excitedly, and they were already deeply engaged in another mindless conversation about the man named Cetrois. Cetrois here, Cetrois there.

"What is it with you two and this Cetrois?" called Michelle.

She began to explain the placement system and the extension of the Celtic cross to the German, who incidentally was named Jutta. She touched on the ancient Egyptian origins of the cards, the Major and Minor Arcana, the principle and its inverse, and all along she intermittently repeated her question.

"Do you want a piece of chocolate?" Helen answered.

Without even dignifying her childhood friend with so much as a glance, she laid the Hierophant on the one. Why did Helen always have to make it so obvious how little she thought of her spiritual powers? Not to mention the fact that Helen knew damn well that Michelle never ate chocolate: it went straight to her thighs.

"I'm just asking! Cetrois here, Cetrois there."

"There is no Cetrois," said Helen angrily.

The waves whooshed on the sand and the seagulls screeched above their heads. The magnificence of the natural surroundings would have calmed and relaxed anyone else. But not Helen.

"Of course there's Cetrois," said Michelle. She held up the next card solemnly and then turned it over. The Magician on two. The Hierophant as the starting point and the Magician in the ascendancy was never easy for Michelle to interpret. You deceived yourself if you mistook religiosity for religion here. "I know him," she mumbled, laying Temperance in the third position. Temperance next to the Magician, it didn't make any sense at all. She'd have to wait. Often the connections became clear only with context. Next came the Hermit, the Star, the Chariot... and finally Michelle lifted her head in the awful silence surrounding her.

Helen and Carl had jumped up and were staring at her. She hadn't expected so much attention. She calmly laid out the rest of the cards. The Wheel of Fortune, the Lovers, the Emperor...

"What?" yelled Helen.

"You know him?" yelled Carl.

What kind of tone was that? She let a few seconds elapse before she looked up again.

"You know him?" Helen yelled.

"Yes, of course," she said, shrugging her shoulders at Jutta, and Jutta nodded knowingly. "But nobody asked me."

She put on a pouty face and contemplated with a friendly, self-possessed look the friendly, self-possessed Emperor on the ten. Would the Emperor bring peace to Palestine? That was the question. The cards seemed to suggest an interpretation, but unfortunately for only half a second. Then Michelle was yanked around by her shoulder. Helen. Next to Carl. Screaming. Up to this point it had been a triumph. But now it was suddenly unpleasant. Michelle would like to have refused to answer or at least dragged her feet about answering the questions that had been so extremely impolitely posed, but if her years in the commune had taught her one thing it was that being yanked by the shoulder represented the end of friendly communication. What was that great saying? The cleverer person gives in!

"The more clever person gives in," said Michelle. She tucked a stray strand of hair behind her ear and began somewhat fearfully because of Helen, who was standing over her, to report that she knew this Cetrois, yes, of course she knew him, and why wouldn't she? Okay, not directly, but... how did she know him? Yeah, how indeed, as if she couldn't figure it out herself. It was obvious given the fact that she hadn't spent time in the last few years in any other location than the commune, and it was there... no! Not a member of the commune, good god, he wasn't a member of the commune... and what was the meaning of all this? Could they please stop shaking her by the shoulder and just let her talk? She was in the process of explaining, and it wasn't as if a second or two mattered. She could only talk if they stopped badgering her, that's the way she was, Michelle, she was how she was, and if they didn't calm down, then it wasn't going to work...

Helen slapped her in the face. It was the first time in her life she had been smacked like that, and it remained unclear as to whether it had a therapeutic effect or not. If one takes an aspirin and the headache subsides, one never knows what really caused the cure. And what emerged in less than a few seconds was that Michelle didn't know who this Cetrois was. She had neither seen him nor spoken to him... no, not personally. He had visited the commune shortly after the massacre. On behalf of an insurance company. He was apparently an insurance agent.

"At first we thought he was a journalist, then a detective or something like that. And then perhaps an insurance representative. Agent. Though that's what the others said, I was asleep at the time. Now leave me alone."

They didn't leave her alone.

"What insurance company?"

Michelle fidgeted, coughed and looked around. All these probing questions. Once again it wasn't enough just to know something. Everything always had to be precise and substantiated, the typical Western affliction. And she didn't know exactly anyway.

"I only know what the others told me," she explained, emphasizing her words with dramatic gestures. Because it had been a dramatic series of events. "I don't have anything to do with it! It was a few days after the horrible attack. The police had searched through everything, for hours, and then this man showed up. Because Ed Fowler... Ed, Eddie, you met him, he had some sort of insurance policy from that English company—"

"Life insurance? Theft?"

"Yes... no. Could have been. He had some sort of insurance policy, don't ask me what it was. I've never paid attention to material things, and Ed himself didn't pay attention to such things either. It was his family, they took out the policy. He's from a filthy-rich family, and they must have wanted, they apparently took out a policy on him, how should I know what kind?" Michelle paused briefly, though only ever so briefly. "In any event, it was in all the papers, the rattan suitcase and the money. The golden suitcase full of cash. Everyone saw it, thousands of people were standing in front of the place and saw that dirty Amadou with the suitcase... and you know how the Arabs are. Gold and jewelry! You wouldn't kill four people for nothing. But it was just a rattan suitcase. Mine, by the way. Had to make them in the fourth grade, yellow with red stars on it. The stars fell off though. And somebody had filled it with paper money. East German. Which wasn't worth anything."

"How much was it worth?"

"A couple of dollars is what Ed said."

"But nobody knew that?"

"Yes, they did. The police—at first we told them everything. In the initial shock. And then Ed realized… they became dollars later on. It'd been dollars in the case. And valuables. Gold."

"And then you tried to scam the insurance company. Is it possible that it was Lloyd's?"

"I don't know if it was Lloyd's. I had nothing to do with it! I shouldn't even have told you about it." Michelle lined the cards up on the patterned bath towel in front of her. It suddenly looked grim for the future of Palestine. She did not want to continue the conversation.

"But you didn't see him?"

"No."

"And how do you know he was named Cetrois?"

"Because the others told me, for god's sake! The ones who talked to him. They said that was his name."

"And he showed up there, knocked on the door and introduced himself as insurance agent Cetrois."

"Yeah… no… no, not as an insurance agent. But that's what we figured out, we're not idiots! I mean, he introduced himself as… I don't know exactly, a journalist or something, I don't remember any more. But it was clear that he was no journalist. That he was there about the money. Because he kept asking about it. Money, money, money! Money here, money there, money everywhere! And now you tell me why *you're* interested in him." Michelle fought back tears and Jutta, who had sat by sympathetically quiet the whole time, took her hand.

39

No Body, No Murder

I mean, of course I'll move my camera. But only if I see a reason to.

CRONENBERG

A LARGE BUILDING and two small ones, in the middle of the desert. Canisades followed tire tracks that split off from the road and led to the buildings. Laundry had been laid out to dry on the roof of one of the small huts. The giant barn was falling apart, sand dunes were creeping up the walls. A garbage pile had attracted two birds. Presumably the estate had stood on arable land twenty or thirty years ago, irrigated either from the oasis or by means of a spring right here that had since dried up. There could be only two reasons for the fact that someone still lived here. Either the owner was crazy, or smugglers were using the old barn for storage. Canisades parked his car. An old fellah immediately staggered over toward him. Based on physiognomy alone, the "crazy" hypothesis was gaining in plausibility. Half blind, squinting badly, one eye glazed over, dull white.

"Misery! Misery!" he began to yell. "Are you the police? No amount of money in the world can make up for it. My sons! Thousands of dollars, thousands and thousands, my noble sons, light of my life, the sun in my winter years! Cradled in my

253

arms, both of them, the young princes. I beg you, no amount of money on earth."

Canisades, who had no intention of trying to make up for anything in the world with money, took a step back.

"Mohammed Bennouna? This is your property?"

The man nodded dramatically. "Dead and gone! Pain in my earnest heart, I do not lie! Once a paradisiacal garden, now a filthy desert. An infidel… fallen from above… this is how he slayed them, like this! With both hands." He swung an imaginary pulley block above his head. "May he rot in the depths of hell… I will not curse. The pain. Allah has challenged me with the toughest test, which is just. But my golden boy, my silver boy, murdered, defiled, gone…"

"Where are the bodies?"

"Can one live with these thoughts? That is what I ask myself. For the broken skulls of my sons, how could it… under no circumstances. The moped is gone, my sons are gone, the pillars of strength in my old age… invaluable! And that doesn't even include the pain in my soul." The fellah fell to his knees in front of Canisades and wrapped his arms around his legs. Despite the scent of alcohol coming off him, it couldn't have been the only explanation. Canisades first tried to step out of his grasp, then cursed at him. The old man crawled after him on all fours.

"Show me the bodies. You reported two dead. And stop drooling on my shoes."

The fellah kept jabbering and it was only when Canisades took out his car keys and threatened to drive back to Targat that he collected himself. Still piteous, but relatively coherently and with grand gestures, he took Canisades around and reported what had happened; or at least what he believed had happened. Apparently he had had two sons. The older was twenty-one (light of my life, the sun in my winter years, etc.) and had been hit with a heavy object (the old man suggested a pulley block);

the younger was sixteen, had run off into the desert and been killed there. On the same day.

It remained unclear how the old man had arrived at this explanation, since he had not seen the murders, and, as it soon emerged, there were no bodies or any signs of the crimes. And the supposed perpetrator, whom the old man persisted in calling an infidel fallen from above, seemed vague and hazy. On the one hand the fellah claimed to have seen him (and even to have wrestled with him *mano-a-mano*), on the other hand he couldn't give any further details about his person except that he was an "infidel" and had "fallen from above". It took a while before Canisades realized the entire episode had taken place not outside beneath the open sky but inside the barn, where the man hadn't fallen from above but rather jumped down from someplace; the proof that he was an infidel apparently rested in the very fact that he was able to commit such a crime. But that was basically it as far as the facts were concerned. Nothing more could be culled from the tirade by the physically and mentally reeling fellah.

After Canisades asked to see the bodies for the fourth or fifth time and then finally jangled his car key again, the old man suddenly changed his strategy, put a puzzled look on his face and tried now to express surprise at the ineptitude of the police. Four days. He had waited four days! Rats came, the sun was burning, so obviously he buried the dead. While the other one off in the desert, like he said … where he, too, was beaten to death … otherwise he would have returned. The gold son, the silver son, light of his old age.

"But you buried one? Show me the grave."

Tears ran down the old man's face. He crumpled to the ground, repeating in other words what he had already said ten times before, and Canisades didn't have to think for too long as to why the fellah was blathering so horribly: obviously he had not only lost track of the one son in the desert, but also had no idea where he had buried the other one. Either that... or he hadn't buried him.

He spoke so persistently about money not being any or much of a consolation for his pain and whatever other nonsense, that Canisades finally gave up on seeing a body and asked to see ID or birth certificates for both sons, because he had a feeling they did not exist.

With great confidence, the old man led Canisades into the smaller of the two huts and showed him an array of written and printed pieces of paper. Canisades was able to decipher some dubious letters, bottle labels, recipes and a TV magazine. The man was illiterate.

Except for a path down the middle, the entire hut was knee-deep in junk, and it smelled worse of alcohol than the owner. The fellah finally pulled a photo out of a little box and handed it to Canisades: the souk in Tindirma and a confused mass of people. A peddler in front of a primitive wooden stand full of bottles, glasses, carafes, canisters. Not far from the peddler, two small children. The large, blackened thumb of the old man trembled as it hovered above the three figures. Me. My son. My other son. Dead and gone.

Both children in the picture were wearing girls' clothing and their faces were soft and feminine. The old man looked a bit like himself.

"Birth certificates," repeated Canisades.

The emotional anguish returned, but instead of any official papers the only thing that turned up in the end was a foul-smelling straw sack that had supposedly been the boys' bed.

What gave the fellah credibility was that he reeked of alcohol and blathered on about sins. It was unlikely that an old boot-legger would invite the police onto his property for nothing. Nobody would voluntarily bring the police in here. The old man's despair was probably real, and the fact that two of his children had disappeared was within the realm of possibilities. But did that really mean they were dead? Had they ever existed? Perhaps, thought Canisades with a look at the photo, the girlish sons disappeared or died years ago, and it was only in the old man's alcohol-pickled brain that they occasionally lingered on, turned up again and disappeared all over again. Final-stage Korsakow.

"Shall we have a look at the barn?" Canisades suggested in order to cut things short. As expected, the old man balked. He didn't want to show him the barn at any cost. With that, the case was closed. It wasn't clear whether there had been a crime; but if there had been one it was obviously what Canisades had suspected from the start: one of the two golden boys had killed the other and run off into the desert. It was no great loss. He wasn't motivated to pursue any punishment.

"No body, no murder," he said, citing the textbook. "As long as you don't know where you buried your boys, there are no boys. And as long as you don't find any bodies here, kindly avoid calling the police again. Otherwise we'll take a look at what you're brewing up there in the barn, got it?"

"There, that's where I buried him, there!" yelled the old man, pointing hopelessly out of the window. Somewhere there, somewhere nearby, not far away, one could look around. His finger trembled, and a shadow scurried past the window. The old man's eyes were far too weak to notice the shadow, and Canisades had his back to the window. The shadow moved toward Canisades' car, stood there and then ducked.

40

The Invisible Royal Brigade

Some people—and I am one of them—hate happy ends. We feel cheated. Harm is the norm. Doom should not jam. The avalanche stopping in its tracks a few feet above the cowering village behaves not only unnaturally but unethically.

NABOKOV

AMADOU HAD HIDDEN in the Salt Quarter for two days, then the bulldozers showed up. He lived on the street, slept on the beach, he was starving. Going back to Tindirma, where he had last lived and where he had shot four people, was the riskiest and stupidest move he could make, but he soon didn't know what else to do.

He reached the road early in the morning and marched easily along. But he had overestimated his own strength. His bare feet hurt, thirst tortured him with every step. When he saw in the distance a large building and several small ones, he crept toward them. At first the property seemed deserted. He was unable to find a spring. Staggering from one hut to the other, he came across an old fellah stretched out on the ground as if he were dead. One eye glazed over, white. But his chest rose and fell. Amadou didn't dare wake the man. Next to his head sat a canister. Amadou quickly grabbed it, took two gulps and then spat it out. Hard liquor.

Coughing and gasping, he rummaged around the rest of the buildings and the barn, and since he didn't find water anywhere, he tried in the end to slake his thirst from the canister. He figured it would work in small sips. It didn't. It burned horribly.

He found a few barrels, a ladder and a broken pulley block. Above him a hatch to the attic. He was just trying to figure out how he could get up there when he heard a sound in the distance.

Peering out of a crack in the wooden wall, he saw a car approaching from the road. It passed only a few meters from his hiding spot and stopped in front of the huts. The driver (light-gray suit, tidy appearance) got out, and shortly later Amadou saw him talking to the fellah. They got to the point immediately. The old man fell to his knees in front of the driver and Amadou heard the word "money". Again and again the old man assailed the driver, again and again the talk turned to money and compensation. Finally they disappeared into one of the huts. Nothing happened. The driver's side door of the car was standing open.

Amadou waited for a little while, then crept to the car and into the driver's seat. The key wasn't in the ignition. He tried to rip off the housing around the ignition lock with his fingernails, then froze when he thought he heard voices. He jumped into the back seat, ducked and covered his head with a sweater that was lying there. Then the voices died down again. He cowered there for a few minutes. Then he anxiously lifted his head and began to search the car. He pulled a few things out from under the driver's seat. Some wire, a pencil, a bottle of water. He drank the water, carefully broke the pencil into two pieces of equal size, twisted the ends of the wire around the two pieces of the pencil and wrapped them tightly. He tested the contraption by pulling on the two halves of the pencil. It made a sound like a guitar being strummed.

"… but I can't do anything on my own. Don't blather at me, light of your life, sun of your winter years! I believe you, I believe you! And the experts will be notified today, I promise. Our special unit for complications… colleagues of the highest level of competence, the Invisible Royal Brigade. They'll find the grave, no question. They always find everything, and then they'll do a full investigation. Without a body we can't do a thing. And your other son, that'll be thoroughly checked out, yeah… of course, on my mother. Do you think I'm telling you nonsense? You're not telling me nonsense, I'm not telling you nonsense, that is my understanding… no, of course not! They're called that because they're *secret*, not because they're invisible. Nobody is invisible! But you'll see, they'll be here soon, and everything will get cleared up. And it goes without saying that you must not speak to anyone about this. Now stop licking my boots… on Allah, on my mother, on anything you want! Go away. God in heaven."

Canisades got into the car, started the engine and headed for the road without glancing back at the old man with the alcohol-blasted brain kneeling in the dust. The wretched stench of hard alcohol hung in the car as if his clothes or the car had absorbed the odor during the short amount of time there, which was hardly possible. A phantom smell. But he didn't think about it too much. And a minute later he was dead.

41

A Yellow Mercedes with Black Upholstery

Ben Trane. I don't trust him. He likes people, and you can never
count on a man like that.

ROBERT ALDRICH,
Vera Cruz

MICHELLE WAS LYING in the bed in her room on the sixth
floor of the Sheraton Hotel and sobbing. Even though
the bungalow had more than enough space for three people,
Helen had insisted on putting her up in the main building,
and Michelle, who knew what that meant, was in her heart of
hearts relieved. Her farewell to Africa was now also a farewell to
Helen, the end of their in any case never really existent friendship. The final humiliation came when her kindergarten friend
counted out the exact fare for the airport taxi and gave it to her,
and Michelle, who some might have said lacked a few things
but certainly sensitivity and intuition were not among them,
no longer doubted Helen's real motivation: jealousy. Raging
jealousy. Helen wanted the handsome Arab man to herself. She
could have him. Michelle wasn't interested any more.

While they slowly began to decompress, and in the relaxed
lethargy that followed the crying fit that lasted for over an hour,

Helen and Carl found themselves headed toward Tindirma. Right up until they reached the edge of the desert, they debated who should enter the commune and make inquiries. Helen won the argument. Michelle's last words tipped the scale. They were very distrustful of outsiders, even more so since recent events, and the atmosphere was so bad that an Arabic-looking man like Carl would probably not even be granted entry. Helen, on the other hand, was at least known as her friend, and obviously it would be best if she herself went with her, but she knew, this horrible place… not for anything in the world. Not to mention that her flight was already booked for the next day, and so on and so forth. She was sorry. Wild horses couldn't drag her there.

In the end she had asked Helen to bring a number of things she had forgotten at the commune, and Helen tossed the scrap of paper with the list on it in the waste basket as they left, saying she could manage to keep two and a half things in her head without a note.

Out in the desert the day was hotter than it had ever been. Carl tried rolling up his window to keep out the hot wind. But it didn't help. A mirage made the kissing camels look as if they were floating above a sky-blue lake.

"There's something over there," said Carl looking to the left, and Helen asked whether he wanted to get out.

"I don't know."

She let the car roll to a stop.

While Carl climbed up the dunes, knee-deep in sand, Helen re-did her ponytail while holding the hairband in her mouth. She saw the stumbling figure reach the highest point of the dune, put a hand to his forehead and shrug his shoulders. Carl wasn't sure whether he saw anything. In the far distance a light-gray spot hovered in the air, probably a rock outcropping made to look as if it was moving by the fluttering heat. Endless desert all around. On the horizon a few dark points which Carl recognized as the barn and huts where all this misery had begun. The urge to go there again alternated with the urge to get back to the car as quickly as possible. For a moment Carl thought the light-gray spot was actually moving now… but then he heard the horn of the pickup and he went back.

Helen parked the pickup in the small street in front of the commune, right by the big gate. Carl watched from the passenger seat as she crossed the courtyard, knocked on the interior door and was let in by a young woman with long hair.

He waited. The heat in the car was unbearable, and after a while that seemed to him an eternity, he got out and bought a bottle of water in a little shop nearby, without ever taking his eyes off the gate of the commune for even a second. He continued to wait. Finally he knocked on the door of the commune.

Nobody answered it, but higher up in the building a hatch opened and a dark-skinned woman with short hair told him it would take a while. Helen wants you to know it's going to take a while longer. Ed was taking a nap, and they had only talked before, and now they were talking in the room of the ouz… and what did he want anyway? No, that's not possible. There was no way they could let him in, and could he please leave the courtyard, it's not public property, they didn't like people in the yard, and by the way why was the gate open? He should shut it behind him.

The hatch closed.

Carl waited a few seconds and then knocked again.

"Can you get Helen for a second?"

The shadow of a woman behind the window making defensive gestures. Nothing happened. He called Helen's name, he walked around the courtyard. Finally he got back into the Honda, searched for a pen and paper and wrote to Helen that he had tried to no avail to get into the commune and was now going to have a look around the nearby streets. He put the note on the driver's seat, looked at it for a second and added an arrow, just to be sure, indicating what direction he was heading: *Down the little alley and past the bread, oranges and pottery*.

Due to the heat the street wasn't very busy. It smelled of fresh-baked goods, it smelled of oranges, and the potter and his assistants were discussing the Olympic question. A beggar was asleep in the gutter. A peddler hosed the remains of fruit and vegetables from the sidewalk, and his cheerful, even-tempered face took on an air of put-on anger as he turned the hose on a group of children creeping toward him in water-soaked shirts. A pregnant woman stood nearby looking as happy and beautiful as the evening. A boy talked with an invisible dog.

Carl made his way down the street toward the mosque, walking alongside parked cars. Now and then he turned to glance behind him. He felt uneasy. Heavily veiled women looked down, and the grilles of the parked cars stared at him like cross-eyed rabbits, emotionless insects, glasses-wearing intellectuals and bureaucratic meat-eaters. Fish-mouthed chrome-flashing Citroëns with pneumatic suspensions gleamed next to old street-beaters with peeling paint. Lilac, mustard-yellow, pink. Carl blinked and grabbed his head. At the end of the row of parked cars a jug-eared Mercedes whose back rear tire sat atop a crushed soda can. It was a green can with white writing: *7Up*. Ants swarmed into the triangular opening. The muezzin called. On the right, men sat in a café rattling dominoes. On the left, backgammon was being played: "And then we turn the plate around and rinse it from the other side, and we repeat that seven times."

A peddler squawked the price per kilo.

"Come on. Come here, have a look, don't be shy, look what I have, take a look, lookie-lookie, come on, step right up, check it out, check it out, have a look, no, no, get out of here, yes, come here, yes, yes, come on over, yes, have a look, have a look."

Without realizing what he was doing, Carl had stopped. He felt a strange sensation in his head and ran his hand over his seven-day stubble. When after a while he snapped out of his thoughts, he noticed that he had been staring for several minutes at a shop window. He focused his gaze and saw a man puttering around inside. It was the window of a barber shop.

On an impulse he went into the shop, sat down on one of the upholstered chairs and asked for a shave. A hot, moist towel landed on his neck. The barber was a small, nimble man and as he scraped Carl's whiskers away he talked, the very cliché of his profession.

Carl didn't listen, and when now and then he did catch something it seemed to be about some criminal case. He stared at his own image in the mirror, and his image stared back at him with a look of concentration bordering on emptiness. A criminal case and its complexities. Carl closed his eyes and saw the green soda can in his mind's eye, beneath the car tire, only he didn't see it the way he had during his walk but rather from the other side, and in the manner of a photograph: square, reduced in size and secured in the photo album of his mind with bright-colored tape.

The barber told him to take it easy. Carl grabbed both arms of the chair and then yelled at the man to be quiet and put his hands over his eyes. A soda can beneath the rear tire in a photo with slightly rounded edges… it wasn't a photo. It couldn't be a photo. The top and bottom of the image weren't parallel. A trapezoid-shaped image with rounded edges and the sharply defined image of a soda can beneath a car tire. What the hell was it?

"And ever since he'd been on the run," the barber continued unfazed. "And if you ask me—turn to the left, please. If you ask me, he had help, from the top. A police transporter like that is no cardboard box. A friend of mine saw him in the

Empty Quarter! He was crossing the street... nearly finished, sir. I asked why he didn't do anything. And do you know what he said? He said what do I care about the Nasrani. So I said, I get it, but what you didn't think of is that there's a reward, and then he said, four Nasrani, he said, the reward could never be large enough to get me involved with that... that's no argument, I said, there's four less, so you might as well take the reward, gone is gone, dead is dead, I said, and then he said..." said the barber and then he said no more. The straight razor in his hand hung in the air for a few seconds above the upholstered chair, which was now empty. A coin jingled into the sink and a towel hung weightlessly in the open doorway for a split second, thrown by Carl over his shoulder as he ran out; then it fell to the floor.

Carl ran the entire way back. As he ran he wiped the shaving cream from his face with his sleeves. He ran past the row of parked cars as if he were following a train of thought backwards. The car with the jug-eared mirrors was still there, and it was still a mustard-yellow Mercedes 280 with black upholstery. A pink Ford in front of it, a lilac Ford behind it. He went around the car. Then he squatted down by the rear tire and looked at the 7Up can and the ants going in and out of the opening. Was it this? Was this the image? He tried to pull the can out from under the tire, but he couldn't. He looked inside the car. He didn't see anything unusual. The seats appeared to be made of leather. There was a brown briefcase holding a packet of paper in the passenger-side footwell. The window was cracked slightly open but the door was locked. A normal car with normal things in it... He kneeled down by the rear tire and looked at the aluminum can. He tugged on it.

"What are you doing?" Two young men were now standing behind him. They weren't police. One was the merchant whose shop the Mercedes was parked in front of.

Carl waved them away and lost himself again in looking at the soda can. He looked at the stream of ants. He looked at the street. He looked at the aluminum.

"Hey, man." Aggressive tone. Very aggressive tone.

"I'm only interested in the can here," said Carl, trying to wave them away like flies.

"You tried to open the door of the car."

"So?"

"Is it your car?"

"What does it matter to you? Is it your car?"

"No, it's not mine. But is it yours?"

"Yeah, it's my car!" said Carl, annoyed. The can moved a little. He bent part of it upward so he could grip it better, and yanked at it with all his strength. He didn't even know what he wanted with it. Ants crawled on his fingers.

The men behind him were whispering. Then one said: "Hey, what makes you think you can talk like that? What makes you think you can talk that way to us?"

Carl again motioned behind his back at them. They should get out of here.

"If it's your car, why don't you just move it forward a little?"

Carl felt something hit him in the back, apparently a soft kick. He thought for a moment and then said: "Good idea." He made a show of pulling his keys out of his pocket as he stood up, patted the dust from his knees and went around the car in the hope that the bothersome pair would take off.

And they did in fact move away, but then they stopped and watched him suspiciously. He stood by the driver's side door and made as if he were sticking the key into the lock while at the same time acting as if he had noticed something interesting at the end of the street. It worked. Out of the corner of his eye he saw the two men wander slowly off. The key slipped into the lock and, with a smacking sound, opened the central locks.

42

Nothing of Importance

ALICIA: My car is outside.
DEVLIN: Naturally.

HITCHCOCK,
Notorious

H E NEEDED A FEW MINUTES to calm down. Once he had settled into the driver's seat his gaze fell first on the right-side mirror, which showed a crushed soda can beneath the rear tire in a somewhat trapezoid-shaped, gleaming chrome frame with rounded edges.

It overwhelmed him. He slumped with his forehead against the steering wheel and the car's horn startled him upright again. He took three or four deep breaths and reached for the briefcase of papers at the foot of the passenger's seat, let it drop and again slumped down. All the tension in his body had seeped out. He didn't feel well. He didn't feel well at all. Suddenly he was no longer sure whether he wanted to know who he was. If he wanted to know at all who he was. A few minutes went by. He looked out of the windshield at the narrow street, the light traffic and the two men, who had sat down at a nearby café and were watching him from there. Next to them a boy punched at the air yelling: "Ouz!"

Dull echoes wafted over the buildings.

The contents of the briefcase were disappointing. The stack of paper that dropped out was blank, about twenty pages, white, unlined. Along with the paper a worn map of Targat, an empty glasses case and nothing else.

Carl went around the car to the trunk. Inside was a colorful ball and a wrench. In the glovebox were two brown glass ampules and beneath the seat a pair of sunglasses, a pen made of polished metal, two bottle caps with the Coca-Cola emblem on them and the handle of a razor. Other than that, just a little notebook and a black wool cardigan with empty pockets. That was it. And none of it suggested at first glance anything about the identity of the car's owner. Not at the second glance, either. The two glass ampules were nine-tenths full of a clear fluid. There was a barely legible label on one of them that seemed to indicate it was a morphine concoction. The notebook was blank, like the stack of papers. The pen wrote with blue ink. The clip of the pen had "Szewczuk" written in script on it. Apparently the name of the manufacturer.

Carl took the pen apart, wrote another squiggle on the notebook with the ink cartridge and then put it back together. He unfolded the map of Targat. In the upper-right corner, contrary to geographical reality, was an inset with Tindirma. He opened the glasses case and closed it again and felt the exterior. He felt the ball. It was sewn together out of many different-colored segments, a ball for children... blue, red, yellow and a washed-out orange that was reminiscent of cut-off fingertips, if one had the inclination to think of it for some reason. The ball seemed to be filled with wood shavings or stringy foam rubber. Carl pushed on it and kneaded it and tried to feel for anything inside. He bit the ball and ripped it open. Wood shavings and more wood shavings. Finally he took the briefcase and then all the other items one after the other, stared at them and turned them around in his hand. He looked through the glovebox again and then under all the foot mats. Beneath the passenger seat he found another small pencil stub and a receipt listing among other things the words for fruit, water, eggs and beef. He looked at the piece of paper as if it were a transmission from another planet and then began to cry.

He threw the wads of wood shavings out of the window with energetic swings, stuffed everything else he had found into the briefcase, locked up the Mercedes and went back to Helen's car. His note was sitting unmoved on the driver's seat; no sign of Helen. The entrance to the commune's courtyard was now barred with a wooden gate. Carl shook it and peered through the cracks. He called Helen's name.

A man armed with a club trotted down the street behind him, screaming. More shouting could be heard in the distance.

Carl sat down in the pickup, crossed out his previous note and instead wrote to Helen that he still didn't know who he was but that they would probably be driving back to Targat in two cars. He had found his own car, a yellow Mercedes with black interior, down the street in the direction of the arrow he drew, and he would wait down there for her at a café within sight of the car. He wrote that he was very happy and unhappy at the same time and that he desperately hoped that nothing had happened to her, Helen. Then he crossed out the word "desperately" and in the end crossed out the entire last bit, since he realized it was written more to himself than to her. He read through the whole note again. In tiny letters and winding several times around corners, his barely legible sentences covered the paper. He pulled the little notebook out of the briefcase in order to rewrite it all from scratch, and when he put the notebook on the dashboard he noticed in the sideways light grooves pressed into the top piece of paper.

He rubbed across the grooves with the pencil stub and a word became visible: CETROIS.

Nothing more. Carl stared at the writing for a long time and then wrote the word again next to the original. The two versions looked exactly alike. It was his own handwriting. Why had he written down that name? Had he been looking for Cetrois before his memory loss, too? Up to that point he had assumed that the person he was seeking was some sort of friend of his, a buddy. In any case, someone who shared his fate, being chased by four idiots in white djellabas. But why would somebody write down the name of a buddy or a confidant—and only his—in a notebook? To visit him? To call him? Nothing sensible occurred to him, and the longer he stared at the letters the more sure he became that Cetrois was no friend of his. At least not one he knew well. Probably a total stranger. Helen had likely been right after all.

Carl waited and drank an iced water in a little sidewalk café with a view of the yellow Mercedes. As he tried once again to remember first coming to and fleeing the barn and, without even noticing that he was doing it, made complicated geometrical shapes in the air with his hand, he noticed a woman at a nearby table staring at him. Smiling at him. Had his gestures attracted her attention? Or did she know him? He looked away, and when he looked back at her she was still smiling. Was it possibly a woman from the commune that Helen had sent after him? No, she didn't look the part, not with her neat, tidy clothes. And besides, it seemed to Carl that he'd seen her enter the café from the opposite direction.

Carl had become accustomed to nodding at total strangers in the last few days. He smiled back. She immediately got up and came over to his table.

"Hello," she said loudly and distinctly.

"Hello," he said.

"You look good," she said, as if they hadn't seen each other in a long time, and to him it made him think—she knew him!

Even if she apparently didn't know him well, since before she sat down in the empty chair she visibly hesitated.

The urge to immediately confide in the woman was unbelievably strong. She had an honest, unattractive face, and nothing about her suggested any sort of danger... or did it? Was he fooling himself? What if she was an acquaintance of Adil Bassir's, a messenger perhaps, sent to remind him of the ultimatum? But no, no, that was nonsense. Her face was far too harmless. And how would she have found him?

He decided to count silently to twenty and then open up to her. And if he let himself talk to her perhaps he would be able to figure out (or she might just tell him) who he was... and who she was. It shot through his brain: maybe she's my wife? But a wife who had been missing for days and who had been threatened with rape and having her son's finger cut off would greet her husband differently. No, she was a close acquaintance, Carl decided, maybe his lover. Though again, she seemed far too honest and upstanding, not to mention ordinary, to be the lover of a violent criminal. The frizzy perm alone. And there was something off about her eyes. Her gaze was as unsteady as his, and when he got to twenty and communication was still stalled, he considered the possibility that she too had lost her memory. She smiled, then looked pensive, then smiled again. Then she looked pensive again. Finally she blushed.

"Don't make me do it all by myself," she said.

Perhaps she was mentally ill.

"I'm happy to see you," he said, making an effort to stay calm while his feet twitched uncontrollably beneath the table. His urge to flee was almost as strong as it had been when he first came to in the attic of the barn. Should he not give more credence to his own body? The woman, who noticed his anxiety, threw her head back and laughed theatrically.

"There's a hotel nearby," she said.

Carl nodded.

She blushed again. She's insane, he thought, she's talking totally incoherently… no. No, it had to be something else. Probably something so simple and obvious that he was missing it. He decided to stop playing games and tell her the truth. It was too late for anything else. He leaned across the table and whispered: "I know it sounds crazy, but I don't know you."

The expression on her face didn't change at all. Had she not understood him?

"Are you married?" she asked.

"What?"

"I know," she said, running both hands through her hair. "I know that it's not normal. The hotel is over there."

She stood up and walked off without looking back even once. Carl, whose hands were trembling so badly he barely managed to toss two coins on the table, followed her. The waiter licked his lips.

43

Sirens

Images of humans, how horrid. Humans don't interest me, if I may be frank.

LUHMANN

T HE HOTEL CONCIERGE didn't even lift his head as he put the key with the number 7 on the counter.

They went up a shabby staircase, down a shabby hallway and into a shabby room. The woman immediately ripped her shirt off. Carl had never seen anything like it. A naked breast… another naked breast… at least if he had he couldn't remember it.

He was powerless.

"Talk Arabic to me," said the woman as they were lying next to each other.

"Why?"

"Talk to me, you wild man!"

"What?"

"Speak Arabic!"

"What should I say?"

"Anything."

"I can't think of anything," whispered Carl in Arabic.

She nodded, slowly closed her eyes and pulled him on top of her. Her face took on a rapturous look. "Keep going," she moaned, and Carl, who noticed she didn't understand Arabic, called her a stupid cow, an ugly old woman, an idiotic perm-girl. As the room rhythmically wobbled back and forth, his gaze fell on the yellow blazer that he'd thrown next to the bed. It made him think of the items in the briefcase, particularly the map. He couldn't keep his mind on the deed at hand. He closed his eyes and tried to imagine it was Helen. He stuck his head in the woman's armpit and knew: this wasn't the first time. He had a wife and child, he had done it with his wife. He forgot to breathe and gasped for air. Finally their motion stopped.

While the woman was showering, he lay on his back in bed and stared at the ceiling. The woman returned with a slam of the door. He heard her drying off, heard her pulling on her clothes. As she did she softly talked the whole time. She said he was a merciless lover, a hard fuck, an animal. She'd said the same sort of things the whole time in bed, too (and she repeated them now perhaps not to seem unstable to herself, as she appeared to be nearly in tears). In parting she approached him and put a finger on his lips, then on her lips, and said: "If we happen to run into each other again: you understand. We don't know each other."

She looked at him until he nodded. Then she left, and he remained lying on his back staring at the ceiling. He could make out the remains of crumbling stucco in all four corners of the room. Concentric rings of water stains extended out from the windows. Their calligraphy-like contours meant nothing to him, which was exactly what most other things and faces meant to him, and he thought about the secret significance of this analogy. He closed his eyes.

After a while he heard sounds from the next room. A moan, as if two people were going at it. Carl didn't want to hear it and buried his head in the pillow. The couple's moan grew louder, though technically speaking only the woman was audible. His mind had added the man. It could also have been two women pleasuring each other. Or a woman and two men. Or a woman on her own. The number of possibilities unsettled him.

He thought about the fact that the same sounds could have been heard a few minutes before from the room where he was now, and suddenly it occurred to him that it could be not just the same sort of sounds but the same actual sounds, the moaning of the crazy woman, that were bouncing back through the walls in a delayed echo. Like a tape recording that someone in the next room had made of them and now was playing back, an echo of his own no longer present lover. He sat up in bed, an ear to the wall. The moaning rose rhythmically for several minutes and then suddenly dropped an octave like a police siren passing by while a second voice wheezed breathlessly, muted. Then it was quiet again.

Carl was relieved to have heard the man's voice, which was clearly not his own. He had spoken Arabic only at the beginning of the whole thing, quietly, and then tried to be silent; out of embarrassment on multiple levels. First, he didn't know the woman, or at least he was quite sure he didn't. Second, he was hiding something from her, though it was hard to say exactly what. And third, he knew that people made noises during sex, but he wasn't sure what sort of noise he would make, and worried about having to hear a bunch of appalling, unknown sounds coming out of himself.

Without meaning to, he fell asleep. Half asleep, he thought he heard an actual police siren go past, told himself that they were after him… and fell back to sleep. Something was picking painfully at the back of his skull. He blinked his eyes open and saw a beam of light in the shape of a crescent moon wander across his retina. Quivering, the crescent glided leftward into the night, quivering. In his dream he saw himself drinking a glass of green tea. He saw himself sitting at a green table, looking at a green building that had a white flag waving atop it. A jeep drove past, he suddenly remembered the soda can again... he jumped out of bed.

From the pockets of his blazer he ripped the ampules, the notebook, the map and the other objects. He spread the map out on the bedspread, used his finger to find the spot where he currently was, and suddenly froze. The hotel was marked with a blue squiggle. The squiggle was somewhat ambiguously scrawled on the entire area... it could also have been marking the commune rather than the hotel. Or another building on the street. No, surely it was the commune! His heart beat wildly. Then he discovered another mark a few streets away, then he saw that places all over the map were marked and circled. "Who would do that?" he said to himself. "A mailman?"

The bulk of the markings were in Targat. Carl counted nearly thirty blue markings. But none of the key places, that is all the places that had played a certain role during the most recent few days of his life (the Sheraton, Adil Bassir's villa, Dr Cockcroft's practice, etc.), were marked. The bar where he had met Risa wasn't marked. The workshop where the two men had trapped him wasn't marked. Helen's bungalow was nowhere to be found. He picked up the pen and circled an area in no man's land in the desert, approximately where the barn was. It was a different shade of blue. He stepped to the window and for a second time took apart the pen and held the cartridge up to the light. Metallic silver, maybe five or six millimeters in diameter. At the front end a narrow bit with a nib fitted over it, and the back a blue plastic plug that proved impossible to open. Here, too, a threadbare imprint of the maker's name: Szewczuk. He looked closely at all the individual parts of the pen again. Two sheaths, a jagged piece of plastic, a compression mechanism, the cartridge—mine in French—the ring and the nib. He pressed the nib between two of his fingers, it bent and then sprang against the window with a click.

Outside, a floor below, Carl saw a group of men running through the street. A straggler trailed along behind them, limping. Carl put the end of the cartridge in his mouth and watched them go by. A distant scream could be heard and then he suddenly screamed himself... a string of fine droplets of blood landed on the window.

He had ripped the plug out of the end of the cartridge with his teeth and hurt his lip in the process. The cartridge fell to the floor. He hopped around on one leg in pain. Then he picked up the cartridge, held it up to his eyes and tried to peer into the dark, open end. He turned the open end downward and shook it. Two long metal capsules with rounded edges fell into his hand. The capsules looked exactly the same. They were perfectly cylindrical, dull silver, and even at first glance appeared so different from the other parts of the pen that Carl didn't doubt for a second what he had found. Around the middle of each cylinder ran an inconspicuous seam. He washed the blood from his lip in the bathroom, then he got dressed and ran out.

44

La Chasse à L'Ouz

Not a single progressive idea has begun with a mass base,
otherwise it would not have been a progressive idea.

TROTSKY

THE FIRST THING he saw out on the street was a young
man with a sickle over his shoulder, followed by others.
There were more and more of them. Carl tried to make his way
toward the commune but soon it was impossible to move up the
street. For no discernible reason, groups of people suddenly
drew together and broke apart again. Young men blocked the
street, ran around, linked arms with each other. At first there
was no discernible goal, but distant calls soon drew the crowd
in a certain direction. Carl saw picks, shovels and axes. Most of
the stream of people was made up of young men the same age
as him. But there were also a few old men, and little children
with bows and arrows ran around the edges and got squeezed
up against the buildings. Not a single woman on the street. Carl
stood still, tried to take a few steps against the stream but was
pushed, jostled and carried along. The blazer where he had
stashed the pen he held firmly against his arm. Pushing his way
to the side of the street, he tried to turn into side alleys, but
streams of people were coming out of all the side streets as well.

Above him a window opened and a toothless old man yelled at the men. Some immediately went toward the window, spitting, jumping up and trying to hit him with fists and sticks, before a woman managed to yank it closed.

The stream along the main road met up with other streams from various side streets and spilled out into the souk. There any sense of direction was lost. The center of activity seemed to have been reached and also to be empty. People wandered around in circles. Formations that had held on the way there fell apart. There was a strange absence of enthusiasm from it all, and Carl found himself reminded of a show he and Helen had watched on TV the night before. An animal show. A glittering, silvery school of fish forms and quickly shifts, and with these shifts communicates second by second the onset of a shark attack. All the faces around him were blank with anticipation.

Carried along, Carl wondered where all the children and adolescents were; he found them on the roofs around the souk, where they were standing with bows and arrows. He himself gave up trying to go against the flow. Just don't stand out.

The restlessness became ever more palpable, and suddenly it seemed as if a standstill had been reached that slowly worked its way backwards through the crowd. A brief hold-up, then a sharp cry, and the crowd shot out of the center of the souk, crashing like a wave into walls and buildings and washing into the surrounding side streets. Carl found himself carried up a set of stairs in the tallest building around the souk, blocked in by other bodies.

From his raised position he looked out into the middle of the nearly empty souk. A couple of clubs and a lonely sandal lay abandoned there, and a slim teen with a contorted leg and eyes wide open, the loneliest person in the world. Bracing himself on his elbows, he crawled along the ground and kept looking around in panic—until his gaze stopped at a side street.

A murmur went through the crowd. Something popped out from between the buildings, something that looked like a giant, dark snout with trembling whiskers.

"Ouz! Ouz! Ouz! Ouz!"

The snout floated a few centimeters forward. Thick, bushy fur, a hanging lower jaw, two gigantic tusks in its mouth. Short, thick legs dangled from the sides of the beast. It bore no resemblance to anything Carl had ever seen before. The triangular head would have looked like a marten's except for the fact that the marten was as big as a truck. Scattered screams—and with blood-red, beady eyes the beast swung in Carl's direction. It seemed to fix on him for half a second. Then, accompanied by the roar of the crowd, it shot across the souk and into a side street on the far side. Men holding up axes followed immediately after it. A few seconds later the beast re-emerged from another side street, ran across the souk again and began to run around in frenzied circles with an ever-larger crowd of people following it. Horror had given way to an urge for action, the urge for action turning into daring and bloodlust. Behind the field of people stumbled the old men, the slow ones, a child on crutches and a few excited unarmed people. Whenever the beast made unexpected moves they screeched excitedly, and when the crowd surged backwards a few were caught beneath and trampled.

A bare-chested man stood directly in its path and was tossed aside by the tusks. Others wounded the flanks of the monster and slumped away, celebrating, accompanied by a rain of arrows. After just two trips across the souk, the animal's pelt was peppered with barbs. The archers stopped waiting for the target to approach and instead took long shots when it was out of range. The arrows clattered to the ground, pattered against building walls, or stuck in the backs of foolhardy attackers. The people who had been trampled tried to crawl away. Nobody helped them.

The ouz was finally dispatched not far from the stairs where Carl was standing. One wave of attack after another broke over the barely still-twitching lump of fur; even the weakest and smallest took part. The giant cadaver fell over sideways and stuck a foreleg in the air like a chimney. A hind leg lay broken and in the beast's dented, ripped-open flanks wooden lathing and beams were visible. But the crowd continued to beat on the mechanical parts, and as the hindquarters caught fire Carl spotted four men in ritual vestments fleeing from the slit-open belly of the beast. Robbed of their original goal, the angry crowd threw itself against the priests and pummeled them until they were able to throw off their vestments in the jostling mob and get away.

Carl stood on the stairs as if paralyzed, clenching his blazer. The men around him didn't move, and he was able to watch for several minutes as the remains of the ouz moved around in the middle of the crowd. Like a giant molecule being pounded by tiny, invisible particles, it moved across the square, flaming. Kicks and shoves moved it along, a teen jumped onto its back and his shirt immediately caught fire. At first it seemed as if the flaming monster was simply rolling around by chance, here and there, but the increasingly loud and strident screams eventually made clear that a goal had been found. With clubs, stakes and kicks the men pushed the fireball into a side street and up to a wooden gate.

Carl couldn't see what was happening beyond, but through the billows of smoke he thought he saw a few Europeans trying to push back the rolling ball of fire with ridiculous kung fu moves. Which obviously did nothing. The ouz was shoved up against the gate, which immediately broke out in flames. Soon stacks of wood and garbage in the inner courtyard of the commune had also caught fire.

Two women attempted to put out the flames with a very green, very silly-looking garden hose. Another one in jeans and a batik shirt shoved bags, carpets and heavy boxes into a large Land Rover. Helen was nowhere to be seen. The flames were lapping at the main building in no time. The Land Rover took a running start in order to break through the inferno but got stuck in all the debris. A triumphant cry went up again and only died down when the fire jumped to other nearby buildings. Two streets of houses were completely burned down.

With trembling knees, Carl made his way down the stairs during all of this. Everything seemed to move toward the fire, and he pushed his way sideways past the crowd and into a small side street. There to his relief he could see that a little blue Honda was not among the small number of cars still parked in front of the commune.

But his relief was short-lived. Because as he looked down he realized his blazer was gone. The arm on which he had been holding it was still cocked, but it was empty. He first ran back to the stairs, then across the souk. A small boy armed with two spears was carrying something bright yellow in the crook of his arm. Carl caught him right in front of the fountain. The boy, not even ten years old, clasped his prize, screaming, scratching and biting, punched Carl in the stomach and tried to escape. Carl shoved him up against the wall of a building. He ripped the blazer out of his hands and searched the pockets for the pen. The pen wasn't there. Not in the right pocket, not in the left. On all fours the boy tried to crawl away. Carl knocked him over with a kick to his side. He put a foot on the boy's throat while he continued to search the interior pockets of the jacket, then the side pockets again. A group of men with clubs began to assemble around them. "He stole something of mine! The filthy little brat robbed me!" yelled Carl as his foot continued to hold down the wriggling boy. Suddenly his finger felt the pen in the right pocket that he had already looked through three times. At that same moment something hit him on the shoulder. Carl reeled, pushed the crowd aside and rushed off with the blazer pressed to his chest.

He heard yelling and screaming behind him, and among the voices was one that sounded very different from the rest. Shrill and questioning. Turning around, Carl recognized a familiar face... but he wasn't sure. His pursuer seemed equally unsure. And in this uncertainty they recognized each other. It was one of the four men in the white djellabas that Carl had seen on the day he awoke in the barn. The man had a nondescript face, was again wearing a white djellaba and was clearing his way through the mob with both arms. And he didn't seem to be alone. Behind him the fat man was also pushing his way through the crowd. Behind him the short one.

45

Moon and Stars

Enthroned on high in heaven he looks down upon us
And pitifully points humankind the way;
And his starry writing upon the heavenly firmament
Declares joy in this world and adverse destiny;
But humankind, world weary and aggrieved of death,
They don't ask about such writing, they read it not.

PIERRE DE RONSARD

CARL'S FIRST THOUGHT was to make for the Mercedes. But even if he managed to reach the car, unlock it and start the engine, he wouldn't be able to move a meter in the clogged streets. He ran without thinking, and when an alleyway appeared on his left that opened onto the desert, he sprinted down it.

Luckily for him, his pursuers turned out to be poor runners. It seemed he had lost them by the second or third dune.

Carl ran and the hot sand that pressed in between the straps of his sandals burned his toes. The memory of his last flight through the desert welled up in him and filled him with panic. Should he keep running? Take a roundabout route back to the car? Bury himself again?

No, he didn't want to return to the oasis at any price. The situation there was too unclear. Maybe later. The sun was only two hand-widths above the horizon, soon it would be dark, then he'd be safe in the desert. It was twenty or thirty kilometers to Targat. He could make it.

Out of breath and with bad cramps in his side, he stopped. He looked around. Silence. The first star appeared and he thought of Helen. He hoped, no, he was sure, that she had left the commune before the situation escalated there. She could have found his note telling of his discovery of his car, and she was smart and pragmatic enough to save her own skin, knowing he had done the same. With every step he stomped more heavily in the sand. His brain kept conjuring up dreamlike images, suddenly he saw himself in a happy future. He had a blonde, unbelievably attractive American wife, two or three hazy children and an interesting career. Neighbors and friends held him in high regard, he was a valuable member of society, and then his neighbor was bitten by a poisonous snake. Carl saved his life by tying off his arm and sucking the venom out. Then four men in djellabas dropped out of a helicopter, shot him and raped Helen.

What made a brain like his come up with daydreams like that? But he was unable to pursue the question any further. He was exhausted from walking and let his thoughts keep running in the same grim circle.

Since Dr Cockcroft had first insinuated—even if only ironically—that Helen could be his wife or lover just having a laugh, Carl had been unable to give up the hope that sooner or later everything would resolve itself in a quick, witty dialogue. When the various plot strands reached their most convoluted, Verdi arias would ring out and champagne corks would pop. Helen would reveal some plausible reason for her game of cat and mouse, and his memories would come out from behind heavy curtains like guests at a surprise party.

He nearly tripped on the corpse. Or the part that was sticking out of the sand. A foot without a shoe, a black sock, a light-gray pant leg. Carl took a horrified step back and looked over at the slope from which he had peered out into the pale-gray hours before. Then he looked to the other side. Sure enough, there on the horizon the gable of the barn was visible.

Holding his breath, he dug out the body and turned it over with two kicks. A man of indeterminate age, with open, sand-blind eyes on his face. The cause of death was clearly a thin wire cutting through his blood-encrusted throat. Both ends of the wire were wrapped around broken halves of a pencil. An Adolphe Menjou-style mustache sat like a dusty butterfly on the rotten flower that was his blue-tinted face.

It could only be Cetrois! So the four men had caught him. While Carl was acrobatically scaling his way down the ladder from the attic. But where was the moped?

Carl walked around the dune in a small circle, then in a larger one, and a larger one still. No moped to be seen. Instead, the parallel tire tracks of a car, leading toward the barn. He crouched down beside the body. Perhaps this was my friend, he thought. Perhaps my enemy. He took a handful of sand and let it trickle into the mouth of the dead man.

Then he searched the pockets of the pale-gray suit, but someone seemed to have been there before him. No keys, no wallet, no personal items. Only a used piece of gum wrapped in foil and, in the right pants pocket, a few shreds of reddish paper. The shreds had been typed on. Carl tried unsuccessfully for a few minutes to assemble them like a puzzle in the palm of his hand, then put them in his own pocket. Once again he went through the pockets thoroughly, and he found a few more scraps of paper and took those, too.

He stayed crouched next to the body, looked from time to time at the horizon and rocked back and forth on his knees like a little child. Then he felt in his pocket for the pen, took it apart and pulled the blue plastic plug out again with his teeth. He let the two metal capsules drop into his hand. It seemed to him as if they could be screwed apart at the seam. But not without a tool. He could barely grip the little cylinders with four fingers, and as he was fiddling with them he thought he saw motion in the desert out of the corner of his eye. He stared at the orange-colored edge of a dune behind which the sun was setting. But everything was calm. He stood up carefully, turned around slowly 360 degrees, and again saw the shadow. Now the orange light was broken in one spot, and at the crest of the dune stood an animal about the size of a marten. It didn't move.

"Aha?" said Carl softly, moving toward it. The animal took a cautious step to the side. Carl thought he saw something transparent on its head. Very slowly he advanced a few steps toward it, kneeled down, stretched out his hand and made a quiet clicking sound that he thought was reassuring. With its head cocked slightly to the side, the ouz trotted up to him. It had two sharp incisors that protruded over its lower lip. In this miniature form it didn't seem at all threatening. As he got closer, the thing on its head turned out to be a crumply piece of paper through which the last rays of the sun were shining. Carl saw letters on the paper. He carefully put a hand under the animal's belly and lifted it up. It didn't move, it just sniffed and made little peeping sounds. "Shhh," said Carl. "Shhh."

The strip of paper had been strapped to the animal's head with a rubber band, and Carl turned the ouz around so he could read what was there: *A man may be born, but in order to be born he must first die, and in order to die he must first awake…* he didn't get any further. With a screech he flung the animal to the ground; it had bitten him. The exact imprint of its two rows of teeth were visible on his wrist, and blood seeped from the wound. It had already run down to his elbow and dripped in the sand. The animal trotted off in no hurry, turned around to look at him from the top of the next dune and disappeared into the twilight.

The pain was incredible, as if the wound had become instantly infected. Carl squatted in the sand, and as he went to brace himself with his right hand he realized that it had been quite some time since he had stopped holding it in a fist. He had dropped the metal capsules. He saw only gray on gray around him, sand and pebbles and dark splotches of blood and otherwise nothing. He ran the flat of his hand over recesses and crevices. He didn't move his feet out of fear of burying the capsules deeper in the sand. He turned his upper body to the right and the left. Cautiously at first, and then increasingly desperately, he ran the sand within his reach through his fingers, raking the surface with ten fingers, feeling the throbbing wound on his hand, and soon was barely able to make out his own forearm in the dying light. The sun had now sunk deep beneath the horizon; the needle-width sickle of the moon was following quickly behind it. Carl remained crouched in his own footsteps for a long time. Finally he braced himself with his unwounded hand and stood up, stretched out sideways and used his foot to draw a circle around himself, the radius of his body length. Then he straightened up, thoroughly brushed off his hands, feet and clothes and took a big step out of the circle. He lay down a few meters away and went to sleep.

46

The Electrification of
the Salt Quarter

Art thou pale for weariness
Of climbing heaven and gazing on the earth,
Wandering companionless
Among the stars that have a different birth,
And ever changing, like a joyless eye
That finds no object worth its constancy.

SHELLEY

DOES ANYONE KNOW what it is like to experience a
night in the desert, alone? To someone accustomed to
spending his nights in a bed, in a house, surrounded by other
houses and people, it is difficult to imagine. And it is even
more difficult to imagine the way the blackness and gloom
tears at the spirit of someone who for days has been able to
recognize no more about himself than he would about a blank
piece of paper.

It's often said that barbarism is the opposite of civilization,
but a more fundamentally suitable word would be loneliness.
It may have been silent and windless during the day, but the
silence grew oppressive during the night. Lying on his back in
the sand, the throbbing, blood-crusted hand on his chest, Carl

looked at an expanse of stars the likes of which he had never seen before.

He saw the twinkle of distant suns that were nothing more than specks of dust in space, and to know that he too was lying on just such a speck of dust and the only thing separating him from eternal, weightless nothingness was a couple of grains and pebbles, a minuscule cluster of matter... the disconcerting scale entered his consciousness and mixed with his fear. Fear that someone could have followed him (or would follow him at first light), fear that he would have to flee without first being able to find the capsules, fear that an overnight sandstorm could blow everything away... and above him the insult of thousands of galaxies to which none of it mattered at all.

Satellites passed overhead in the night. Something larger, maybe an airplane. The image of eighty sleeping bodies onboard a Boeing, ten kilometers above him, heightened the painful feeling of abandonment. It got cold. Carl dug himself into the sand, and over the course of the night he buried himself deeper and deeper. He had disturbing dreams that he was unable to remember after the fact.

In the light of the morning, the circle he had drawn in the sand the night before turned out to be an oval double spiral around a rumpled center. He went around the circle but was unable to spot the capsules anywhere. He examined his sandals to make sure they hadn't got stuck in the contours of the soles, and then he began to carefully sift the sand on the lee side of the circle. He let the sand trickle from one hand to the other, twice, three times, and then tossed it up with the wind at his back. He worked hour after hour, going through the top layer of sand by his knees, moving slightly forward, and then kept sifting. The sun rose higher and higher, and Carl squatted, sweating and thirsty, in his little trough. He became ever more despondent. By around noon he had gone through more than half of the circle and still not found a thing. Afraid he might overlook the capsules in a moment of inattention, he was now sifting each handful four and five times before tossing it onto the little mound behind him. His increased diligence left him worrying that he hadn't been thorough enough before, so he started a second mound of the sand he had sifted five times in case he needed to sift through the less thoroughly sifted sand of the first mound.

The sun had already passed its high point when he saw a flash of metallic silver among the grains of sand, and while Carl, still sweating and distraught, was trying to calculate how many hours of work he still had ahead of him given the fact that it had taken half a day to find the first capsule, the second capsule turned up only a few handfuls later like a child thief who doesn't dare run away when one of his little accomplices has been caught.

Carl put both capsules back into the cartridge, closed it again with the blue plastic stopper and wondered whether maybe some other spot would be safer. In his wallet? In the pocket of his blazer? Or should he just go ahead and swallow them? He took the keys, notebook and ampules of morphine out of his side pockets, stuck them in his Bermuda shorts and clipped the pen into the inside pocket of his blazer all by itself. As he was still concentrating on doing all of this he noticed a flickering figure coming toward him across the desert. A grubby white djellaba, it was a very old man.

He came directly from the direction of the barn and yelled something incomprehensible from a long distance off. This time he wasn't holding a trident, but Carl recognized him anyway, and while Carl tried to analyze the man's gait and the level of threat he represented, he also noticed that the sense of recognition was not mutual. Babbling loudly, the old man stomped up the dunes, calling Carl the invisible royal brigade, seemed extremely happy about his appearance and, gasping and coughing, expressed his hope that he would soon be able to hold the bodies of his two sons in his fatherly arms.

He was nearly upon Carl when he suddenly stopped short, yelled "my golden boy!" and fell to the side of the body in the sand. It took nearly ten minutes for him to realize his mistake. No, his son had never worn a light-gray suit. Only a djellaba. And where was the moped?

It was a question Carl could not answer for him, and all that he was able to learn from the old man's hour-long barrage of words could be boiled down to three sentences: that the old man had apparently lost two sons, one of whom had been beaten and the other had gone missing. That he was hoping for the aid of a highly secret division of the police in his search for their bodies. And not to be overlooked: he was searching for his moped.

With his blazer wrapped around his head as protection against the heat, Carl continued to march westward. The burning thirst he had felt since he awoke reached an unbearable level as soon as he could make out the edges of the shanty town on the horizon. He staggered weakly between the first two corrugated-metal huts, ran into a grubby shop, bought a liter-bottle of water and downed it while still standing up. Followed by a second bottle. With the third bottle open, he wandered around behind the building and pissed while calling to the shopkeeper to ask whether there was a phone anywhere nearby. Indeed there was, in a plywood booth two streets down, where someone ran some kind of café, it was a black plastic phone.

Carl had himself connected to the Sheraton. Helen's voice came over the line. Helen! She was not hurt, she was fine, and before she could explain to Carl how and why she escaped the blaze he screamed into the phone that he had found the "mine"... yeah, the cartridges, mines in French, were in his pocket, two tiny capsules inside a pen, he repeated, inside a pen… yes, he was sure these were the mines, and she had to come pick him up right away, in the easternmost outlying section of the Salt Quarter, the last filthy café on the main road through the huts… he was waiting for her there. The biggest street. The widest. At the easternmost point. A plywood booth with a phone. He heard his own excitement mirrored in Helen's voice, heard her tell him not to move, she'd be right there, and when he hung up the waiter was standing behind him holding up a bowl of overcooked soup as if it were a selection of the finest spices. It was on the house.

A stack of boxes facing the street served as an improvised table, and Carl sat down with his soup. He put down his blazer and closed his eyes. For the first time since the incident in the barn he felt good, felt as if he was in the clear, even though he knew that the things he still had in front of him—handing over the capsules to Adil Bassir, negotiating for the return of his family, clearing up his identity—might be the toughest of all. But the uncertainty was gone. The horrible uncertainty.

He ate and drank, brushed off his clothes, emptied the sand from his pockets and once again double-checked the contents of the inner pocket of his blazer. He washed his hands with a little of the drinking water and splashed the rest over his tortured feet, and looked down the street. Sand-colored children played with a sand-colored soccer ball between sand-colored huts… filth and ragged figures, and it occurred to him how dangerous it was to have a white, blonde woman who didn't know the area drive here. On the other hand, Helen had already proved herself fearless on more than one occasion; and anyway, there was nothing else that could be done. He watched a dog spinning in a circle, chasing its own tail. The soccer ball landed with a clang atop a corrugated-metal roof. Then a gaggle of children with battered wooden tablets and tattered notebooks crossed the road looking like an image from a volume of children's poetry, one with sentimental verses about bygone ages and decorated with bister sketches: golden suns, golden youth. One boy jumped on another's back and pointed the way with a crutch. Giggling little girls transcended continents and centuries. One child hopped along behind the others with one leg and no crutch.

"Monsieur Bekurtz, où est-il?"

The book of poetry slammed shut as one of the children lurched toward Carl and noisily demanded a baksheesh. The waiter came out and whipped at the mischief-maker with a dishtowel. He called the children filthy vermin harassing his customer, scum, the god damn spawn of the god damn Salt Quarter. They made faces as they ran away, and the waiter threw a handful of pebbles at them.

Carl stared at the waiter and said: "What?"

"Yes?"

"What did you say?"

"That they should get out of here."

"No, god damn… the god damn Salt Quarter?"

He shrugged, threw another handful of pebbles, furrowed his brow.

Carl said: "But isn't this the Salt Quarter?"

"Sir!" said the waiter indignantly, pointing out over the shacks of his proud neighborhood, and before he was able to express his sense of insult any further Carl had already sprung to his feet and run to the telephone. He had himself connected to the Sheraton again. The waiter followed him warily, stood directly behind him and periodically held up his hand, rubbing his thumb and forefinger together. The telephone operator said: "Connecting you now."

The Empty Quarter. He was in the Empty Quarter.

"Answer!" said Carl. "Answer!"

At the beginning of the 1950s bulldozers had for the first time plowed a broad swath through the mud huts and corrugated-metal shacks of the massive slums around Targat and separated a small section in the north from the Salt Quarter. The action came to be known as the first purge. Since then the Salt Quarter and the Empty Quarter treated each other like rival football teams. They were still somehow lumped together, still spoke the same language and still lived in the same filth, but thanks to a swath between the two quarters of several kilometers in width, each came to believe theirs was a different sort of filth. Residents of the Empty Quarter developed feelings of arrogance and superiority as a result of the fact that power lines and even a telephone line were run past the area one day, which they quickly tapped into. This allowed the Empty Quarter to gain such a significant edge in civilization that it almost achieved legitimacy enough to save itself and was spared from purges two through four while its sister slum to the south sank ever more deeply into squalor.

After a few minutes of silence, the voice of the operator came on the line again and said that nobody was answering at bungalow 581d.

Carl ran back outside. Or tried to. The waiter grabbed his arm. Oh right, the bill. He pulled out a few coins, looked around for his blazer, and his blazer was gone. He stared at the waiter. The waiter turned the palms of his hands upward. Two sweaty men on the street. Above the tin roofs of the Empty Quarter hung the leaden midday heat and a fading chorus of school children's voices. Shrieking school children, happy school children, running school children in possession of a yellow piece of women's outerwear which sadly yielded them nothing more than a cheap pen.

Hour after hour, until late into the night, Carl walked around first the Empty Quarter and then the Salt Quarter. He offered a lot of money for the blazer. People looked at him like he was crazy, shrugged their shoulders, knew nothing. He saw no sign of Helen, whom he had sent to the wrong place. There was an easternmost extension of the Salt Quarter, but no broad street there, no huts, no telephone, nothing that would have matched his description. If Helen had tried to find him around here she would have given up long ago. Carl collapsed next to an evening garbage pile. Two dogs sniffed him, a chicken clucked at him. He pulled the ampules of morphine out of the pocket of his Bermuda shorts, held them up to look at them against a light, and couldn't decide whether it was a sufficient dose to kill himself.

47

Chéri

According to the conception of primitive men a name is an essential part of a personality; if therefore you know the name of a person or a spirit you have acquired a certain power over its bearer.

FREUD

H E STUMBLED ALONG the harbor front. Sat down on a mooring bollard. Watched ships sailing away. My life, he thought. A boy stopped in front of him and spat a brown lump of phlegm into the air which he watched so attentively as it fell to the ground that it seemed as if he had never before studied the effects of gravity with such clarity or he thought the effects wouldn't possibly apply in this particular case. Carl waved him over and asked whether he went to school in the area. And if so, where exactly. The boy laughed. He made angular gestures. He was deaf-mute.

No, the cartridge was lost for ever. Carl knew it. He would never find Cetrois, and besides Helen there was no other person he trusted. As he dragged himself toward the Sheraton, he considered stopping at Dr Cockcroft's practice despite his distinct aversion.

A fruit cart was blocking his way through the narrow alley. Next to him somebody was hawking shoes. Behind him he heard a hoarse voice.

"Charly, hey."

He turned around. At first he didn't see anyone.

"Freeze, you idiot, you asshole! Hey!"

Half hidden by a column, a haggard woman stood leaning against a building. A ravaged face. Her shouts created an odd contrast to her motionlessness.

"What did you say?" He took a few steps back toward her. Only when he got closer did he see how young she was. Sixteen at the most. Bloody marks on her forearm, her face and neck pockmarked with boils.

"I said asshole."

"Before that."

"Idiot. You idiot." She pushed herself upright off the wall.

"You said Charly."

"I said idiot. Asshole, Charly, chéri, you piece of shit. My love. Do you have anything with you?"

She reached out for him and he shrank away from her.

From her gestures and behavior he couldn't tell whether she was a prostitute, a crazy woman or another nymphomaniac.

"We know each other," he said tentatively.

"You want me to blow you?"

"That was a question."

"That was also a question."

"Why did you call me Charly?"

She shoved him by the shoulder and then started to curse him.

A few passers-by stopped and laughed. The men in the café across the street straightened themselves up to be able to see better. Carl saw two policemen at the next crossing, only a stone's throw away. He didn't like the situation. The girl wouldn't stop insulting him, pushing him and at the same time offering her services.

"I don't have any money."

She patted his pants pockets and grabbed his crotch as the crowd hooted approvingly. He jumped back. She pulled him into the next building entryway. Down a long hallway, into a small room. A mattress sat on the floor with no sheets. The memory of the honest woman in Tindirma immediately disappeared. Suddenly all the girl's verve seemed to have abandoned her. She stood in the middle of the room, shaking.

"Do we know each other?" Carl asked again, suddenly quite sure they did know each other.

"Do you have anything with you?"

"Do you know me?"

"You want me to act all psychotic?"

"You said Charly."

"I can call you Alphonse if you want. Or Rashid. Herr General. I'll blow you."

She grabbed at his pants. He held her hands.

"You have something with you!" she screeched excitedly.

"I don't want anything from you. I just want to know whether you know me."

She continued to rant. Her unsteady gaze, her desperate, uncomprehending manner... no, she didn't know him. She was a deranged, drug-addicted street kid. Carl reached for the doorknob and the girl screamed: "Freeze, you fuck! You can't leave now! If you and your piece of shit friend can't get your shit together—"

"What friend?"

"You want to have a three-way? I'll go get Titi."

"What friend?"

"You disgusting pig."

Standing at the door with his hand on the knob, he continued to ask questions, to no avail. All he heard was a stream of curses. Carl let go of the knob and tried one last time. In the most casual tone he could manage he asked: "When was the last time you saw Cetrois?"

"Huh?"

"Just answer."

"You want me to piss in your mouth?" She tried to shove her forefinger between his lips.

He jerked his head away.

"Lie down, I'll sit on your face and piss in your mouth."

"When did you last see him?"

"Who?"

"Cetrois."

"Hit me. You can hit me. As hard as you want. I'll shit on your chest. I'll suck your brain out through your cock. I'll do whatever you want."

"Then answer my question."

"What question?" Tears ran down her ruined child's face. She fell to her knees yammering. "Give me the stuff. I know you have it."

He put his hands into the pockets of his shorts and said, emphasizing each word: "Do you know Cetrois?"

She whimpered.

"Do you know where he is?"

"You sick, psycho, piece of shit."

Why didn't she just answer? Or if she didn't know him, why didn't she just say she didn't know him? He lifted her chin, pulled one of the brown ampules from his pocket and watched the girl's reaction.

"Simple question, simple answer. Where. Is. He."

For a moment she stared at him apathetically. Then she launched herself at him. Her feather-light body bounced off his. He held the hand with the ampule high in the air.

"Answer."

"Give it to me!" She jumped at his raised arm, swore like a

sailor, ripped at his clothes. Finally she tried to climb up him with her eyes fixed on the fist he was holding aloft.

"You can have the stuff… even if you don't know. But you have to answer. Do you know me?"

"I'll shit in your mouth."

"Do you know Cetrois?"

"You sick pig!"

"Where is he? What is he doing?"

Whining like the siren of a fire engine, she hung from his neck. She beat on his back with her little fists. Her breasts were beneath his chin now, the smell of female sweat, despair and vomit. Maybe it was that smell, maybe it was the bodily proximity, maybe it was the way it went without saying that every communication would come to nothing, but he suddenly had the feeling that this woman was closer to him than he would have liked. In the worst-case scenario, she was his lover from another life. Parallel to that and almost simultaneously, he had the feeling that she didn't know him at all. That she didn't know anything at all. That she was just crazy, a prostitute with a brain destroyed by drugs, who didn't know him or a friend and who addressed every potential client as Charly. And begged for stuff. Maybe Charly was the slang term for a client around here? And had she even really said Charly? Had she perhaps said chéri right from the start?

"Give me the morphine," she yelled, falling to the ground and writhing around in self-humiliation like a three-year-old child.

"You can have it," he said with a look at the nearly illegible label on the ampule. "Just answer one question. Do you know me?"

She sobbed.

"I have two of them." He pulled out the other ampule. "If you don't know me—do you know my friend?"

"You pig."

"When did you last see Cetrois?"

"You psycho piece of shit. You filthy trash."

Psycho. For the third time. What was that about? Was it just another curse word for her, or did it have some sort of meaning? Was she in therapy? Was he her psychologist? Or was he a known madman and she one of his victims? No matter how many times he asked, he got just as little answer. As an experiment, he let one ampule drop. Glass shards, a cry of despair. The girl lunged to the ground and licked up the fluid and slivers of glass with her tongue.

"Do you know me now?"

"Fuck your mother!"

"Do you know Cetrois?"

"Give me the other one!"

"Where is he? What is he doing? Why don't you answer me?"

She ranted and screamed, and it slowly dawned on him that she knew nothing. She didn't know him, she didn't know anyone. She had simply addressed him with a random name on the street, and he fell for it like the stupidest mark in the world. With a remnant of sympathy, he threw her some money and left.

"You want to know what Cetrois is doing?" she yelled after him.

He looked at her crouching on the floor. She was pulling glass splinters from her tongue and laughing, blood trickling between her lips.

"You want to know what Cetrois is doing right now? I'll tell you what he is doing right now. He is standing in the door and refusing to give me my stuff. That I already paid for! I paid for it, you pig! I pissed in your mouth, you piece of shit. I fucked you a hundred times, I've had it with your games. It belongs to me! It's mine, it's mine, it's mine, it's mine, it's mine."

He didn't believe anything for a moment. His gaze fixed in the distance. Cetrois.

The next second his body collapsed under her weight. She had jumped on him and pulled him to the floor. They rolled around. The second ampule had long since slipped out of his hand. The girl didn't notice and bit his empty hand. He elbowed her in the face and tried to get away from her. Glass broke beneath his back.

The sounds that came from her were no longer human. Pushing him aside, she began to mop the floor with her tongue, trying to catch the last droplets as they trickled down between the floorboards. Stunned, Carl headed for the hall.

A glance back: bloody misery.

A glance forward: a fist in his face.

He was dragged into the room and slammed up against the wall. A powerful, black body. A full head taller than him, wearing a colorful West African dress, arms as thick as tractor tires. A woman. She bore no resemblance to her emaciated friend, but despite that the professional relationship was immediately clear. The black woman pressed a hand against his throat and screamed: "What did he do to you, my dear? What did he do to you? The evil man!"

She yanked Carl down by his hair and rammed her knee into his face a few times. He felt the wound on the back of his head open up and collapsed. The black woman dropped on top of him; she must have weighed at least a hundred and fifty kilos. The druggy wreck came toward him from the side, wiping blood from her mouth with the back of her hand, and swung a chair leg through the air. The leg caught Carl's shoulder first, a second time it hit him on the shoulder, then in the face. He tried to turn himself beneath the black woman. His shirt was ripped over his head. A warm taste of iron in his mouth, agile hands in his pockets. He passed out. He awoke in a gutter. It took him nearly an hour to cover the ten-minute walk to the Sheraton.

48

Ockham's Straight Razor

I like horses, but I'm riding on a mule.

GERHARD BANGEN

H E GAVE NO EXPLANATION, just slipped past Helen into the bungalow, took off his shirt and shorts, and went into the bathroom and turned on the shower. He stood motionless for nearly twenty minutes beneath the lukewarm water. He dried himself off on his way toward the bed, let the towel fall to the floor and fell lengthwise into bed.

"You can't be serious," said Helen. "You didn't really lose the cartridge, did you?"

"I'm Cetrois."

"You're not serious?"

"No. I don't know."

She kept asking questions, he answered drowsily and incoherently. He pulled the covers over his head and fell asleep.

When he awoke it was pitch-dark and his heart was racing. It seemed as if he hadn't slept for even a second. But the clock said it was almost midnight. He felt around with his arm; the other half of the bed was empty. A weak rectangle of light surrounded the door. He found Helen in the next room in the bright glare of the ceiling lamp, her blonde hair pinned up.

The telephone and a steaming cup of coffee on the table in front of her. In her hands a notebook that she quickly closed when Carl entered the room. The TV was on with no sound.

They sat silently opposite each other for a while. Then Helen turned the TV off and asked again in a quiet voice whether he had really recovered the cartridge and then lost it again, and Carl said: "I am not Cetrois."

"How could you just leave the blazer sitting there?"

"I can't be."

"Why didn't you follow the school children?"

"I did follow. But the woman was totally out of her head. She can't know me, she must have just said any old name."

"What did the children look like?"

"And she wanted morphine from me."

"I asked you something."

"What?"

"What the children looked like."

"Who cares what they looked like?"

He kept talking and repeated his last few sentences, and though at first he didn't believe it and he had no explanation for it, there was suddenly a very different tone to Helen's voice. She kept interrupting him; there was little left of the calm and relaxed manner of the last few days. On the one hand, that seemed understandable in the face of the latest developments. But on the other hand, Carl had the feeling that there must be another explanation for the change in her tone. Her questions came quickly and pointedly, almost as if it was an interrogation, and the only thing she was interested in was how he had found the cartridge and under what circumstances he had lost it again, while Carl kept insisting on trying to return to the episode with the prostitute. For some reason he had assumed that the question of his identity would animate Helen as much as it did him, but that was obviously not the case. How many school children? What were they wearing? Why hadn't he waited in the Salt Quarter? Empty Quarter, what was the Empty Quarter? First of the purges? What capsules? Two capsules with a seam in the middle? In a pen that said "Szewczuk" on it? And what kind of yellow Mercedes was it again?

"I'm not interested in any of that," said Carl, worn out. "What I want to know is who I am. I don't care about the capsules, I don't care about my supposed family, all I care about is *who I am.*"

"What I'm interested in is how someone can allow an object that holds the key to his life, his identity and everything else to be stolen by some little kids." Helen seemed irritated. She was getting loud, and so was Carl, and after they had yelled at each other for a few minutes Helen suggested they separate the two topics, his identity and the cartridge. She considered the cartridge significantly more important... but by all means. As far as she was concerned, identity first.

Carl didn't answer.

"Your little prostitute," said Helen. "Go ahead."

"No, you start."

Helen turned away, shaking her head, and Carl, who knew he was acting childish, chewed on his lips.

Their shadows sat mutely beside each other on the black TV screen. After a while Carl's shadow reached for the hand of Helen's shadow but she pulled her hand away.

"Go ahead."

"But I've said everything now! It's just that it can't be. Cetrois went into the desert on a moped. I'm not Cetrois. The girl is mistaken."

"Or the four men are mistaken."

"How's that possible? And you didn't see this girl." Carl described his encounter with the drug addict once again, down to the last detail, making sure to vividly emphasize how disturbed she was, and Helen interrupted him and said: "She wanted morphine from you. And you had some with you. Was that a coincidence?"

No answer.

"Did you tell her that you had some, or did she ask?"

"She asked."

"And what exactly did she ask for?"

"For… stuff. Did I have any stuff. And then I pulled out the ampules and she wanted them. And at that point she said morphine."

"You didn't say morphine?"

"No."

"And did it say morphine on the label in big letters?"

"No. It was written on the ampule, but it was barely legible."

"She couldn't have read it."

"No. But what else could it have been?"

"Cocaine. Cosmetics. Saline."

"She must have guessed it. She knows her drugs."

"If I can just recap: this girl, who addressed you on the street as Charly, wanted stuff from you. And you happened to have stuff on you. At which point she said morphine, and what you had happened to be morphine. You don't seriously think that she doesn't know you, do you?"

"I—"

"And the fact that she just cursed and swore instead of answering your questions, even though you promised to give her the ampules if she answered. Why would she do that?"

"Because she's a halfwit."

"That is one possibility. Another is that the question is half-witted. I mean, you ask incessantly about yourself and what your name is. You won't find many people who will simply answer the question 'what is my name' with 'you're so-and-so'. And then you ask about Cetrois. You ask a hundred times whether she knows Cetrois and where she last saw him—I would call that psycho shit, too. Right? What would you say?... Do you know Helen? Answer. Do you know Helen? Helen Gliese? When did you last see her? Where is she? What is she doing? Answer, little man."

Carl had buried his head in his crossed arms, and he didn't lift it now as he groaningly said: "But the four men at the barn. I didn't mishear them. I listened to exactly what they said, Cetrois went into the desert. Cetrois drove into the desert on the moped. They were far off. But I understood every word."

"Then tell me exactly what they said."

"I already told you. That Cetrois drove off into the desert, that they'd found a lot of money... and that they'd bashed in someone's skull with a jack."

"Someone?"

"Yes."

"They said they had bashed *someone*'s skull in?"

"Some guy."

"*Some guy*?"

"Yes."

"And did they say why they bashed his skull in?"

"No. Or actually yes. When the fourth man showed up they said the guy was in the barn. They wanted him to tell them where Cetrois had gone. But he didn't tell them... and then the carjack."

Helen had stood up and was opening cabinets and drawers in the kitchen as she continued to call questions to Carl. She asked about the old fellah and what he'd been wearing, asked about his two sons, the color of the rattan suitcase and the location of the window in the attic of the barn. She asked about the size and shape of the hatch in the floor, the nature of the pulley. The height above the floor, the number of pulley blocks, the length of the chain. The weight of the ladder.

She returned with a paper and pencil, pushed them across the table and said: "Draw the floor plan. The entire barn and the huts… and where exactly the window was upstairs. And the entrance. And where you were lying when you woke up… right. There? You were lying there with your head in this direction? So this is where the crack in the wall was that you were looking through?"

Helen turned the sketch ninety degrees, took the pencil from Carl's hand and drew a stick figure where Carl had put an X to mark the spot where he'd awoken with the wooden gun on his back. They looked at the map for a while and then added compass points to it.

"And the four men were here?"

She drew four stick figures next to the barn. One of them had a stroke of pencil lead in his hand to indicate the carjack, one was off to the side a little next to a jeep.

"And the jeep came from this direction, right? From Tindirma? And they were following you, so you probably also came from Tindirma. Doesn't matter. So somewhere between here and the oasis they found the case of money or the loose money that made them stop, so they weren't directly behind you, but a ways behind you."

"Yeah, so?"

"Just a second."

"None of this changes the fact that I can't be Cetrois."

"I think I've got it." Helen looked at the drawing for a while longer. Then she looked at Carl. "You had on a djellaba, right? Over your checkered suit. That you took off when you were fleeing. Did it happen to be white?"

He nodded.

"The four men also had white djellabas on. The old fellah had on a dirty-white djellaba, the dead man under the pulley did too. Let me guess: the guy on the moped was dressed no differently."

"That's speculation. But fine, whatever you're getting at, it won't work—"

"Just a second. You flee from your pursuers into the barn. You are here and they are here, and now the question is, what do they see? They see from far away someone in a white djellaba go into the barn and then someone comes out on a moped. Black hair, white djellaba, the same way their brothers look. So naturally they think it's you, Cetrois."

"That doesn't work."

"I wasn't finished."

"But it doesn't work because they beat in my skull. And if they cracked my skull they must have known that it couldn't have been me on that moped."

"And how do you know that they cracked your skull?"

"Is that supposed to be a joke?"

"They said they cracked somebody's skull."

"Right, some guy! But not Cetrois."

"That's what I'm talking about."

A blank, uncomprehending face.

"I don't know whether you have forgotten," said Helen, "but you weren't the only person in the barn with your head smashed in."

She drew a stick figure in the square of the hatch in the attic floor.

"But I hit him! With the pulley."

"How do you know that? You said it was six meters or so. The hatch was four or five meters above the floor and the pulley was maybe two meters above the hatch. And the chain ran around several blocks. That would make quite a racket, don't you think? Or was it silent? No. And how quickly did the pulley block set in motion when you hit it with the ladder?"

"Like this." Carl lowered his hand. "First slowly, then it really got going."

"And you think a man waited below for the thing to crush his skull while the thing rattled and started to fall in slow motion from six meters above him?" Helen drew chain links in the hatch and on the circular head of the stick figure. "He would look up. If someone was standing there he would look up. If you ask me, there are only three possible reasons he wouldn't look up. First, he'd deaf. Possible, but not likely. Second, he's sleeping. Which, given the noise you had already made up to that point, is also highly unlikely. And the third possibility is he's dead already. Unconscious or dead. Because someone had already whacked him with a carjack."

Carl scratched the back of his head.

"And look at your wound. Do you know what a carjack is? If somebody hits you with one of those your head is nothing more than mush. What you have is a cut, there's no way a carjack touched you."

She turned the paper around and drew another stick figure on a moped at a distance from the barn and wrote "Cetrois" in quotation marks above the figure.

Carl said nothing.

"If you ask me, it makes total sense," said Helen. "Of course, I can't say it with certainty. But when there are multiple possibilities, go for the simplest. First, I don't believe that you misunderstood the men. Second, I don't think you misunderstood the girl. I would assume there were three parties."

She pointed to the three parties on the paper one after the next. "You are one party. Your pursuers are a second, and the fellah family is the third. An old man with two sons. You follow me so far? And I am assuming that at the moment in question only the two sons were in the barn. Maybe the old man as well, but definitely the two sons. Pulley son and moped son. And then you show up. You are fleeing the men, and you storm into something that looks like an illegal distillery with something that

looks like an assault weapon. I'm assuming the reception would
be none too warm. You're crazed because you're being followed,
and the sons are crazed because they are bootleggers and you're
running around with a weapon that, as you yourself said, looks
deceptively real, even up close. And is it light in the barn? No,
it's dark. So you have an AK-47 and no matter what you tell
them they know that trouble is on the horizon. Maybe you ask
for help, maybe you even threaten them. And maybe they also
see your pursuers coming and take them for your backup, so
as a precaution one of them smacks you from behind. They
hoist you up into the attic with your minor wound… or maybe
you had already climbed up into the attic and it's up there that
they catch you and smack you, doesn't matter. And now they're
really panicking. They've cracked one person's skull and there
are three more on the way. So son number two grabs the moped
and races off into the desert. Maybe to get help, maybe just to
get away. Doesn't matter. When the men pursuing you reach the
barn, only son number one is still there, and they ask him where
Cetrois is and he doesn't answer. Because he doesn't know. So
they crack his skull with the carjack, which they soon proudly
report to the fourth man. While you are lying unconscious in
the attic and the man on the moped has basically saved your
life. Because they chase him next. They probably catch him,
too, somewhere back there, and realize he's the wrong man, so
they come back to look for you. But Monsieur Cetrois has left
in the meantime, and the upshot for the old fellah is: one son
killed, one disappeared. Mystery solved."

Helen drank the last sip of coffee and went into the kitchen
to make a fresh cup.

Baffled, Carl stared at the sketch that Helen had covered
with arrows and Xs.

"And the wooden gun? Why would I be running around the
desert with a wooden gun?"

"I would suggest that you ask yourself that question."

Carl tried to go through everything again in his head. He counted the stick figures, he picked up the pen and read the word Sheraton on it. The certainty and ease with which Helen dismissed all his objections offended and confused him. He found it difficult to picture everything in chronological order. How was Helen able to put all the puzzle pieces together so effortlessly? Was she really able to? He felt obligated to find a mistake. With his finger on the stick figure that was supposed to be him, he said: "When I was at Adil Bassir's, he spoke of *two* men." He avoided using the word sausage. "Two men, me and my partner."

"He must not have been there."

"No... but up to now I thought Cetrois was my partner. If I'm Cetrois, who is my partner?"

"Is that an important question?" Helen opened the coffee can and looked around for the measuring spoon. "Or can we turn to the question of whether it was really *school children* who stole your blazer?"

"I'm not sure what makes you so confident."

"What did the children look like?"

"Forget the children! What is it with you and these children? You're not going to find them anyway."

"I'll tell you what it is about them. As far as I know there are no schools in the slums."

"And what made you think of all of this?" Carl asked without addressing her point. He lifted the drawing and waved it in the air.

"Because the personal description fitted. In the commune. Fowler and the others described a man almost exactly like you. Checkered suit, thin, thirty years old, one meter seventy-five tall. A bit Arabic-looking. Although that was all they knew. They didn't know anything else. What you were doing there at the commune you either didn't say or they didn't understand. You must have introduced yourself as a journalist, but then you only seemed to ask about the valuables, the suitcase of cash and all that, so they figured you were from the insurance company that they were in the process of trying to defraud. Cetrois, insurance man. Or extremely incompetent journalist. Something like that."

49

Foul Thoughts

Alert! Alert! Look well at the rainbow. The fish will rise very soon. Chico is in the house. Visit him. The sky is blue. Place notice in the tree. The tree is green and brown.

E. HOWARD HUNT

H E CRAWLED BACK into bed late in the night. Helen tucked him in, sat for a while on the edge of the bed and stared at him with a look that, had his eyes not already been closed, would not have sat well with him.

Still, he spent the night—the last night—peacefully. Early in the morning he was pulled out of bed. Someone had him by the neck and dragged him into the other room. With a voice that was neither inquiring nor upset, but rather just cold and cutting, Helen said: "What is this? What. Is. This."

Carl stood beside her in his underwear with the worn-out elastic, in front of him twelve scraps of paper loosely assembled into three rectangles. He recognized them immediately. A thirteenth piece lay to the side. It was slightly singed but was of the same material as the rest and had the same red pattern. Three ID papers. Three Officers of the Virtue Committee.

Leaning over them, Carl suddenly said: "What is that?"

"It was in your shorts. I was going to have them washed. Don't lie to me now."

Carl rubbed his chest with his hands and, still not sure why Helen was so upset, he told her about finding the IDs on the body in the desert. Or rather, the pieces of paper. A body in a light-gray suit and a wire noose around his neck that he had stumbled across... that's where he'd got these. In one of his pockets.

"And what is this?" Helen tapped her finger on the sections of the IDs typed out with red ink.

Carl read and stopped short: Adolphe Aun... Bertrand Bédeaux... Didier Dequat.

"A, B, D!" said Helen loudly. "One, two, four!"

"Shit."

"Yeah, shit, Monsieur *Cetrois*. Now stop telling me shit about where you got these. Don't tell me any more shit. You shove that story about the body up your... You've played the amnesiac long enough, and now, please: Do. Not. Lie. To. Me."

Carl picked up the singed piece of paper. It said "Nom:" and after looking at it for a second he put it back on the table and repeated the story of stumbling upon the body. A wire noose. Two halves of a pencil... and an Adolphe Menjou mustache. The dead man had a Menjou mustache.

"Bullshit," said Helen. "You are talking bullshit."

"You don't really believe that, do you?"

"What?"

"That I've only been pretending to have lost my memory."

"I believe what Dr Cockcroft believes."

"How do you know what Dr Cockcroft believes?"

"Because you told me, my dear boy. Are you suddenly really suffering from memory loss? Tell me where you got these things, and don't say from a dead man. Have you had them the whole time? Who are you? You had them the whole time, didn't you? You knew all along who you were, and—"

"I can show you the corpse."

"No."

"Yes, I can—"

"No, you can't! Do you really think I would drive into the desert with you now to look for a dead man with a Menjou mustache? It's over. The trip to the Salt Quarter was enough. That's when I began to think something wasn't right. That you're a liar. A liar and a faker. Don't look so offended. And in case you can't imagine how I see things I'd be happy to tell you."

"Helen."

"What are the facts? The facts are—no, listen to me. The facts are: I pick up a man at a gas station in the middle of the desert who says he's lost his memory. I believe him. I take care of him. I'm not put off by the fact that he doesn't want to go to the police. I'm not put off by the fact that he doesn't want to go to the hospital and that a specialist says that an explanation for such memory loss doesn't exist."

"*Probably* doesn't exist."

"Probably my ass. But it's nice that you want to talk about probability. I was just about to get to that. So I'm taking care of this man. I'm taking care of this man whose identity is completely in the dark, a man who claims not to own anything more than the things he has on his person, along with the singed corner of an ID the crucial part of which was burned by some hippies. What is the probability of that? And he'd barely been with me before he was kidnapped by a gangster boss. He had a letter-opener jammed through his hand and even under extreme pain didn't reveal the fact that he'd lost his memory or that he had a friend named Cetrois. Or believed he did. For days we desperately searched for this Cetrois, and it emerges that it is the man himself. What is the probability of that? And we'd barely found that out when our man turns out to be carrying three IDs in his pocket. Three silly, forged IDs which match wonderfully the fourth, silly, forged ID burned by the hippies. And how did they suddenly turn up? He found them on a corpse in the desert, a corpse with, and I quote, *a Menjou mustache*, that he happened to stumble upon among the dunes, and all of this yesterday—without ever paying much attention to the IDs or bothering to mention them to me. The man who pours his heart out to me every night—this one thing he forgets to mention. I happen to find the things in his pocket. What is the probability of that?"

"It's not too probable, but—"

"And last of all, our man is searching for a mine. What kind of mine? He doesn't know. But due to a happy coincidence he suddenly finds or at least claims to have found his mine, which it turns out is the ink cartridge of a pen, actually of a ballpoint pen, a quote *cheap ballpoint pen*, and this fucking pen, which has all the fucking answers to all his fucking problems, he allows to be stolen in the Empty Quarter by, and I quote again, *a schoolboy*, while he sends me in the car to the *Salt Quarter*. You still have your wallet, the money I gave you, the second key for the bungalow, you have all of that. The only thing gone is the blazer with the pen. What is the probability of that? Put yourself in my place. I mean, do you think I'm an idiot?"

Helen's voice had lost any sluggishness or droning. She spat out the final sentence in a staccato that sounded like a machine gun.

Mystified, Carl looked her in the eyes. Was she really as sure as she was making out, or was she just testing him? He didn't know. And what if she were right? Was it possible that, despite not having been there and using nothing more than combinatorics, everything Helen had figured out was true? Was it possible, as Dr Cockcroft had suggested, to fake something without realizing you are faking it? Was that the incvitable conclusion to be taken from the scraps of paper?

It felt for a moment as if he might go crazy. He tried to work his way back through the memories of the last few days to what he had learned about his life and to try to reassemble it all into another somehow also consistent whole, but he wasn't able to. It was no longer a question of thinking, it was a descent into a fog. How could Helen cast a glance at the strewn paper scraps and so unambiguously see what it was she wanted to see, namely an image full of contradictions and improbabilities?

The possibility of losing the trust of the only person he was close to put him in a panic. He groaned. He fell silent.

"If that's all you have to say, then that's it," he heard. "It's over. I helped you in every way I could, but I'm not going to shelter a liar. If you want to tell me what these IDs are and how you got them and, most importantly, who you are and where the cartridge is, then you can tell me now. Tell me. This is the last chance. Who are you? And what is with the fucking cartridge?"

His mind was racing with no result. Helen swished the paper scraps off the table with a swat of her arm. "Fine," she said without any noticeable emotion. "I'm going to the beach. You can wait until your clothes come back from the hotel cleaner, but you'd better be gone when I get back."

She grabbed her bathing suit and two towels from the bathroom, then went to the phone and had herself connected to the US. Carl sat slumped on a chair trying to straighten things out in his mind. Through the fog came the contours of other unexplained details. The wooden gun. A fake gun, a fake ID. The fog began to cause physical pain. He knew he was lost without Helen. He heard her speaking to her mother and he stopped trying to figure out an answer and just tried to think of something he could say that would calm her down. He had told the truth throughout, but the truth was improbable. He knew it himself.

"It is certainly unlikely," he began again. "But I want to ask you something. If I had really wanted to deceive you, if I had really known all along about those IDs in my pocket and wanted to lie to you about where I got them—would I really have come up with something so absurdly improbable as a corpse with a Menjou mustache? With a wire around its throat? Couldn't I have simply come up with something much more plausible?"

Helen's answer came straight back: "Like what?"

She took her hand away from the telephone, which she had covered for a few seconds, and began talking again.

"No, nobody, mother," she said.

"Yes, fine," she said.

"Then I wouldn't have tried this morning," she said.

Carl attempted to imagine what Helen's mother was saying on the other side of the ocean. Then he thought about the wooden gun again. He went over it in his head again and again.

"Yeah… yeah. No, it didn't turn up and won't ever turn up. I'm sure. I called the company, they're sending a new one. Three new ones would be better, of course… three are always better than one, yeah… immediately, when else? I'm going to the beach now… the same everywhere… yeah. Carthage is good. Say hello from me," said Helen and hung up.

"Who is Carthage?" asked Carl.

Helen didn't answer.

"Who is Carthage?"

"My dog. Remember: when I return, the bungalow is empty."

She put her beach bag over her shoulder and left.

Carl picked the scraps of paper up from the floor, reassembled them with trembling fingers and saw what he had seen before: ridiculous IDs from a ridiculous "Virtue Committee". He swished them off the table again, went out onto the terrace and watched an already small Helen as she disappeared between the pine trees. The ocean rolled onto the beach in small waves.

Helen was barely gone when a man appeared on the path and stopped among the trees. He was very far away, but Carl had the impression that the man was staring at him. One or two minutes, then the man turned around and went back down toward the beach.

Carl flopped down on a deckchair. He felt leaden with fatigue. Something had worn him out to the core. The thoughts no longer raced through his head, they just limped around. Out of fear of further angering Helen for not following her order, he pressed himself out of the chair with a groan, trudged down the path to the second terrace and climbed over the railing there. Teetering on the downslope side, he scoped out a suitable spot to sleep in the undergrowth and then nestled himself among some genista shrubs. The light was grainy. He lay on his stomach. Then he turned onto his back. From time to time he sat up in fright, as if a thought had hit him, but each time lethargy overwhelmed him again. He didn't feel capable of making any decision. His gaze wandered to the swaying treetops between which the evening sun hung like violet-colored glass, and he wished he were dead.

50

Contrazoom

Concerning the gods, I have no means of knowing whether they exist or not or of what sort they may be. Many things prevent knowledge including the obscurity of the subject and the brevity of human life.

PROTAGORAS

H IS DREAMS WERE STALKED by endless herds of stiff, wooden goats inside which timber worms worked dressed as priests. With a swat of his hand, as if he were casting out ghosts, he sat up in the morning light.

After he had stewed for fifteen minutes or longer, he walked up to the bungalow. Twenty or thirty steps below the terrace he hesitated. He crouched behind a tree and cried. And waited. Finally he knocked on the door. He put his eye on the outside of the peephole, knocked again, and then went around the building and looked in the window. The blinds in the bedroom weren't down. The bed was empty. Helen's suitcase was no longer on the dresser.

With the second key, which he still had in his pocket, he opened the door. He called Helen's name. Went from room to room. Everything was cleaned out. There was a hotel form on the nightstand, not filled out. The only thing left was the gleaming chrome machine with the Polish writing on it that they had taken together from the workshop, which sat on the sideboard. And a basket of fruit.

Next to the despair he had felt when he first awoke in the barn and realized that his memory wasn't coming back, this was the worst moment. And he didn't know whether or not she had left the bungalow in such a hurry because of him. She had never spoken of her travel plans.

The main key had been turned in to reception, as a hotel staff member told him with a maximum of courtesy, and the bungalow was paid for another two days. There was, however, no information about the hastily departed American business-woman. What businesswoman? This morning? No, the night porter was no longer in the building.

Carl sat on the terrace of the bungalow, ate an apple and looked out over the pines to the ocean. He opened the refrig-erator. The freezer drawer. He read the technical data printed on the chrome machine again. A movie flickered gray on the television. For a second time he gathered the scraps of paper out of the trash can, but didn't puzzle them back together. He shook the bedcovers. He lifted up the pillows. He found a sweater under one and he held it to his face and breathed through it for several minutes before putting it on. He looked under the bed.

There he found wood chips from a broken pencil and a pink hairband with a few long blonde hairs stuck in it.

Carl found an empty shampoo bottle in the bathroom, and he kept finding himself back in front of the gleaming chrome machine. Why had Helen confused it with a mine? Had she really? He examined the built-in two-pin plug on the side and looked around for a cable that he could repurpose. The cable of the lamp on the nightstand was attached, but the television had a twin wire. But the plug didn't fit the chrome machine.

Resigned, he dropped onto the sofa and changed the chan-nels of the TV with his feet. Test pattern, test pattern, movie.

"Now you listen to me. I'll say this once. We are not sick men."

He took a bite of the apple core, chewed once and spat it onto the television.

Beneath the wet apple remnants Helen's face flickered on the screen. Carl closed his eyes for a moment and when he opened them again it wasn't Helen. It wasn't even a woman. It was Bruce Lee. With dancer-like ease he passed through a light-filled rectangle into a dark room and punched with the side of his hand the larynx of a man who you could tell by his laugh alone was obviously evil. Just like Helen had done. Exactly the same.

Carl walked down past both terraces to the beach while coughing and spitting pieces of the apple core and shaking his head. A few pale Europeans were sunning themselves. A squall blew their towels around.

Carl sat down in a sheltered spot among some black volcanic rock that formed a natural boundary on one side of the property and stared at the waves as they went about their timeless business.

Diagonally below him, two Berbers squatted in blue scarves. A young girl of perhaps twelve and an old woman with a face like a skull and eyes like holes. The old lady was holding a thin stick that was covered in a black paste. She pressed the girl's head to her breast, clawed at one of her eyes with her index and middle finger, and ran the stick across her eyelid. The girl opened her eye, now circled in black, and blinked.

The more Carl thought about it, the less he could take issue with any of Helen's allegations. She had followed logic, and logically speaking she was right. Everything that had happened during this short life he was able to remember was unlikely. An almost frightening abundance of improbability. His family, his buddy, the wooden gun... the Polish machine. Nothing made any sense. He tried to recall the words of the men in the workshop and detected a glance from the girl with the blackened eyes.

The old woman was dyeing one of the girl's hands with henna, and Carl wondered what had possibly convinced an American cosmetics company to send one of its employees to a country where people seemed satisfied with black and red paste. Helen would have to put in a lot of effort to sell anything here... and suddenly he was struck by something about her list that was off. He froze. Helen's telephone list. That she had prepared while he stayed behind on the beach and Michelle read her comics and read tarot cards with the German tourist. When Helen went up to the bungalow it had been between ten and eleven in the morning. She wasn't there long, maybe fifteen minutes. And during that time she had apparently called friends and acquaintances in Paris, London, Seville, Marseilles, New York and Montreal and asked them to look for the name Cetrois in the phonebook... the names Cetrois, Cetroix, Sitrois, Setrois. Why was this just occurring to him now?

A ship was sailing on the horizon, beyond which at great distance lay America. The time difference to New York must have been six or seven hours, meaning Helen had called there between three and five in the morning. It wasn't impossible. But was it *likely*? And what kind of friends were they? Maybe there were freaks who weren't bothered by being woken up in the middle of the night to look in their phonebook for a series of non-existent French names. But Helen didn't seem like the type to hang out with freaks. And once this thought had got into Carl's head, a veritable flood of other inconsistencies occurred to him.

That Helen had searched his things was the least of them—he had after all also searched her things. But why did she have handcuffs, leg irons and the other thing that looked like a baton and certainly was one? How had he seriously believed that she needed them for sexual purposes? And how as an employee of an American cosmetics company did someone learn to crush a man's larynx with a single blow like Bruce Lee? Didn't all of it point to some sort of law enforcement training? The more Carl thought about it, the less doubt he had. Helen, who had accompanied him day after day, had practically shadowed him—why had she never shown even the slightest sign of her professional duties? Totally coincidentally her sample case had fallen into the ocean as she disembarked from her ship. During a skirmish on the gangplank. A *schoolboy* had ripped it from her hands.

"You're paranoid," he heard Helen's voice say in the back of his mind, and at the same time he remembered her peculiar unconcealed interest in the mine, only the mine. He was sure. In his mind he pictured Helen coming through the door in some nebulous uniform and putting his hands and ankles in cuffs… but there was one thing, unfortunately, that contradicted all these illusory images in his head. And that was the circumstances of their meeting. He had stumbled upon her at the gas station in the desert. She couldn't possibly have known that he would turn up there. And he had approached her, not the other way around.

Exhausted, he slumped in front of the television. He sat there without moving until the late news came on. Dr Cockcroft's bearded face popped into his head. Hadn't he had the same doubts about the doctor? Hadn't he raised a flood of objections against him and in the end everything, and hadn't he wanted to see him as a charlatan, just not the one he actually was? Maybe he really was paranoid. He thought about it for a few minutes and then jumped up and went through all the drawers in the kitchen. In the utensil drawer he found a large knife, a small screwdriver and a flashlight. He took them and went out into the night and crept down the serpentine path to the next bungalow.

No lights were on and as far as he could remember none had been on during the last few nights, either. The blinds were shut, the place discernibly vacant. He shone the light on the front and the garden, convinced himself that nobody was watching him, and broke open the mailbox with the knife and screwdriver. He found a shrink-wrapped packet from the hotel to the next guest, some ads for restaurants and dive schools, the same ones that had been in Helen's mailbox. He found all sorts of things. But he did not find a flyer for a psychological practice.

While he was still staring at the papers in his hand, the garden lit up. On the other side of the street, a few steps up the hill, a light had gone on in the upper floor of one of the buildings. Two slender figures moved toward each other behind floral curtains. Carl thought for a second, marched over to the place with the bundle of ads in his hand and rang the doorbell. After a while the door opened a crack. Quiet music could be heard.

"Have you looked in your mailbox in the last few days?"

"Sorry?"

"Have you looked in your mailbox in the last few days?"

The door opened wider. A young man and then a younger man looked at him a little confused. They were both wearing bathrobes, and the hair of one of them was wet. Their gaze was drawn to Carl's gestures, particularly those gestures made with the hand holding the long knife. They listened very earnestly and answered just as earnestly. Yes, they had been here for quite a while, nearly half a year, and they had regularly emptied their mailbox. One of them was a journalist and communicated regularly with Paris… and there hadn't been any trouble with the mail thus far. They were professionally dependent on it, they hadn't received a flyer for a psychology practice. No, they were sure. They would have remembered. They would be happy to have another look if he—what was his name again—would like.

Carl waited at the door with his head hanging. One disappeared into the house while the other waited at the door and fiddled with his bathrobe, which kept opening. So they were neighbors… interesting. And a psychology practice, really? That was connected to the Sheraton? For tourists? No, he could scarcely imagine it, sorry. Not that he had any problem with it, he himself had been to therapy several times, in New Jersey by the way, though more out of curiosity rather than because of an actual problem. But he was shocked that the same sort of thing was available here. Psychology in Africa, wasn't that a bit like trying to sell refrigerators to Eskimos?

Carl strained to look past the man into the dark of the house.

The other man returned with a stack of ads and opened envelopes and confirmed apologetically that they had no such flyer.

"But you received one, or what? And now you need psychological assistance? No?"

Both men began at the same moment to laugh in a very odd way, and Carl, who wasn't sure whether they were being friendly or making fun of him, quickly left.

He tossed the knife, the screwdriver and the bundle of papers he still had in his hand into some bushes and wandered up the hill along the little alley. Nobody had received a flyer, there had been no flyer. Only at Helen's had there been one. In the only mailbox in the city where somebody with *real* problems was staying.

Carl had trouble finding the street where the practice was located. Only when he found the door he had tried in vain to unlock with his own key after leaving Dr Cockcroft did he recognize it.

There were no lights on. The door was open. Carl first pushed the doorbell and then felt around for the light switch in the hall. But the light didn't work, not in any of the rooms. Carl rummaged through the entire building with the flashlight. All the furniture was gone. His surprise was limited. The three-legged table on the top floor was the only thing left. Both of the books were gone, too.

Carl opened the window with an indefinable sound of despair. He braced his elbows on the windowsill and looked out over the street into the night. The stars. The people, the buildings, the practice. Dr Cockcroft, Helen, the Polish machine. The corpse in the desert. He went back into the room and sat down on the floor with his back to the wall. Just as before, he had the feeling that he might be able to find something if he just thought things through, but whenever he tried to connect the various threads they got tangled in his hands and then a strong gust of wind blew through his thoughts that not only blew apart the connections but sent the threads themselves off into the air. All that was left was paralyzing darkness, and thinking about it was as painful as banging his head against a wall.

In the few days he was able to remember, he had experienced more absurd things than many people did in seventy years. And now he was running the risk of losing this new life again. Helen gone, Dr Cockcroft gone, a doctor's practice that perhaps never existed. The cartridge stolen, Bassir's ultimatum expired… and someone might possibly have been cutting off his son's finger or raping his wife at that very moment.

He found it difficult to think of words to express his emotions. Not to mention for his situation. He didn't know if he could feel anything at all. He turned around and hit his head against the wall. Half numb, he went back to the window and looked out. Dark shadows stood on the dark corners. One of the shadows was watching him. Or at least it seemed that way to him. Anyway. Either his pursuer or his paranoia hadn't disappeared. He shone the beam of light from his flashlight on his own face. They might as well see him. They should see that they were being permitted to see him. They should see that he didn't care. They should go ahead and come for him.

51

Marshal Mellow

Two Vietcong prisoners were interrogated on an airplane flying toward Saigon. The first refused to answer questions and was thrown out of the airplane at 3,000 feet. The second immediately answered all the questions. But he, too, was thrown out.

WILLIAM BLUM

B UT NOBODY CAME and, overwhelmed by fatigue, Carl finally lay down on the floor and tried to sleep. He wasn't able to. A quiet banging sound kept him from falling asleep. He closed the window, but the sound reverberated like a heartbeat through the walls and ceiling. It robbed him of his last ounce of sanity. Finally he got up, went down onto the street and looked around. He took a few steps in the direction of the Sheraton, then, following an impulse, instead followed the sound. It led him to a building behind Dr Cockcroft's office, above which hung a defective neon sign. The walls on either side of the entrance were covered with layers of posters, Jimi Hendrix, Castles Made of Sand... Africa Unite. And pasted sideways across everything by the hundred was a freshly inked image of a rectangular face with a monstrously broad jaw, around which three smaller heads and various musical instruments circled like swirling thoughts.

Marshal Mellow and his Skillet Lickers—Life!

While Carl read the dubious English, the pulsing rhythm went silent and muted elation rang out from the interior of the building. Two Bedouins with joints in their hands made their way around him, and then a busload of tourists who suddenly showed up pushed toward the entrance, pulling Carl along. He tried for a moment to escape the surge of bodies but gave up once he was past the ticket table and pressed into a thick wall of dry-ice fog.

The contours of a large hall were discernible from time to time, filled with a mix of people that was unusual for the area—Arabs, Americans, tourists, rowdy teens, men and women. There were even a handful of local women. A single spotlight cut through the fog, on stage stood a rectangular man with a monstrous chin wearing an American naval admiral's uniform (if Carl wasn't mistaken), he tapped the microphone and began to talk in a very soft voice. He talked without moving his body and only part of his face. His hands were wrapped around the microphone, his jaw set. Only his lips moved, like in a poorly synchronized cartoon. As Dixieland sing-song filled the room, Carl ordered a water at the bar and breathed the THC-saturated air. He heard scattered applause and enthusiastic screeches behind him and through it all, unwavering, the soft voice of Marshal Mellow talking about impulse control, four-year-old children, deferred gratification and character, about the Korean War, blood and thunder and the Marshmallow Experiment. It remained unclear for a long time whether the speech was propaganda or the introduction to a song. On the one hand the words seemed dark and incoherent, on the other hand his talk was getting the hippies at the front of the hall worked up. The drummer threw a young man who had climbed onto the side of the stage out over the crowd into the third or fourth row. Women screamed.

The band members on bass, guitar, synthesizer and drums were also wearing uniforms (lower-ranking), and their square jaws gave the impression that they might actually be affiliated with the armed forces. These were not times when the American military could expect to be met with enthusiasm or even polite applause abroad or at home for that matter—and certainly not in front of this random collection of hippies—and Carl wondered if perhaps they had actually hit upon their ironic stage clothing because of their chiseled physiognomy and not the other way around.

The drum played a little roll and the whole room immediately pressed forward, pulling Carl along. Two women got up on the speaker towers; they began to spin around like chess pieces. Suddenly Carl felt his T-shirt being pulled up in the back. Two arms wrapped around his midriff, and because he had been staring at the two pretty women for too long his first thought was that there was a pretty woman behind him now. But the downward patting motion of the hands quickly made clear that he was mistaken. He tried to turn in the crowd. A dark shadow ducked down behind him and continued cavalierly to pat his pants. Carl struck at the head with both fists and a thin young man slowly emerged from the darkness below. Three vertical scars ran from the forehead to the chin of his beaming face.

"I had to check to see if you had a Claymore in your pants, man. Don't get upset... but apparently you still haven't bought one."

Risa, known as Khach-Khach. He smacked Carl on the shoulder, grinned even more broadly, and seemed genuinely happy. In the din around him, Carl couldn't make out every word. Marshal Mellow took a step back from the microphone and looked at his fellow band members.

"Can I buy you a drink, you hobby terrorist? What do you want to have... about the whole thing? Listen, I'll sell you one for... but first the song... the song...oh, man. Geeshie. Mellow is... but Geeshie... ferried over specially with the boat."

He steered Carl toward the stage by his hips. The hall had got quiet. Mellow now had a cigarette in his mouth and was sort of shadow-boxing with the microphone stand. The Americans in the audience shouted obscenities, the Arabs joined in, some fearfully, some excited about the intensity of the foreign words. Then a bass line boomed out and the room set in motion as one. Someone collapsed directly in front of Carl. Hands pressed to ears. He himself was pushed forward and to the side. He dropped his cup. Two black men in colorful pants and batik tops shoved their way through the crowd with their elbows. A sludgy, psychedelic rhythm poured out of the speakers, the slowest, sludgiest rhythm Carl had ever heard, like a hypnotized dinosaur stomping unknowingly over flower children and a meadow full of butterflies in a gently rolling landscape. Above the proceedings opened up a sky filled with the suns of a million spotlights and out of those heights came the falsetto voice of Marshal Mellow, naked and featherless, squawking as it flitted downward, a tiny, prehistoric bird landing on the dinosaur's neck and tossed around. Carl wondered whether somebody had slipped something into his water.

He couldn't follow the lyrics or the music or understand the crowd's excitement. The appallingly loud speakers did nothing but scare him and he tried to plow his way out of the mass of people. He felt Risa's hand on his shoulder. He shook it off. Suddenly a jolt went through the room. A girl with thin brown pigtails had entered the stage or been thrown onto it. She was wearing a knee-length skirt, a tight green T-shirt and apparently no bra. Intensifying calls of "Geeshie, Geeshie!"

Marshal Mellow had stopped singing. The girl stood at the edge of the stage and stared out over the heads of the audience. Then she lifted her T-shirt to her neck, let it down again, and left the stage. The room exploded. The bass came thick and fast. Carl saw to it that he got out.

A man was lying on the floor of the dark corridor that led to the exit. As Carl went to step over him he grabbed Carl's ankle with both hands.

"Let go."

"What are you looking for?"

"Let go of my foot."

"You trying to find Geeshie? Wait in the back. I'm her manager."

With his free foot he kicked himself out of his grasp and then walked down the hall and up two steps. He opened a door and found himself in a store room full of drinks.

The supposed manager had in the meantime managed to stand up and blocked Carl's way back out.

"What are you looking for?"

"The exit. Get out of the way."

"You're not looking for the exit. You're looking for yourself."

"What do you want?"

"What do *you* want?"

"I just want to get out of here."

"That's what we all want."

As if he'd been struck by a gust of wind, the manager collapsed to the floor and grabbed at Carl's leg again as he fell. Carl stepped over him like a pair of scissors and as he did so he noticed that on the shoulder and chest of the jacket the man was wearing were dark threads, as if it were a military jacket with the badges of rank ripped off.

"You guys are really military, are you?"

"Come here my pretty warrior. As you know, I am the man who is your father."

A door suddenly opened in front of Carl. That was the exit. The door slammed closed again. Carl limped toward it, pulling the manager along behind him, and felt for the door handle. There was no handle. He banged on the door.

"What is going on? Why is it closed?"

"It is closed because it is closed," the manager explained solemnly.

The boom had fallen silent and all that was audible was the muted voice of Marshal Mellow.

"Horrible," said Carl as he tried to free himself.

"No truer words were ever spoken," confirmed the manager. "The dumbest, deafest singer the world has ever known. And I am wise. I'm Geoffrey Weise. I wrote the songs. Ask me a question, you friend of truth."

"Why is that door closed?"

"My hand is shaking. Shit, my hand is shaking." The man looked at his elbow, horror-stricken.

"Why is that door closed?"

"The door is closed because it is closed. And now the door is open. Think about that."

And someone did indeed open both sides of the door at that very moment, and Carl ran out onto the street, dragging the manager behind him.

"If you don't take acid you don't know who you are."

"I don't know anyway. Let go."

"Do you take acid?"

"No."

"That's what I mean. Here, lick this, chéri. Lick it, lick it."

With helplessly jerky motions, as if he were trying to re-enact an educational film on epileptic fits, the man fidgeted his way across the road while trying to fish something out of his bag at the same time. This finally gave Carl the chance to flee.

"You were looking for the exit and you found it," called Geoffrey Weise after him. "Do you realize how symbolic that is?"

Gasping, with trembling knees, Carl stopped at the next crossroad. He looked around and wasn't sure where to go when he once again felt someone poke his shoulder from behind. Or rather, gently massage his shoulder, not poke it.

"Hey, hey, hey," said the beaming Risa, holding a set of keys in Carl's face. "Can you drive, hobby terrorist? I need someone to drive me to Tindirma. Ten dollars, or a mine with a big boom. Or both. Okay?"

52

Tuareg

Soon they will die—
Yet, showing no sign of it,
cicadas screech

BASHO

CARL TURNED DOWN the offer at first, but then he remembered the yellow Mercedes that he had left in Tindirma and he reached for the keys.

Risa dozed almost the entire way through the desert with his face against the passenger-side window. The Salt Quarter appeared in the headlights followed by the earthen road, the brick camels, the gas station, Tindirma.

Burned-out ruins filled the streets around the commune. Families sat next to their furniture in the street and slept. Carl found the Mercedes undamaged except for some ash on the windshield, and Risa, who tried to take him to a bordello in an apparent attempt to thank him, added another ten dollars to the promised ten when they parted and said: "If you change your mind. Life is short."

Life is short. The sentence was nothing more than an empty cliché, but Carl couldn't get it out of his head. He didn't take his foot off the gas for the entire ride back. He raced. The gas station, the brick camels, the earthen road, the Salt Quarter. A kilometer or two before the souk and already within sight of the Sheraton looming above the sea of houses, he turned onto a sandy, rocky road. The Mercedes trailed a meter-high cloud of dust behind it that was lit up spectacularly by the morning sun, and by the time the cloud had settled on the little workshops, fruit stands, the souk and the steam bath of the Ville Nouvelle, a white convertible with four men inside had already parked between the bath and the war memorial. A strikingly nice car, it was an Alfa Spider with red leather seats.

The driver of the Spider had put a paper plate of meat on the dashboard in front of the steering wheel and reached for it with both hands. He was short, slender and wiry. There was something choleric about the way he moved, even while doing something as harmless as eating. He shoved dripping pieces of meat into his mouth with both hands. Then, as the cloud of dust surrounded him, he suddenly stopped chewing—with his cheeks stuffed, looking like a cow interrupted while grazing—and spat part of his food out onto the tachometer and turned as the dust cleared and looked at the other occupants of the car.

Next to him, in the passenger seat, sat a burly black man with his head nearly shaved, cursing and wiping sauce from his knee. In the back seat, behind the black man, was an equally stocky but light-skinned man who stuck his hand up in the air at the sight of the Mercedes. Next to the light-skinned man was a somewhat older white-haired man who seemed no less agitated but more strong-willed than the others, and he was loading a pistol. Adil Bassir.

Difficult to say why they were parked there, what they were waiting for and what they wanted. Perhaps it was just one of those coincidences that shouldn't trouble anyone much in a novel and that in real life contribute to the invention of the idea of fate.

A second later the paper plate flew out of the car and with a howl of its V-6 engine the Spider headed down the earthen road, skidded sideways toward a mud-brick wall on the opposite side, and then shot off after the cloud of dust.

The Alfa Spider had a top speed of over 200 kilometers per hour, but in the narrow alleyways, on the pothole-littered earthen road and with the thick cloud of dust in front of it, it didn't get above sixty. It lagged further behind the Mercedes and then caught up, pedestrians ran out of the way, and when the dust cloud finally cleared in front of the Spider's hood, among the huts on the outskirts of town, the Mercedes had disappeared.

The driver slammed the brakes, threw the car in reverse and raced back to the previous intersection and jerked his head around, ninety, ninety, and two hundred and seventy degrees: four perplexed men in an Italian sports car full of food remnants.

Two children were standing on top of a tower made of car tires. Bassir hid his weapon between his knees and yelled: "Which way did he go?"

The children stared. They were maybe eight and nine years old. Their feet and teeth were black, their clothing tattered. Flies clung to the face of the smaller child, at the corner of his mouth, beneath his nostrils, on his eyes and forehead. The larger one was holding a mushy lump in his hand that looked like barley bread; he had been chewing it and had taken it out of his mouth. The skin of his arms shone with the purity of youth, the color of chocolate, but the hands of both children were red and raw with eczema as if they were regularly bathed in acid. The stench of a tannery wafted out from some nearby yard.

"The yellow Mercedes!" shouted Bassir, gesturing at the vanished dust cloud. "Which way!"

No answer.

"Julius," said Bassir, handing the pistol to the light-skinned man. He jumped out of the car and with a step was standing in front of the children.

"Which way!" he asked now.

Coal-black eyes staring into the barrel of the pistol.

"The yellow Mercedes!"

He held the pistol against the ear of the smaller child. The boy stammered incomprehensibly. A fly took off from the corner of his eye, alit on the pistol barrel and scurried along it excitedly.

Julius repeated his question a second time, jerked one of the boy's arms up and shot him in the elbow joint. The child fell over immediately, without a sound, his legs writhing around on the ground. The other boy stood there with his mouth open.

"Which way?"

The larger boy gulped but offered nothing more of an answer.

"I don't think they understand you," said the black man from the passenger seat. "Fucking Tuaregs."

He yelled a question at the boy in Tamajaq. He immediately raised his trembling arm and pointed down a side street behind the men. There were rows and rows of huts along it, and beyond the last one the boxy shape of a parked Mercedes 280 SE gleamed in the sunlight.

53

The Five Columns

If a hare, a goat or another animal passes before a praying person the prayer remains valid. The jurists are in agreement that only three entities annul a prayer: a grown woman, a black dog and a donkey.

ABDUL-AZIZ IBN BAZ

CARL, WHO HADN'T EATEN a proper meal in an eternity, saw the little souk off to his right, felt in his pocket for his money and parked the car. He had only made it a few meters into the rows of merchants and was standing in front of a display of fresh bread when he heard screams behind him. A shot rang out. Above the heads of the shoppers he saw the nearly shaved head of a huge black man making his way toward him using his arms like a freestyle swimmer to clear the way. Behind him two more men shoving their way through the crowds. The smaller of the two was holding up an Uzi and the man with white hair was smiling. Carl knew immediately who they were and didn't need to think long about what they wanted from him. The ultimatum had expired. He fled into a cluster of people in the hope that they wouldn't shoot at him. And in fact they did not shoot, but the people all ran off screaming. Everyone ran into buildings. For a second Carl was alone on the street with his pursuers. He sprinted into a narrow street and realized too

late that it was a cul-de-sac. A door closed in his face. At the
exact same time a second shot rang out.

Carl threw himself to the ground. Clay exploded out of a
wall directly in front of him and sprayed in his face. A burst
of machine-gun fire went over him. He threw his arms over
his head and looked past his armpit at the men following him.

A snapshot: from a horizontal position in the street. His
own body sloping away from his armpits. A lost shoe was in
the picture, not his own. At the entrance to the cul-de-sac the
body of the smaller man hung in the air, his bent knee nearly
touching the ground, the weightless Uzi above hands thrown
high in the air just like the famous photo from the Spanish
Civil War. Next to him Adil Bassir colliding with the nearby
wall with an awkward swing like a marionette. The right side
of his face displayed a mix of relaxation and surprise, the left
side was being blown away in the form of mincemeat. The
black man was not in view. The pursuer who had got closest
to Carl, Julius, was lying two meters away in the sand, a lifeless
arm stretched out toward Carl's foot. A cherry-red bubble of
blood coming from his mouth.

Despite the freeze-frame of the images, the soundtrack continued incongruously on: bursts of machine-gun fire, shots from
a small-caliber handgun, screams. A nine-millimeter. American
accents. Two uniformed personnel grabbed Carl and dragged
him to a green Jeep Wagoneer. Or he ran along behind them,
he was barely conscious of what was happening. He came to
again while staring at the waffle pattern of a rubber mat at his
feet. The rubber mat was between the driver's seat and the back
seat of the jeep. On the waffle pattern: sand, balls of paper,
hair and a chewed piece of gum. And his own feet.

Sand and paper balls hopped and jumped in the rhythm of
the jeep. A hand on the back of his neck kept him from lifting
his head. The hand belonged to one of the uniformed men,

one with a brownish, nearly olive complexion and built like an armoire. He spoke two sentences of Arabic to Carl, high Arabic with a light Syrian accent. The other uniformed man, who had spoken in American English, sat in the front passenger seat and seemed to be in command. Four stars on his epaulets: were these guys really military? Wasn't one of them a member of Marshal Mellow's band? The bassist?

The driver was the only one Carl couldn't see. He was only able to see between the seats that he wasn't wearing a uniform but rather striped trousers. A girlishly small gloved hand held the gear shifter. A hairless wrist… in his feeble state of mind Carl thought for a second it might be Helen, coming to his rescue.

The man in the passenger seat yelled. The Syrian pushed Carl's head down more, the jeep leaned into the turns.

"Everything okay?"

"You got him?"

"Are you hurt?"

"You got him?"

"I've got him."

"You okay?"

"Yeah. You?"

"Yeah."

"Anyone following us?"

"All dead."

"I said: anyone following us?"

"No."

"You sure?"

"I got them all."

"Are you hurt?"

"Who, me?" asked Carl.

"Are you hurt?"

"No."

"Turn right up here."

"Who are you?"

"You'll come to a bridge. Take another right after the bridge."

"Who are you?"

"Slow down."

"Where are we going?"

Carl tried to lift his head. The Syrian pressed his hand into his neck even harder and said something about security. Carl complained even though it wasn't clear to him why he was the only one hunched over. He could see that the driver and the man in the passenger seat were sitting upright, and the Syrian, too, who was half again as tall as Carl, wasn't taking cover. Apparently his life was more important than theirs.

Only now, several minutes after his rescue, did he feel the tingly process of disintegration in his bones and the way his deadly fear had turned his body to jelly. Sobbing hysterically, he thanked his rescuers in a tone that seemed miserable even to him. They didn't react.

"Left there?"

"Yeah, I'd say that's the left we want."

"The wide street there?"

"That's the wrong one, I think."

"You think?"

"Ninety per cent."

"Then I'm turning left."

"There's the synagogue."

"That's a different synagogue."

"What if I just take a right?"

"No."

"You say no?"

"I agree."

"You agree?"

"Do you want to tell me who you are?"

"Calm down." That came from the front seat.

When Carl tried to lift his head again the Syrian twisted one of his arms behind his back. He tried to defend himself and got a punch in the ribs, then he felt his wrists being handcuffed behind his back.

"Is he making trouble?"

"Wait a second."

"You got it?"

"Of course I got it."

"If he starts making trouble the syringe is in the back."

"It broke earlier. But it doesn't matter, he's not causing any trouble."

"He can't scream."

"He's not screaming."

"If he screams, put something in his mouth."

"What the hell?" bellowed Carl.

The Syrian pressed a balled-up handkerchief into his face and tried to stuff it into his mouth. Carl turned his head back and forth. "I'm not saying anything," he said through clenched teeth.

"Quiet down, quiet down," murmured the driver in a voice that seemed vaguely familiar to Carl.

He thought for a moment and then said toward the driver's seat: "I know you."

"It would be strange if you didn't. It's not anterograde amnesia. And now keep quiet."

"It's you? Why are you doing this? What do you want?"

"Easy."

"What do you want from me?"

"What do you want from me?" mimicked the man in the passenger seat in a simpering voice.

"I said quiet down."

"What is this all about?"

"Okay," said Dr Cockcroft. "Gag him."

"I can't get it in his mouth. He's clenching his teeth."

"Stop him from floundering around like that."

"But I can't get it in."

"So just leave it as long as he stays quiet. Are you going to stay silent? Or do you want to keep jabbering?" Dr Cockcroft jerked the wheel sharply a few times to make Carl's head loll from side to side.

He was silent and tried to concentrate on the noises outside the vehicle.

The windows were all closed despite the heat. The muted sound of traffic on the main road, passing music, the calls of a water salesman. Horse hooves. While waiting at an intersection, the din of many voices and along with it extra pressure on his neck from the Syrian.

At some stage the Syrian asked how much longer it would be and the man in the passenger seat mumbled something. Carl saw his angular jaw from below and was suddenly convinced it was the bassist from the band.

"Approximately," said the Syrian.

"About an hour to get out of the city. Then about two more. And if the road cuts out before the mine, we might need the whole night."

"It's nearly time for the Maghrib prayer."

Nobody responded to this statement, and the Syrian added: "When the sun is down we have to stop for a few minutes."

"You must be out of your mind." The bassist. "Just see to it that you do your job."

"That won't work."

"What won't work?"

"I'll quit."

"What?"

"If I can't pray then I'm out."

"So pray."

"You have to stop."

"Are you crazy, man? In the middle of the city, with a hostage back there who's not even gagged, just so you can fucking pray?"

"I can stuff something in his mouth."

"Better yet, pray in the car."

"It's not allowed."

"Of course it's allowed. Now shut your mouth."

"Ah," said the Syrian with forced self-certitude. "So that's how it is. I'm supposed to shut up." He rummaged around in his pocket and then stretched his arm out toward the front of the vehicle. "I'm getting out. Here's the hundred and the twenty. Stop the car."

"Keep the fucking money, you can't quit now."

"Watch me."

"You can pray in the back seat. Rattle off your verses, bow down and stop bothering us."

"It won't work. Even if I wanted to. Don't you see where we're going?"

"We're going where we want to go."

"We're going west. Mecca is—"

"Good god, we're going west! So pray to the west," barked the bassist. "The earth is round after all."

"I don't have to put up with this." A strained pause. "This is an outrage."

"What's an outrage? That the earth is round?"

"Stop the car."

"Keep going."

During this exchange of words Carl felt the pressure of the hand on his neck diminish. He cautiously lifted his head and looked out of the vehicle. The buildings of the Ville Nouvelle. Shouting, the bassist turned around and banged the handle of his gun on Carl's head.

"Do. Your. Job."

"Then stop. If I can't pray, I quit."

"Do you want more money?"

"Your narrow-mindedness."

"What?"

"I said: your narrow-mindedness."

"What about it?"

"Your Jewish estimation of money! You think you can manage everything with money! Money, money, money."

"I'm happy to have you work for us for free."

"I've never met an American who was any different. The only thing that matters to you is mammon. You don't pray, you don't know the five columns, your salvation is—"

"Five columns, don't spew that crap."

"It is a holy obligation, and the holy obligation—"

"But not in every situation?" Dr Cockcroft intervened. "You wouldn't pray during a war if there was an Israeli tank rolling toward you."

"Though that would explain a lot," mumbled the bassist.

"I've never missed a prayer, not in twenty years. And we are at war."

"That is debatable."

"Your war, maybe. I am just an employee. You pay me—but I don't have anything to do with the whole thing."

"Wow, you don't have anything to do with the whole thing!" With feigned excitement the bassist turned to Dr Cockcroft. "We've hired the man they call Pliers and he has nothing to do with the whole thing! His salvation has nothing to do with the whole thing."

"I'm getting out at the next traffic light."

"There are no more traffic lights."

"I'm getting out anyway. Stop."

Nothing happened for a while, then the Syrian opened the door on his side. Carl could hear the road rushing by. A melee ensued, Carl's clothes were yanked, and he used the opportunity to lift his head and have a look around. They were driving on the six-lane Boulevard of the May Revolution that connected the Ministry of Commerce to the civilian airport. They were just passing a bus station and for a split second Carl looked into the eyes of a woman who was waiting there and watching traffic go by. A frizzy perm, neat clothing and an upstanding, ordinary face. The woman from Tindirma. He nodded desperately at her with his head. She acted as if she saw nothing.

The bassist clubbed Carl and the Syrian with the pistol grip from the front seat. Dr Cockcroft sped up. The Syrian closed the door.

"I'm a faithful man and a good Muslim—"

"Even a faithful man and good Muslim is allowed to skip prayers once. You can make up for it in two hours."

"That's against the rules."

"And I suppose kidnapping and torture are not against the rules?"

"You do it, too."

"What do we do? What kind of bullshit logic is that?"

"Is it consistent with your religion?"

"I'm an atheist."

"You said you were a Jew."

"I said my mother was a Jew. But she believed in God about as much as she did in the superiority of Aryan cock. And now tell me how you can do your job and still believe that Allah will be enraged because of one measly missed prayer? Do you think you'll meet your maker one day and say: Hey, I'm the guy they call Pliers, but everything I did is excusable because an atheist Jew and a bearded, piece-of-shit psychiatrist also did it?"

"You Americans just don't understand. Prayer is holy. Nothing is holy to you."

"The question isn't what is holy," said Dr Cockcroft. "The question is whether you are with us or not."

Carl didn't hear anything more for a long time. He could only guess what was being negotiated with glances. Finally the doctor's voice: "What if I turn around briefly? Would that be a compromise? We could pull off up ahead. Then we can turn around and drive eastward on the avenue for a few minutes and you can pray up here in the front seat, and then we'll turn around again. Does that work? Stopping here in the middle of Targat is not an option."

Twenty seconds in order to save face. Then: "I need absolute silence."

"Of course, silence, no problem!" yelled the bassist, and looking between the seats Carl saw Dr Cockcroft touch the bassist's forearm with the tip of his finger.

Then it was quiet for a long time. The jeep turned right. And then right again. Carl listened to the changing sounds. Heavier traffic. Construction. Beeping mopeds.

After a few minutes the painstakingly restrained voice of the bassist: "What's the story? Are you going to start or have you already? We can't go any further east."

"The sun is still up."

"What?"

The Syrian tapped on the side window. "There's a red glint."

"Have you lost your mind? The compromise was that we would turn around. Now that we have, kindly pray!"

"Only after the sun has set."

"What, what, what, what, what? You said it was time for your fucking evening prayer."

"I said it was *nearly* time. It will be time any minute now. When the sun has set."

"The sun has set, man!"

"The red glint has to be gone."

"What about them? Look! What are they doing?" The bassist turned around agitated.

"They're no Ja' faris."

If the bassist's tone up to this point had been a mix of threatening and hysterical, now it became bewildered.

"Do you know where we are going? Do you think this is some kind of vacation trip? If we drive another five minutes in this direction we'll be in East Targat."

"What's the problem? I'll keep his head down."

"Cockcroft, turn the fucking car around."

"I can't turn here."

Carl heard a rooster crow.

"Pray!"

"Don't make a fool of yourself." The Syrian was getting a second wind. "You can't pray as long there's a red glow in the sky. It's haram."

"Haram!"

Dr Cockcroft's voice, which was also no longer so calm: "Why is it haram? Those people are doing it."

"That's the way it is."

"But why? Does it say so in the Koran?"

"I don't know."

"You don't know if it's in the Koran?"

"I know that's the way it is. And that is enough."

"How do you know that?"

"How do I know, how, how? Because I know. It's haram at sunrise, too, at sunset, and when the sun is at its zenith—haram."

"In other words: it's not in the Koran, and you don't know where it comes from."

"I don't need to know where it comes from. My father prayed that way, my father's father prayed that way, the father of my father's father prayed that way. Islam isn't like your churches, where one person tells everyone what to do."

"Which part of 'we are atheists' did you not understand?"

"Atheists or Christians, it's all the same. Nothing is sacred to you. And my sacred duty demands—"

"Sacred duty! You haven't even read the Koran. Can you even read? Sunrise, sunset, haram—what do you know."

"Since the people around us are praying," Dr Cockcroft said, trying to placate, "it is apparently a question of interpretation. And in this dire moment, in this quasi-military situation, and since we are currently heading toward the troops based in East Targat, I'm sure that an exception—"

"Open to interpretation, exactly." The Syrian's voice kept getting more and more calm, more polite, and he managed to come across as noticeably smug even with his modest English. "There are these schools of jurisprudence and those schools of jurisprudence. And in the Ja' fari school, you wait until the red glow is gone from the sky."

"Why?"

"That is a stupid question. Only a Nasrani would ask such a stupid question. It's not about why. It is about something greater than why. Why does God allow evil? Why do clouds float in the sky? Why doesn't America win the World Cup— why, why, why?"

"If you don't know," said Dr Cockcroft, "then I'm going to turn around."

"I know," said Carl. He stared at the rubber mat at his feet. The silence in the vehicle didn't seem to invite him either to speak or to shut up, so he continued talking. "It's because of the natural religions. In the Near East, where they come from. They didn't want the prayers of the orthodox believers to be mistaken for worship of the sun."

The Syrian patted his ventriloquist dummy's neck appreciatively. "That is exactly the reason." And he added boastfully: "Along with a hundred other reasons."

The bassist groaned. Dr Cockcroft drove slowly on. Shortly afterward Carl saw the Syrian take off his sandals. Carl's head was pulled sideways and wedged between the back of the passenger seat and the Syrian's knee. Then the Syrian's hand left the back of his neck, though not without a shove that made clear that any further movement would not be tolerated. Carl felt some jostling above him, then ninety kilograms leaned over him in the direction of Mecca.

Carl's upper body slowly slid sideways beneath the rhythmic motions above him. His mouth ended up near the door handle. He stretched out his neck.

After three or four futile attempts he managed to get the handle between his teeth. He waited for the moment when the prayer was over and the Syrian was getting himself upright again. The car took a sharp left and Carl opened the door, and with the help of the centrifugal force managed to wriggle out of the car. Two fists tried in vain to keep him in the vehicle. Kicking his feet wildly, Carl spilled out onto the street in front of a braying mule and, despite the handcuffs, landed on his feet and started running off. In the wrong direction. Directly in front of him a two-and-a-half-meter-high wall, buildings to the left and right. Behind him already the pursuers: screeching brakes, two car doors, at least two pairs of military boots stomping in the sand. They were already too close. He had no time to think about alternatives. There was a burned-out car propped up on blocks in front of the wall. With his hands still cuffed behind his back he took a running start and used the trunk and roof as a springboard, smacking with his hips into the top of the wall. For a moment he and his life hung suspended in air, then his upper body tilted cumbersomely over and down and he landed head-first in a giant pile of dates.

Merchants jumped up. Veiled women—a market—in the middle of a huge, gray tent. Carl rolled around in the fruit and looked up: nobody was jumping after him. He looked right and left: wall as far as he could see. He turned onto his back, pulled the handcuffs down around his seat and into the back of his knees and then pushed the chain under his feet. Another look up: still nobody. Screams around him. An old woman pulled on his clothing, held a smashed date in her hand in protest and yelled. He pushed her aside and bounded off. The screams immediately grew louder. Merchants and market women in billowing abayas came at him, and Carl noticed a door in the wall just a few steps away—through which came three men, smiling. Dr Cockcroft leading the way.

Carl impulsively pushed his way between two spice stands and scattered the colorful bags. He bumped into two sheep halves, jumped over a pile of unripe pumpkins and stumbled into a contraption of rope and sticks. A giant tent collapsed on top of him. Ear-splitting noise. A mass of people covered in gray linen heaved around him. The squawking women could still be heard but no longer seen, and when Carl managed to extricate himself from the tent cover, the first thing he saw was a drawn pistol.

The pistol was in the hand of a mustachioed policeman. Next to him, still partially covered in the tent cover, a second policeman with the remains of a broken water pipe in his hand, behind him the market women, behind them the Syrian, the bassist and Dr Cockcroft. Carl was so overcome by his luck that he gave his pursuers a look full of schadenfreude.

The Syrian whispered something to the bassist, the bassist whispered something to Dr Cockcroft, and Dr Cockcroft pulled a wallet out of his pocket and tossed it to the policemen.

As the valiant public servants were still examining the contents of the wallet, Carl felt himself being pulled by his handcuffs through the masses and shoved into the jeep with a kick.

BOOK FIVE

The Night

54

The Rattan Chair

All the Libyan nomads bury the dead in the same manner as
the Hellenes, exccpt the Nasamonians; they bury their dead in
a sitting posture and take care, when a sick man breathes his
last, to put the body in that position, and not on the back. Their
houses are constructed of asphodel-stalks, wattled with rushes,
and portable. Such are the customs of these people.

HERODOTUS

A GAG IN HIS MOUTH, a plastic bag loosely over his head
and the cuffs once again bound behind his back. His feet
bound together with the bassist's belt. To Carl the drive seemed
to last for ever. Aside from a few commands related to the directions, nobody said a word. The sounds of the city faded away
and soon there was nothing more to hear than the noise of
the jeep itself. Rocks pattered against the undercarriage. Carl
was sure they were driving through the desert. At some point a
sharp left turn and then a steep uphill climb. Serpentine. More
serpentine. The vehicle braked to a stop.

Strong hands pulled Carl out into the night. He was laid on
the ground and tied to something by a long rope around his neck.
He managed to glimpse out from under the plastic bag and saw
he was tied to the bumper of the jeep. He screamed into the
gag and felt two, four, six hands patting him down, yanking on

his clothes and searching his pockets. They removed his shoes and socks. They opened his pants and grabbed him between the legs. He writhed around. The plastic bag was taken off his head. They put his shoes back on. Then he heard the three men walk away. The wind carried snippets of words to him. Finally they returned. Dr Cockcroft shone a flashlight on Carl's face, double-checked the rope holding the gag in place, and then he and the others got back in the jeep. Apparently to sleep.

Carl didn't sleep. The balled-up rag in his mouth turned overnight into a giant, slimy lump. His jaw might as well have been paralyzed. He had long since lost feeling in his bound hands and feet.

He was happy to see the bassist get out of the vehicle at first light of the breaking dawn.

Dr Cockcroft did some exercises. Knee-bends, jumping jacks, push-ups. The bassist complained about the working conditions. The Syrian pressed his forehead to the ground and praised the All-Merciful. After each of the three had eaten an apple, they untied Carl from the bumper, took the belt from around his feet and pulled him by a long rope up the mountain, over the crest and down into the next canyon—and toward the goldmine. Practically the exact same path he had taken with Helen a few days before.

He had already had an idea of where they were taking him during the night when he'd seen the shape of the mountain, a black triangle against the starry sky. But he had rejected the thought again and again, and for a while, even as they approached the little plateau on the opposite side of the valley, where the windmill, a couple of casks and Hakim III's cabin stood, he still thought it could all be a coincidence. That's how strong his belief was that there was nothing to be found in the mine.

Some twenty meters below the cabin at the entrance to the tunnel, they laid him on his stomach behind a boulder, bound his feet with a rope that was then pulled up his back and secured to his neck, and left him there.

The gag in his mouth still seemed to be swelling. He fought to breathe through his nose, writhed around and groaned. The sun rose over the crest of the mountain. He thought he could hear voices above, but he was unable to turn his head that way. Then it was silent for a long time. Then the bassist came down the hillside, confirmed that the prisoner was still in the same spot, and disappeared again. Finally all three of the men returned, untied the rope at Carl's back and took the gag out of his mouth. Apparently he could scream now if he wanted to. He didn't scream. He would hardly have been able to anyway.

The Syrian filled a carbide lamp with water from a water bottle; what was left of the liquid he sprinkled on Carl's face.

Cockcroft, whom Carl had long since stopped addressing as doctor in his head, said a few words in a language Carl didn't understand, and the bassist answered. Then they led him up to the entrance of the mine and pulled him into a tunnel marked with a soot-black palm and four fingers. There followed a left hand with index finger and ring finger, and a right hand without a thumb. No sign of Hakim and his rifle.

The beam of the lamp fell on a rusty metal door set into the rock at an angle. Carl could not remember having seen it before. The Syrian opened it with a powerful tug. Beyond was a medium-sized room. Picks and shovels, iron rods and ropes, large wooden crates with the following inscription on them: "Return to Daimler Benz AG factory Düsseldorf". Smashed rocks, dust, slings. The toolshed of a miner.

In the middle of the room a chair, the seat of which was made of woven rattan. They sat Carl on it and tied him up. And they didn't just tie him up, they secured him completely. Nearly an hour went by before the Syrian and the bassist were satisfied with the results. Then Carl's elbows were bound together behind the seatback, his feet and ankles tied to the front legs and many meters of rope wound around his upper body. They wrapped a rope around his neck from behind. There were even ropes around his thighs. Finally the Syrian took the handcuffs off and tied his wrists together with painfully thin twine. At this point Carl was only able to move his head a little bit and wiggle his fingers. He was sweating with fear. Cockcroft and the bassist left the room without a word; they pulled the door closed behind them. The Syrian lit a cigarette, smiling. Carl was on the verge of passing out. Then the Syrian, too, left the room.

The carbide lamp belched smoke. The room was silent. Carl pulled and tore at his constraints. Sweat dripped from his chin. When the men returned the Syrian was carrying a metal case the size of a portable radio, which he put down next to Carl. The bassist was swinging a burlap sack that looked like a shopping bag from which he pulled a tangle of blue and yellow cables. He held it up for a moment like a schematic display of the human circulatory or nervous system and then handed it to Cockcroft.

"Why do they always leave it in this condition?" asked Cockcroft while trying to untangle the cables and moistening two electrodes attached to them. "Only because it doesn't personally belong to them. It's the element of human nature that will doom communism."

He handed the untangled cables to the Syrian, who plugged them into his gray case. Then they began to fight about where on Carl's body to attach the electrodes. The bassist and the Syrian agreed that the genitals were the preferred location, though because of the ropes, getting the electrodes to that spot was hardly possible. The ropes in the area of his hips made it impossible even to open his pants. They would have to have removed the constraints in order to place the electrodes.

"Then the head," said the Syrian.

"Head is always a good bet," agreed the bassist.

Cockcroft objected. His knowledge of electroconvulsive shock therapy was limited to, as he hinted, an article in a Russian-language psychology journal he had read the previous night, but he claimed that after this reading he was utterly convinced that shocking the brain could be beneficial for various conditions, most notably epilepsy, depression and paranoid psychosis—though never in cases of memory loss. On the contrary, it could lead to additional damage to the memory, and the purpose here was neither to damage the memory nor therapy, but rather a form of truth-seeking. Whether and to what degree there existed lapses in memory was by necessity a part of what they were trying to find out.

The others could say little to challenge this, and after they had all agreed to limit the electrodes to the extremities and neck, a new disagreement broke out over the question of whether or not the electricity needed to be routed around the heart.

Carl followed as if in a dream the discussion being conducted before his eyes in big words and poor arguments. The phrases that Cockcroft and the bassist trotted out, as well as the discourses that swayed the Syrian, created an increasingly surreal impression, an impression of rote knowledge and previous experience. And the fact that through it all the protagonists didn't cast so much as a single glance at the audience just added to its school-theater-like air.

The Syrian argued emphatically for a combination of the left hand and right foot, for the very reason that the current would cross the heart. The bassist pointed to his own groin and explained that using the left hand and right foot would also be an alternative way to ensure the current ran across the genitals, which seemed important to him, while Cockcroft ultimately prevailed with: right hand, right foot. And under no circumstances have the current cross the heart.

In the meantime the Syrian had taken another item out of the burlap bag, a gleaming black semicircular box with two knobs on it that looked like the foot pedal of a sewing machine and quite possibly was one. With a spiral cable he connected the small black box with the large gray one. An indicator light came on.

"Are we ready?" asked Cockcroft.

55

The Black Box

LUKE SKYWALKER: Your thoughts betray you, Father. I feel the
   good in you, the conflict.
DARTH VADER: There is no conflict.

Return of the Jedi

"WE ARE GOING TO ASK YOU a few questions," said the dubious psychiatrist, who had sat down on a long Daimler Benz AG crate directly in front of Carl. At his feet lay the black box. Further away, in the darkest corner of the cave, the bassist stood and smoked a cigarette, a glowing tip. The Syrian was squatting between the electrical connections on the ground.

"Very easy questions. Answer only with yes or no or clear, declarative sentences. Do not ask counter-questions. You have already been asked all the questions we have for you. At least most of them. But we have reason to believe that the answers we have got from you to this point do not bear a particularly close relationship to the truth. Which is why we are asking them again. And I will begin with the easiest of all: What is your name?"

"I don't know."

"Truly? If you are already struggling with this relatively easy question—do you have any idea what is in store for you?"

Cockcroft had leaned forward. Crumbs of tobacco clung to his beard. "I repeat: What is your name?"

"I don't know."

"That is your final word?"

"You know that I don't know."

"Don't speculate about the extent of my knowledge. I know more than you think. Answer the question."

"If you really were a doctor you would know."

"I am a doctor. Do you remember *my* name?"

"Cockcroft."

"Dr Cockcroft."

"But you're no doctor."

"You are mistaken. But that isn't the question. The question is: Who are *you*?"

"Do you know?"

"What did I say about countering questions with questions?"

"But you know, don't you? You know who I am? Or what I did? Why don't you just tell me?"

"Because you haven't even answered question number one. And you now have one last chance to do so." Cockcroft lifted his foot, held it a few centimeters above the black box and repeated in exactly the same tone as the first time: "What is your name?"

"I! Don't! Know!" yelled Carl.

The foot hung in the air indecisively for a moment then stomped down. Carl's body seized up in panic. His head flew back, he forced air out of his nose intermittently and sucked it in again through his back teeth.

He had tensed all his muscles in anticipation of the electric shock. The absence of pain brought tears to his eyes. The bassist, who had come closer, watched Carl's reaction contentedly, the Syrian watched with squinted eyes and Cockcroft with a furrowed brow. He turned the gray case off and then on again and pressed once more on the switch. With a slight time lag, Carl tensed up again. Again no pain. Cockcroft looked Carl in the eyes, waited a few seconds, and then made three quick, irregular motions with his foot. Carl tried as best as he could to tense up in the same rhythm and to groan. Cockcroft shook his head. With a few swift kicks he dispatched the black box out of view. It was silent for a moment. Then irritable stomps on the switch.

"The guy doesn't feel a thing," said Cockcroft.

The men examined the connections, shook the gray case and turned it over. They took the electrodes off Carl's skin, held them up to their own forearms, wet them with spit and stuck them on again. They ran their hands along every bit of cable. The Syrian pulled out the connector plugs and polished the metal clean. They jiggled the contacts, they unscrewed the foot switch and put it back together and tapped away on it. After excruciatingly long minutes they finally discovered a regulating screw on the back side of the gray case. Relieved, the Syrian turned the potentiometer all the way to the right, and the bassist said: "Are we ready?"

They turned back to the prisoner. Cockcroft closed the circuit and Carl flew in his chair into the wall.

It felt like liquid explosives had been pumped into every artery, every vein, and they were silently detonating.

"Amazing given the fact that he can't move at all," said the Syrian. Together with the bassist he righted the chair and checked the ropes.

Then they discussed whether they should turn down the potentiometer or weigh down the chair with rocks. Carl struggled for air the whole time and came to with the sensation that he'd been hit in the throat by a millstone.

The next thing he was aware of was a chunk of rock in his lap. A blinking indicator light. A smile framed by a beard.

"We've come to the exciting part of tonight's program," said Cockcroft.

56

Electricity

Our story deals with psychoanalysis, the method by which modern science treats the emotional problems of the sane. The analyst seeks only to induce the patient to talk about his hidden problems, to open the locked doors of his mind. Once the complexes that have been disturbing the patient are uncovered and interpreted, the illness and confusion disappear... and the devils of unreason are driven from the human soul.

HITCHCOCK,
Spellbound

H E TALKED ABOUT EVERYTHING he knew, and he talked about the things he didn't know, too. And he still didn't know what they wanted to know from him. They asked what his name was and where he lived. But they didn't want to know what his name was and where he lived, they wanted to know whether he was ready to admit that he was faking, so he admitted it. Then they repeated their question, what was his name, and he said he didn't know and they gave him electric shocks. He said his ID paper listed the name Cetrois, and they gave him electric shocks. He said he might be named Adolphe Aun or Bertrand Bédeaux, and they said his name wasn't Adolphe Aun and it wasn't Bertrand Bédeaux and it definitely wasn't Cetrois, and they gave him electric shocks. He said he didn't know his name and he said he did. He made up names and stories, and when he'd had enough shocks he made up other names and stories and begged them to stop, and screamed out everything he knew about himself in the hope that they would recognize his goodwill, screamed out his entire life story from the barn up to this moment, and they gave him electric shocks. They said that wasn't what they wanted to know and repeated the first question, and the first question was the question of his name, and he said his name was Carl Gross. And they gave him electric shocks.

They asked what a car and a boat had in common, and gave him electric shocks. They asked what he had been doing in Tindirma and whether he remembered the tyrant of Acragas, and had him count backwards from a thousand by thirteen. And gave him electric shocks. They wanted to know if he'd got out in the desert and whom he had met there. And gave him electric shocks. They asked the name of his wife. They asked him if he knew the joke about the skeleton in the cave and the spies and why he had approached Helen at the gas station rather than the German couple in the VW bus. They asked for a personal description of the women he'd been with at the hotel, and a description of the objects in the yellow Mercedes. They asked who Adil Bassir ("Adil who?") was and what his relationship to him was. How it came about. They asked about his friend. They asked his name. And gave him electric shocks. They asked how he was able to find his Mercedes in Tindirma given his memory loss and gave him electric shocks. A soda can? A barber shop? A pen? They asked about details, pointed out contradictions or claimed they had pointed out contradictions, and gave him electric shocks.

They seemed sure that he knew what they wanted from him, or they tried to give the impression they were sure in order to make him think they weren't going to give up interrogating him until he had told them everything. As if they wanted him to identify the most important things, as if they were afraid to influence him. Almost as if they themselves didn't know what it was all about. But he had already said everything ten times over and told them what he could remember and he no longer knew what to say, and he asked them what they wanted. And they gave him electric shocks.

What did they want? The same thing Adil Bassir had wanted, of course. Whom they'd shot. The mine. But what mine?

If they were looking for this mine, why were they interrogating him? They'd already found it. And if this was about the two things in the pen, why had they brought him *here*? It made no sense. He drifted off, answered mechanically, images appeared in his head. One recurring image was of him falling from a tall building and landing with a pleasant thud. Nothing before and nothing afterward, no story, just the fall and the thud. Another image was the old man with his musket. With an eye peering through his sights he stormed through the metal door and started shooting. Cockcroft's head burst apart like a bearded watermelon, next up were the bassist and the Syrian. And they gave him electric shocks. They weren't even daydreams. Carl wasn't doing anything to dream them, but he also couldn't do anything to stop them. Someone snapped his fingers in his head and the door opened silently and Hakim of the Mountains administered justice. What had they done with him? Had they eliminated him? Bought him off? Was he one of them?

He was unable to think about it. He was in pain, and when he wasn't in pain the anticipation of pain coursed through his body and erased any thoughts. He had the feeling that his life depended on these thoughts, depended on his ability to concentrate and to logically figure out what they had done with the old miner, he who was the only one who could still rescue him, and then again he felt that his life didn't depend on that after all and that the old man was part of a system totally independent from his thoughts. And then it occurred to him. What this was all about. It wasn't about the mine. It wasn't about gold, either. There was no gold here. But there was something else. Something hidden. That they couldn't find. He raised his gaze, looked Cockcroft in the eyes and said: "I'll take you there."

"Sorry?"

"I can't take it any more. I've had enough." Carl tried to sound confident, and because he knew his facial expression would give him away, he let his head loll back and forth on his chest. "If you untie me I'll take you there."

"*Where?*"

"It's deeper into the mountain. I can't describe it. A tunnel with just one finger. I know where it is. I'll take you."

A few long seconds went by, then came the next shock, and Carl's head jerked around.

So that wasn't it either. What the hell was it they wanted here?

"May I ask a question?"

"No," said Cockcroft, stepping on the switch again. "And you may not ask whether you can ask questions."

"Why here?" Carl shouted. "Why are you interrogating me here of all places?"

"What kind of a question is that?" Cockcroft furrowed his brow as he looked at the prisoner. "Do you want to be tortured in a public market? I don't want to test your middle-school intelligence too severely, but what we're doing here isn't exactly compatible with the laws of this country. Or with the laws of our own country, by the way."

And so it continued. In response to the question of why he had been in the Empty Quarter, he said he preferred the Kinks to the Beatles; in response to who he worked for, he said he liked the Beatles better than Marshal Mellow; and to the question of what his real name was, he answered that the line judge would condemn them. And they gave him electric shocks.

The pain was boundless. Not to be compared with, say, a toothache, which concentrated a person's soul into a single point. It was more a back-and-forth surge, a theatrical piece taking place partly in his body and partly on the faces of the audience. The shrieking finger, dead legs, ax blows to the neck, the throbbing stone walls. Carl felt his heart muscle pushing against his chest. The headaches during the pauses didn't seem to be just in his head but rather in his entire body and even the space around him. He lost consciousness for a long time and came to again. The seconds before he had passed out were the nicest he had experienced in a long time, the minutes after he awoke a half-dark room at dawn with the remains of a nightmare still lingering. Lying in sweaty sheets, the glaring sun on the shades of Helen's bungalow, the screech of seabirds and the slow realization that he had not awoken from the nightmare. He tried to recall his psychological state just prior to losing consciousness and take himself back there, observing himself as if he were another person. But Cockcroft and the Syrian were watching him too, trying to hinder him from doing that very thing. They reduced the electric current and didn't allow him to slip away again.

"… talk a little."

"Like reasonable, civilized human beings."

"Nothing more."

"Here it is."

"School children."

"Seriously."

"Your name."

"And real psychology. Six semesters."

Sentence fragments that made no sense.

Nothing happened for several minutes. It looked as if they were on a break. Thick cigarette smoke, three glowing tips. Cockcroft was talking. Carl tried to switch over from body to mind. Snippets of thoughts. He thought of Helen and the fact that she had left without leaving any message. He thought of the ocean and the fire in Tindirma. Of Helen's pickup. Had she really left, or had they kidnapped her as well? Could he possibly get a sip of water? And did it make any sense to co-operate or did every attempt at answering just unnecessarily prolong this mortifying procedure? In his mind he saw himself lying in silk sheets, and suddenly he knew why they were here.

It was so easy that it hurt: he hadn't been imagining the fact that he was being followed over the last few days. They had followed him—hadn't Cockcroft even said so himself? They needed a remote location where they could interrogate him in peace. And since they had been following him the whole time and were thus hot on his heels when he and Helen made their trip here, they, too, had stumbled upon the old mine. An ideal spot for their purposes. They could just buy off Hakim or maybe they got rid of him altogether. "Or he wasn't even here!" Carl inadvertently said out loud, brooding over whether this theory was sound. No counterarguments occurred to him, and therefore he concluded the pen must be what this was all about. Not the mine, clearly the pen. And the two things. The metal things.

"The things," he said aloud.

Cockcroft leaned his head and looked at him.

"The things, the capsule things," said Carl. "I have them."

He had hardly uttered the words before he was 100 percent sure that he had hit the nail on the head. The capsule things, that was what this was all about, and they were interrogating him here because they'd come across the location while following him. He would have beamed with joy and confidence if it hadn't occurred to him that the capsules, which he had lost, couldn't help him in the slightest. And it never occurred to him that it would be impossible to follow someone in this barren landscape without being noticed.

57

The Stasi

A tale told by an idiot, full of sound and fury, signifying nothing.

SHAKESPEARE

"THE CAPSULE THINGS," said Cockcroft, smiling derisively. "You have the capsule things. Is it possible that we need to take a little break?"

He signaled to the Syrian and the bassist and they both left the room. Laughter could be heard out in the tunnel.

Cockcroft leaned toward the prisoner. He took a last drag on his cigarette and politely blew the smoke upward. He sat opposite Carl with a grim look on his face, his legs crossed. One foot was planted next to the black case, the other rocked in the air while Carl was totally preoccupied trying to concoct an acceptable location for the capsules. He didn't want to give the impression that he was thinking about it and he blurted out: "I gave them to Adil Bassir."

"I don't know what you mean by capsule things," said Cockcroft, "but as long as we're conversing here so nicely, I would like to draw your attention to a little fact that seems important to me and that you must not be aware of. And I don't mean the fact that Mr Adil Bassir and his three henchmen would hardly have been chasing you with guns blazing and flags waving if you had already handed over to him what you described as the capsule things. No, I mean the fact that I spoke for two hours yesterday with Professor Martinez, an expert in this area. *The* expert. It's not easy to get international calls through from here, and it costs a fortune, but Professor Martinez is, at the risk of sounding immodest, in complete agreement with me. Global amnesia is out of the question. As much as it pains me to have to tell you, your skills are wholly inadequate to fake global amnesia. And when my two colleagues return in a minute, we will demonstrate that by somewhat more painful means. You can look forward to a new master of ceremonies. Because unfortunately I am too sensitive for what is on the way. But we still have a few minutes, just the two of us, and if you want to tell me something at the last minute after all… No? All right, suit yourself. It would have looked good in my personnel file. But it's up to you. So we'll just wait for the return of the specialists. Silently if you want. Or shall I tell you a joke?"

"Is it part of the torture?"

"Ascertaining the truth. You're doing splendidly."

Cockcroft leaned both arms on the cushion behind him, looked somewhat inscrutably at the prisoner, and finally said: "The CIA."

Carl closed his eyes.

"The CIA, the KGB and the Stasi make a bet. The Stasi is the Ministry of State Security, in case you don't know. The German intelligence service. Did you know that? Ah, you're not speaking to me. Doesn't matter. So, the CIA, the KGB and the Stasi make a bet. There is a prehistoric skeleton in a cave, and whoever can come closest to finding out the exact age of the skeleton will be the undisputed winner. The CIA man goes in first. After a few hours he comes back out and says that the skeleton is about six thousand years old. The judges are amazed. That's damn good, how did you manage to make such a precise estimate? The American says: chemical analysis. The KGB man is up next. He re-emerges from the cave after ten hours: the skeleton is approximately six thousand, one hundred years old. The judges: excellent, you are even closer! How did you do it? The Russian says: carbon-dating. The Stasi man is the last to go. He stays in the cave for two days. He crawls out completely exhausted: six thousand, one hundred and twenty-four years old! The judges' jaws drop. That is the exact age, how did you figure it out? The Stasi man shrugs: he confessed. Don't you think that's funny? I think it's funny. Or another joke that you will like for sure. A high-ranking Israeli military officer is looking for a secretary."

"I don't want to hear it."

"What can you do to stop me? He is looking for a secretary."

"I don't want to hear it."

"And he asks the first applicant: how many characters can you type per minute?"

Carl closed his eyes, turned his head from side to side and hummed "La la la".

The bassist and the Syrian returned. The bassist had a Tupperware container in his hand. He painstakingly opened it and pulled a sandwich that he handed Cockcroft over his shoulder. Cockcroft took a bite and said with his mouth full: "I've been telling this joke for years, and it's one of the best I know. Pardon me." He brushed some crumbs from Carl's pants. "Everyone I've ever told has laughed, and you will be no exception. Listen to it closely, and when the punchline comes, laugh as a sign of your mental maturity. So he is looking for a secretary."

Two or three jokes later, Carl no longer knew whether he was still conscious or dreaming. Through his gummy eyelids he thought he saw motion by the metal door. The handle slowly moved and the door opened a crack. Or had it been like that the whole time? No, it had just opened. And it opened wider, millimeter by millimeter. Carl tore his eyes away and looked Cockcroft in the eyes.

Cockcroft and the bassist were sitting with their backs to the door. The Syrian had sat down on the gray metal case, looked at his feet, which were playing with the blue and yellow cables, and then a sluggish, smug, droning female voice said: "Sorry to interrupt. Can you tell me where to find the tourist information?"

58

The Vanderbilt System

Many areas of the human brain are not used, which points to
the fact that our evolution is based on a long-term plan, the
fulfillment of which lies far ahead of us.

ULLA BERKÉWICZ

THE CELTIC CROSS wasn't working. Because of the simple
fact that the folding tray-table in the back of the seat
in front of her was too small. No more than six cards could
fit on it, and then only if they were laid out in a rectangle.
Even as she was riding out the jet's take-off with intense gulps,
closing her eyes and thinking of childhood memories, she had
already hit upon the idea of spreading the cards out on the
carpeted floor toward the rear of the 727. But they hadn't
been in the air for even fifteen minutes before businessmen
in double-breasted suits, tourists in comfy pants and mothers with children began to block the aisle to the bathrooms.
If she had laid out the cross there, she would have to have
begged the pardon of all those people, justified her activity,
answered beginner's questions and put up with attention or
incomprehension. Ed Fowler would have managed it. And if
Ed had been there, Michelle would have felt strong enough
to manage it, too. But some days—and this was one of those

days—just looking in the eyes of a stranger was enough to unsettle her.

She rubbed the tray-table clean with the heel of her hand. She ignored the fat, wheezing man to her left and didn't take so much as a glance out of the window at the white clouds beneath which yawned the abyss. But she didn't close the shade either, so as not to disturb the flow of energy. She concentrated entirely on the tray-table. Two times three cards; there was no more space. In a pinch she could have used a small cross, but Michelle hadn't had good experiences with small spreads. Small spreads—for small problems. When it came to major opening questions you needed more than four cards, otherwise the results were too vague. At the commune she had always used an expanded Celtic cross with thirteen cards when making any important decisions, but that was impossible here even if she used the armrests, her thighs and the little patch of open seat between her legs. She pushed the shaky tray-table up to its closed position and then lowered it again. A smaller deck of cards would have been helpful, she thought, a sort of travel deck. Cards the size of a matchbook, with miniaturized versions of the images. With a little business savvy you could probably get rich off an idea like that. You could sell the decks at train stations and bus stations, on ships, at airports or duty-free shops, anyplace where space was tight. Or supply them directly to the airlines! Then the cards could be distributed to open-minded passengers during boarding, along with newspapers, fruit and wet-wipes. The stewardesses could demonstrate the Celtic cross along with the emergency procedures. Michelle closed her eyes and pictured herself in a blue uniform, demonstrating use of the cards. When the cart with food and drinks clattered past her she ordered a coffee. The fat man beside her ordered two whiskies, downed them both, glanced at Michelle and then fell back into a wheezing half-slumber. Spittle dangled from his slightly open mouth.

Michelle's urge to find out something about the future grew ever more intense. What if she did try a small cross? She looked around. Most of the passengers were busy with newspapers or books. A stewardess was collecting plastic cups at the back. Suddenly Michelle had an idea.

She stretched her back, straightened her hair and then shook awake the man next to her, whose head was almost leaning on her shoulder by this point. Would he mind if she used his tray-table? The man looked at her dumbfounded. The spittle tottered on his chin. Then he turned away with a grunt.

When Michelle was sure he was asleep again, she carefully laid six cards on his tray-table and six on her own. She thought for a while and then placed a card on the armrest between the two seats. Her eyelids flitted. What was she to make of the pattern?

The two cards at the far left were clearly recognizable as the layers of consciousness, the past, above the male, no the female principle, beneath that the father. The next pairing was childhood and youth, the internal and external perspectives, environment and self, hopes and wishes, future mental and physical development. And the lone card on the armrest? It had to be the neuralgic connection between everything, the current state of the self, the nexus... the opening question.

For a long time Michelle held the rest of the deck in her lap. She pressed her back into the seat and let the spread of cards sink in, like an artist stepping back to size up her work. It was nice. But would it perform its function? She decided first to ask the question about the Boeing 727, as a performance test so to speak.

Except for a minor irritation on the right side, the results were comforting. The plane had been developed and built by the company Boeing in adherence with all specifications for aircraft construction and drawing upon the highest engineering practices, it had a considerable number of failure-free flight hours under its belt and almost as many ahead of it, and in between, as the pilot so to speak, on the armrest between the seats—the Emperor. The prospects for a transatlantic flight couldn't have been better. The irritation on the right side signaled at most some sort of minor repair in the distant future, maybe a loose screw in some unimportant part of the plane. Maybe on the exterior surface… or more likely a cosmetic repair on the interior. A defective seatback perhaps. *Nothing to worry about*, Michelle tried to tell her fellow passengers with the strength of her thoughts. She looked around. Most of them were asleep or burrowed behind their newspapers.

Next she laid cards out for Helen, for which she reintroduced the Hanged Man into the deck, though it did not make an appearance. Here, too, the spread pointed to good results. Equipped with the best assets, Helen Gliese developed her ambivalent character in her earliest youth. The grotesque face of her cynicism peaked out between the Fool and the Devil. Severity, coldness, resolve. Qualities that, annoyingly, never put men off, indeed they seemed to attract them.

Michelle searched for signs of a new life partner with Arabic roots, but to her relief was unable to find him. Not that she begrudged her friend for Carl, but their connection was star-crossed. That was clearly noticeable. On the armrest the High Priestess, and to the right Michelle barely dared look: all six cards there were reversed.

The fat man snorted himself awake, threw a glance at the mess on his tray-table and slumped back to sleep. Now Michelle laid out the cards for herself, then for Edgar Fowler. Then for her mother, for her dead father. For Sharon, for Jimi, Janis and finally, over the middle of the Atlantic, for Richard Nixon, too. Everything that emerged was tremendously telling, far more telling than the usual pronouncements of the Celtic cross. Michelle's enthusiasm over the results was such that she nearly woke the man next to her a second time. She needed someone to talk to. In her imagination she saw members of the media approaching her. She gave interviews. Professional journals in America snapped her up. A young man with eyes as black as coal, brown hair falling over his brow, and rimless glasses, with a recording device with a leather strap thrown over his muscular shoulder, his facial expression filled with sympathetic pain. As with most of the other interviews that Michelle had already given, his first question is also about the great suffering that forever marked her life back in the Sahara. But, with her eyes closed and shaking her head, Michelle made it clear that she didn't want or wasn't able to talk about it. Even after all this time. It ran too deep.

"Then, Miss Vanderbilt, on to the question that will probably excite our readers most. How does one—or to put it another way—what circumstances led to the discovery of the six-card spread that among insiders has in the Western world nearly displaced the Celtic cross, with its weaknesses in interpreting congruence?"

She thought for a long time, glanced at the air vents above her, and finally corrected the likable young man. Even though it was referred to by nearly everyone as the six-card system these days, it was actually the 727 system. Many people also called it the Vanderbilt system, or the V system for short, but she herself, as the inventor of the system, preferred the original name. Even though the cards were basically laid out in a 6-1-6 spread. But the original name conveyed the place of discovery aboard the airplane as well as the spread, plus one, the plus one because of the higher power working at high altitude, symbolically speaking, hence 7-2-7… a cold chill ran down Michelle's spine as she suddenly remembered that 616 was the number of the beast in the Codex Ephraemi. It was incorrectly given as 666 in the Bible, but older writings and palimpsests contained the original number that, veiled for the ignorant and falsified by the powerful, was changed to the comparatively more harmless six. She felt dizzy. There it was again, the numen that seemed to make its own way out of the depths and reveal itself if one was just a little open to these sorts of phenomena. Michelle hadn't quite finished answering the first interview question when the stewardess served their meal.

Plastic containers abutting one another, wrapped in plastic, on a plastic tray. While eating, the fat man made remarks of a profane sort that Michelle was unable to follow. Minutes later he fell asleep again, and her gaze fell on a loose screw on the bottom right of her seat. She smiled. She wasn't the slightest bit surprised.

She looked at the Sun with its eight flickering yellow and red arms, and later she offered to read the cards for the fat man for free. At that stage he'd already been awake for a while, and without ever changing from his sleeping posture in the slightest had been following the activity on the two tray-tables through squinted eyes.

"What is it?" he grumbled, and Michelle explained it to him with the serenity of someone who had five of her favorite cards in her future. He immediately lifted his hands up defensively.

"I can understand," said Michelle. "It scares most people to learn something about themselves. Because they are afraid they're not up for that kind of insight. That it's too deep for them."

"What?"

"Life," said Michelle. "The past. The future. The connectivity."

"You're interested in my future? In that case you're interested in more things than I am."

This last sentence struck Michelle as dark and inscrutable, she didn't immediately understand him, and the man continued:

"I already know my future. You don't have to tell me. My future is like my past, and my past is a pile of shit. You see this?" He pulled down the collar of his shirt to reveal a few thin scratches on his neck and below.

"Were you on vacation?" asked Michelle cautiously.

"Vacation! Shall I tell you what happened to me among those kaffirs?" Ignoring the fact that Michelle was shaking her head, he began to tell the story of his stay in Africa. Michelle tried to keep her facial expression under control. If at first his narration was reasonably consistent and even mildly amusing, it quickly became abhorrent and downright criminal. Only because of her good upbringing did she not dare to constantly interrupt his flood of words.

"So, the cheapest room," he said, and described in great detail his room and hotel, the clogged toilet, the bad food, the beach, the climate and the nights in the bars, many nights and many bars, and for some reason that Michelle could not figure out, always women in the bars. But none of it mattered, he said so himself, as he was nothing but an auto mechanic from Iowa and his ancestors had emigrated from Poland, that's right, Poland, and he was a decent man—cross his heart—decent was his middle name. He didn't make a lot of money, and this was his first ever vacation, but definitely his last one in horrid Europe.

"Africa," Michelle corrected.

"Africa," said the fat man. "It's all the same." A misunderstanding. Why else would a man come here? Because he'd been told that here—he pointed at the floor of the plane—the old and new worlds met. The women pretty, the morals loose, the parties bizarre. And the most important thing, as that Austrian neurologist correctly figured out, was that—and here he used a word ending in "ism" that Michelle had never heard. She wanted to ask about it but hesitated, and then by the next sentence came to think she must have misheard it, because the fat man went directly from "ism" to the declaration that you could hardly write home about the banging out here. There had only been one single fuckie fuckie and—bam!

Thirteen cards flew simultaneously up into the air like a scared flock of birds. For a second Michelle grasped at the cards before her hands sought out something solid to grab hold of, and even as her body was still being flung around in her seat, she was less surprised by the jerking of the plane, of whose sound condition she had already convinced herself, than by the fact that she had suddenly thrown her arms around the fat, sweating man and was screaming for dear life.

"A pothole," said the drunk-sounding pilot over the loudspeaker. "We are flying through an area with turbulence."

"Turbulence," said the fat man as if he hadn't even noticed that a young, extremely attractive woman was hanging from his neck like he was her last hope. He helped her gather up the cards, she apologized, and he continued with his story without any discernible change in tone. A fortune, he said, it had all cost a fortune, and even the African women in the bars, even the smallest, even the blackest... they knew what he was after. And instead, nothing but foul smells, bugs, heat. Because what was more expensive than a woman? Michelle didn't know. Two women, that's what. And that's when it happened all of a sudden.

He coughed gruffly, covering his mouth with a napkin, and then stared at the dark-yellow discharge the way a child might look at a toy.

"I'm enjoying your story," said Michelle, still unsure what it was about, though she found having to watch him scrutinize his phlegm more unappetizing than anything he could possibly say.

He gathered himself noisily, stuck the napkin in the crack between the two seats and stuffed it down with the palm of his hand.

Anyway, he said, that's when the man came up to him. Who seemed like a local. Or kind of in between. Dressed oddly, almost like a clown. And asked him to accompany him to his place.

"Not what you think!" he bellowed, shoving his face very close to Michelle's confused-looking face.

Actually the man was only looking for an interpreter. And toward that end he had gone around to the people lying on the beach and asked if any of them knew Polish. And even though he himself didn't really understand Polish, he'd spoken up. After all, his grandparents. And your, you know. And he had as a child. There were certainly things you could say here about languages and the ability to learn them. But anyway, he, like his entire family, was practical—and now he had lost his train of thought.

"The man," said Michelle, "the man whose place you went to."

"Right, the man with the place. And the pink Bermuda shorts. They had gone into the place and there in the middle of the room stood a machine. A gleaming chrome machine that he, even without any knowledge of Polish, immediately recognized as an espresso machine. Gigantic, the kind used in a cafeteria. Or a bar. Polish letters. Nothing particularly unique. But expensive. And now things got mysterious."

The word mysterious had its dependable effect on Michelle, and she tried to sit leaning in, crossing her legs, which was barely possible even with the tray-table closed. The fat man stood up because he thought she wanted to go to the bathroom, and it took a moment to clear up the misunderstanding.

"And then," said the fat man, "he just vanished." The man, that is. He just wanted to know what type of machine he had there in his own place. Then he rushed out of the bungalow without any explanation or words—and that was it.

"That's crazy!" said Michelle, disappointed. She had no idea why the man was telling her all this.

He was silent for a while. Then he smiled.

"Now, of course, you want to know what *I* did," he said. Michelle would like to have had longer to consider whether she really wanted to know or not, but she found herself suffering from some sort of mental hiccup and nodded with wide eyes.

"I'll always be my mother's son," said the fat man. And wasn't the whole thing a sign. He went back down to the beach, where he was able to watch the bungalow. The door of which was still open. Until evening. And when the man never reappeared, he rented a handcart and hauled the machine off and exchanged it for money, whether that was right or wrong. It brought in eighty dollars, a tenth of its value at most, but since it had been his last day and all. Then off to the port for a full house. Two blacks and a white.

Beg your pardon, she said, and he repeated: two super blacks and a white. The white one only as an alibi. She'd have to excuse him, but a man was a man and he couldn't do anything about his preferences. In his case as black as coal. As black as hell. Or nothing at all. And, to cut to the chase, the end of the story was, they tried to kill him. He pulled down his collar again and drew his thumb across his neck.

He came to in a gutter with no luggage, no money, no clothes, passport or airline ticket. Half a day at the American embassy. That was his past. And the future looked exactly the same, because that's the way they were. Women. Always. His misfortune. For his entire life. He could be just as unfortunate without any cards being dealt.

He snuffled, coughed heavily again, looked searchingly at Michelle, dark brown from the desert sun, yes, her skin nearly black, and he suddenly smiled at her in such an awkward, solicitous way—a way that seemed to her rather common in men of his age, the result of a natural process, especially in combination with excess weight and thinning hair, in a way that also had an oddly childlike and innocent effect—that Michelle assumed he must hardly have been aware of the look on his face, or at least of the incongruity between his bloated, aged face and his youthful intentions.

But she didn't avoid his look either. On the contrary, she held his gaze. Like a highly sensitive instrument, she watched the smile spread across his face, watched as it froze, watched as it ebbed, insecure and twitchy, from his face again and disappeared. She watched as the big, strong man turned away from her, unsettled by her confidence, then turned back to her and tried once again to muster his leering smile, and the entire sequence, the inscrutable man in his animal awkwardness, reminded her so much of the lovable bull terrier she'd had as a child, found beneath the Christmas tree (covered in drool, a blue bow tied around its belly, with a light-brown leather leash) as a replacement for a canary that had died, that she felt an affinity germinating inside her which, surprisingly, she found herself embracing rather than opposing as her familiarity with the fat man increased, as it was as sure to do during the rest of the flight as the sun was to set each day. His wedding gift to her was a solarium. The marriage was long and happy.

59

Operation Artichoke

And in such a war, it is a Christian act, and an act of love, to kill enemies without scruple, to rob and to burn, and to do whatever damages the enemy, according to the usages of war, until he is defeated.

LUTHER

"JUST A JOKE," said Helen. She entered the room in white shorts, a white blouse, a white sunhat, white canvas shoes and with a large jute shoulder bag. She glanced at Carl over Cockcroft's shoulder and then pulled from her bag a pair of green rubber gloves, a thick Arabic newspaper and a pair of pliers, all of which she handed to the Syrian.

The Syrian opened the paper, took out the sports section and spread the rest carefully out on the floor.

"How are you?" Helen asked, then pulled out a black plastic bottle. "You thirsty?"

She unscrewed the bottle top, sniffed the opening and handed it to Cockcroft, who also sniffed it. Then the three of them—Helen, Cockcroft and the bassist—stepped out of the room. Even though the door wasn't closed all the way, Carl couldn't make out even a word of their conversation. When they returned, Cockcroft gave the Syrian a signal. He pulled himself away from the unpleasant match results of the Primera Division, stuffed the sports section into his waistband and stationed himself behind the rattan chair. He wrapped his vice-like hands around Carl's head. From the front, the bassist grabbed Carl beneath his chin, and Helen put the black bottle to his lips while holding his nose at the same time.

"Open your mouth. Open up. Open up. It doesn't taste good but it's not poisonous."

It really did taste bad. And it really wasn't poisonous. Something very medicinal. Bitter. Soapy.

Once she had poured most of the contents of the bottle down his throat they let him go and stepped back quickly. Yellow fluid surged out of Carl, and as he was still gulping and coughing they undid his restraints. He flopped weakly to the ground. They ordered him to undress, but his red and blue arms no longer responded to him. They kneeled over him and took off his clothes. Then they dragged him over to the spread-out newspaper and tried to get him to crouch down above it. But he kept falling over. Finally the Syrian held him upright by his hair. The two of them reeled back and forth.

Helen wiped a few splotches from her blouse. Cockcroft balled up an empty cigarette pack. The bassist rolled up his sleeves.

"Want me to take over?"

"How long does it take?"

"What does it say on the bottle?"

"Do you feel anything yet?"

"No."

"Give me the bottle."

"Do you feel anything yet?"

"When did he last go?"

"He hasn't."

"What about before?"

"The day before. And then not again. If you paid attention."

"Now watch. Watch. Whoa."

While Carl emptied the contents of his gut onto his heels and the newspapers, the Syrian shook him by the hair as if emptying a bag.

His grip loosened a little while later, and Carl fell limply to the side. His head thudded to the ground. He stopped moving. Little black dots moved directly in front of his eyes. Ants. He heard a clicking noise and looked over the stream of feelers at the bassist, who was putting on the green rubber gloves. Carl had kept himself together for a long time but now he started to cry.

Using a pocket knife, the bassist poked around in the excrement. Squatting in front of the newspaper with his hands hanging between his knees, he used the blade to cut up little chunks of dung and smear them on the paper as if he were spreading butter on bread.

Cockcroft, Helen and the Syrian stood behind him with their arms crossed. That they were engrossed in something warm and foul that had just left his body filled him with great melancholy. There was something symbolic about this act, something horrid, a dark inkling that they might also separate him from other parts and products of his body and seize them. Carl's gaze returned to the ants.

After the bassist had spread the excrement across the entire newspaper like Nutella across a giant piece of bread, he proclaimed with the facial expression and inflection of an eight-year-old: "Nothing here," and three sets of blue eyes and one set of black eyes turned to the man lying naked on the floor, sniffling.

With her foot Helen shoved Carl's clothes over to him, and after he had more or less dressed himself they tied him up in the chair again.

"So, on to the second option," said Cockcroft. And then to Helen: "He's yours."

60

Legends of Perseverance

> There has been a good deal of discussion of interrogation experts
> vs. subject-matter experts. Such facts as are available suggest that
> the latter have a slight advantage. But for counterintelligence
> purposes the debate is academic.
>
> KUBARK MANUAL

THE NARROW BUT VERY STRAIGHT line of black dots
swarmed past the right side of Carl's chair toward the
back of the cave, where he could no longer follow them with his
eyes. On the other side they headed off under the metal door
to freedom carrying orange-colored granules.

While Carl was still thinking about the fate of the ants,
Helen sat down facing him. The rest had left the room. She
pulled a cigarette out of a pack but did not light it, instead she
began to talk in her strangely lifeless, half-comatose way while
gesticulating with the cigarette in one hand and the lighter in
the other. She crossed her legs, and Carl yanked at his restraints
as if he were in pain. In fact they had not tied them as tightly
as they had the first time, and his right hand, which he could
barely still feel (he didn't dare look at it), was working its way
out of the cords one millimeter after another. He said: "You
know that I don't know anything," and Helen said: "I don't
know anything." As if to show him that she did not wish to be

interrupted, she pulled the black case over with her foot and then lifted it into her lap, where it rocked back and forth on her white shorts and bare thighs.

"Where do we start now? You might be asking yourself why such an uproar is being made over such a trifle. Because whether you realize it or not, it is a trifle. To us, anyway. Any student knows the system, and the whole thing isn't so sophisticated that a few smart people couldn't put their heads together and assemble it. But it's sophisticated enough that we can't set up a raging export business with it. Nor do we want to. Not to mention that other crap would be transported via the same route." Helen held up the cigarette and lighter then let both arms fall again. "You're not the first who has tried. You're just the first that we caught. Or the second. But the first living one, so you will be the first to share his knowledge with us. Because, as you probably understand, this little game isn't about *whether* you tell us the truth. That's not up to you. What is up to you is only the point at which you decide to tell us the truth. You can keep tormenting yourself, you can drag things out, but you can't avoid the inevitable. If you have been well trained in how to act in the case of interrogation scenarios—which we have to assume is the case—you know this as well. You know that you can hold out for a while against blunt force with willpower, autosuggestion and similar tricks. Assuming you are good at it. Maybe a day or two. Maybe even three; stranger things have happened. Carthage," she motioned behind her with her thumb, "claims to know somebody who held out for five days. But I don't believe it. It's just one of those legends about the brave soldier who despite being burned with glowing coals doesn't betray his brigade, his homeland, his family, and who is subsequently immortalized in monuments, where he's depicted with two intact marble eyes staring off onto the horizon, happy still to have all four limbs. But those are either legends. Or the interrogators were inept. In most cases they were inept. And at least in this area I can put your mind at ease." Helen put the cigarette between her lips, lit it and blew the smoke up at the ceiling, gouged with chisel marks.

"And I can make your decision somewhat easier for you, too. By telling you what we know. So you don't think there's anyone or anything you need to conceal. Or could conceal. Because, what do we know? We knew the handover was to take place in Tindirma. And approximately when. We knew who was handing it over, but not to whom. There was a reservation at the hotel for a man named Herrlichkoffer. Herrlichkoffer is German and it means something like splendid suitcase. You know the name? No? I actually believe you. We located this splendid suitcase at the airport in Targat and followed him to Tindirma, and we lost him there. He didn't turn up at the hotel. Obviously we could have picked him up before that, but we didn't know whether he had the thing with him. Or where it is. We didn't even know exactly what it was or in what form it would be transported. We knew only where it came from, which research facility it came from. Then it took us nearly twenty-four hours to find the man again. But apparently nothing had happened in the meantime. He sat day after day in a café as if he had an appointment that someone failed to show up for. We put a guy in front of the café with a radio link in his ear and he reported: nothing. Either he was blind, or our man had got suspicious. But perhaps he also wasn't our man at all. And then came the massacre. In the commune. And that's where we made a teeny weeny mistake. Though anyone else would have made the same mistake. Because, what was it, after all? A group of communists and hippies and longhairs, politically confused, four dead, a bunch of money missing… of course, we thought, we're after the wrong guy. We needed to get into the commune. But our people didn't manage to get inside. They had cut themselves off from the outside world, what with all the press and everything. And mourning. And when it emerged that an old college friend of mine was inside, they had me brought in. I was in Spain at the time. But after I'd paid a visit to the commune and Michelle explained to me that money hadn't actually been involved, that it had just been a crazy, sex-crazed Arab, this Amadou squared, at that point we'd completely lost the trail. Herrlichkoffer had disappeared into thin air, and the criminal potential of those hippies wouldn't have been sufficient to smuggle a chocolate bar through Swiss customs. So, the case was blown. My thoughts had already wandered toward home when this Arab crossed my path. At the gas station in the middle of the desert. Bleeding, disoriented, seeking help and apparently on the run. I only picked you up because I had an inkling. I thought, who knows. All your talk of memory loss, I knew that was bullshit. My first thought was: just a sob story to elicit sympathy. An Arab looking for a white woman. I was ninety percent sure. At least that's what I reported the first night. But I wasn't entirely sure. We weren't entirely sure for a long time. It wasn't until Bassir grabbed you... what a catastrophe. A few people here nearly lost their jobs over that. A hundred men following you, and they just stuffed you into the trunk of a car. I've never seen such a collection of idiots. A bunch of amateurs. The whole team. We didn't even have twenty-four hours to put it together and get to the desert. I couldn't even get a flight, I had to come by ship from Spain. Two others got delayed in New York. All the things that our little Torah pupil had to do all alone! The flyer for the psychologist's office. I nearly keeled over when I took it out of the mailbox. Introductory rates! That's how it went the entire way. You really have no idea what it is like to try to put together a team in August. Two of us couldn't even speak French. We didn't have an Arabic translator at first, we had to fly one in from Belgium, and he's lying in the hotel with a stomach bug. Our radio man is hard of hearing, comes from Iowa, and thought he was in Libya for the first forty-eight hours. Two nearly died of thirst while searching for the mine. And Herrlichkoffer was already dead before we were able to connect with him. A minor mishap. On and on. And the fact that Bassir could just pluck you away—like I said. An unbelievable foul-up. But the fact that you kept throwing yourself into the arms of this collection of idiots should make it clear to you that you're not the brightest bulb, either."

Helen flicked the ash from her cigarette and smiled. It was the same clinical smile she had smiled on the terrace that time, just after she had finished her gymnastics routine and turned to Carl and he realized for the first time that he was in love with her.

"Believe me, I prayed every day, heaven, I prayed, please let him be as dimwitted as he looks. Nobody expected that. Three times," she held up three tautological fingers, "I was ordered three times to cut things short and break out the gray case. It took every ounce of effort to hold that off, three times. He'll lead us there, I said."

Carl jerked at the ropes. He felt a snap and crunch in his right hand and closed his eyes.

"And if you think that this is it, if you think we'll just leave it after a bit of talk and psychology and a couple of paltry zaps of electricity... do you think that? Do you think this is some kind of cute little play with a cave and a harmless electrical device and a blonde out of a cigarette advertisement working you over a little verbally? I promise you, that is not the case. I'm going to ask you a few more questions. And you can act coy like some kind of silver-screen diva. It's up to you. But then—"

With a cry of pain, Carl yanked his shoulder up. And his hand was free.

61

A Little Stochastic

What is the evil in war? Is it the death of some who will soon
die in any case, that others may live in peaceful subjection?

AUGUSTINE

THE SMOKE HAD CLOUDED the air like milk-glass. Helen
leaned her upper body back. "What's this?" she asked,
coughing briefly. "We'll tie that back up."

She tied the hand down again and then had Carl tell the
whole story over again from the beginning. Everything she
already knew. And everything that he, aided by the electric
shocks, had told Cockcroft, the Syrian and the bassist. Every
detail. When he was finished, she said: "And now the whole
thing again, backwards, point by point."

"Have you fallen under the spell of the psychologists?"

"From the moment you met the prostitute to the moment I
left you alone in front of the commune."

"If you still don't know whether I have amnesia—"

"You don't. Now start talking."

"Then why are you testing my memory?"

"I'm not testing it. Start."

Carl furrowed his brow, and after a while Helen said: "I
already told you, you're not the brightest bulb. This is not how

you test for amnesia. This is how you test for poorly constructed lies. So. Your prostitute."

He stared at Helen. He looked at her knees, he looked at his own knees, and then he looked her in the eyes again.

She nodded to the switch in her lap, and Carl told the whole story backwards. The prostitute who called him Cetrois, the morphine, the walk through the port. Before that the Salt Quarter, which was actually the Empty Quarter. The little café. The school children in front of the café and the stolen yellow blazer. The telephone booth. The waiter with the overcooked soup. Before that the desert, the old fellah, the corpse with the wire around its throat. The question of the moped and the paper scraps in his pocket. Running away, the men in white djellabas following him. Tindirma. The riot. The fire in the commune, set off by the animal the size of a truck. Carl talked about the mass panic and the spot where he had watched it all, he talked about the shabby hotel and (in all detail) about the respectable woman in the hotel. About the green soda can and the yellow Mercedes and the things inside it. The ball, the pen and the pad of paper with "CETROIS" on it. And at the very end, the note he left for Helen on the passenger seat of the pickup.

Helen listened to it all, and when he was finished and looked up like a fifth grader after an oral exam, she wanted to hear it again, forward. And then again, backwards. The fact that she didn't raise her voice or make use of the black case gave Carl a glimmer of hope. It seemed he might be believed if only he could just string together the details in the same order, or the other way around.

The only comment Helen made was a sneering grin at the point with the happy school children, and the more times he used that adjective, the more strange and unlikely it seemed even to himself that he would just lose the blazer together with the cartridges inside it. He no longer doubted the fact that this was all about those cartridges. He began to include explanatory words in his sentences, and as he was describing in vain for the fifth or sixth time running after the yellow blazer, he added a detail he had left out up to then: the ouz. How it had suddenly appeared on top of the dune at dusk and bitten him, with the paper crown on its head, and how he had nearly lost the cartridges right then, in the sand, in the most ridiculous circumstances possible… as if the unlikeliness of this event might explain the unlikely subsequent loss. A mathematical law, a cosmic fluke. He begged her to look at the bite wound on his wrist, and Helen stood up and walked around Carl's chair with her hands folded behind her neck.

"Who trained you?" she asked barely audibly when she was behind him, and "Is that all you want to tell me?" once she was seated again on the wooden box. "National pride, idealism, religious dogma, whatever other baubles and tinsel the intellectually unenlightened decorate their world view with and make it so empirically difficult for adults to cast off—I don't know what motivates you. But you should think it over. When I said I was going to ask you these questions *once*, I really meant it. And when I said it was a trifle, that doesn't mean it isn't important to us. It is very important."

"More important than a human life?" Carl mustered the energy to ask.

"Are you talking about yours? Nothing is more important than a human life." Helen ran her index finger down Carl's stained sweater. "Even when it is the life of a liar. Or the life of a smuggler. An idiot and a career criminal. Every life is priceless, unique and worth preserving. Says the lawyer. The problem is, we're not lawyers. We are not of the opinion that a life can't be weighed against other goods or other lives. We're more like the statisticians, and the statistics say: there is perhaps a one percent chance that things are the way you say they are. That you don't know who you are. That you just happened to be in the wrong place at the wrong time, multiple times. School children, corpses in the desert with wire around their necks and IDs in their pocket and all the rest. It could all be true. But there is a ninety-nine percent chance that's not the case. That it's all bullshit. That a man reached his hand out for something that didn't belong to him. And that he didn't lose it, but rather passed it on. Or hid it. Ninety-nine percent. Ninety-nine percent chance that we are protecting world peace. Ninety-nine percent chance that our little investigation will serve to maintain a peaceful cohabitation without nuclear weapons. Ninety-nine percent chance it's for the survival of Israel, for happy children, grazing cows and all that other shit. Ninety-nine percent chance that this isn't about *one* human life but about millions of them. Ninety-nine percent for enlightenment and humanism and one percent that our shameful interrogation is an example of a return to the Middle Ages. Honestly," said Helen, lifting his chin gently with two fingers and looking him in the eyes. "A hundred to one. Or a million to one. How should we proceed? What do you think? I can give you a tip. The statisticians traditionally operate dispassionately."

"You know me. You've spent time with me."

"You don't even know yourself. So you say."

"But why should I have told you all that I told you?"

"Because you're stupid?" said Helen. "Because to the very end you had no idea whose car you had got into? Because you thought the blonde, gum-chewing woman would continue to help you? We don't even know if these cartridges exist. Or in what form—"

"You know," said Carl. "You know that I don't know anything."

"I'll know when we're finished here. When we are finished here and have tried out all our pretty machines, then I will know. Then I will believe you and apologize—which has a one percent chance of happening. But you can believe me: when we are finished here, you will have said everything you know. Because I'm afraid we're the good guys here. And you are not. Whether you realize it or not. But you've got yourself into it, and you have something that belongs to us. That we discovered. Our scientists. And that's why we are the good guys: we built the bomb and wreaked havoc with it. But we learned from that. We're the adaptive system. Hiroshima shortened the war, and you can argue about Nagasaki—but it's not going to happen a third time. We will stop it from happening a third time. In our hands the bomb is nothing more than an ethical principle. Put the same bomb in your hands and we'd be heading toward catastrophe that would make everything else look like nothing more than a minor headache by comparison. And why am I telling you all of this? I'm not saying it because I think I can convince you. If you were susceptible to rational argumentation you wouldn't be here now. I'm telling you because I want you to know where we stand."

She opened the top button of her blouse, wiped sweat from her collarbone with two fingers, then lit another cigarette.

62

The Deepest Hole

They came to the river of pus and the river of blood, intended as traps by the dark lords. But the brothers caused their blowguns to swell as they had the madre de cacao tree and simply floated across without a care.

POPOL VUH

T HE GOAT HAD DISAPPEARED; the loose end of the chain lay on the bank. The shadows of the rock formations that Carl still had in his head swayed in the light. The Syrian, with his pant legs rolled up, dragged him into the middle of the sludgy pool. He fished out the chain and bound it around his neck with a lock. "It's too long," said someone, and the Syrian pushed Carl's face down until it was nearly touching the water, then opened the lock and wrapped the chain around again. Cockcroft, Helen, the bassist and the carbide lamp looked out from the bank. They encouraged him to talk. He remained silent.

Cockcroft squatted down, looked into Carl's eyes for a long time and said: "No idea is so great that it's worth dying for. We've been open with you up to now, and I'm going to be open right now, too. Existential despair is the goal of our methods. To put you into a state of existential despair. There are varying theories about it. Until recently the assumption named after Hanns Scharff generally held sway, namely that *too* much despair is counterproductive to eliciting the truth and causes people to make things up. But that's no longer agreed upon, and as far as we're concerned it's toast. Still others, and I'm talking about people worthy of being taken seriously, suggest on the other hand that the obdurate, and in particular the anal-retentive, become more obdurate and in the end utterly shut down when subjected to an excess of despair. But this, too, has been disproved. Current theory holds that deep existential despair is the gold standard..." And on and on.

Carl had long since stopped following it. It was all just blather, the one hundredth showing of the tools. He felt his way down the chain, which was secured to an iron rod attached to a rock deep down in the mud. He closed his eyes.

"See you tomorrow," someone said. Helen. And that was apparently the closing statement. Because the light wobbled away together with voices and footsteps, and Carl remained there alone in the dark. He sought a stable position, shifting around in the knee-deep water. The length of the chain between the surface of the water and his neck was barely fifteen centimeters. It was so short that he couldn't prop himself up on outstretched arms, and if he tried to rest on his elbows the water came up to his chin. He tried to stay calm. He screamed.

He propped himself up on his left side until the muscles cramped, then he propped himself up on his right side until the muscles cramped. Then he rocked from side to side until he was sapped of all strength. Which happened quickly, and he realized he wouldn't be able to hold out for even an hour. But after an hour he was still alive and rocking back and forth.

At first he was able to brace himself on each elbow for five or even ten minutes at a time, but the intervals quickly shrank. Like a person carrying a heavy suitcase through town, switching it from hand to hand until finally unable to hold it in either one. He tried to lean his shoulder against the iron rod, he tried to mound mud into a pillow. His stomach muscles gave out, his back muscles gave out, and when he realized where this was leading he tried to drown himself. He rolled onto his back into the warm, gurgling silence. The mud. The held breath. The obsidian above his closed eyelids. He saw the desert. He saw a yellow cloud. He saw a green flag. A gulp of the disgusting-smelling broth splashed into his mouth and he shot back up again spitting and choking. He yanked on the chain. He pulled on the iron rod. Left side, right side. Submerged. As with every monotonous, stressful activity, he didn't concentrate on what he was doing but how he did it. He began to lecture himself and couldn't suppress the thought that he was standing at a lectern in front of hundreds of students giving a speech about surviving in muddy pits if fate (or its human representative) staked you unforgivingly in such a spot.

This is the manner in which you prop yourself up, he said, and not this way. The joints A, B and C need to be in such-and-such an angle in order to minimize fatigue and thereby maximize endurance. Thereafter in logarithmical, abbreviated intervals will follow cradling and rocking, which in turn will be followed again by the modified technique of propping oneself up… and so on and so forth. Even the most recalcitrant student had opened his notebook by this point and was taking notes. It was a little like being in an orchid garden of physiology, but the professor's lectures about the ideal bracing positions were so captivating that even his colleagues dropped in to hear them. The length of the lectures was unusual as well. They went on for hours and days, weeks and months and many semesters, and always sitting in the back row sat a gum-chewing blonde with large breasts and a strange facial expression.

In one of his moments of clarity Carl was coming to terms with his own death when for the first time, inspired by this line of thinking, he thought he might not be alone in the dark. They knew—surely they knew—that a person in his circumstance would quickly drown and take his knowledge with him. So there must be someone there observing him, eavesdropping and holding a protective hand over him. One of the four of them. Carl had heard their voices and footsteps fade away, he had seen the light die, but he had not paid attention to whether it had actually been the footsteps of four people leaving.

He went totally silent, but the other side, too, held its breath. But he was sure. Behind a gravestone of night, a bundle of blonde locks.

He had been talking to himself on and off, and now he raised his voice. He spoke to his relatives, lamenting his fate, said goodbye to his father and mother, and fell into the water sobbing theatrically. Dramatic blubbering underwater. He thrashed his arms and legs, stopped thrashing them and lifted his head silently. And breathed. It took all his strength not to groan, not to gasp and not to move. His trembling caused tiny ripples in the water. He heard them lap against the bank and heard the echo of them lapping against the bank and then the echo of the echo of them lapping against the bank. And nothing else. Nobody appeared. He repeated the experiment a few more times and forgot it was an experiment. He was really speaking to his father now, and his father put his hand on his neck and led him down a long tiled hallway that smelled of chlorine. A white terrycloth towel sat folded atop the radiator. Two girls in blue bathing suits stood by the railing of the diving board and looked at him with exaggerated indifference. One of them was going into the eighth grade and was the love of his life. He spat water, came briefly to his senses, and screamed and snorted that he knew what they wanted to know. He had always known, and the cartridges from the pen hadn't been stolen from him after all, he had them in a hole in his tooth, they didn't need to wait until tomorrow.

"Until tomorrow!" droned the echo.

63

Spatial Orientation

And be constant in praying at the beginning and the end of the day, as well as during the early watches of the night. For, verily, good deeds drive away evil deeds. This is a reminder to all who bear God in mind.

SURAH II: 114

THE NEXT DAY he was still alive. He didn't know how he had managed it, he didn't know whether to be happy about it, but he felt no sense of relief when he heard the footsteps of several people. He felt nothing aside from thirst and pain. A piece of excrement floated somewhere beside him in the water. His face was swollen and flecked with mud. If it was true, as one of the voices hidden behind a light claimed, that they had left him for only one night, then his sense of time had slowed down by a factor of five or six.

Beneath the light he saw three pairs of shoes. Brown shoes, brown shoes, women's shoes. Nobody with rolled-up pant legs.

"Unfortunately Carthage took the key with him. But we have this."

Cockcroft squatted down on the bank. Helen's hand held a bolt-cutter. A huge, peaceful sheep floated through the cave and nibbled at Carl's back.

"Ksch," he said.

"And has it occurred to you now what you want to say? No? Because we're winding up this post, and it could be a few years or even decades before a human being makes it down to this cave again. So get it off your chest: want to give us something for the road? Nothing? Do you think this is funny? It's unfortunate. Very unfortunate."

Cockcroft talked, Helen talked, and then Cockcroft talked some more. But as for answering any more questions, Carl felt capable of doing that only underwater. At one point they said they were going to leave him there alone. Then they said they'd give him another chance. Helen put the bolt-cutters down next to her on the bank of the pool. He drank a little of the muddy water. The three silhouettes sat there motionless, watching him.

"Think it over." Helen leaned forward and splashed a little water at him with her finger.

"I'm dying," he said.

"You're not dying. You know the story about the rat that was thrown into a barrel? It can take days."

"Fuck the rat. Shit. Fucking rat." He tried to splash back but was unable to bridge the three meters that separated him from Helen.

"You should at least have enough sense to use your last conversation to make a statement that isn't completely meaningless."

He thought for a moment and then said: "You make me want to throw up."

The silhouettes stood up. The beams of the swaying lamps caused shadow boulders to swell in the room. Footsteps. Goats. Darkness. He waited.

He had imprinted in his mind the location where the bolt-cutters had been left. Three and a half, maybe four meters away from his outstretched arm on a flat rock on the bank.

In order to take off his pants he had to keep submerging in the water. He shoved them over his hips with both hands. His left hand, which the ouz had bitten, hurt much worse than the right, which Bassir had stabbed the letter-opener into. Mud stuck his eyes together. He hoped it was mud.

He ripped his sweater over his head and tied an arm to a leg of his pants. It was an exhausting tug of war, which probably had to do with the fact that his mind was already running on emergency power, or the fact that his sense of spatial orientation was once again greatly diminished by the darkness; either way it took for ever for him to realize the sweater was stuck on the chain and was unusable for his purposes. He untied the pants and pulled the sweater back and forth. He tried to rip it lengthwise but his fingers couldn't hold it tightly enough. Wafts of mist were drawing over his eyes. He screamed, and some sort of synesthetic foul-up transformed his scream into colors. He knew he didn't have much more time. So he let his sweater be a sweater and tried it with just the pants.

He knotted one leg closed and put some mud into it, then tested the weight. Then he measured the distance. He figured: maybe thirty centimeters of chain plus half the breadth of his shoulders plus an outstretched arm plus the length of the pants, which was about a meter and a half. All together a maximum of three meters. It wouldn't reach.

He swung the pants forward by one leg, lasso-style, and heard the other end smack down on water. Same thing on the second and third attempts. He didn't even reach the edge of the bank. Maybe it had something to do with his throwing technique: resting on his left elbow, half lying down; prior to each throw the pants hung in the water somewhere behind his right shoulder and came out crumpled and sloshing. Once he even swung the weighted leg into his head.

Before the fourth attempt he draped the cloth carefully over his right shoulder and then tried to shot-put the weight in the tied leg instead of throwing it; it was risky. Because he had not only to shot-put the weight but also hold onto the second, slippery leg with one and the same injured hand. If that end got away from him it spelled his certain death.

He concentrated for a long time and then shoved his arm out in the dark. Immediately there was a sound of impact on the bank, a wet smack on rock. He pulled the lasso in and shot-put it four or five more times in slightly different directions. He hit the bank each time. But nothing more. He lay flat in the water, pulled the chain taut and believed himself capable of freeing himself from this misery by working systematically. The series of impact sounds on the bank organized themselves in his head into a sort of rescue map that he just needed to carefully go over, grid square by grid square, and he'd be sure to hit the bolt-cutters at some point. These moments were displaced by an inkling that the bolt-cutters were far beyond his range. Then he also thought he'd lost his sense of orientation again in the dark. He turned himself like the minute hand of a clock and threw the pants in all directions, only to realize that in three-quarters of the cases he was unable to reach the bank.

Even so, the direction that he had originally thought to be the correct one was still vaguely recognizable as a result. The bank where Helen had stood, spoken to him and put down the bolt-cutters was the closest.

He continued to try, but the sound of a sand-filled pant leg hitting a metal tool continue to elude him. From time to time he yanked on the chain around his neck, as if he might magically be able to conjure up the sound of clanging metal. He talked to himself, and at some point the mist before his eyes suddenly lifted and he could see dark trees around the pool. The trees stretched their leafless branches into a gray sky; snowflakes fell from above. The pool froze over. He slid across it and away. His mother scolded him to be more careful, a young woman with brown eyes. And then the dog showed up. The dog leaped on

him like a huge woolen glove. The Christmas tree lit up and
caught fire and tipped over. A doctor examined him, putting
a wooden tongue-depressor in his mouth. He was allowed to
keep the tongue-depressor afterward. Candies sat in a glass
bowl as a thank-you, the teacher demanded an explanation
of prime numbers, and at the edge of the jungle lived talking
apes who hunted people, stuffed them and exhibited them in
museums. He remembered the Statue of Liberty on the beach,
in the sky above, a twitching piece of lint on the camera lens,
snake-like greetings from the realm of the dead. Forty-eight
hours with no sleep.

Carl came back to his senses because he had choked on
water. He coughed, spat out slime and began an idiosyncratic
act. His elbows swung back with momentum, the hands balled
into fists, then with the fingers spread, forward, an upward shovel
motion at the end. Again and again. The two, the three… and
the seventeen.

He looked once again at the blackbird that had strayed into
his nightly room, and a man with a gold wristwatch opened the
window and let it out. The smell of a burned cake. A young
man who shoved the wrong end of a cigarette into his mouth
and then, engrossed in conversation, lit the filter. The grandfather, washing the car, frozen for ever in faded colors, except
the water continuously spraying out of the hose for all eternity,
silver on the hood of the car.

He mechanically gathered the drenched pants. He wondered what they had done with Hakim of the Mountains.
Shivering-cold, he tried to pull the sweater back off the chain
and onto his body. After many futile attempts he finally suc-
ceeded in squeezing himself into the wet clump and pulling it
down over his head.

The noises fell silent for a moment and a thought staggered
toward him, club-footed: if it was possible to get this bit of

cloth over his head—wouldn't it be possible to push it all the way down his body and pull it off below his feet? There in the dark he didn't dare to answer the question. His ability to think spatially had shut down.

He saw himself as a comic figure attached by his neck to a huge weight that had the shape and size of the earth. It wouldn't work this way. But the other way? Out of the two to four holes that in his mind made up a sweater, out of how many would he have to extricate the numb, swollen lump of flesh that he himself was in order to make use of the cloth? He didn't know. He'd just have to do the experiment.

Lying down underwater, he shoved an arm up past his throat. That was easy. But the trouble began with the second arm. It got stuck in the neck opening just below the elbow. His body was as inflexible as the sweater was resistant to being ripped. Carl tried to free himself again but he couldn't get his arm any further or get it back out. He sank into the mud in his straitjacket, floundering around like a fish out of water. He gasped for air. He plunged. And all of a sudden his other elbow shot past his face. Snorting, he writhed up out of the water. Both of his arms were pressed together above his head, and his forearms danced as if imitating a rabbit's ears. He struggled. He fell over. Then the sweater jerked down over his chest and stole his breath. With a last muster of strength he ripped the sweater down over his hips while still underwater. The rest was easy. With the sweater in his hands, he paused for a moment and tried to relax.

Then he searched for his pants so he could tie them to the sweater, but the pants had disappeared. Three, four times Carl crawled around the iron rod without locating the pants, and when he finally found them the weight had disappeared and the knot in the one leg had untied.

He made a new knot and realized how short his lasso had suddenly become. He untied the knot and re-did it closer to the end, but it was still too short. Groaning, he felt from one end to the other and it became even more confusing. Something seemed to be missing from the pants, and there was a big cloth hanging in the middle. Writhing around on the pants couldn't have ripped them, could it?

Searching for unseen overlooked knots, tangles or pant legs, he let the cloth slide through his hands. But he couldn't feel anything else. He thought he had lost his mind. He pounded on his blind eyes. And only when he pushed the cloth up his face and ran his tongue over it did he feel what his numbed hands could no longer feel, that it wasn't the cloth of his pants but something knitted. The sweater. He had been holding his sweater the entire time.

"This time let's keep track," he muttered to himself, and because the sound of his own voice had a calming effect on him, an effect like being addressed by someone whose sanity remained less impaired than his own, he continued to talk to himself.

"First let's put the sweater here," he said, laying it over his shoulder. Then he felt around. He was still unable to find the pants and said: "No problem. No problem at all. If they're not over here, then they are over here. Or here. Or here."

He laid himself out as flat as possible on his stomach and used his foot as a hook, stretching it out and dragging it around the iron rod in a circle. And sure enough, a long piece of cloth did get tangled around his ankle, at which point he immediately assured himself that the sweater was still on his shoulder. It was.

"Great," he said, "terrific." He tied the sweater to a leg of the pants.

Then he measured the length of his lasso and was disappointed. It was barely one and a half times his arm span. The knot took too much cloth. But he didn't dare make a riskier knot. If it came apart and one of the two pieces of clothing flew off, he was doomed.

Before he undertook the first attempt, he took a short, solemn break. Then concentration and the proven shot-put method: with the familiar smacking sound, the wet cloth struck rock.

But he had now lost all sense of orientation. For the next attempt he turned ninety degrees to the right: the same wet smack. The third try was a mistake; he had forgotten to turn. Another wet smack... and this time mixed with a light metallic clang. Frozen in shock, he held his throwing arm outstretched for several seconds in the dark before he dared to start slowly pulling in the lasso. Slowly, then even more slowly. He heard the scrape of metal against stone. Then the sound lost its metal component.

Carl weighted the leg with additional mud and took another throw. This time he missed the bolt-cutters. But that was no problem. His pains had disappeared. Strange chemical transmitters held back by the body until the last moment suddenly surged through his brain.

With new strength and confidence Carl shot-put the weight into the dark and felt at the last second the end of the arm of the sweater, which he was supposed to hold onto, slip through his clammy fingers. Silence for a moment. Then he heard the slosh of wet cloth landing, accompanied by a taunting clang.

It didn't take Carl even ten seconds this time to confirm that the pants and sweater were completely beyond the reach of either his hands or feet out there in the infinite dark distance of the rocks, further than the bank of the pool, further than his own life.

He realized that until this moment he had believed himself immortal. He wrapped the chain around his neck. He pushed his face into the mud. He banged his head against the iron rod. With a scream he shot back out of the water. He screamed the name that had been on the tip of his tongue the whole time. Now it echoed off the walls into the void.

64

Aéroport de la Liberté

Blond hair actually bestows cleverness; the less that is sent into the eyes, the more remains in the brain with its fluid nourishment and endows it with cleverness. The brown-haired and brown-eyed, and the black-haired and black-eyed, they force that which the blonds push into the brain, into the eyes and hair.

RUDOLF STEINER

T HEY'D ARRANGED A TICKET for her on the eleven o'clock flight. The others had already left the evening before. Helen packed her things, took a taxi and reached the airport in the north of Targat at eight. There she learned that because of technical difficulties the flight had been canceled. There were seats left on two Air France flights leaving soon afterward, one to Spain and one to the south of France, but she had to rule them out because her weapon made her dependent on flying aboard an American airline.

After a bit of back and forth (and protests from other passengers, who didn't have as much luck), she was rebooked on the night flight. Now she had twelve hours. She deposited her baggage in a locker and found a nice, exotic-style European café on the upper floor of the airport building. She read the *Herald Tribune* and a French newspaper that someone had left behind on a table. She was relieved not to stumble upon anything familiar while flipping through either paper.

The cup in which her coffee had been served was white porcelain and had a pattern around the rim of tiny blue sickles alternating with stars. It was the same make as the ones in the kitchen cabinet of bungalow 581d, the same make she had put out on the breakfast table each morning for several days. Two settings. She stared into space for a while and wondered what her life would be like in thirty or forty years. Her life, the extent of her happiness and, potentially, how she might remember this current episode, how she might remember this backward, half-civilized, violent, dirty country in North Africa that she hoped to leave behind for ever in a few hours.

The probability that the nameless man was still alive was close to zero. He had already looked bad the last time they checked on him. And since then another thirty-six hours had passed. You didn't have to be a pessimist to predict that the surface of the water had settled above him for ever by this point.

The airport loudspeaker paged Mr and Mrs Wells to the Air France ticket counter. Helen peered out of the panorama window and saw among the swarm of white, blue and sand-colored Arab buildings around the airport a neon sign that held her attention.

She looked at the clock, called to the waiter and paid. Then she went to her locker and glanced over her shoulder at passers-by. Inconspicuously she took two heavy objects from her travel bag and shoved them, still hidden within the locker, into a plastic bag. She left the airport with the plastic bag, crossed the street and stopped in front of the neon sign she had seen. It was a car rental office.

The cheapest car was a sand-colored Renault 4 with a dashboard gearshift. Helen choked the engine a few times before she left the thick traffic and headed off on the dirt road to Tindirma. She stepped all the way down on the gas. The view of the two kissing camels affected her like looking at a dusty box of childhood memories.

What exactly she intended to do—if she intended anything at all—she didn't know herself. The assignment was over. Nothing definitive had been uncovered, but it had been determined that the transfer of the plans had in all likelihood been unsuccessful. After descriptions of the multifaceted complications, headquarters had ordered a withdrawal overnight, and the *problem*, as it was now called, was to be left on his own in the mountains. The man could not be released.

So what did she want now? She parked the car in the familiar spot, climbed over the ridge and looked across at the mine entrance, the windmill and the barrels on the opposite ridge. She did not see the cabin. There was just a blackened spot. As she crossed the canyon below she was met with a light scent of smoke.

She took her weapon out of the bag, swung out the cylinder, slipped her fingers into the frame, looked down the barrel, closed the cylinder again, shoved the gun and a flashlight into her belt and carefully climbed up to the little plateau.

The charred beams of the cabin had collapsed into a pile. A wisp of smoke rose from the middle. Helen looked around. The only explanation she could come up with was that Cockcroft and Carthage had tried to get rid of any evidence. They'd been the last ones there. But that didn't seem very likely to her. She cocked the hammer.

It was a humid, overcast, late afternoon, and she felt slightly terrified about entering the darkness—because of the darkness. In theory it didn't matter what time you entered a pitch-dark cave, day, evening or night; but the thought of darkness falling above while she was wandering around in the dark beneath the earth, and that she wouldn't emerge into the light but rather to a dark, starless night, a night that looked the same as underground, made her uncomfortable in a way that might have caused someone more simple-minded than Helen to wonder whether feelings of shame and guilt were playing hide and seek in the harmless landscape and lighting conditions.

"Nonsense," she said to herself, and followed the artificial beam of light into the tunnel. Occasionally she turned into a side tunnel in order to study the hand markings, and her level of excitement rose step after step. She started calling Carl's name even before she made it into the deepest cave. No answer. Just darkness and silence and the briny smell of the pool.

The first thing she saw in the beam of light was a muddy, tied-up bundle of clothing lying atop the bolt-cutters, surrounded by a circle of moisture. Helen immediately recognized what had been attempted—and had remained merely an attempt.

She stood on the bank of the pool for nearly a minute holding her breath. She called his name again. She heard the droning echo of her voice, and a shudder ran down her back. But it wasn't a result of the thought of what might be hidden beneath the glassy-smooth surface of the water that made the hairs on the back of her neck stand on end, it was the sound of her own voice. More precisely, the memory of the repulsion she'd had for her voice since she was young. The strangeness, the insecurity and the little thought: how much time has passed. How young I was. And how pointless it all was.

She had no idea why this made such a strong impression on her at this particular moment. And it passed quickly.

She sat in the car for a long time without turning the key in the ignition. She smoked two cigarettes and watched a fly on the windshield. Then she started the engine and switched on the high beams.

65

Further Events

I F ONE WISHED, one could with a clear conscience end this chronicle of none-too-pleasant events at this point. Not much more happened beyond what has already been reported.

A key went missing at the Sheraton Hotel. A man in the Empty Quarter made a fortune when he was able to sell a cheaply acquired espresso machine for ten times what he had paid for it. A young, light-skinned woman (of Norman extraction) and her three-year-old child were found in the mountains with their throats slit. An amulet in the shape of a demon was found in the gaping hole in the boy's throat. The crime was never solved.

Neither Spasski nor Moleskine won the Nobel Prize. Their renown faded away, even if you wouldn't guess it from the magnitude of their Wikipedia pages. A united Africa was never founded.

The police superintendent of Targat felt forced to replace his three half-Arab, half-European officers, Canisades, Polidorio and Karimi, with less well-trained officers. Canisades' corpse was discovered in a desert no man's land in the vicinity of an abandoned liquor distillery, with wire around his throat. He had been sent there to investigate the disappearance of two fellah sons who had mistakenly been dragged into the quadruple murder in a pastoral commune. Hanged for Canisades' murder was an old bootleg distiller who had no sons, no alibi, and, if one is entirely honest, no motive.

Amadou Amadou headed south, sold a car with a bloodstained driver's seat to some nomads on the road to Nouakchott and was last seen in the vicinity of Dimja, where his trail went cold.

Karimi left the police force in 1973 after he was pulled from his bulldozer by residents of the Salt Quarter during the fifth purge and nearly stoned to death. He was treated for nearly two years in a French hospital specializing in spinal injuries. Afterward he returned to the coast in a wheelchair, just as misanthropic as before. He turned down a position in the Interior Ministry. For nearly a year he helped pour drinks at his brother's bar and scared off the customers, until he was granted a modest pension and took up oil-painting.

He came to painting almost accidentally during one of his outings down near the port. In a shop window he noticed a painting set with a cluster of marten-hair brushes surrounded by zinc tubes that looked like plump, colorful sausages—for tourists, and overpriced. Using advice from his old contacts he was able to negotiate to buy the set for an eighth of the original price and applied himself henceforth to magical realism.

He was able to sell a few paintings, took part in minor exhibitions, and landed a spot in a group exhibition at the Jeu de Paume in Paris in 1977. The exhibition catalog is difficult to come by, but any interested party can still find a painting rakishly signed *Q. Karimi* in the Targat police presidium today. It has adorned the entrance hall for thirty years at this point, attending to the space with an appealing composition of handsome female faces, grisly skulls and ghostly bare trees circled by bats. The artist died of pneumonia in 1979.

Finally Polidorio, as we remember, set out for Tindirma in his Mercedes on a Saturday morning in 1972 and has been missing ever since. Photos of him were put up all over Targat and Tindirma for a while, then after a while only in Targat, and then, finally, only in the police presidium there. He was declared dead in 1983 and this declaration has to this day never been contested.

In a letter, Heather Gliese wrote that her mother led a happy and fulfilled life and remained spry and healthy until she died peacefully in her sleep a few days before her seventy-second birthday. She was survived by four grandchildren, her library comprised 8,000 volumes in several languages, and a recurring nightmare that plagued her for a time in middle age and led to an unpleasant form of insomnia disappeared on its own in the end, without the aid of a therapist.

One could end the book with a few last harmonious notes. Perhaps a brief description of the landscape, a panoramic view of the jagged silhouette of the Kangeeri mountains in evening light, valleys swathed in pink and lavender mist, ravines filled with crimson shadows, a few bats, a picturesque mule. Ry Cooder playing guitar. A windmill enters the screen from the left.

Of course, if one were utterly fearless and in the right mood, one could also take another glance at a figure not entirely insignificant in this story, a man whose convoluted fate has had us on pins and needles for quite a long while, a man who fell beneath the wheels of fate neither by his own volition nor entirely by accident, but rather solely and exclusively because of a process of false logical deduction; through the belief in the innocence of a guilty party. A man with memory loss.

Shall we? A quick glance at the camera assistants, fleeting shoulder shrugs on both sides, and the camera is already zooming in on the opening of a mine which was already recognizable as a tiny dot on the opposite mountainside but now quickly looms larger in the picture, darker, until the entire screen is swallowed and with a mix of tracking shots and complicated special effects we travel deep into the mountain.

If we had a night-vision device available to us, we would now see the flickering silhouette of a human figure in a muddy pool. Circling the pool, the shaky image would show us the cramped upper body from all sides, would show the man who had for many hours been struggling desperately with thirst and sleep and death. Then a quick cut to the face, devoid of all hope. We could exhibit the familiar mix of voyeurism and empathy with regard to this person's suffering, could watch him to the point of his ultimate death or his highly implausible—given the well-known circumstances—rescue.

Of course, we should also admit that we do not have access to such a night-vision device. And even if we did, what good would it do us in reality? It's dark in the cave, so dark that there isn't so much as a shimmer of residual light in the depths of this mine that could be intensified by whatever technical means. Complete, all-permeating, impenetrable darkness surrounds us, so that we must kindly ask the reader to imagine the following in his or her mind.

66

Beautiful Memories

The ball I threw while playing in the park
Has not yet reached the ground.

DYLAN THOMAS

CARL PROPPED HIMSELF UP on his left elbow. He propped himself up on his right elbow. He remembered once swimming out into the gray sea one morning at first light. It must have been the Atlantic or another great sea. He was surrounded by yellow fog which had grown more dense over the water, nothing but yellow fog everywhere, and the shore had long since disappeared. He hadn't really lost his orientation, but an abstract, nameless fear suddenly rose in him. Alone at sea and with nothing to grab hold of anywhere around him, nothing but bottomless water below, in a world without shape, swathed in yellow gauze, he had believed that he sensed death. He could still hear the brooding seagulls on the shore, but what if they had taken off? He swam back, and when he had swum what he took to be twice the distance he thought it would be to the shore, he heard the gulls behind him. Horrified, he changed direction again. His body was getting cold, his muscles were growing weak, and it occurred to him that the smartest thing to do was to stay in one spot and wait for the sun to burn off the fog so he would be able to muster his last remaining strength to make it back. But in a panic he didn't think he was capable of it. He swam further and further in the direction he'd already gone, and just when he thought he was done for, the fog lifted and he saw that he had been swimming parallel to the shore the whole time just a stone's throw from land.

Now, in a muddy pool in the depths of a mountain, buried beneath kilometers of rock, this seemed one of the most serene memories of his entire life. He wished he could die in the ocean beneath the yellow light of an indifferent sun, swallowed up by clear salt water. Spray splashed in his face, telegraph poles flitted past, both hands gripped the steering wheel.

A sandblaster was aimed at his windshield. He wrapped a piece of cloth around his head and opened the door. A bucket-load of sand blew into the car; he closed the door.

He kept coming to his senses, and then saw the shadows on the bank of the pool. He thought pensively for a while about how you could tell whether you were already dead, and realized a man was sitting next to him.

"Hot here," he said, and Carl, who had no desire to talk with ghosts, said nothing in reply. He was looking at a green building on the other side of the street, above which a green flag waved.

"Hot here," the other man repeated.

"Yeah," said Carl grumpily, then he submerged himself and butted his head against the iron rod. It barely even hurt any more.

"What's the story?"

"What?"

"Your name!"

"Huh?"

Carl looked around fearfully. But nobody was there, only a little girl who put a glass of mint tea on the table in front of him. He practically burned his tongue. He waved his hand back and forth above the hot tea and then asked: "What's *your* name?"

"You first," said the ghost.

"You started this."

"What?"

"It was you who started."

"Fine," said the ghost, imitating Carl's swatting hand motion. "Herrlichkoffer."

"What?"

"Herrlichkoffer. Not so loud. Or Lundgren. But for you, Herrlichkoffer."

"Herrlichkoffer for me."

"Right! And now write your name here—here—here."

The ghost shoved a pad of notepaper across the table. Was this some kind of experiment? Or did they really want to know his name now? He began to write, but before he had even written seven letters the other man had already jumped up and run off down the street. "Your notebook," Carl called after the crazy man, but he didn't hear him. And he hadn't only forgotten his pad and pen, he had also not paid for his tea. The girl asked Carl whether he was going to pay for it.

He put money on the table and she swept the coins from the table into her dirty, little hand, and at the end of the street a Chevrolet braked to a stop and four men in white djellabas got out. He saw her by chance... and the next image was: he was running. Running away from the men toward his car, saw that the Mercedes was blocked in, saw a white djellaba on the passenger seat and threw the door open. Threw the djellaba on and tried to blend in with the throng of people on the street. Screaming. The men. The desert. He practically stumbled over a boy lying face-down in the sand. The boy lifted his head listlessly. His face was swollen, the skin on his forehead cracked. He was wearing a blue uniform jacket with gold braiding and had an assault rifle in his hands. He had no pants on. A light-blue sock hung around one of his ankles. A question mark of dried blood below his nose.

"A—a," said the boy barely audibly.

"What?" Carl turned to look for his pursuers. Then he looked at the boy again.

"A—a."

"What?"

The boy dropped his head, gulped with his eyes closed, and then opened his mouth with a clicking sound.

"At—ta," he groaned. He cried.

"I don't have any water," yelled Carl, took the gun from his hands and motioned over his shoulder. "Tindirma. That way."

He ran. As he was running he threw the rifle sling over his head and reached for the safety catch. The gun had no safety catch. It was made of wood.

67

The King of Africa

We did not create the heaven and the earth, and everything between them, for amusement. If we wished to create a diversion, we could have initiated it without any of this, if indeed we were to do so.

SURAH 21: 16–17

HIS SKULL BANGED rhythmically against the iron rod, and then all of a sudden he thought he felt the rod give. "To arms, citizens," he mumbled, pulling weakly at the chain and falling over sideways. He got back up and pushed the rod back and forth with both hands but couldn't tell whether it was just his soggy hands that were giving or if perhaps the footing of metal was indeed loosening.

Carl yanked and shoved the rod like a child who feels a loose tooth in his mouth and then touches it and pushes and pulls it for so long with his tongue that he loses feeling not only in the tooth but in his tongue and whole mouth and can no longer tell whether the tooth was ever really loose. He threw his body against it, swung back and forth and kept the mechanical motion going despite appalling pain, until his strength finally flagged. He didn't dare test the result of his efforts for a long time, but when he finally straightened his upper body he pulled the rod out of the rocky ground with virtually no effort.

He flopped down on all fours on the bank, hit his head on a rock, and lay for a long time sobbing in the darkness.

He had no trouble finding the narrow tunnel out of the muddy cave: around a large boulder, that's where the ascent began. To the right and left he could feel chisel-mark-covered rock walls—the passageway was barely shoulder width. The chain around his neck and the iron rod attached to it dragged along behind him. The noise stopped every few seconds when he froze in order to stretch his arm out into the darkness ahead. His desire to flop down on the spot and sleep was incredibly strong, but it was surpassed by his will to leave the darkness behind as quickly as possible. As expected, the passageway soon broadened. He could tell by the echo.

If he remembered correctly, he was now in a cave about his height from which various other tunnels branched off. He had no idea how many other tunnels and which one was the right one. Deciding quickly, he crawled down the next tunnel to the right, which immediately started to ascend. It went through the rock in long, serpentine curves. Then came a short flat section, then it ascended again. Carl could feel his waterlogged skin sloughing off and bleeding. He tried to stand up two or three times, but his fear of unseen chasms always sent him immediately back onto all fours. He was also too weak to walk. All of a sudden a pile of debris blocked his way. He felt around. His left hand sank into something slippery and smelly. He tried to climb over the debris but it went up to the ceiling. A horrible thought gripped him.

"They couldn't have!" he yelled. "They really didn't need to do this!" He made his way back to the cave abysmally slowly, reeling, slithering, scooting and scrambling all the way, and once again went to the right. He was barely sentient at this point.

The next tunnel went steeply down and the one beyond did as well. He crawled only a few meters into each before the slope convinced him he wasn't going the right way.

The next tunnel went up. "This is the right one, it must be," he said, scraping along one hand after the next. He kept dozing off for seconds at a time. The passageway went on and on. Up, then a flat section, then up again. Then a pile of debris blocked his way. His left hand hit on something slippery and smelly.

He heard himself scream like a two-year-old, and once he had calmed down again he tried to figure out what the slippery stuff was. Whether it was rotten or whether it might be edible. But after a day and a half in a muddy pool his senses were numb. He couldn't figure out what the stuff was, and the fact that he'd even thought about it made him realize that his final mental and physical breakdown was very close at hand.

Back in the cave he marked with a stone the dead-end tunnel he had now crawled up twice. Then he tried to think of how many passageways went out from this cave. Was it three? Or four? He didn't know. He couldn't remember. In order to be sure, he took another painful crawl counterclockwise around the cave. One that went upward… another that went upward… then came the one that had been marked. So only three passageways! A dead end, a tunnel that ended at the muddy pool, and one that led to freedom. Must lead to freedom. But which one? The one on the right? The one on the left? His ability to think logically had abandoned him. It would certainly be possible by light to memorize the layout of a room with three exits. But three passageways in a pitch-black cave that you can only feel was nothing short of an amorphous nightmare. It seemed to him that the tunnel not directly next to the one he had marked must be the right one. But then it occurred to him that with just three exits, they were all directly next to each other. He heard himself wheezing in the dark. His intuition was adamant that he should go left, but that same intuition told him that his spatial orientation was so muddled that he shouldn't depend on intuition at all, and so he went to the right once again.

The tunnel he headed into went down steeply for ten or fifteen meters, then flattened out and then came to a cross-shaped intersection.

Both side tunnels were long, as Carl found out, and petered out. He marked the entrances and crawled on. His last hopes were fading. At least in the mud he had been struggling against something concrete, against water and metal. Here he was struggling against nothingness. Stuffy, hot, labyrinthine darkness that was swallowing him up. Had already swallowed him up.

Other passageways went off to the right and left. He couldn't find stones that he could mark them with, so he left them unexplored. At some point he turned into a passageway he took to be wider than the others. There were chisels and stones at the entrance, and he tried in vain to carry some of them in his mouth. He would have had plenty of use for them. Tunnels suddenly branched off every few meters. To the left, to the right, ascending and descending, and at some stage he collapsed and lay down. His face on the cool stone. He would never get out of this labyrinth without help. He just hoped to be able to nod off and die peacefully, but the finality of death kept him from falling asleep. Maybe just to the end of this broad passageway. He dragged himself along on his shredded hands, elbows and knees through a long, sustained curve—and then it brightened.

It was a surreal, otherworldly, disembodied light. It didn't touch any objects, it just hung before his eyes like fog. He turned his head back and forth, but the fog of light turned with him. In the middle of the fog a point. He stared just to the side of it and the point became more distinct. With the last of his strength he crawled another twenty, thirty meters toward it, until he assured himself that the shimmering point increased in intensity as he went closer so that it could only be a reflection of the light from the distant exit. Then he collapsed.

In a single dream that kept endlessly repeating, he saw himself drinking from a bottle of water that Helen handed him.

When he opened his eyes, he was in complete darkness. The point of light had disappeared. He blinked and looked all around. The point was still gone. But he did not panic. The sun has set outside, he told himself, the entire world is dark. And he fell back to sleep. His body was feverish. His mouth was dried out and as hard as wood. And when he finally felt himself coming to, he was afraid to open his eyes for a long time. He was sick from hunger and thirst and pain and anxiety. But the shimmer of light was there again, and it was brighter than before.

As he crawled toward it he began to recognize the first contours. After two bends he was able to make out the ground he was moving over. He hoisted himself to his feet. The iron rod swung back and forth into his knees. The air improved, the rocks took on shapes and colors, and finally he was able to see a bit of sky in the not too far distance, framed by jagged stone.

He shielded his eyes from the dazzling light with a blood-and-mud-encrusted arm. He stopped on the narrow plateau where the miner's cabin sat. He breathed like a tiny bird. The windmill spun. Morning had just broken.

For a long time Carl just stood there and looked out at the comforting, deserted world, a world of violet mountain tops, valleys immersed in pink and lavender, ravines filled with purple shadows. A bat shot over Carl's shoulder and into the mine. He thought he heard a quiet knocking. The sound was so quiet that he wasn't sure whether it was coming from the wooden cabin or from his left temple.

At the same instant the vitally important questions returned: Where can I get water? How can I get medical help? And most important of all: How can I get out of here?

The door of the cabin crashed open, banged into a rock and slammed shut again. Someone was romping around inside. The door opened again, and Hakim of the Mountains came hopping out, naked except for a tattered pair of underwear dangling around his knees. He looked horrible. His feet were tied together with hemp rope. Dried excrement clung to his flanks. His wrists were tied, too, but the rope connecting the two of them had been severed. He hopped awkwardly out into the morning, his underwear slipped further down to his ankles. The Winchester under his arm. He stared at Carl. He shouted.

"We know each other," yelled Carl, holding up his bloody hands in a peaceful gesture.

"Indeed," said Hakim, cocking the rifle. "Fucking American!"

"I'm not with the others! I'm not one of them!"

"Of course not—and I'm the King of Africa."

"I didn't do anything to you!"

"You didn't do anything to me! No, only your wife, that stinking pile of camel dung!" shouted the old man, aiming, and putting a bullet between Carl's eyes.

Struggling to keep his balance, he hopped twice on the spot, then hopped back into the cabin and undid his ankle restraints. At about noon he packed his belongings, dragged Carl's corpse into the cabin, poured gasoline over everything and threw in a lit match. Then, with his bundle, he climbed down to the low-lands, Hakim III, the last great miner of the Kangeeri massif.

68

The Madrasa of the Salt Quarter

Tremblez, tyrans, et vous perfides
L'opprobre de tous les partis,
Tremblez! Vos projets parricides
Vont enfin recevoir leurs prix!
Tout est soldat pour vous combattre,
S'ils tombent, nos jeunes héros,
La terre en produit de nouveaux,
Contre vous tout prêts à se battre!

'LA MARSEILLAISE'

ARMS STRETCHED OUT to the sides of his body as if he'd been crucified, a blue plastic canister in one hand and a rusted wrench in the other, Jean Bekurtz stood on the roof of the school building looking eastward and waited for the sun to rise.

Jean was the offspring of a family of French civil servants and had fought in Indochina as a young man and—as his mother confided to the family doctor—had not emerged entirely free of damage.

After the removal of General Navarre, Jean stayed in the Far East for a time and then began a restless life of travel that took him to many places in the world, just not back to France. Finally, around 1960, he wound up on the North African coast, the first harbinger of a generation who saw their primary mission as calling into question their parents' lifestyle.

He made a modest profit selling leather sandals, hats, suntan oil, beach towels, key chains, T-shirts, handmade jewelry, sunglasses and, once in a while, pot, to the tourists. It wasn't an overly fulfilling life, but it probably would have gone on that way for quite a long while if not for the fact that Jean met the charismatic Edgar Fowler III by chance one day on the beach at Targat. The two of them stumbled upon each other, and they recognized something in each other immediately. Left Siddhartha, right Feltrinelli, soul brothers, and all that remained in Jean's head about the first weeks of their friendship was, for good reason, nothing more than a hazy glow. They lived together in a tiny little room with an ocean view (Jean's recollection) or a view of the mountain of garbage (Fowler's recollection), they were interested in Italian films about the exploitation of women by society, played around with a children's chemistry set and read ever more obscure writers until finally they hit upon the idea (though the how and why of this venture remain obscure) of founding a commune in the desert that would fund itself by growing vegetables.

Fowler provided the general ideological orientation of the project and in no time at all recruited a substantial number of exceedingly good-looking young women while Jean primarily handled the farming concept.

As a child of the city he didn't have the slightest idea about what he called at that time the wonder of nature, but his enthusiasm was contagious. He could be seen mornings waltzing barefoot through the blue-green millet sprouts breaking through the hard desert soil with a yellow plastic watering can in his hand, or holding lectures about the incomparable feeling of working the earth by the sweat of your own brow and sharing the well-earned payoff in solidarity with like-minded people.

It was Jean's exuberant, sometimes fanatical enthusiasm that held the community together at first, and it was also Jean who first lost his interest in vegetables again.

The unbearable sun coming over the Kaafaahi cliffs and the even more unbearable sand! The tedious planting of seeds that just didn't want to grow and had to be constantly sprinkled with water that needed to be endlessly, exhaustingly hauled in! This wasn't his idea of the wild life.

The first rifts developed among what had grown to eight other members of the commune, and as a result of ideological differences and after endless discussions about the practice of sexual freedom and the fact that, in his mind, it was not being practiced freely at all among the people Jean described as quote unquote adults, after just a few weeks Jean became the first member who had to be banished from the commune, personally excommunicated by his friend Edgar Fowler. That was in 1966.

Back in Targat, his old business in trinkets was sluggish. Jean had competition now: there were suddenly a dozen longhairs living on the beach. He was forced to switch to selling opium; the police now took three-quarters of his earnings. He couldn't afford a room. He fell into a bad state. It was second only to Dien Bien Phu as the worst period of his life. He was even entertaining thoughts of returning to France when one beautiful day a broke American approached him and tried to trade him a surfboard for his daily fix.

Jean had never seen anything like the board before. The contemplative form, the dazzling whiteness. Later that same evening he paddled out into the open ocean on his stomach. He found the new perspective thrilling, the freedom, the meditation of the waves. He closed his eyes, and when he opened them again and saw dark clouds on the horizon it didn't bother him. When the wind shifted and turned into a storm, it didn't bother him. As the swells grew higher and steeper and swept him from the board, he found it incredibly humorous for a few seconds. Then he began his fight for survival. He had immediately lost any sense of orientation. Underwater he crashed against the rocks and gasped for air in the thunderous spindrift. Finally a breaker tossed him up onto land.

In his completely smoke-addled mind he exaggerated the danger he had found himself in, greatly, and while he was still lying on the beach wheezing and coughing and watched as the water also spat out his board then sucked it back in and spat it out again, the moment intensified in him into a ball of radiant clarity. This wasn't a fight against rice-eating gooks any more, this wasn't a scheme of some petty veggie commune, this was the omnipotence of omnipotent nature, a decisive moment. The ocean had shown him what it was capable of, and he, Jean Bekurtz, had shown the ocean that he could come to terms with it. The fine line, the great light, the sentence written across the sky: you must change your life. And he changed it.

Every day he paddled out when the surf was up. It took him about two weeks before he was able to stand up and glide a few meters down a wave, and in the following years anyone who vacationed on the beach at Targat would see him standing on his board regardless of the weather, his arms pressed to his sides or at his back or folded across his chest. Sometimes he sang while surfing. Jean had stopped smoking and was so clear-headed that clear-headed wasn't even the right word for it any more. Sun-browned skin stretched over his muscles, saltwater and sun bleached his hair.

It went that way for nearly three years without him ever experiencing a moment of doubt. He was the first waverider these shores had ever seen, and there are probably still pictures in European and American photo albums from the time of a longhaired, Apollonian, tender young man practicing balancing with alternately joyfully shrieking, frightened, wide-eyed, cheeky or simply shocked ten-year-olds in the water near shore. *Targat 1969.*

But this life ended just as abruptly as it had begun. An emaciated Spaniard with two heavy suitcases had put up at the pension where Jean lived. This Spaniard had booked passage on a ship and was too weak to carry his own luggage. His bottom jaw had been eaten away by cancer, tumors grew on his neck, and his breath already smelled as if it was from another world. As he confided in Jean, he wanted to go back to his homeland to die, it was too late for medical treatment.

Smiling, Jean took both suitcases in one hand and his surfboard under his other arm and carried it all down to the harbor. Sitting between the bags on the pier, smoking, as the ship slowly grew larger and larger on the horizon, the Spaniard told Jean his life story. He spoke very quietly and gracefully, somewhat incoherently and with his mouth half closed as if trying not to breathe out too much of the afterworld into this one.

For eight years he had held a teaching position in the Salt Quarter, the only teacher there. Though to call it a teaching position would be overstating it. The head office never checked in at all, and as for the pay, he might almost as well have been working for nothing. Visibly straining, he described a few episodes of his pedagogical existence. He wiped the sweat from his face and tumors, held out his arm to show how big the children were, and added a few platitudes about eyes filled with curiosity, untainted minds and the bright laughter of children. Strictly speaking, the crux of all of his stories boiled down to the bell-like laughter of children. How he had educated them, how he had given them hope. How they called him Monsieur So-and-so and rewarded his jokes with their laughter. The gratitude in their grime-encircled eyes. Now their education would for ever go unfinished.

He mimicked their sad little faces at his departure, coughed blood onto the pier, and Jean had no trouble discerning the message behind the message. People like the Spaniard and himself could sniff each other out from a long way. He let the sick man give him the location of the school and a description of its environs, waved cheerfully one last time as the ship departed, and two days later the Salt Quarter had a new teacher.

Jean Bekurtz had no more pedagogical training than his predecessor, but anyone could read, write and do math.

The classroom was a mud-brick square with no windows, light came only through the open roof, half covered with mats. The tables and chairs were from the beginning of the colonial period. Some still had slogans from the Khan war scratched into them. When too many children turned up to class they had to sit on canisters they brought with them, or they leaned one-legged against the wall. The front wall was newly adorned with a chalkboard in the form of a black-coated surfboard with both ends cut off.

The Spaniard had not exaggerated. There were too many pupils to count. Even on holidays charmingly bedraggled, trusting kids turned up to be entertained, and Jean sat them in his lap and gave them lessons in Greek history. When he had extra money he bought popsicles or chocolates or other things little hearts desired. They played with an old soccer ball during breaks, and if one of the little brown things managed to dribble around Monsieur Bekurtz he would pick them up and give them a wet kiss on the forehead as penalty. "You make me crazy!" he would yell, and the bell-like laughter of children answered him. Though for the most part they did indeed do school work.

The legendary thirst for knowledge of the underprivileged proved only half true. Like anywhere else, one and a half of them were intelligent, five were somewhat gifted, and the countless remaining students were charmingly simple. Some of the oldest and mistreated only came to class because they were too weak to work, because they were treated like dogs on the street, and because there was no room for the dregs in the distant Koran schools.

There were no school books. To pass on the love of reading and solving math problems, Jean clumsily recreated the smattering of knowledge he had retained from his own childhood, read from dime-store novels, or sketched diagrams from magazines on the blackboard. He found a schematic drawing of a cow in a pamphlet from a Franco-Belgian dairy corporation, and added to it four stomachs with implausible functions and sang the praises of appreciating nature. A dead starling lying on the threshold of the school one morning was dissected with a pocket knife, its wings compared to those of a Boeing. A fantastically complicated diagram of a combustion engine found in a motorcycle magazine and crudely recreated in chalk looked down at the children for weeks and was studied in every detail. Depending on the mood, some seventy excited children transformed themselves for weeks at a time into veterinarians, pilots and auto mechanics. The fact that none of them would ever actually have the chance to get into any of these fields was something that Jean spent long, lonely nights putting out of his mind. He awoke those mornings with a headache and it took great effort to keep his flicker of idealism burning after a night of such thoughts. He became sentimental over the years.

When he stood on the roof at dawn and rang the jerry-rigged bell, when he saw the beloved wretches hurrying toward him from all directions, when they came into his building chattering and giggling, singing and waving, sad and cheerful, he knew all the toil was for naught. Their destiny amidst the mountains of rubbish was foregone and irrevocable from birth, as though the religion they adhered to was for once more than a tall tale, and the naively colorful, bright hope of education and freedom that

Jean was trying to seed in their souls lit dully and unsteadily, weak and easily extinguished in a world benighted by superstition and patriarchy. But they were lit! And Jean, who in the course of his life had begun many things and failed to follow through with them, stayed true to his purpose. He was the teacher of the Salt Quarter, and he remained so year after year.

Class began at sunrise in summer as in winter. The first hour was devoted to the Latin alphabet, a ritual Jean had adopted from the Spaniard. A as in Advancement. H as in Humanism. There were very few words with Q. Jean wrote on the board and the pupils wrote with chalk on wooden tablets that belonged to the school. The tablets were as smooth as if they'd been sandblasted, and they were wiped clean with rags at the end of the lessons.

In early 1972, at which point Jean had already been in the Salt Quarter for two years, there was a minor revolution in terms of writing. Abderrahman, the son of the water salesman, got hold of a pencil somewhere and for the sake of showing off began to write on pieces of scrap paper. Thereupon Khalid Samadi, the local baker and thus far above a water salesman, paid a great sum to acquire for his son a pencil stub and a small spiral notebook with half the pages still blank. Just a few weeks later only the poorest of the poor were still writing on the wooden tablets.

The best method to get hold of a writing utensil was to undertake the four-hour march to the coast and to ask tourists there for them. "*Pour l'école, pour l'école*" was an argument to which the mysterious Europeans seemed far more open than to "*J'ai faim*" croaked from an empty stomach. They accepted the risk of getting lost in the city of more than a million, of getting caught or carried off by soldiers or other riff-raff, or of never again returning for whatever other reason. Beyond the harbor lay boxes of squished vegetables, it was possible to pick up an hour's work in the Ville Nouvelle if you were lucky, and in the southern part of the city the danger of being thrown into a truck equipped with bars like a jail cell was highest. Every third trip ended in tragedy. Like insects drawn to a light, however, the children still tumbled over the barrier of rubbish toward the bounty beyond.

One of the four Mohammeds wrote with a sharpened wooden stick that he dipped into home-made ink derived from coffee grounds. Rassul owned a felt pen that he constantly spat into the top of so that greenish fluid would emerge from the tip. But the king of the alphabetized was Aiyub.

Aiyub was a leper of limited intelligence. He didn't know his family and lived in a hole in the ground covered with cardboard. He was too weak to make the journey into town: a mine had blown off his lower left leg. He was the last pupil still writing on a wooden tablet until one day with great show he pulled a pen out from beneath his djellaba. The pen was made of polished metal that glinted so smoothly and dully and nobly that it might even have been silver. No, it definitely was silver! Because there were strange letters on the clip, an unpronounceable word that amazed even the teacher. Nobody had ever seen a writing utensil like it. You could make the tip of the pen poke out, and by pressing a mechanical gadget the push-button at the back would pop out. If you held the pen to the back of another student's neck and pressed on the mechanical gadget you could inflict a funny little pain.

Aiyub looked after his pen like a treasure. For four weeks he held it with two hands when he slept, until he passed away from dysentery and his best friend Buhum inherited the precious object. Buhum couldn't read or write; he traded the pen to Chaid for a picture of the footballer Johan Cruyff and a peppermint candy. Chaid lost the pen to Driss because he bet that Hitler had been French. Driss had no greater desire than to see a naked girl take a pee. And so the pen ended up with Hossam, who had a sister.

Hossam was as stupid as a sheet pile in water, and he took apart the mechanism. He stretched the metal spring and lost a part of the push-button mechanism in the sand and pricked his sister in the eye with the empty barrel. Shrieking, his mother swatted the diabolical thing out of his hand and threw it out the door. Hossam was writing on a wooden tablet the next day again. People later found individual parts of the pen in the sand beneath the corrugated-metal shack. Hossam's little sister dug out the cartridge and used it as a spine for a wobbly straw doll, her favorite, so it could sit upright.

This little sister answered to the name of Samaya. Samaya was seven or eight years old and of unrivaled beauty. An old Tuareg, a man so old that he had been cradled in the arms of the last king of the Massina Empire, said that to look at Samaya's face was to comprehend Allah's creation. She was the first one to school every morning. She was barely more intelligent than her brother, but she had the angelic quality of heart that earns one eternal life. There wasn't an evil thought in her, her purity unblemished. When the fifth purge compassed the Salt Quarter, Samaya ripped herself free of her fleeing mother's hand and ran back into the shack, where her beloved doll was. Together with the doll she was buried beneath a toppled wall of the structure. A bulldozer rolled backwards over the spot. It lifted its shovel like a priest raising the Ark of the Covenant, showed it to the infidels, and then dumped the entire contents onto the mound of rubbish.

AFTERWORD

"He Confessed": Thoughts on Wolfgang Herrndorf's Sand

THE SURPRISE German literary sensation of 2010 was Wolfgang Herrndorf's road novel *Tschick* (translated into English as *Why We Took the Car*), heaped with awards, translated into many languages, and before long assigned reading in Costa Rican schools. The press quite rightly saw *Tschick* as a German *Huckleberry Finn*—a comparison Herrndorf himself soon wearied of—while the critic Gustav Seibt, one of Herrndorf's earliest admirers, described the book as hearkening back to the romantic era, marked by that atmosphere of sheer reverie, music, emotional surrender, the wafting call of the post horn, wanderlust, nostalgia, fireworks descending upon nocturnal gardens, and foolish bliss that Thomas Mann discerned in the poems and stories of Joseph von Eichendorff. Be that as it may, *Sand*, the novel that Herrndorf wrote next—it was to be the final novel he saw into print; diagnosed with an incurable cancer, he committed suicide at the young age of forty-eight in 2013—must be considered the antithesis of *Tschick*, almost a revocation of the earlier book. *Sand* has a romanticism of its own, the cool, dark Romanticism of the Gothic tale, but it is as sharply contoured as a work by Poe.

Merely to summarize its plot, an idle endeavor with most books, is to embark on an adventure—an adventure that Herrndorf, who lamented the dying art of writing book reviews without spoilers, indirectly discouraged. Nonetheless, it can't entirely be avoided here. Initial reviews of *Sand* judged it to be enigmatic and baffling, leaving many questions unanswered. Nothing could do the book a greater injustice. *Sand* demands a good deal from the reader, but all in the form of one thing: attention.

The setting and time are clear: It is the summer of 1972, when the Palestinian terrorist organization Black September took Israeli hostages at the Munich Olympics, though those events merely flicker at the margins of the novel. The scene, a thinly veiled Morocco, is the North African port city of Targat on the edge of the Sahara, not far from the oasis Tindirma, where dropouts from Western society have formed a commune.

It is also clear that the genre of the book can't be pinned down— and that this is not of the slightest consequence. No one gives a hoot about genre. All bad novels are alike; each great novel is great in its own way.

WHO IS THE HERO?

The characters pose greater difficulties. In chapter two (of sixty-eight) we learn a great deal about Polidorio, a police officer, only to see his trail peter out in chapter twelve. There is an ongoing search for a gentleman by the name of Cetrois, who has some super-important item in his possession, but up to the very end Monsieur Cetrois fails to turn up. And even the simple question of the identity of the book's hero turns out to be a knotty one, which is why most reviewers have steered clear of it.

The question is so tricky because the hero, who does not appear until page eighty-nine, has been hit on the head and lost his memory. He hasn't the foggiest notion who he is. He makes do by calling himself Carl, after the label in his jacket (in the blog that Herrndorf wrote while terminally ill, he noted the offer of a complimentary suit from the designer Carl Gross, and mused that perhaps he should have lingered longer on his descriptions of the Alfa Spider). Until the grisly end, Carl is left in the dark about his real name and his past. He knows nothing about himself; when he learns that Tindirma's Mafia boss, the smuggler king, has taken his wife and small child hostage and is threatening to murder them, he can worry about them only in the abstract, because they are strangers to him.

Unlike Carl, readers can fortunately leaf back and review the characters Herrndorf introduces in the first eighty-eight pages. Two peculiar policemen crop up at the beginning—the above-mentioned Polidorio and a certain Canisades—and, as one reviewer wrote, "soon vanish from the scene again, one due to his insignificance, the other due to a noose around his neck."

This is almost correct. Canisades is strangled by a murderer who escapes while being transported to his execution. That other, seemingly insignificant policeman—begone, fear of spoilers, the book has been out long enough!—that other police officer, Polidorio, is Herrndorf's amnesiac hero.

CES TROIS NE FONT QU'UN

An early review of Georges Perec's *La Disparition* noted that there was something odd about the book. Something off-kilter, something bizarre. The reviewer had failed to realize that the book contains not one single letter *e*.

Readers of *Sand* miss something equally important by overlooking the novel's basic construction, which is as discreet as it is compelling. The web of clues is so densely woven that readers really can hardly avoid stumbling over it. Carl speaks the local language and looks like an Arab, but thinks in French. Polidorio studied in Paris and in the heat of an argument is reviled as a *pied-noir*; his grandfather was an Arab. Carl is surprised to find that he understands German and can even read it in Gothic type; Polidorio spent his youth in Switzerland. Carl is judged to be about thirty, while Polidorio is twenty-eight. Even as he accosts people in the city, Carl goes unrecognized—because Polidorio (with his unloved wife and a child conceived in 1969) had arrived there from Paris just eight weeks before. The only people who recognize him are two colleagues from the police station and a drug-addicted prostitute who curses him for failing to supply her with morphine from the evidence room; Polidorio, who spent every other night at the brothel, was in the habit of doing just that.

Why does Carl give his name as "Bédeaux" under torture? Because it is one of the made-up names that Polidorio enters into French colonial-era papers in chapter two. Again and again the amnesiac has flashbacks to the police officer. He experiences a sandstorm using the same words as Polidorio does before him. And the decisive moment of his life comes to him in a dream as a fragment of memory. Carl sees the green house with a green flag that stands opposite the café where, as Polidorio, he had been unlucky enough to drink his tea next to a Swedish secret agent who mistook him for his contact person. Lundgren, the agent, requests that Polidorio write his name in a notebook, and the name Polidorio employs is Cetrois —Polidorio is Carl is Cetrois, the three seemingly separate characters one and the same—at which point a ballpoint with an inner life of its own also changes hands. Lundgren, already befuddled by sunstroke, composes a mental telegram announcing the completion of his mission ("*VC accomplished stop the desert is on fire stop C3 hit upon oil*"). Shortly after, he is lying slain in a pond.

An accident, as we learn later on; the CIA had meant to capture him alive and interrogate him under torture. Lundgren, you see, was transporting microfilm with blueprints for an ultracentrifuge. An Arab power aspires to build an atom bomb, and Israel and the CIA want to stop it. This is the backstory of a thriller whose boldness extends to its total disregard for political correctness. "The Arabs are stupid, lazy, and smelly," Herrndorf said as he described *Sand* in an interview, unfurling the slurs with relish, "the Europeans, without a single exception, are arrogant racists and pederasts, the Americans torture whoever crosses their path, and the people pulling the strings are—naturally—the Jews."

HEADACHES

But whatever the hero's name is, how did he end up with amnesia? For one thing, though he may be the only sympathetic character in the novel's huge cast, he is not exactly Einstein. To be precise, he has an IQ of 102, as he learns from an old French middle-school questionnaire. And so it takes him a while to grasp that his friendly American helper Helen, with her karate skills, might not be a cosmetics saleswoman after all; that the office of the scruffy psychiatrist Cockcroft is a bit on the unusual side; that the "mine" everyone is after is the ink cartridge (*la mine*) in the pen that someone left in the Mercedes whose central locking system—in a moment set up with great elegance—opens with a click at the very moment Carl-Polidorio, clueless as ever, is playing around with his key near the lock.

Being kindhearted, but not all that bright, Polidorio alias Carl has made a mistake. Four people have been massacred in the hippie commune near the oasis. The chief suspect, the sexually uptight son of a fellah, denies the deed, though all eyewitness reports and other pieces of evidence point to his guilt. In a cheap thriller he would be innocent all the same, and this is precisely the false hunch that seizes the police officer Polidorio. To get to the bottom of things, he drives to the oasis in his Mercedes and questions the inhabitants of the commune one more time. Afterwards he drinks that fateful tea next to the Swedish agent, is pursued, leaves the pen that was slipped to him in his Mercedes, and flees into the desert, ending up in an old distillery where he is knocked out and loses his memory.

The belief in the innocence of a guilty man—that, the narrator declares toward the end of the novel, is the reason for his hero's ordeal. This really lets the cat out of the bag. Whoever still hasn't figured out that the hero is the same police officer reported missing after driving out to the oasis ought to realize it now. And enjoy one of the hidden payoffs that fill the book to bursting: it is this brain injury, of all things, that has relieved Polidorio of the excruciating headaches that used to afflict him punctually at four each afternoon. In this regard Carl is free of complaints; in other respects he has more than enough. Though he never does learn that the bodies of his wife and three-year-old son have been found in the mountains.

LUNDGREN HAS A PROBLEM

But why did so many reviewers feel that they had lost their way in a labyrinth? *Sand* has a clear chronological framework in which every single day can be dated. As Herrndorf once wrote, he would have regarded it as a catastrophic error if, say, August 23, 1972, had actually been a Tuesday. But within this framework, rather than tell the story in chronological order, he jumps about, taking little sidesteps and backsteps that lend the book its tension and incredible momentum. Here is how the Swedish agent is introduced: "And now Lundgren had a problem. Lundgren was dead." First Lundgren is lying dead in the pond; then he arrives in Targat, travels to the oasis town by shared minicab, and then, when it breaks down, by donkey cart; he very professionally avoids the hotel he had booked, gets too much sun, grows more and more careless, lets himself lust after the twelve-year-old waitress, asks the toothless old Arab who has been sitting for days outside his pension, "Already fucked your sheep today?"—a man from the wrong side, Lundgren's bad luck—and chats with a stranger to whom he hands over his ballpoint pen.... A rondo that ends back up in the pond.

Herrndorf provides information in a way that is staggered, rhythmicized, slightly delayed, quasi slantwise. But he provides us with everything we need. Novalis demanded that in poetry chaos should glimmer through the veil of order; in Herrndorf's case it is just the opposite. Herrndorf wrote that he was tempted to offer a reward of 100 euros for each loose end a reviewer could prove and not just claim, and he wasn't risking a cent. There isn't much superfluous information in *Sand*, but there's no missing information either. Readers must draw the connections themselves, like a connect-the-dot puzzle that reveals a clown in a pointy hat. Though in this case what is revealed is not a clown but the grimacing face of the devil.

THE MOANING IN THE NEXT ROOM

When pulled off successfully, as E. M. Forster illustrates in *Aspects of the Novel*, plot, the story of a novel—which should be enigmatic but never misleading, organic in construction and free of dead weight—has an aesthetic dimension and a particular beauty of its own. The reader's memory hovers above it, continually weighing and sorting things anew, glimpsing new threads and new chains of cause and effect, and at the end—hey presto, the plot's beauty is revealed.

Forster could never have read *Sand*, of course, but his remarks are so pertinent to the book that it's as if he'd had a chance to. Anyone with a weakness for artfully constructed plots is in for a feast here. Everything adds up, and everything comes full circle, albeit in the most perfidious way. But Herrndorf's greatness is not confined to the plot. Other things are more important—the force of his imagination, the scintillating intelligence that suffuses each page, the wealth of detail. Herrndorf started off as a painter and carried his ingenuity over into this other discipline: in the shimmering heat of the desert, everything is seen, not merely asserted, and there is nothing without color, sharply drawn shadows, texture. The tone is cool and laconic; the psychology is cool and comic. Indeed, comedy is his silver mine and his veritable elixir. At times even the excessively precise thoughts, the meticulous logic have a comic element. Lying in a hotel room with a sex tourist in one of the few moments of relief, Carl hears a couple moaning in the next room; a moment later he realizes that he can't actually hear the man's voice, he is merely imagining it. From which he concludes: Next door there might be a woman with two men. Or with another woman. Or a woman by herself. Later, after his companion has gone, he hears more moaning from next door, and muses that it might not just be similar moans but in fact *the same* moans they had just uttered, recorded on tape in the next room and played back as a delayed echo. Details like this, weird and beautiful in themselves, make up the nonfunctional surplus that lends a major literary work that je ne sais quoi of abundance, indeed of freedom.

AIMABLE-JEAN-JACQUES

But it is a different woman who plays the main role in Carl's short life: the American Helen Gliese. Her name, as Herrndorf's writer friend Kathrin Passig has pointed out, recalls the planet Gliese 381d, which is earthlike but disappointingly cold. Herrndorf characterizes Helen Gliese by saying that a stranger could pick her up at the port if you described her in two words: "pretty and stupid"—though she is neither one nor the other. Helen is the smartest of them all, and since she has an unpleasant voice and her facial features are slightly off, as her friend and tarot-card reader Michelle tactlessly points out to her, she decides to pursue a career as a secret agent as a way of proving something to herself.

Herrndorf doesn't spell this out, but he provides enough dots to be connected to make a portrait. Helen Gliese has a daughter named Heather who tells the narrator about her mother's later life in an epilogue inserted before the novel's denouement. What is this all about? First of all, why are we suddenly hearing from a first-person narrator, and second of all, why is he exchanging letters with a fictional character? The voice of a first-person narrator had already chimed in back in chapter eight, someone who, like the real-life author, was seven years old in 1972. The boy is staying in a hotel in Targat. "My parents had rented a two-room apartment on the ninth floor," we learn, "and when they sent me out, as they so often did, in order to be able to carry out secret things behind closed doors, I explored the sprawling grounds on my own." The narrator, who wore lederhosen back then, inside which his parents pinned tiny plastic bags, can no longer recall whether he spotted the blond American tourist and her one-armed taxi driver from his hotel room on the last day of August 1972. But a photograph of her bungalow door supposedly hangs over his desk today.

Then at the end of the novel we hear from Heather, who, disconcertingly enough, appears in the acknowledgments of the German edition alongside real people like Sascha Lobo and Tex Rubinowitz —admittedly, also alongside an "Ebbesand Flutwasser" (Ebbsand Floodwaters). Perhaps there are more real-life facts in this novel than its pulp-fiction quality would suggest—indeed, what if the world itself often behaves like pulp fiction?

The author's true alter ego may be hidden in a cameo. In the pseudo-office of the pseudo-psychiatrist Cockcroft, Carl flips through an encyclopedia to explore the different meanings of the word *mine*. The last entry concerns an author by the name of "Mine, Aimable-Jean-Jacques" whose humorous miniatures depict "the vacuousness of cosmopolitan society." This is easily recognizable as Herrndorf's *In Plüschgewittern* (Storm of Plush), his debut novel set in Berlin, just as Aimable's later turn to "adventure novels with trivial elements" represents the work we are reading, one well worthy of enshrinement in the encyclopedia.

MINES AND MIENS

On arriving at the port, Helen loses her suitcase because a child begs her for a ballpoint pen. Earlier, Polidorio stirred his coffee with a pen before taking painkillers to ward off his impending headache. Helen's taxi driver, who has lost his right arm, points to the stump and declares, "Mine." Carl marvels at the wealth of meanings in the word *mine*, then discovers the deadly ink cartridge in his own pocket. His blazer, with the pen in it, is stolen by slum children who are being tutored by ex-commune-dweller Bekurtz. Carl is tortured in a private goldmine because he is unable to hand over *la mine* with its explosive contents. Concealed in the ballpoint pen, it passes through the hands of Bekurtz's pupils—the same ones who begged Helen for a pen at the port—and finally ends up as the silver spine of a doll made of straw. To rescue this beloved doll, little Samaya wrenches herself free from her mother's hand just as another wave of demolition is sweeping the slum, and is buried beneath the rubble of a shanty that is being bulldozed. "It lifted its shovel like a priest raising the Ark of the Covenant, showed it to the infidels, and then dumped the entire contents onto the mound of rubbish."

It is the last sentence in the book.

FAVORITE SUBJECT: TORTURE

"Two Vietcong prisoners were interrogated on an airplane flying toward Saigon. The first refused to answer questions and was thrown out of the airplane at 3,000 feet. The second immediately answered all the questions. But he, too, was thrown out."

This quote from William Blum is the epigraph to chapter fifty-one. Epigraphs light the way into each chapter, elusive and misanthropic; another is by Vladimir Nabokov, proclaiming his distaste for happy endings. "Doom should not jam. The avalanche stopping in its tracks a few feet above the cowering village behaves not only unnaturally but unethically."

Nabokov would have been happy with *Sand*, and not just as a grandmaster of plot. Here there is not the least hint of a snowball stopping in its tracks above a mountain village. Everything takes the worst possible turn, with one exception. Near the end of the novel, one character is in a plane en route to a long, happy marriage—Helen's former friend Michelle, the esoteric airhead who, before departing, correctly divines the hero's future from her cards.

Carl's fate will be quite different from hers. The Swedish agent, before meeting up with his problem in the pond, at least grasped for a moment that he ought to be careful, "Favorite subject: torture." Carl is less fortunate, reeling from one disaster to the next until at last he finds himself in pitch-blackness, chained down in a subterranean lake, and has to save himself from a slow death by drowning—a particularly grisly fantasy. He escapes against all the odds; then, as in *No Country for Old Men*, something happens to break the implicit pact between author and reader.

Herrndorf's greatness is in things that lie beyond the pale, and his delight in detail doesn't flag when things turn gruesome. The word *delight* is wide of the mark, though; his descriptions of horror have nothing to do with sadism. It is the same moralism, balancing on the edge of despair, with which Nabokov has juvenile delinquents torment the hero's son to death in *Bend Sinister*.

But didn't we just say that comedy is his elixir? Profound horror converges with comedy in one place: the absurd. The doctor torturing Carl, who is tied to a chair, tells him a joke between electric shocks. Well, what he calls a joke. About a competition between the intelligence services: the winner will be whoever can make the best guess about the age of a prehistoric skeleton lying in a cave. With their scientific methods, the CIA man and the KGB man get closer and closer to the correct age—about 6,000 years, no, 6,100. The Stasi agent emerges from the cave after two days, exhausted: 6,124 years! How did he find it out so precisely? The Stasi man shrugs: "He confessed." That same doctor, trying to untangle the wires of the electroshock device, complains: "Why do they always leave it in this condition?...Only because it doesn't personally belong to them. It's the element of human nature that will doom communism." The book abounds with this sort of sarcasm. And, as *Pulp Fiction* showed, another intersection between horror and comedy is burlesque. In the car on the way to the mine where Cockcroft will resignedly untangle the electrodes, a dispute breaks out between the CIA agents in the front and the Syrian torture expert, known as "Pliers," in the back. Carl is lying on the floor, tied up. The Syrian wants to pray; the others argue, unwilling to make an extra stop with their sensitive cargo, and ask whether he couldn't pray in the car if they point it toward Mecca. No sooner said than done—but then the pious Syrian refuses to start praying, claiming that it is haram because the sky is still touched with red. Well, why is it haram? The atheists in the front don't know, the pious Muslim doesn't know, no one knows except the hero, huddled on the floor, who answers for the Syrian: it's because of the nature of religions; the Ja' faris don't want to be confused with the Middle Eastern sun-god worshippers.

This scene, as nightmarish as it is burlesque, casually raises the ancient question of theodicy.

THE CROSS AND THE ARK OF THE COVENANT

"Why does God allow evil?" This question is posed by the Syrian in a list of what he sees as senseless "why" questions—after the haram awkwardness he wants to teach his atheist CIA colleagues the lesson that "why" questions are always stupid. "Why does God allow evil? Why do clouds float in the sky? Why doesn't America win the World Cup?"

Here, with characteristic bathos, Herrndorf has concealed a central issue of his book. At a crucial moment in *Tschick* two crutches are left sticking up by the side of a field like a cross, and the hero's father, with pointed subtlety, is called *Josef. Sand* also begins by signaling the sacred. In the first sentence, the ex-commune-dweller Bekurtz is standing atop a brick wall, torso bared and arms stretched out to the sides "as if crucified." And the final sentence cites the Old Testament: the bulldozer lifts its shovel like a priest raising the Ark of the Covenant. Nor does the third great monotheistic religion escape the wave of demolition: Samaya, the girl lured back into the house by the diabolical cartridge, has an angelic goodness of heart, her purity is without blemish, and to gaze into her face is to understand Allah's creation. But we know how it all will end: as rubbish.

At the end the hero's son is found murdered in the mountains, with the amulet of a demon thrust down his throat. It is the signum of the entire novel. Its original title was not *Sand*; it was *The Desert of Evil*. The evil of the world is the true theme of this great antitheodicy disguised as a thriller. A world that is the scene of the events described cannot be ruled by a god who is both mighty and good. The desert of evil is the diabolical world of reality, governed by stupidity, cruelty, and sheer contingency—the world in which it makes no difference whether someone confesses or not, because he will be pushed out of the airplane one way or the other; the world in which a six-year-old's childhood ends with his parents and grandparents, four sisters, a brother-in-law and all his relatives, two other Tuareg families, a handful of rebels, and several bystanders being laid out in a row in the desert sand and staked down before an army tank rolls over their exploding bodies.

THE LAST CRY

Herrndorf's novel does leave one question open: the question of meaning. That meaning is hard to sift out from the sand of the desert, the eternally uniform *nihil*. But perhaps there is one tiny glittering particle to be found. It is an elementary feeling, not subject to reason: compassion for living creatures.

Even Helen, who abandons Carl manacled in the underground lake, feels a hint of this emotion at the end. She is waiting for her return flight to the States at the Targat airport, and the departure is delayed. In the café, the blue-patterned china reminds her of her breakfasts with the man whose amnesia she refused to believe in. She rents a car and drives back to the mine to see Carl.

And in so doing, she is following his summons. For in the moment of his greatest despair Carl cries out in the darkness, he calls out the name "that had been on the tip of his tongue the whole time. Now it echoed off the walls into the void."

Is he crying out for Helen? According to Herrndorf's widow, he uttered a different name: his own. Staring death in the face, the scales fall from Polidorio's eyes, and he sheds his amnesia and finally grasps his true identity. But it is not quite true that he calls his name into the void. Helen—whose name goes unspoken—does come; she does not find Carl, but at least she has heard him. In the cold of the universe there are some residual rays of empathy.

Herrndorf has written the greatest, grisliest, funniest, and wisest novel of the past decade. He is *aimable* indeed, and his work will endure.

—MICHAEL MAAR
Translated by Isabel Fargo Cole

OTHER NEW YORK REVIEW CLASSICS

For a complete list of titles, visit www.nyrb.com or write to:
Catalog Requests, NYRB, 435 Hudson Street, New York, NY 10014

* *Also available as an electronic book.*